Tories and Patriots

A Novel of the American Revolution

Martin R. Ganzglass

A PEACE CORPS WRITERS BOOK

ALSO BY MARTIN R. GANZGLASS

Fiction

The Orange Tree

Somalia: Short Fiction

In the American Revolutionary War Series

Cannons for the Cause

Non-Fiction

The Penal Code of the Somali Democratic Republic
(Cases, Commentary and Examples)

The Restoration of the Somali Justice System, Learning From Somalia,
The Lessons of Armed Humanitarian Intervention,
Clarke & Herbst, Editors

The Forty-Eight Hour Rule, One Hand Does Not Catch a Buffalo,
A. Barlow, Editor

For Marc
Who taught me to persevere

A singed cat may make a good mouser.

Private Joseph Plumb Martin
Eighth Connecticut Continental Regiment

Part One
The Battle for New York

Chapter 1 - The Hanging of a Tory

The hastily constructed gallows was a simple inverted L. The rough hewn, brown weathered upright beam appeared to have been torn out of a stable stall. A thick, dirty rope hung from the narrow and newly-planed tail. It loomed ominously on a platform, the freshly made planks interspersed with worn grey ones, expropriated from nearby abandoned sheds. The entire structure stood five feet off the ground providing the people assembled at the Bowery, a clear view of the hanging. Five regiments of regular troops of the Continental Army were lined up in front of the scaffold. Militias held back the vast crowds on the other three sides of the execution grounds.

Will Stoner waited in the third file of the four hundred soldiers of the Massachusetts Continental Artillery Regiment, their backs to the New Yorkers massing behind them. Sweat saturated Will's linen shirt underneath his dark blue wool coat. They had been standing in the warm June sun since nine that morning, having marched smartly to The Bowery from their red brick barracks on lower Broadway. Sergeant Merriam marked the end of their line. The tall thin figure of Corporal Isaiah Chandler was to Will's immediate left. Will took comfort from the older man's presence, recalling how he had nursed him back to health in Lieutenant Hadley's home in Boston. That had been only three months ago, he thought. Three months since his beating by a thuggish mob of patriots who thought he was a Tory spy, and his rescue by Hadley with the aid of Will's friends in the Marblehead Mariners.

The Artillery Regiment, in the center of the line of troops in front of the scaffold, was part of General John Fellows' Brigade. General Washington himself had ordered the entire Brigade to attend the hanging of Sergeant Thomas Hickey, a member of his own headquarters troops, the General's Life Guards. Will was not sure whether the Brigade was there to witness the hanging or to prevent armed New York City loyalists from rescuing the convicted traitor. He held his loaded musket tightly across his chest. He wished he had been issued a pike or at least a bayonet. In these close quarters, he didn't think his musket would be of much use.

The 14th Continentals, the Marblehead Mariners, looking smart in their short blue jackets and white oiled canvas breeches, were drawn up to the left of Will's regiment, at the corner, almost to the side of the gallows. He looked in vain for his friends, Lieutenant Nathaniel Holmes, Adam Cooper and others. Colonel John Glover, the Mariner's commander, sat motionless on his horse in front of his regiment facing the gallows, his red hair tied back with a black ribbon protruding from the bottom of his blue tri-corn.

The militiamen across from Will and on the sides surrounding the scaffold platform stood in their homespun clothes in an undisciplined lounging stance. They were armed with an odd mixture of muskets and fowling pieces held askew at all angles. Some casually rested the stocks on the ground.

Almost the entire population of the city, said to be twenty thousand, had turned out for the hanging. Ordinary citizens filled the long grassy field closest to the gallows platform and up the slopes of the hill a hundred yards away. Most were men, young and old, some well dressed on horseback, others common laborers and n'eer-do-wells. Several barefoot boys had climbed the nearby trees for a better view. Here and there, like butterflies among moths, a few women in their colorful bonnets and dresses sat in carriages fanning themselves.

"Oh, the Tory traitor will soon do the gallows dance," a man's voice said from behind Will.

"How do you know that," his companion asked.

"Look at the knot on the noose," the first man replied, pointing with his dirt encrusted finger past Will's right ear. "'Tis a gallows knot, they have tied. It will strangle him. The hangman's knot breaks the neck," the man said with authority.

"Serves him right, the treacherous bastard," his companion said. "Trying to poison General Washington and his staff. I heard he put arsenic in the General's food. It could have killed Mrs. Washington too."

"True enough," a third man chimed in. "They say their plan was when the Redcoats landed, Hickey and his conspirators were going to seize the General and his staff, while the Tory traitors among us blew up our powder and then turned the cannons, loaded with grape shot on our troops".

"I do not see," Sergeant Merriam said in a loud voice to Isaiah and Will, "how one can both plot to poison General Washington and to seize him." He snorted derisively. "General Howe would like nothing better than to take our General back to London for trial."

"And what do you know about the whore-faced Tories of New York," the first man responded, noting that Sergeant Merriam's Boston accent marked him as a stranger. "Before you and your fellows arrived, Mayor Matthews and the Royal Governor were entertaining British Naval Officers in their homes with their elegant balls and dinners and such, while the Redcoats and their ass bag sympathizers threatened and terrorized decent patriots in the city."

"Good thing they caught Mayor Matthews," his companion added. "They should hang him next."

"And Governor Tyron too," another man shouted. "I heard he escaped to one of those ships of the line in the harbor. It mounts seventy four guns I am told, ready to bombard and burn New York to the ground."

"Would you not think, the Royal Governor would want a city to govern," Sergeant Merriam said loudly, turning his head to partially look at the men behind them. "If the city is filled with loyalists, why would he burn their homes and property?"

Merriam leaned closer to his friend Corporal Chandler. "If these men were true patriots instead of undisciplined rabble and gossip mongers, they would either be in the militia or working on constructing the fortifications in Brooklyn. All they are good for is spreading rumors."

"You may make all the smart talk you want," the man who had spoken first yelled at Merriam. "The city is crawling with armed traitors, scheming away in their secret meetings, ready to rise up on a given signal. The only way to rid us of those pockey scum is to hunt them down like rats and ride them on a rail."

"Oh we had some grand Tory rides this past week," his companion said, laughing. "There were so many of the traitors, we almost ran out of rails, tar and feathers."

Will shuddered remembering how close he had come to being tarred and feathered in April and his narrow escape from the mob. Adam, his friend from the Marblehead Mariners had carried him away from the frenzied crowd, while Lieutenant Hadley and others had held them at bay.

"Steady lad," Isaiah said, noticing Will rub the faint scar over his eye. "You are in uniform and one of us now. General Putnam's men made short work of these ruffians, dispersing them and putting an end to their mob justice. These fake patriots are long on talk and . . ."

He was interrupted by a drum roll signaling the arrival of the prisoner and his guards. A uniformed drummer boy, no older than ten, led the troops into the square. A small round snare drum hung from broad white straps that crossed his narrow chest. He bit his lower lip concentrating on maintaining the beat with two hardwood sticks. Behind him, forty soldiers marched ten abreast in four rows. The long bayonets on their muskets glinted in the late morning sun. Hickey, bare headed with his hands tied behind his back, followed, with two Lieutenants of Washington's Life Guards next to him gripping each arm, their long unsheathed swords held upright in their free hands. Another forty soldiers and an officer on horseback brought up the rear. The entire procession came to a halt directly in front of the scaffold and faced the gallows. The officer rode forward, dismounted and climbed the platform. The crowd was quiet as Hickey was led up the stairs.

Commands rang out and the regulars came to attention. The militias behind the gallows shifted into some semblance of military order. Will watched the officer on the platform.

"That is Captain Gibbs, Commander of the General's Guards," Merriam whispered. "A Massachusetts man."

Gibbs unrolled a scroll of paper and read it in a loud clear voice.

"By Order of General Washington, with the concurrence of Generals Heath, Spencer, Greene and Putnam, in conformity with the verdict of the Court Martial of the 26th of June of One Thousand Seven Hundred and Seventy Six, duly and properly convened, finding Sergeant Thomas Hickey guilty of mutiny and sedition, said Thomas Hickey shall be stripped of all rank and insignia and hung by the neck until dead." Gibbs tucked the scroll in his waistcoat and nodded to the guards. "Bring the prisoner forward," he commanded.

The prisoner stood bareheaded, his black hair unkempt and his cheeks covered with a bristly stubble. He was stocky, about five feet six, with a wide flat forehead, a narrow chin and a tight thin line of a mouth, which seemed mismatched to the rest of his head. He looks so ordinary, Will thought. Like any common soldier. What could have driven him to try and kill the Commander in Chief?

Hickey smirked as Captain Gibbs drew a straight razor from his jacket. He mockingly bared his neck as if preparing to be shaved. Gibbs ignored him and methodically cut the buttons off Hickey's uniform and then his Sergeant's stripes.

The sound of the razor slicing through the wool fabric was like a saw rasping through soft wood.

One of the guards lowered the noose and placed it over Hickey's head while the other brought a wooden stool and helped the prisoner, his hands still bound behind him, to climb up. The Officer attempted to tie Hickey's feet around the ankles. The condemned man kicked the Officer's hand away. He made another failed attempt before Captain Gibbs waved him off.

"Does the prisoner wish to say any final words before the verdict is carried out?" Gibbs asked.

If there were to be an attempted rescue, it would have to occur now. Will sensed the tension in the troops near him. He gripped his musket tightly and scanned the people massed on the hills. The crowd shifted, pushing forward. Will felt the pressure from those behind his file. He kept his eyes forward and hoped the movement was from their eagerness to see the execution.

Hickey looked out over those in front of him, their faces upturned, watching him. He swiveled his head slowly within the looseness of the noose, taking in the people to his left and right. He made an effort to look at those behind him, but decided against trying further, given the narrowness of the stool. He smiled, as if pleased with the enormous numbers who were present. He licked his lips, seemed to be marshaling his thoughts and then bellowed out, "God damn you all. May you all be blown to hell."

"No priest for this one," some one from the crowd yelled back.

"I have no need for one," Hickey shouted back. "They are all charlatans."

Those were his last words. Captain Gibbs kicked the stool out from under Hickey with his booted foot. Hickey's body jerked down, his legs moved wildly as if he were trying to run on air, his neck seemed to stretch up from his violently twitching shoulders as his entire body struggled against the rope tightening around his throat. His eyes bulged frantically and blood trickled from his nose. His death spasms made his body turn on the gallows and as his back now faced Will and the others, a dark brown stain appeared on the seat of his pants.

"He was a Tory shit all right," someone yelled from the crowd. Others laughed at the now limp corpse hanging from the gallows.[1]

"Hang all the Tories," someone shouted and the crowd took up the chant. The people farther back on the slopes began to disperse. Those closer pushed toward the platform trying to get a better look at Hickey. The uniformed troops of General Fellows' Brigade held their lines awaiting orders. The militias simply dissolved into the crowds pressing forward. Will thought the Brigade would soon be engulfed by the surging mob and forced to give way.

He heard a shouted order by Colonel Glover. The Marblehead Mariners executed a sharp left and the crowd parted instantly, creating a path for the disciplined and armed men, led by their fiery Colonel on horseback. Will's Regiment followed and quickly closed the space between them and the rapidly marching Mariners. They moved smartly down Bowery Lane toward lower Manhattan.

As they marched down Division Street, past the Commons

and turned on to Broadway, with St. Paul's Church on their left, Will assumed they were returning to barracks. It was past two in the afternoon with the sun high in the sky. He longed to shed his wool uniform for his work clothes of a more comfortable, looser fitting hunting shirt and linen britches.

Ahead a crowd of men, urged on by some whores from the Holy Ground, the city's infamous brothel district, stood in front of a grey stone building. They reluctantly gave way on the street to the approaching soldiers. Several of the mob held lit torches as others threw paving stones against the shuttered windows of a building. There was the distinctive smell of rum and ale in the air. One man was trying to pull down a wooden sign, depicting an elegantly clad hunter with a musket.

Lieutenant Hadley halted the column, jumped up on the granite stoop and struck the man hanging on to the sign in the stomach with the hilt of his sword. The man collapsed in a heap, his head hitting the pavement.

"There will be no more rioting and destruction of property. You men disperse or we will arrest you."

"This is Gilbert Forbes' gun shop," one of men closest to the Lieutenant shouted. "The bastard is a Tory conspirator in the plot to kill General Washington. We should burn his place down." The others, made braver by the liquor they had consumed, moved forward, shouting "Burn it down, Burn it down."

"Sergeant," Hadley shouted to Merriam. "Arrest this man," he said, placing his booted foot on the spokesman's chest and pushing him forcefully down the steps. Merriam and a few men rushed forward and pulled the man to his feet and thrust him back into the ranks.

"I do not give a whit if this shop belongs to Thomas Hickey's own father. There will be no looting and arson. Disperse immediately, or we will arrest you." Hadley remained standing at the entrance to the locked shop, his sword drawn.

The crowd withdrew several feet. The men in the front row insolently weighed the stones in their hands, judging the distance to the line of troops facing them, who were now drawn up in a line to protect the store.

One of the whores stepped forward, one hand on her hip, the other holding a wooden tankard. "Come disperse with me to the Holy Ground," she yelled to Lieutenant Hadley. "Or if you are not up to it," she paused winking and letting the men in the crowd get the joke and laugh, "that young handsome soldier on the steps with you will do." She pointed at Will who blushed despite himself, causing the mob to laugh at his discomfort.

Hadley shouted an order from the stoop and the front line dropped to one knee and pointed their muskets at the crowd. The second line, standing behind them, took aim. At the sound of two dozen hammers being cocked and the marching cadence of more troops coming down the street, the crowd sullenly backed away.

"Save your courage for when you face British troops," a man shouted over his shoulder, before retreating up Broadway. There was a murmuring in the ranks at the affront to their Lieutenant.

"Leave them be," Sergeant Merriam said. "They are just words spoken by drunken, lazy layabouts, besotted by rum and whores. General Washington should close down the Holy Ground, all of it. The brothels and the rum shops. These strumpets and drunkards are an affront to God." He glanced back at the eight soldiers, they had left guarding the gun shop. "They should be coming with us to the barracks instead of performing extra duty to protect against drunken louts egged on by poxied trulls" he said, still angry over the confrontation.

Will was washing his face and neck, using the water from the rain barrel behind the barracks, when Nat Holmes found him.

"Great news, Will. Tremendous news indeed for you." Lieutenant Holmes, wearing the short dark blue jacket with the red color and cuffs of the Marblehead Mariners, beamed at him.

"Yes, well tell me," he said grinning back at his friend.

"I have come from the wharf at the end of Stone Street on the west side. An Albany sloop docked this morning. Mr. Luyken van Hooten was on board and with him," Nat paused for dramatic effect, "his lovely daughter Elisabeth."

"Have you seen her, I mean them? " Will said, hurriedly putting on his shirt and grabbing his razor.

"No, but they will be staying with Colonel Knox and are probably there now."

"What shall I do, Nat," Will asked, confused. "I cannot call on her."

"Certainly you can and must. I will talk to Lieutenant Hadley. Go. Hurry, get back into uniform. And make sure it is clean. Then I will walk with you to Colonel Knox's headquarters."

The Colonel's headquarters were at Number One Broadway. It was a large three story red brick building with a dark green tiled roof. Nat, with Will driven by his eagerness a step or two ahead, approached the sentry at the entrance. It had been the previous winter when he had last seen Mrs. Knox, at a dinner in Nat's honor, at the Colonel's quarters in Cambridge. Nat had invited Will as his friend to attend. Will had felt out of place as a mere teamster but Mrs. Knox had been exceedingly gracious. They had discussed Fielding's novel, "The History of Tom Jones," and Mrs. Knox drew from him his feelings for Elisabeth. And now, Will thought, Elisabeth was here in this building.

"Lieutenant Holmes of the 14th Massachusetts Continentals and Private Stoner of the Colonel's Own Regiment, wish to call on Mrs. Knox," Nat said confidently to the sentry. Will stood next to him, smoothing out his dark blue regimental coat, and fiddling with the pewter buttons on the coat's white facing and cuffs. His white stockings, below the knee band closure were reasonably clean. He looked down at his scuffed brown boots, protruding from the short gaiters, and regretted he had not had the time to polish them.

The sentry winked at Will. "Lieutenant Hadley said you might be by. According to the Colonel's orderly, Mrs. Knox is entertaining two women but would be pleased to receive both of you." [2]

They were escorted up to the second floor, their boots resounding on the hard wood floors and ushered into a large sitting room. Three ladies were seated on a banquette, their backs to a wide bay window that looked out on the harbor. Mrs. Knox rose and held out her hand.

"Why Lieutenant Holmes and Will Stoner. How handsome you both look. Come let me introduce you." She beckoned them into the room. Will noticed she had not lost weight since the birth of her daughter. He followed Nat into the room, almost bumping into a chair, his eyes fixed on Elisabeth. She was more beautiful than he remembered her from the crossing of the Hudson River last January in Albany. The late afternoon sun, coming in from a corner of the high window seemed to illuminate her solely for his eyes. Her honey colored blond hair was tied back with a colorful flowered scarf. The lace ruffle on her dress and bodice blended with the whiteness of her skin. She approached him with a slight smile on her face, her blue eyes dancing with mischief.

"I should reprimand you for not writing to me more frequently," she said. "Or for not wearing the scarf I gave you when we last met." She paused. "But I am so glad to see you Private Will Stoner, I could hardly be angry for more than a moment."

"Even though I was unable to write, you were always in my thoughts," Will replied, surprised he was not tongue-tied or blushing.

"Well said, Will," Lucy said. "Oh dear, where are my manners. This is Catherine Greene, General Greene's wife. She is staying with us while her husband is at camp in Brooklyn." Will followed Nat's lead, bringing his boots together and bowing slightly from the waist, before returning his attention to Elisabeth.

"And where are you staying," he asked her.

"Mrs. Knox has graciously asked me to stay with her. Father has business to conduct. We will only be here for one week."

"It seems I cannot get anyone but Catherine to call me Lucy, but then again I call her Kitty. Mrs. Knox sounds so old and matronly. So," she said pointing her finger at Nat, Will and Elisabeth, "you must call me Lucy or you will not be entitled to tea and sweets."

"If you so require, I will comply," Nat said, adding her name Lucy as an afterthought.

"Of course, it is not real tea, but our patriots' brew of sassafras and other herbs," Mrs. Greene said.

Lucy gestured to Nat that she intended to occupy one of the chairs facing the window. Nat dutifully held it out for her as she settled her plump body on the cushion and indicated Nat should sit next to her, leaving the banquette for Will, seated between Kitty Greene and Elisabeth.

Will was intoxicated by Elisabeth's presence. He breathed in the smell of her hair, felt the air from her mouth when she talked, heard the rustle of her skirt as she moved. One week to see Elisabeth seemed both a boon and a burden, a gift of time which would end all too soon. He heard his own voice but for the life of him, it didn't register what he was saying. He saw Elisabeth put her hands to her mouth, her eyes opening wide with concern.

"Yes," Nat said. "Will was severely beaten. That is where he lost your scarf."

"And were it not for the Marblehead Mariners, it would have gone worse for me." Will related the story of his rescue on the wharf and being picked up from the icy pavement and carried by Adam Cooper to safety.

"I never heard that part from you when I visited while you were recovering in Lieutenant Hadley's home," Lucy said, a mild reprimand in her tone. "My dear Harry told me Will had joined the Regiment and I was glad for that," she explained to Kitty and Elisabeth. "It is so good to have old acquaintances from Cambridge and Boston." She hesitated, her eyes misting over. "It would have been a blessing for my mother and sisters to see our daughter. She is asleep in her crib in the next room," she said, pointing toward a door to her left. "Otherwise I would play the proud mother and show her off to you two gentlemen, who knew me when I was first pregnant with her."

"She is a beautiful baby," Kitty Greene affirmed, beaming at Lucy.

While he had only lost his brother to the Tories, Will realized when the British evacuated Boston, Mrs. Knox's entire family had left for Halifax.

A serving girl brought in tea and tiny little sugar coated cookies. It had been a long time since Will had eaten anything dainty and sweet but he restrained himself and took only two. Barely enough to chew on, he thought, washing the sugary crumbly dough down with the weak hot tea.

"Now, Will," Lucy said. "We must make the most of Elisabeth's time in New York. I will ask Harry to give you as much leave as possible. Someone else can dig the fortifications for a while. How long have you been here?"

"I arrived with the rest of the Regiment at the end of April," Will responded suppressing the urge to end with ma'am. "Since then, I have been stationed at The Battery and briefly out in Brooklyn at Fort Putnam. We have been digging the gun emplacements for when the British come."

"My husband was first ordered by General Washington to Newport, Rhode Island," Lucy explained to Kitty and Elisabeth. "He supervised the building of fortifications there before continuing on to New York. Well, I will talk to Harry tonight and we will see what can be arranged for you. At the very least, for the next week you could be assigned to do something in the city rather than being sent across the river to Brooklyn." She smiled at Elisabeth and Will, pleased to play the role of facilitator for the young couple.

"But for now, I must end this delightful afternoon and reunion. Kitty and I have to call on Mrs. Washington and we must get ready. Your Elisabeth will care for baby Lucy." She stood up and Nat gallantly pulled her chair back.

Will rose, nodded to Mrs. Greene and turned to Elisabeth. "I will see you tomorrow and every day for a week. I promise, after the week is out, I will write more frequently."

She held out her hand. It felt so soft and smooth in his, he wished he could keep the memory of that touch forever. "And I promise to make you a new wool scarf and not to wait for your letters to write to you," she replied, inclining her head with a smile.

Elisabeth stared up at him. He looked at her, imprinting in his mind the vision of her light brown eyebrows arching over her expressive eyes, the delicate shape of her ears peering out beneath her hair and scarf, the angular profile of her nose, her lips not too full yet not thin and the whiteness of the skin of her neck. Regretfully, he let go of her hand and whispered "good night."

Outside, in the dusk of the summer evening, Will set the pace as they walked quickly up Broadway. "I wish I were the best artist in the colonies and could draw her image. I would carry it always. How can I miss her so when I just left her?" Will said. Nat, shorter than his friend, raced to keep pace.

"The same way I miss my beloved Anna. We are to be parents in

January of the coming year," he said breathlessly. Whether it was due to the fast pace or excitement over the blessed event, Will could not tell.

Will stopped and grabbed his friend by both shoulders. "That is good news, Nat. I am overjoyed for you."

"And I for you," Nat replied. "For the coming week, I am certain Mrs. Knox will prevail upon the Colonel and you will have time with your Elisabeth. You do not need me to escort you to call on her, do you?" he asked with a grin.

"No, I will call on her tomorrow at the first available instant. Good night, Nat," he said as they parted at his Regiment's barracks.

"Good night, Will." He watched his friend ecstatically dance up the stone steps before turning and continuing on his way.

Chapter 2 - A Mighty Fleet

Will rose earlier than usual the next morning. It was Saturday. He was eager to finish feeding and exercising Big Red and the other horses in his care and call on Elisabeth after breakfast. He wondered if he could arrange to go horseback riding with her. Perhaps on Sunday, after regimental services, he could take her around The Battery and then north along the Hudson River with its views of the cliffs and woods of New Jersey. They would need a picnic lunch. [1]

He was startled out of his reverie by the booming sound of an alarm cannon from The Battery followed by the pealing of church bells. Hastily leading Big Red back into his stall, he left the Regiment's barn and dashed out into the street. Men stood on the roofs of nearby buildings pointing to the south and east and shouting about ships in the Lower Bay. Down below on cobblestoned Broadway, crowds of men and boys passed on the news about sails in the harbor before racing toward The Battery. He heard fragments of their agitated voices as they surged past: "Maybe fifty ships, all men-o-war," "hundreds of them," "Troops in flat boats coming ashore," "Hessians for sure."

A disorganized group of militia came out of a side street, carrying their muskets and quickly became entangled in the crowd running toward the harbor. At the sounds of musket fire from the direction of The Battery, the mob hesitated, blocking movement in either direction. A majority turned and ran back up the street away from the harbor. Many of the militiamen fled with them.

Will hurried back to his barracks. A few merchants had already stationed wagons in front of their stores. Prudently, they positioned their horses facing up Broadway for a fast escape. Several black servants, dripping with sweat in the early morning summer heat, carried heavy barrels and boxes of goods from cellars and shops. He heard women screaming from inside a brick building, about what he could not make out. Over the shouting and commotion, church bells rang incessantly, as if a crazed person was attached to the pull ropes.

Inside the three story barracks all was disciplined but frenzied activity as some two hundred soldiers, crammed tightly together in rooms which had been stripped of all furniture when the Tory owner fled, rushed to get ready. Some men sat on the bare wood floor pulling on their boots, others headed to the front parlor, now the arms room for muskets and bayonets. Will found his blue regimental coat and rapidly changed from his trousers into his buff colored knee breeches and waistcoat. He grabbed a musket, affixed the bayonet, slung the haversack over his shoulder and hurried outside to line up with his gun crew. When his company was assembled, they marched to Colonel Knox's headquarters, a few blocks down Broadway, clearing the crowds of tradesmen, laborers, boys and individual militia members in front of them with their disciplined cadence.

They stood in even lines in front of their Colonel's Headquarters, awaiting orders. They did not have to wait long. They were being sent across the East River to Brooklyn and dispersed to the various forts to man the cannons. Will, as part of Lieutenant Hadley's company was going to the Cobble Hill Fort. He wished he had been sent to The Battery or even the fort on Governor's Island so as to be closer to Elisabeth. Together with those in the Regiment assigned to the other forts in Brooklyn, Hadley's men wheeled in ranks on his command and marched across the bottom of Manhattan Island, turning north past Black Sam Fraunces' Tavern at Bridge Street and continuing up to Maiden Lane to await being ferried across the East River.

As they reached the dock, Will saw a flat bottomed boat, mid-river, the rowers struggling mightily against the strong flow of the out going tide, carrying Colonel Knox and other officers and their horses toward the opposite shore. Several boats had left the Brooklyn side from higher up and were rapidly approaching the ferry dock taking advantage of the swift current to carry them down river to the Manhattan landing. They were filled with women and children, a few men, horses, cows and wagons loaded with furniture and other possessions. They were fleeing their small farming communities. Wet from the spray, miserable and frightened they came ashore, clogging the pier, blocking the flat-bottomed transports and delaying the troops' departure to Brooklyn.

Twenty men of Will's company finally embarked on one of the boats. They stood, tightly packed together, the press of their bodies steadying them, their muskets held high in the shoulder arms position, as the boat rocked sideways, before the rhythmic strokes of the five pairs of rowers propelled them forward. Will spread his legs to balance himself better. The men rowing were not in uniform. They were not the Mariners. He wondered where Nat and his friends were now. And where was Elisabeth? What if the British Regulars got past Governor's Island and landed at The Battery? There were no more sounds of musket fire. He hoped it meant the shots he had heard were nothing more than ill-disciplined militia discharging their weapons. He suppressed the thought the silence meant the invading troops had already overrun The Battery.

Once ashore, they stood in ranks before marching up the steep hill from the river to Brooklyn Heights and inland toward the Cobble Hill Fort in the distance. Their wool uniforms were wet from the salt spray. Even though it was almost noon and hot, Will was thankful he had kept his linen hunting shirt on under his waistcoat. It kept the wet wool from rubbing against his skin. Lieutenant Hadley, riding his white mare, caught up with them at the top of the slope. He dismounted and walked with his men, falling back occasionally to talk to Sergeants Otis and Merriam. They passed an occasional wagon fleeing toward what its occupants deemed to be the safety of the city, the women downcast and quiet, the young children leading a cow or goat and skipping excitedly around as if on a great adventure.

Will was well familiar with Cobble Hill Fort. It was named for the hill outside Boston by some Massachusetts men under General Greene's command who had arrived in New York before the main army. It had taken ten days for Knox's artillery regiment and the rest of the army to march from Cambridge to New York. They arrived the third week in April. After a few days rest, they had been sent across the East River to Brooklyn to work on the construction of a series of defensive forts, in anticipation of a British invasion. Will's Regiment joined thousands of troops, citizen volunteers, drafted laborers, slaves and paid substitutes, digging trenches, erecting earthen works and making thick walls of stone, logs and dirt.

For the remainder of April and much of May, Will's company had been at Cobble Hill. From daybreak until dark Will cut trees and trimmed branches, swung a pick axe and carried stones, and dug and moved dirt to create the corkscrew road leading up to the fort. His tall frame became wiry and more muscular, his arms brown from the sun and thickened in the forearm. Every day was the same, except for Sunday, when there were services that were sometimes held by the regimental chaplain. Usually, they were led by Sergeant Merriam who interspersed the bible readings with warnings about the evil sins of temptation that awaited the men across the river in the taverns and brothels of the Holy Ground in New York.

Once the Cobble Hill Fort was completed, Will and the others returned to New York for the cannons. For several days, they towed the gun carriages down to the river, loaded them on the ferries and crossed over to Brooklyn. Upon landing, they pulled the artillery up the steep muddy road leading to Brooklyn Heights and beyond to the line of forts extending from Red Hook, west of the Gowanus swamp to Wallabout Bay north of the ferry landing. Will was proud that, while other gunners had a team of four horses, Big Red with just another horse in the traces, could pull a brass eighteen-pounder.

Will had delivered cannons to every Fort except Fort Defiance at Red Hook. First, he had gone to the one closest to the East River, Fort Stirling. Then to Fort Putnam, just to the north, and the other forts in the defensive line facing the Jamaica and Flatbush Roads which ran east-west from the flatlands of Brooklyn to the East River. All in all, Will estimated there were more than one hundred pieces of artillery distributed among eight forts, and he had hauled many of them, together with cannon balls, powder boxes and supplies in the summer heat of May and mid-June.

It was late afternoon as the twenty men, led by Lieutenant Hadley and their two sergeants approached the familiar corkscrew road leading up to Cobble Hill Fort. The round fort stood naked on the hill, all trees having been cleared around it for construction and to provide a clear field of fire. A light wind was blowing from the east and they were greeted by a stench worse than any barnyard or stable the men in the unit had ever smelled.

"What is that stink?" one soldier exclaimed in disgust. He was in Sergeant Otis' unit, which was in the lead. "'Tis enough to make one retch."

"Nothing more than the shit of one hundred men shitting for one hundred days," another said loudly. "The militia's own perfume. Does it not bring back memories from their camps in Cambridge?" he said, as if recalling the sweet smell of freshly scythed hay. Several of the men shuddered, recalling the bloody flux which had infected the Army besieging Boston. Others pretended to have severe coughing fits from inhaling the noxious odor.

"Look smart," Sergeant Merriam said, turning his head to look at the soldiers behind him. "No sloppy marching. We are the Colonel's regiment, not a misfit bunch of farmers and mechanics with their fowling pieces." Although they had been marching for two hours with only one ten-minute rest, they stood taller and their cadence became sharper.

The closer they got to the fort, the worse the smell. Will heard the steady buzz of flies. The droning sound came from the shallow trench beneath the front wall of the fort. He looked up in time to see a militia soldier hoist himself up on the wall, drop his pants and let loose a stream of diarrhea to the trench below.

"You there," Lieutenant Hadley shouted from horseback. "What is your unit?" he asked sharply.

The man turned and looked down at Hadley. "This is my unit," he said, wiggling his bare ass and disappearing over the wall.

The men murmured angrily at the insult to their Lieutenant. They marched in cadence into Cobble Hill Fort, mounted the parapet, and as ordered divided up five men to each of the four eighteen-pounders. This was the first time they had a view of the harbor. Sergeants Merriam and Otis quickly dismissed the men recognizing their eagerness to see the British fleet. They pushed and jostled the militiamen none to gently to make room for themselves on the wall.

Below them to the east, in the Lower Bay, was the British fleet, their ships so numerous, the masts looked like a floating forest. [2]

Lieutenant Hadley unpacked his telescope and surveyed the Bay. "Just a few miles below the narrows. At least fifty ships." He was silent, his lips moving slightly as he counted. "Two with fifty guns each, the name on the closest one is Centurion. I cannot make out the other. There is a forty gun ship, name of Phoenix." He trained his glass further down the bay. There are sails well beyond Sandy Hook. I am unable to tell from this distance the type of vessel." He turned and looked back toward the waters off Governor's Island. "No transports or men of war there," he said calmly. "I doubt there was any landing at The Battery this morning."

Will was relieved. Elisabeth was not in any imminent danger. He shielded his eyes and studied the large fleet in the lower bay. He looked questioningly at Sergeant Merriam.

"I have never seen so many sails and I have been to Boston harbor when it was filled with merchant and fishing vessels." He lowered his voice so the nearby militia-men could not hear. "The Lieutenant counted one hundred and forty guns on three men of war. Just three. That is more cannon than we have on all the forts in Brooklyn and New York. And not enough men to crew them all."

They remained seated on the wall, resting from their long march, drinking watered cider eagerly from their wooden canteens. Lieutenant Hadley turned to his twenty men and addressed them informally. "Their fleet is still assembling. I want the cannons inspected. Take especial notice of the vents, and the condition of the powder boxes, rams and sponges. Report to me if any charges are wet or damaged. We must be ready for the enemy." He trotted briskly down the steps from the parapet and across the fort's yard. He disappeared in to a small wooden cabin, partially hidden in the lengthening shadow of the northeastern wall.

The two Sergeants ordered the men to their guns. They pushed their way past the loafing militiamen still gawking at the fleet in the Lower Bay and talking among themselves.

"First task men," Sergeant Merriam shouted to his two crews, "inspect your assigned equipment."

Will moved briskly to the eighteen-pounder. It sat squat and ugly on its bulky heavy oak carriage, pointing east, over the wall, toward the British men-of-war in the distance. The other three men in the crew moved confidently to their usual places; John Baldwin, the vent tender, Simeon Webb in charge of the sponge and ram, and Levi Tyler the wormer and loader. They had been together when the Continental Army seized Dorchester Heights and positioned their cannons to threaten the British fleet in Boston Harbor below. Will had been a natural addition. They trusted him to be the powder handler because of his quick reaction to the unexploded shell on Nook's Hill. It was his job to carry the canvas charges and the cannon balls to Corporal Tyler as the loader. They were short-handed so Will also served as the powder box handler, being responsible for the security of the charges at all times.

Will pulled his hatchet from his haversack and pried open the cover to the powder box. He knelt down and lifted the top layer of canvas powder bags, placing them on the wooden lid, instead of the ground. A few of the militia came over to watch. Will ignored them, concentrating on examining the canvas bags for any leakage or moisture. Sergeant Merriam walked over and felt the seams of the bags for himself.

"You men," he said to the militiamen crowding in close to satisfy their curiosity, "return to your posts or step back and let us do our work."

"This fort is our post, you fat old church warden," a scraggly militiaman replied, spitting on the ground. He pulled the flaps of his worn knee length country coat back to reveal a sword hanging from a dirty brown sash around his waist.

Merriam grunted in seeming assent, and with surprising quickness grabbed the worming pole and swung it, catching the man at the knees. He went down with a cry of surprise and pain. Merriam turned the pole around and poked him hard in the stomach with the blunt end.

"Now you men clear the gun positions. That is an order," he said, still holding the wormer pole in his hands. Will bent down and retrieved his Sergeant's tri-corn as the militiamen helped their comrade up. Sullenly, they left the parapet. Merriam smoothed his thinning hair back, wiped his broad forehead and plumped the tri-corn back on his head.

"Forgive me, dear God for losing my temper," he muttered to himself. "They are ill-disciplined fools, who will run at the first broadside," he said, resuming his inspection of the canvas powder bags. Will picked up the wormer and made sure the iron spiraled coil was firmly attached to the pole. He gave it to Tyler who stuck it down the cannon. The iron came out clean from the barrel. "Not a surprise. These cannons have not been fired since they were put in place," he said. He stepped back as Simeon thrust the dry sheepskin-covered sponge down the barrel. "Good thing I am sponging a cold barrel," Simeon said, going through the drill. "There is no water in the artillery bucket."

"Make sure the sponge is in good condition and tightly bound to the pole," Merriam ordered. Simeon nodded and inspected the seam of the sheepskin and the leather thong that joined it to the long, well worn staff.

Lieutenant Hadley came up the parapet stairway, followed by a portly man, resplendent in a brown jacket with red facing and gilt buttons. Two majors, similarly attired, waited attentively in the background. The contrast between the uniforms of these officers and their men in the Connecticut militia was stark.

"Sergeants," Hadley called for Merriam and Otis. Will remained at the cannon within earshot.

"This is Colonel Fisher Sage of the Fourth Connecticut State Levies. He will be your commanding officer in my absence in all matters except cannon maintenance, drills and firing procedures." The Colonel nodded and looked at the twenty men in the gathering darkness.

"My God, look at that." Sage said, pointing over Lieutenant

Hadley's shoulder to the Lower Bay. The British ships had hung lanterns on the bow and stern to mark their positions. It seemed to Will as if a thousand fireflies had congregated over the water, bobbing in place, in an orderly manner. Here and there lights from a cabin in the stern of some ship, or slivers of bright yellow escaped and danced on the black of the water. The light from amidships must be from the open gun ports, Will thought

"If we had some of our marksmen stationed on shore, the lanterns would be fine target practice," Sage said.

"Below the Narrows, the British Men-of-War would be more than 250 yards away," Hadley replied. "When they try to pass the Narrows, then they will be in range of our cannons and riflemen."

He turned and addressed the Sergeants and his men. "Tomorrow, move the two cannons protecting the fort's entrance to face the Upper Bay. I will return to the city tonight. With luck, our wagons should arrive tomorrow with tents and our equipment. Tonight you will have to make do. Private Stoner, a word with you," Hadley said, motioning for Will to follow him as he descended from the parapet.

"I am certain Elisabeth is safe but I will make inquiries when I am at Colonel Knox's headquarters." Will nodded his thanks. He held the reins while Hadley mounted, wishing he were going with him to see Elisabeth. The Lieutenant wrinkled his nose. "We will have to do something about the lack of sanitation in this fort," he said, before trotting his horse through the open gates.

The men spent the night on the parapets, sleeping propped against the dirt and stone walls. They preferred to be higher, cooled by the breeze off the bay, instead of in the hot and filthy still air of the fort's compound. They were awakened by sound of reveille and drums beating the Connecticut Levies to assemble in the compound. They watched the militia straggle up, forming ragged lines with noticeable gaps where others had not yet appeared. The Levies struggled through the manual exercises, some with muskets and fowling pieces, others with poles or sticks substituting for actual firearms.

Sergeant Merriam shook his head. "These men are a far cry from the Connecticut Continental Regiments. This militia will not be able to defend this fort," he said emphatically. "Our cannons alone will not stop the Regulars. I pray General Greene knows to reinforce each fort with Continentals who will hold the line and stand firm." [3]

Will leaned against the wall next to Corporal Isaiah Chandler, who was part of Sergeant Otis' gun crew. "I have seen militia give a good account of themselves," Isaiah said. "Although," he added after a moment's thought, "it was from defensive positions. And it will be Hessians and Grenadiers storming the fort. That is something to look forward to, Will."

"We were ready for them on Dorchester Heights," Will said. "We have grape shot and canister waiting for them here, as well." He had liked Isaiah ever since the Private, recently promoted to Corporal, had taken care of him in Lieutenant Hadley's house in Boston. Although he was older than Will by more than a dozen years, a tradesman and married man as well, Will appreciated his company.

"So, Providence has saved them by a storm to meet their fate on these slopes before Cobble Hill Fort, just as you were saved by Lieutenant Hadley and your Mariner friends, to be the instrument by which their destruction will take place? Is that your thought?"

"No, Isaiah," Will shook his head. "You confuse me with your talk," Will said. "All I mean is we were ready for a battle once before and now we are ready again."

Isaiah put his arm around Will's shoulder. "Permit me, as the one who nursed you back to health, to confuse you. Here, share my breakfast. We shall break hard biscuits together if we are able to break them at all."

Without cooking pots and supplies, the men of the gun crews ate their cold breakfast. Isaiah cut his biscuit in half with his bayonet and offered part to Will who ate it and slowly chewed on three more. There were only two left in his haversack. He looked out over the wall as the sun came up, casting its rays on the vast British fleet. More ships had passed Sandy Hook and moved up the Lower Bay, hugging the shore of Staten Island, just below the Narrows.

Sergeant Merriam squinted down the bay. "Tis far more than fifty ships now."

"Wait until the Levies finish their drills and mount the parapets. They will shit in their pants instead of over the wall at that sight,"

Corporal Tyler said. Merriam scowled at his language but the rest of the gun crew chuckled at the joke. Will smiled, glad to be part of a crew who acted as if they were unafraid and would hold firm against advancing troops. He wondered if he would stay at his position, or would he run if others panicked and fled. He had never been in battle before, nothing had happened at Dorchester Heights, and the bombardment at Nooks Hill would be nothing compared to a charge by Hessians and Grenadiers. He realized he was more afraid of how he would react, than of the enemy troops.

He was startled by a volley of rifle shots, followed by an answering sound of muskets. The firing continued, the gunfire blending together, interspersed with brief periods of silence, as whoever was shooting reloaded. Will heard shouted orders behind him and the militia raced up the parapets and stared off at the empty green countryside, their muskets pointed toward the distant Narrows.

"There is nothing to see," Sergeant Merriam said to the gun crew. "The shots came from down at the shore. Quickly, finish eating. We need to move these cannons and be ready."

Will washed down the last of his hard biscuit with diluted cider from his canteen and fell in with the rest of the gun crew. It was a struggle moving the two brass eighteen-pounders that guarded the fort's entrance to the eastern side. Each of them weighed close to a ton and was mounted on a heavy oak gun carriage, itself more than two hundred pounds. Will felt a sense of urgency, to get the cannons in position so all four could fire over the top of the works, and concentrate their fire on one ship when it passed through the Narrows and entered the Upper Bay. Or it could be depressed to send grape shot and canister into troops charging up the slopes in front of the fort. The men removed their regimental coats, both because of the heat and their desire to keep some part of their uniforms clean.

With much grunting and effort, they turned the cannons until the guns were parallel with the wall and attached ropes to the heavy oak carriage. Then, they formed two lines, each man facing the muzzle of the cannon. Pulling on the ropes, hand over hand, with several men behind the cannon pushing from the back of the carriage at the breech, where the weight was the heaviest, with others levering the small hardwood wheels over the rough ground, they inched the big guns along the parapet. Will was glad the two crews were working together. "Tis a much better placement than firing through embrasures," Sergeant Merriam said, after the second cannon had been pulled into position. "Aimed from here on high with a flat trajectory, they will smash down on the decks of those ships foolish to sail too close."

A single musket shot rang out on the far side of the fort facing Red Hook, followed by a ragged volley. Will and the two gun crews grabbed their muskets and waited for orders. There were shouts of "Hold your fire, Hold your fire," and all was quiet again. Colonel Sage stormed along the parapet, talking to one of the majors Will had seen the night before.

"I want these men drilled and drilled and then drilled some more. There will be no more firing of muskets without a proper order. No more shooting at shadows. Is that understood?"

"Yes sir," the major said as he brushed past Will's gun crew.

"Colonel Sage, Sir," Sergeant Merriam called after him.

"What is it Sergeant?"

"We will be doing dry fire drills ourselves."

The Colonel waited for Merriam to continue, unclear as to his meaning.

"The gun captain shouts out "Give Fire," after the cannon is primed. I would not want to confuse your men with that command."

Colonel Sage walked closer to Sergeant Merriam to satisfy himself Merriam was not being insubordinate.

"In battle of course, many orders are given," he acknowledged. "It will be good practice for my men to hear competing commands. You may go about your drills, Sergeant."

Sergeants Otis and Merriam let the men rest a few minutes as the Connecticut Levies began their drills in the compound below. It was slightly past mid-day when they began their own dry fire gun drills. They worked in shirt-sleeves, their muskets stacked with their Regimental coats to the side. Will carried the powder to the cannon, handed it to Levi Tyler, the loader, who laid it on the ground instead of placing it in the muzzle. Simeon Webb shoved the rammer down the barrel, grunting as if forcing the imaginary canvas charge in place.

After Sergeant Merriam as the gun commander had yelled "Give fire" and pretended to touch off the charge, Tyler wormed the cannon, Webb swabbed it for real, dipping the sponge in the artillery bucket and Will carried the canvas charge back to the powder box and the entire process was repeated.

Will fell into the rhythm with the others, sweating in the hot sun, feeling his forearm muscles ache as he ran with the charge from the powder box to the cannon, its brass shining brightly enough to make him squint. Maybe, he thought, when the battle came, he would do things automatically and his fear would not take hold. Levi Tyler winked at him as he handed the canvas charge back to Will. He was a lean man, with a long nose, and ears too big that protruded from underneath the tri-corn, pushed too far down on his head. Strands of greyish black hair had come loose from his tail and stood out like bat wings trying to hide his ears from sight.

"We are using the same charge each time," Tyler said. "Better check the seams for wear and tear at the end of the drill." Will nodded. They took a rest, each man seeking the little shade they could find on the parapets. Will drank thirstily from his canteen and glanced around the wall. Some of the Connecticut militia had been assigned spaces along the parapet and were trying to look reasonably alert, although they talked among themselves and pointed at the growing number of masts in the Lower Bay.

After a brief rest, they resumed their drills. This time, Sergeant Merriam worked with another crew and Corporal Chandler became their gun commander. Their pace became faster as they got back into the rhythm, functioning as one rather than five individuals. Will wondered what would happen to their efficiency if one of more of them were killed or wounded. Chandler called for them to break and Simeon cupped his hands in the artillery bucket and splashed water on his face. Isaiah nodded at each of them and they took turns cooling themselves with the water. While the rest of them leaned against the wall, Simeon filled the bucket from the well in the fort's compound, sloshed himself one more time from the pump and clambered up the steps to the gun position. He was a big man, slightly taller and much broader across the shoulders than Will, with a beak nose like a raptor, small deep set eyes and mottled skin. His long thick arms made him the ideal man in the crew as the sponger and rammer.

There was a cry from the western side of the fort, "Wagons approaching." Sergeant Merriam was the first to recognize Lieutenant Hadley leading three wagons laden with their tents and equipment.

"Into your uniforms and line up at your positions. Look smart for the Lieutenant. Hurry now," Sergeant Merriam shouted as the men scrambled to put on their jackets and tri-corns. They stood rigidly at attention as Hadley rode into the fort, followed by the wagons. On command they descended the earthen steps from the parapet. Will was part of the unit carrying the powder boxes with fresh charges to the gun emplacements. He struggled on the bottom corner of one of the heavy boxes, hoping the Lieutenant had seen Elisabeth and would have the time to talk to him before he left. Hadley had also brought crates of grape shot. It took six men to carry them and by the time all of the crates had been wrestled up the steps and placed behind each of the four cannons, the Lieutenant was nowhere to be seen.

Will finished pounding the tent stake into the ground with the back of his hatchet and stood up stretching his aching shoulder muscles as Lieutenant Hadley strode out of Colonel Sage's cabin. It was dusk and a yellow candlelight cast an irregular rectangle on the ground before the door closed behind him. Sergeant Merriam started to call the men to order, but Hadley waved him off.

"Gather round men and I will tell you what I know. This morning, the Regulars attempted a reconnaissance landing near Gravesend and were repulsed by our riflemen." The men cheered. "I have brought Colonel Sage General Washington's Orders of the Day. We are all commanded to do our duty, to remain alert and to follow orders. Specific orders for all Fort Commanders are to ensure proper sentries, to send out scouts and to pay for and bring in food supplies from the surrounding countryside. The wagons which accompanied me carry vegetables and melons purchased from nearby."

He looked at the men in the early evening dusk. "I believe we have time before the enemy land their troops. We have strong forts and cannon. And well drilled crews," he added smiling. "General Washington is aware the Artillery Regiment lacks men. He has ordered every non-artillery company to detach two men. I have shown the order to Colonel Sage. He will assign four men. Sergeants. It is your responsibility to train them. I want them integrated into our crews and reasonably trained by four days hence, by this Friday." [4]

The men disbursed to start their cooking fires and unpack their kits that had arrived on the wagons. Will anxiously sought out the Lieutenant who caught his eye and motioned him away from the tents.

"Elisabeth is safe, Will. She left with Mrs. Knox and the baby before noon yesterday morning. The Colonel was beside himself until Mrs. Knox and their infant daughter were safely away. They are most probably safely well north of the city, nearing the border with Connecticut by now. From there they will make their way to Boston."

Will sighed with relief. "Thank you sir for the news." Hadley rubbed the stubble on his square jaw and put his arm around Will's shoulder. "There is more. Mr. Van Hooten has asked the Colonel for you. I do not know for what purpose. There is a meeting of the Officers with the Colonel at Fort Greene tonight. Perhaps, I will be able to tell you more tomorrow."

Will was torn by conflicting emotions. If Elisabeth's father wanted him, it only could be to escort his daughter farther north to safety. He thought of the pleasure of riding Big Red beside her carriage for several days. He would see her every night at the inns they would stop at, and every morning when they resumed their journey. He felt an initial flood of relief at the thought he would avoid the battle that was coming, followed almost immediately by a flush of shame at his cowardice. Abandoning his comrades before the first Redcoat had even landed. He saw Elisabeth's smiling face beaming up at him in Mrs. Knox's sitting room, her expression changing to one of disgust at his lack of courage.

"I would prefer to remain with the gun crew," Will said.

"Of course you would," Hadley snapped. "I would have preferred to be at Bunker Hill but was ordered by the Colonel to assist in building the redoubts around Roxbury," he said bitterly. "You will have to follow orders, whatever they are," he added more gently. Will knew the Lieutenant had not yet been tested in battle. He wondered whether he too was afraid. They walked back toward the cooking fires in silence.

Sergeant Merriam and the gun crews had started two fires, one for the cooking pot and the other for the spit. A large piece of meat dripped fat into the flames, causing them to dance to the music of the sizzle. Will ate greedily, using the flat broad spoon he had brought from Schoharie rather than the narrow one he had been issued upon enlisting. He sopped up the remains of the vegetable stew with a piece of bread and licked his fingers. He looked hungrily at the remaining meat on the spit and stew in the pot, knowing they were being saved for the five men from their unit on sentry duty. The Lieutenant had not trusted that vital duty solely to the Connecticut militia.

Hadley rose to leave. "There is some melon, sir," Merriam said.

"This has been a wonderful repast gentlemen but I must leave to meet with the Colonel. The melon will have to wait for another occasion." He bowed in mock seriousness.

"One more instruction Sergeant. Colonel Knox told me General Washington is concerned many of the troops will be unfit for combat due to sickness- the bloody flux again. Colonel Sage has not taken our Colonel's suggestion to improve the sanitation at the fort. I believe an order will come from General Washington himself in a day or two. In the meantime, dig a vault in one place, away from the water and set an example for the militia."[5] Sergeant Merriam nodded. Will heard the wooden gates creak open and the drumming of the hooves of the Lieutenant's mare as he made his way down the corkscrew road from the fort.

The next day was spent drilling all day with the new additions to the gun crews. At first, it was as if the Connecticut levy, Private Oliver Strong was all left feet and the opposite of his family name. He tripped constantly, dropped the canvas charges most of the time and was always in the way. The men, who had worked so smoothly the day before, with Sergeant Merriam as the fifth man, became frustrated with Strong's ineptitude and more irritable the higher the sun rose in the sky. Merriam would not let them quit.

"We are not going for speed. We are training to task," he said. "Slow down and get it right," he admonished as Will stood at the powder box watching Strong strain to grip a charge and stagger to hand it to Simeon. Strong stood in the wrong place, blocking Simeon from getting to the rammer. "The Grenadiers will be up this wall and across the opposite one before we get a shot off," Simeon said, pushing Strong out of his way and reaching for the rammer.

"Be quiet," Merriam commanded, thinking for the moment. "The problem is we are dry firing. Strong is staying in place waiting to take the canvas charge back to the powder box. In a live fire drill, he would be back at the powder box." He took Strong by the arm and walked him away from the cannon near where Will stood. "From now on, Strong will hand the canvas charge to Tyler and return immediately to the powder box." Tyler wiped his forehead, grinned at Strong, showing his brown uneven teeth, and waved to identify himself as if dealing with an idiot. Strong said nothing, bent down, hoisted a canvas charge in both arms and ran the few steps to the brass cannon and handed it to Levi. "Well done," Tyler said to Strong's back.

After this change, the drills became more efficient, but still not as fast as the day before. They practiced it again and again, with Baldwin serving as both vent tender and firer. When Strong had the routine down but seemed close to collapse from the exertion, Merriam switched him with Will as powder box handler, which meant all he had to do was stand in position and watch Will carry the charges to Tyler. By the end of the day, all of the crews were exhausted physically and mentally.

Will looked forward to the evening meal, hoping Lieutenant Hadley would return with news and orders. He imagined himself, standing tall in front of Mr. Van Hooten, telling him calmly that he could not serve as escort for his daughter to the safety of Connecticut and beyond. His duty called him to stand with his comrades and fire shot and shell at the advancing enemy. He took those heroic thoughts with him to the parapets where he stood sentry duty until midnight.

Wednesday morning, July 2nd promised to be another hot day. They began their practice drills early to avoid the midday sun. Strong joined them as the crew clambered up the steps and took their positions around the eighteen-pounder. From eight to ten they drilled over and over again, Will relieving Strong as the Connecticut man showed signs of exhaustion. Sergeant Merriam had just signaled a rest for all crews when there was a shout from one of the sentries. "Their ships are under sail." None of the gun crews moved as the militiamen broke ranks and ran to the far side of the parapets.

"I suppose we should see what this is about," Sergeant Merriam said, nodding to his crew. Will stood up. The Lower Bay was filled with ships heading against a light tide up the Narrows, their clean white sails uniformly billowing in the wind. They hugged the Staten Island side and many of them dropped anchor. Soon, the water was filled with flat-bottomed landing barges as the transports disgorged row after row of red-coated soldiers and deposited them on the far shore. [6]

"If we had cannon at the Narrows, it would not be such an easy landing," Merriam observed, as some of the transports had trouble holding position and drifted closer to the Brooklyn side. Will felt some relief the troops were landing on Staten Island. That meant no battle at Cobble Hill Fort was imminent. The Connecticut militia were trying to count the transports, troop carriers and troops and were becoming increasingly agitated.

"There must be more than ten thousand of them. Look at the transports waiting to come up from the Lower Bay."

"Ten thousand," another scoffed. "I would wager it is double that number. And see, there are horses coming from that ship," another said. "I did not think they would bring cavalry."

"They brought their whole army," a man near Will said. "They crossed the ocean with more troops than we have raised from all of the colonies," he said, a note of desperation in his voice. "There are more British troops than people in Boston," another cried.

Sergeant Merriam called the gun crews to order, directed the militiamen around the gun emplacements to move away, and resumed the drilling. They stopped shortly before noon, when Lieutenant Hadley arrived. "Good work men," he said as he walked the parapets, stopping at each gun crew. Will looked at Hadley who mouthed the word later and opened his telescope. Two men of war had passed the Narrows into the Upper Bay and signal flags flew from their masts.

"Hah. The wind has picked up some and the remaining transports cannot follow. They are forced to embark further down. Still it is an unopposed landing," he said, the disappointment clear in his voice. "And it should not have been."

He snapped the telescope closed in frustration and saw Colonel Sage on the parapet. "I have orders for you, sir," Hadley said and followed the Colonel down to his office in the fort. Sergeants Merriam and Otis resumed drilling the crews. This time, Strong carried a cannon ball forward after the charge had been rammed home to make the exercise more realistic.

"Careful not to drop it on your foot," Merriam shouted to Strong. "It will break the bones." In response to the caution, Strong spread his feet wide to lift the ball and winced in pain as he strained his back. They drilled throughout the afternoon as clouds blew in from the east and blocked the sun from searing their skin. During breaks, they watched the continuous lines of boats ferrying troops from the transports to Staten Island, the red coated figures disappearing inland into the woods. Just before dusk, the wind became more brisk and a few drops of rain began to fall.

Will was in the tent with the rest of his gun crew when the rain increased in intensity. "It will be hard biscuits and cold meat for dinner tonight," Tyler said, reaching into his haversack. Will felt the gnawing hunger in his stomach and tried to ignore it.

"'Tis a strange way to form a gun crew when the newest recruit returns to another unit to eat," Tyler observed, studying a piece of cold beef on his knife before taking a bite. "We would share what we have, even though it is not much tonight," Simeon Webb said.

Lieutenant Hadley pushed back the tent flap and ducked inside. He removed his tri-corn and shook the water from it, looking at the five men inside. "There is room for another cot in here, right men?" They all nodded, thinking Hadley would be spending the night with them. "Until this battle is joined and over, the new men will be living with their gun crews. General Washington's orders to all units. Besides, you will have more room tonight. Will is coming with me."

Will looked up surprised. Hadley nodded and Will put on his coat and closed his haversack. "Leave the musket here. The new man may need it." Will felt ashamed as if he were leaving the fort for an area where there was no danger of battle. He shook hands with each of them.

"Good luck lad," Sergeant Merriam said, holding on to his arm. "I will pray you return to us safely." Will followed Hadley into the yard, turning up his collar against the rain.

"Well, Will, we rode before in a storm worse than this at Dorchester Heights and had no shelter but a canvas oiled cloth." He mounted and pulled Will up behind him. "Tonight, we can look forward to our brick barracks on Broadway. And tomorrow you will meet with Mr. Van Hooten."

Will leaned forward, locking his arms around Hadley's chest, as the mare trotted out of the fort.

"What am I supposed to do?" he shouted to be heard over the wind and driving rain.

"Mr. Van Hooten will tell you. That is all I know," Hadley said. As they reached the bottom of the corkscrew road, Hadley kicked the mare into a gallop, leaving Will to his own thoughts, fears and uncertainties.

Chapter 3 - On A Secret Mission

Brigadier General Timothy Ruggles sat comfortably in the wide wooden chair, the buttons of his waistcoat open, as his man servant pulled off Ruggles' polished knee high black boots. It had been five days since His Majesty's troops had disembarked on Staten Island. Today's lunch with General Howe and his staff had gone well, helped along with excellently prepared roasted fowl, fresh vegetables, most welcome after the long voyage from Nova Scotia, and good claret. He found General Howe to be a reasonable man, genuinely receptive to advice from educated Colonials with political experience and particularly one such as he, who had served in the military as well. The British General had given him command of the three companies of the Loyal American Associators, good Tories from Massachusetts who had temporarily left their homes, sailed to Halifax with General Howe's Army and now were ready to put an end to this nonsense of armed resistance to the Crown.[1]

Ruggles was confident it would all end here, in New York City. As he had predicted to General Howe on the voyage down the east coast, the people of Staten Island would welcome the King's troops. No cowardly sniping from behind stone walls and felled trees on narrow roads as during the retreat from Lexington and Concord. General Howe and his senior staff were now welcome guests at the finest homes and estates on the Island.

The farms and countryside were prosperous with no sign of rebellion.

The arrival of the British fleet and the Army would reassure the good people of Long Island and New York City their King would protect them and their property from this rebellious rabble. And those who were waiting to see which way the wind was blowing would flock to support the Crown after having observed the power and might brought to bear on their behalf. More than one hundred and thirty ships, at least forty ships of the line, twenty five thousand of the finest and best-equipped troops and more on the way. They would crush the rebel army, capture its leaders and end the rebellion. Then, he could return to his law practice and business interests in Boston, perhaps even be given a Royal appointment in appreciation for his services.

General Howe seemed to have accepted Ruggles' persuasive arguments, seconded by Governor Tyron. This was not an army of invasion or occupation. Not in New York. It was here to protect and defend his Majesty's subjects. They must extend a hand of friendship to those loyal to the Crown and deal firmly with those who have rebelled. When the Army crossed the Narrows to Long Island the troops must not steal food and livestock, as was the custom in European wars. He told General Howe and his officers, these are not European peasants but men of English stock and blood who welcome and support the troops. All property must be protected, all goods paid for, all women respected. Ruggles was afraid these orders would not be given or enforced. Already there had been complaints about young women being raped, not by just common soldiers but officers as well. General Howe had promised to investigate and convene court martials promptly.

Ruggles walked to the window of his second floor room. It had a fine view of the Narrows and off to the left the brick buildings of New York City. It was getting dark. He removed his wig, running his fingers through his thin hair. Something nagged at him. While General Howe understood the need to treat loyalists fairly, the younger officers were too full of themselves, too eager to show the rebels the sword and let what may happen to the civilians. They were egged on by General Grant who espoused with vehemence his position of no quarter and a war of destruction, laying waste to the land like the British wars in Scotland, to terrorize the populace into submission.[2]

The officers and men General Howe had chosen to reconnoiter Long Island were hot blooded cavalry, young bucks eager to prove themselves, and bursting with energy after being cooped up on ships for weeks. General Howe had agreed Ruggles could assign one of his Loyal Associators to land with the Cavalry on the Island, east of Oyster Bay. Ruggles was confident his man would carry the message to the farmers and landowners- the army had arrived to protect them. And he would serve to restrain those among the cavalry who might otherwise be inclined to obey their more violent natures.

He had selected his young aide, John Stoner to accompany the reconnaissance party, unwilling to spare any of his regular officers whose company he much enjoyed on the hunts and at the lavish dinners given by the landed gentry of Staten Island. Ruggles judged John to be of solid character although a bit plebian and unworldly. True, he thought, Stoner had been overly zealous in Boston but that had been a hostile environment, created by undisciplined mobs of common laborers and mere tradesmen, stirred up by a few radicals, who wrote incendiary and insulting broadsheets, harping about their rights and refusing to pay their taxes to the Crown. Stoner's use of force against these lower class ingrates who had rejected the lawful appointed King's representatives, put them in their place before the British troops departed from the city. A lesson they deserved, Ruggles thought, rationalizing Stoner's rampage among the warehouses and tradesmen's shops near the harbor.

On the other hand, the people on Long Island had estates and were landed gentry with strong mercantile ties to Britain. He had a few words with John, following the dinner with General Howe, before Stoner left with the others and boarded the transport. They would be landing on Long Island sometime early tomorrow morning. He rubbed his eyes, suddenly feeling tired, his joints aching. He stared off into the dark toward New York City, watching the glow of a large bonfire, flickering like a small candle in the distance. The sooner this rebellion was quashed the better. He was getting too old for campaigns in the field.

—⁂—

John Stoner felt the aloofness of the twenty troopers in the predawn darkness as they sailed across the Lower Bay. Embarking on a sandy beach, they ignored him, first exercising their mounts to banish the horses' stiffness and nervousness from being on a ship again. Without a word to him, they divided up into hunting parties. He tagged along with one group, recognizing they tried to lose him by riding at full gallop and jumping over hedges and brush. He was a better than adequate horseman and had managed to keep up. That seemed to have earned his hunting party's grudging respect. In the early evening, they regrouped in a wooded copse of ash and oak, lit fires and roasted the deer, hare and pheasants they had killed.

"So, tell us, General Ruggles' man," one of the officers sneered after the meal. He was propped against his saddle, his long legs stretched out in front of him. "If we find a prosperous farmer with fresh cheese, butter and a well stocked larder, we must leave him alone or else you will report us to your master?" Some of the others moved closer to the fire. He looked around the group, the flames casting shadows on their unfriendly faces. He wanted to ingratiate himself with them. He craved their acceptance. They were from aristocratic families with wealth and connections. They represented opportunities for him, both here and in Britain. He had grander aspirations than to become the chief clerk to a frugal Boston merchant. Joining Ruggles' Loyal American Associators had been just a first step.

"And if we find some plump young lass and give her a stroking, will you be acting the observer scribe, taking notes for use at our courts martial?" another officer asked.

John felt the situation could turn ugly, unless he quickly established himself.

"Gentlemen," he began, licking his lips. "You are fresh from Britain and may not be aware of how much we endured when surrounded by the rebel army in Boston. And how those of us in Boston, loyal to the Crown, treated the rebels and their supporters who abused us."

"Pray enlighten us," the officer John knew as Lieutenant Chatsworth said sarcastically. John rapidly told of the terrors inflicted by mobs calling themselves the Sons of Liberty and the Committees of Safety and how, before leaving Boston, in carrying out General Howe's orders, the Loyalists had taken revenge on known rebels and rebel supporters. He told of the looting of homes of silver and jewels, fine glassware and bottles of wine, of taking what they wanted, and forcing women as well, exaggerating the number of rapes and his participation in them, knowing none of them would deign to verify his story. When he had finished, he could see they looked at him differently. He had defused their animosity toward him as a potential informer. Now, they were inclined to view him more as a likely co-conspirator.

"My point gentlemen is on Long Island, there will be plenty of opportunity, as we reconnoiter the roads and terrain, to enjoy the hospitality of true Loyalists and to punish those who actively support the rebellion. If Long Island is anything like Boston, the King's loyal subjects will be quick to direct us to those who have threatened and oppressed them. If you exercise your righteous wrath on such people, there will be nothing for me to report to General Ruggles."

He knew he had won them over when the officer who had called him Ruggles' man, passed him a canteen of red wine.

—⁓—

On Wednesday, July 9th Will Stoner stood with the small contingent of Colonel Knox's Headquarters Guard on The Commons, just north of St. Paul's Church. It was a little after 6 pm and the July sky was beginning to darken. There were several other regiments drawn up in full dress uniform. Behind them crowds of civilians noisily pushed forward, many of them holding freshly printed broadsheets of the Declaration of Independence. When the news had reached the City a few days ago, people had celebrated in the streets. Now, the reasons for the break with Britain would be read to the troops. Will listened, catching some phrases, missing others as the words were lost in the noise from the crowd. He would get his own broadsheet and study it in his leisure.

The officer, mounted on a large grey horse, finished reading, stood up in his stirrups, lifted his tri-corn and called for three cheers for General Washington. The troops responded loudly and remained in their positions as the crowd of militiamen and civilians, seemingly with a single purpose surged down Broadway, shouting insults about the King and death to all Tories. By the time Will and the Headquarters Unit arrived at Bowling Green, where the large statue of King George III dominated the square, the crowd had lit a huge bonfire and attached ropes to the King's laurel wreathed head and his horse's neck and body and were vigorously pulling in different directions, shouting and cheering at the effort. A few men with iron bars had climbed the statue and were attempting to pry the gigantic mounted figure off its pedestal.[3]

Will walked past the boisterous mob to Colonel Knox's headquarters, saluted the sentry and climbed the stairs, directed by the clerk to the room Mr. Van Hooten used as his office. He knocked, waiting for permission to enter and opened the door. Elisabeth's father was seated at his desk. Adam Cooper, in his Marblehead Mariners' uniform, sat across from him. He turned to see Will and jumped up to embrace him. Will felt his friend's strong black arms grip him tightly.

"What are you doing here," they both asked each other simultaneously and broke into laughter.

"Sit down Will," Van Hooten said, without rising. "I was awaiting your arrival." This was Will's first opportunity to see Elisabeth's father up close. Elisabeth definitely took her looks from her mother although she had her father's sharply defined nose. He was middle aged, stout and solid, with a slight bulge where his waistcoat was buttoned over his stomach. He had a long head, accentuated by his balding high forehead, thick lips appropriate for his wide mouth, and a heavy, bony chin. It was his eyes which drew Will to him, black as coal, dark and piercing, concealing his thoughts but taking in everything around him.

"Do you speak Dutch, Will?" he asked abruptly. Will shook his head. "'Tis a pity," Van Hooten said. "We may have need of a secret language."

"I speak a little and understand more," Adam said, to both their surprise. They waited for him to explain further. "There was a freed slave from the Dutch West Indies in Marblehead, a cooper like my father. I learned some of the language from him." He grinned, pleased to have shocked both of them.

Van Hooten spoke quickly and Adam responded haltingly.

"Amazing," Elisabeth's father said, smiling as if he were a teacher assessing a pupil who had shown promise where none had been thought to exist. He sat in the chair, silent for a moment evaluating how Adam's ability could be useful.

"I have undertaken the task of traveling to farmers and their communities in Brooklyn and some of the towns further east on the Island," Van Hooten said. "It is not important you know the reason for my journey. It was thought wise for me to have companions for protection but who would not arouse suspicion." He looked at both of them. "You, Will, are to be my nephew, from upstate New York, helping me with my business. I am told you are good with horses. You will be our driver. The Colonel has given orders for you to take any horse and wagon of your choosing." Will nodded, already thinking of harnessing Big Red to a sturdy wagon he had seen in the stables.

Van Hooten turned to Adam, sitting smartly in his Mariner's uniform. "You, Private Cooper will play the part of my man servant. Colonel Glover recommended you as a man of sound judgment and prudence. Also one I would want at my side, if the need arose." Adam inclined his head in acknowledgment. "We will leave before dawn tomorrow. The fewer eyes watching our departure the better our chances for success. Colonel Glover will have the Mariners ferry us across the East River to assure further confidentiality. Will, see to the food and supplies for a week's duration."

There was barely a faint pink glow in the cloudy eastern sky when Will finished hitching Big Red to the wagon on the Brooklyn side of the river.[4] A few of the Mariners who had ferried them across waved goodbye as Will urged Big Red up the slope of the heights, on to the road past Brooklyn Village. They passed the Dutch Reformed Church and the Ferry Tavern and headed east on the Flatbush Road as the sky showed a sliver of orange light in the distance. Van Hooten sat next to Will on the wooden bench. Adam lay against the sacks of provisions in the bed of the wagon. Elisabeth's father had two pistols concealed in the haversack between his feet. His musket was with Adam. For appearances sake, neither Will nor Adam carried any firearms. Will's knife was in a sheath on his waist. Adam hid his in his boot. Will drove in silence, intimidated by Elisabeth's father's presence next to him and unsure what to say or how to even begin a conversation.

They rode without speaking for much of the first morning, greeting with a touch of hand to hat, the occasional farm wagon or rider too late for the Brooklyn Ferry, The awkward silence made Will nervous. They passed fields of wheat, not quite ripe for harvesting, grazing cattle watched over by Negro farmhands, and small wooded glens of tall oak, slender ash and wide branched chestnut trees. By late morning they reached the intersection with the Shore Road. Van Hooten indicated they would stop at the crossroads tavern. A large wooden sign swinging overhead in the gentle breeze with a carving of a fat man in a white apron identified the establishment as Baker's Tavern.

"Tend to your horse and then join me inside. Adam best you remain with the wagon and mind the haversack," Van Hooten said, climbing down from his seat and walking around stiffly to flex his legs, before going inside. When Will entered he saw it was also a small general store, with shelves, some empty, some stocked with cloth, others with a few tools and implements. He recognized the hay and corn knives, iron candle hooks and augurs, different types of hammers and hatchets, all for the neighboring farmers. Although it was not yet noon, Van Hooten was seated with a group of men at a rough-hewn table, drinking from a tankard.

"Ah, nephew," he said, beckoning him over. "Ask our landlord for bread and cheese and hard cider for you and Adam, as well as a half-bucket of oats for the horse. You may graze him in the pasture behind the kitchen when you are done." Will ignored the curious looks of the men, mumbled "Yes, Uncle," and went outside to sit with Adam in front of the stable.

"What do you think this is all about?" he asked Adam, as he cut off a piece of cheese and offered it to him.

Adam took off his slouch hat and scratched his short curly hair vigorously. "It is more than a pleasant ride in the countryside and less than a pitched battle," he said, smiling up at Will, who was standing to ease the crick in his back. "We are armed too heavily for the first, and not enough for the latter. I hope we are sufficiently provisioned against the danger only Mr. Van Hooten knows." He spat on the ground.

"And I do not like acting as another's servant, nor seeing slaves doing their masters' bidding in the fields, under the watchful eye of a white overseer with a whip in hand."

"You are playing a part Adam," Will said gently. "It is for a cause and a purpose. Keep your temper under control. You are still a free man and my friend Adam who taught me how to catch fish in the ocean."

Adam snorted and said nothing. Will moved under an eave to escape the hot sun. Adam sullenly remained seated in front of the barn staring at a large bug on the ground struggling to carry a piece of straw.

About two hours later, Elisabeth's father emerged with another man who by his clothes appeared to be a person of wealth. The two of them engaged in an animated discussion away from the tavern entrance, as Will hitched Big Red and brought the wagon around. Van Hooten hoisted himself up on the seat and nodded to Adam in the back.

"We will take the Flatbush Road east, pay the toll if we must although we carry nothing, and stay the night at an estate before proceeding on. My acquaintance from the tavern has assured me we will be well received at this person's home."

"Who is he?" Will asked, sensing Van Hooten was in a more talkative mood.

"A man whose family came from Connecticut and settled here, first to farm and then to do business. He has ties with some of the shipping companies in New York. I have heard of him and maybe even sold some of my flour, salted butter and other commodities to his agents."

"And where will we go then?" Will asked probing for more information.

"That depends. My intention is to find the merchants and those who provide services to the landed gentry with large wheat farms. I have been told it would be advantageous for me to ride further east toward Jamaica and perhaps beyond to Hempstead. The wheat grown on those plains is of excellent quality too."

For what advantage, Will wondered. Was Van Hooten seeking

to purchase wheat for the army in New York? That seemed unlikely. And why seek out the merchants and not the landed gentry? It made no sense to Will.

"After tonight, you and Adam must exercise greater caution. Be more observant of our surroundings. Listen to the talk of people in the inns and stables and servants' quarters," he said turning to Adam in the wagon bed. "The entire British Army is across The Narrows. They may have their own spies on this side. And Tory sympathizers as well."

"Their own spies." Will noticed Van Hooten's slip. Because we are the American spies, he thought.

"Now, Will. Inform me about your adventures after you left us in Albany. Elisabeth told me before she departed with Mrs. Knox, you were severely beaten in Boston. I also understand your brother is a Tory supporter."

Hesitantly, Will related his adventures hauling the cannons through the Berkshires and arriving in Cambridge. In the beginning he felt awkward but gained confidence as Van Hooten asked him a question or two, encouraging him to elaborate or clarify a detail. By the time he told of his rescue by Adam and the Mariners in Boston, it was almost dark and they were passing orchards of apple trees and vegetable gardens of summer squash, melons and greens, announcing the presence of the estate where they would spend the night.

—m—

John enjoyed the next few days, pleased by the troopers' acceptance. During the day, they rode past lush fields of wheat and corn, grazing cattle and sheep, across a vast plain, hunting at will, taking note of the flat terrain and the condition of the roads, running east to west from South Oyster Bay toward The King's County and the heights of Brooklyn on the East River.[5] It was clear, even to John, the Island could support vast numbers of troops with mutton and beef, poultry, eggs, cheese, grain for bread, and even fresh fruit and vegetables. In the evenings, with smoke from the green wood on the campfires to ward off the mosquitos, and canteens of wine and silver flasks of brandy being passed among them, the troopers questioned him about the rebels, who were they, did they have any military training, and were the rumors true about the riflemen -they could shoot a man out of a saddle at two hundred yards.

John had the same opinion as General Ruggles, although unlike the General, he had never been in battle. It did not stop him from confidently giving his views that the militia were ill-disciplined and would run at the first charge, they were afraid of the bayonet, they were especially fearful of cavalry and the Hessians, and many would desert. He predicted General Howe would break the back of the rebellion in New York by defeating the rebel army and capturing its officers, many of whom had been tradesmen or merchants in civilian life. This provoked first incredulity and then derisive laughter among the troopers.

As they moved further inland and encountered different roads, they split into three groups of seven taking separate routes, one tracking back near the Bay, another heading further north toward the Long Island Sound, and John's group riding west toward the more populated areas in the center of the Island. By unspoken agreement, when they met farmers or travelers on the roads, John would greet them and make inquiries about the road they were on, passes or alternate routes and inns or estates where they might stay. They were directed by one friendly fellow to the town of Hempstead where, he assured them, they would be most welcome.

The town consisted of a stone church with a tall wooden spire, a general store and inn and a scattering of well-constructed modest farm houses and cultivated garden plots. The most prominent structures were two large red brick mansions at either end of the town, equidistant from the church. The farmer had been correct in his assessment. They were graciously welcomed into the house of Joseph Markham, who insisted his neighbor and good friend, Robert Clarke, the owner of the other mansion, share his good fortune and host some of His Majesty's officers in his home. Markham arranged for a joint dinner in his elegant manor. John marveled at the fine wood flooring covered with Scotch rugs, dark mahogany and cherry furniture with polished brass handles, the glass chandeliers, flowered wall-papered rooms and the finely woven curtains, all of which he saw impressed the cavalry officers as well. The dinner was enhanced by the presence of the Markham and Clarke daughters, who delighted in the attention of the officers, ruggedly resplendent in their scarlet jackets with gold trim, white breeches and polished boots. John thought the girls a little too bovine and not much to look at. Nevertheless, he was jealous of their flirting with the troopers and angry they paid no attention to him in his drab country coat.

After dinner, the men gathered in the study. A few of the troopers wistfully glanced toward the adjacent sitting room and the female voices and laughter coming from within. They listened as Markham described the situation in their town, how a year ago, the northern part had declared "independence" and formed North Hempstead. It was now a hotbed of rebellion. "Can you imagine it," he said with disdain. "We all met in St. George's Church and they said they did not like our toasting the King, or our Minister praying for the good health of His Majesty, or our refusal to sign their petitions. They were incited by this man, Peter Onderdonk. As his name implies, he is of Dutch descent," Markham said disdainfully. "They formed their own town and now have their own militia and threaten us with violence."[6]

Clarke had listened to his friend with growing nervousness and agitation. He was a small man, elderly with a thin narrow face. The yellow fabric of the ornate armchair in which he was seated exacerbated his unhealthy pallor. "What Joseph says is true. I am afraid to ride out to inspect my crops without at least two of my blacks to accompany me. Our women must be escorted at all times, to protect their honor. An afternoon picnic in our orchards is now fraught with fear for my three dearest daughters. It is no longer possible to enjoy a delightful summer outing. When these rebels encounter us, they jeer and make all manner of threats. And we have done nothing except remain steadfast in our loyalty to the King," he said spreading his arms in dismay.

"Well," Lieutenant Chatsworth said, standing and pouring himself another sherry from the cut glass decanter. "Perhaps at dawn, we will pay a visit to this Dutchman and teach him some manners. You will be so kind, gentlemen as to give us directions so that we may call upon this lout." Joseph Markham nodded. Stoner looked at the other cavalrymen. Their eyes glittered, partly from the wine and port, but he thought more in anticipation of coming action. He determined he would play a part as well and further earn their respect. He carried a pistol and knew how to use it. He had done so before in Boston. The cultured sounds of the clavier drifted into the study and they eagerly adjourned to the sitting room where one of Clarke's daughters was seated at the keyboard.

They rose and were mounted before dawn. John nervously sat on his horse, waiting in the darkness. He opened and closed his saddle bag, making sure his pistol was inside and at the ready. He knew the six troopers would eagerly take the lead and he could safely stay in the rear to avoid danger. He followed as the cavalry cantered down the road leading to North Hempstead.

Markham and Clarke had described Onderdonk's house as the fieldstone building next to the Dutch Reformed Church. John saw the dark stubby spire rising above a round stone structure and then the two-story home nearby. He was alarmed to see lights in the side windows and in the barn behind. He had hoped they would surprise the Dutchman. Were the farmers beginning their chores, or somehow had they been warned? If the militia of North Hempstead had been alerted, he was afraid they would open fire at them from the darkness behind the stone walls of the fields and from the shadows of the buildings. He peered nervously around him and hunched forward close to his horse's neck to present a smaller target. The troopers rode forward, erect in their saddles.

As they trotted into the un-gated yard, the front door opened and three figures emerged, silhouetted by the candlelight and flames from the fireplace within. The larger man of the three stepped forward. He held a lantern and made sure it illuminated the pistol he had in his other hand. The other two, stayed closer to the door, one had a pitchfork, the other a pike.

"Who are you and why do you disturb us?" the leader said. His voice was deep, the simple English words spoken with a thick accent.

"We are looking for the rebel Dutchman Onderdonk," Lieutenant Chatsworth shouted, bringing his horse to a halt in front of the man. The other five troopers spread out in a line on either side. John remained in the rear to the left near the barn, ready to spur his horse back down the road if there were militia inside. He removed his pistol from the saddlebag, pulled back the hammer and held it tightly in his free hand.

"I am Pieter Onderdonk," the man with the lantern replied. "And again, I pray who are you?"

"I am Lieutenant Chatsworth of His Majesty's 16th Light Dragoons. And I am here on behalf of the King's loyal subjects, to teach you a lesson." At that, Chatsworth pulled back on the reins so his horse reared in front of Onderdonk, its front hooves pawing the air near his head. The Dutchman reflexively took a step backwards. From his vantage point, it was unclear to John whether Onderdonk meant to raise his pistol, but his arm came up in a threatening manner.

Chatsworth spurred his horse forward and simultaneously slashed at Onderdonk with his sabre cutting him on the side of his head and neck. Onderdonk dropped the lantern as he crumpled to ground. The two men with him turned to run into the house for protection. They were shot in the back as they fled. Chatsworth leaned down from his saddle and picked up Onderdonk's still-burning lantern and rode toward the barn, swinging the light beside him. John saw a shadow at the corner of the barn emerge and take aim. Quickly he raised his pistol and fired. Chatsworth reined his horse in and then came forward slowly holding the lantern high. The light revealed a Negro servant slumped against a tree, his chest bloody and a musket by his side.

"Thank you John," Chatsworth acknowledged calmly, as he passed Stoner. He flung the lantern in a high arc into the hayloft of the barn. He waited until he was satisfied there was an orange glow visible through the open loft door. John heard women's screams from inside the house.

"Let us see what sport awaits us in there," Chatsworth said, clapping John on the shoulder as they tied their horses to the railing. John felt his cock harden as he stepped over Onderdonk's body in the yard and followed the Lieutenant inside.

Chapter 4 - Encounter at The Rising Sun

For the next few days, Van Hooten, Will and Adam continued east on the Flatbush Road, staying at inns before turning north on the King's Highway. Their pace was slow, which puzzled Will, although Van Hooten seemed satisfied. One night they stayed in a manor house in Flatlands, above the junction of the Flatbush Road and the King's Highway. The owner was clearly a loyalist and Van Hooten spent the dinner and evening hours discussing crops and shipping costs to England, before retiring early. The next night, they slept at a wealthy merchant's home in New Lots. This man's sympathies lay with the patriots' cause and he and Van Hooten stayed up late, drinking wine and talking until almost dawn.

All along their way, they encountered farmers travelling west. Their wagons were laden with fresh vegetables, kegs of cider, early sweet corn, melons and ripe summer apples. Prices were high they told Van Hooten. Demand was great. General Washington's army's needed to be fed. They were in a hurry to get to the Brooklyn Ferry, cross to Manhattan and sell at an advantage.

Will sensed these farmers would also sell to the British when they arrived on the Island, desiring nothing more than to make a profit. One farmer, with his Negro slave beside him on the wagon, told of British cavalry raids on farms to the east. He was not against the Crown, he said, nor was he with those who called themselves patriots.

All he wanted to do was to live in peace and sell his crops to whoever was willing to pay the going price.

The man reminded Will of his father, a person devoid of principles, his actions dictated solely by his desire to make money. He had not thought about Thomas Stoner since writing him in April, before joining Colonel Knox's Regiment and marching south from Boston. He had no regrets. His father, he knew, only rued the loss of his Will's labor on their farm and had no concern for his well-being.

Although it was the heat of the day and the road was bumpy, Van Hooten was in a good mood. He had established solid contacts with several of the merchants and was impressed by their commitment and sense of "probity", as he put it.

"Contacts for what purpose?" Will asked directly.

Van Hooten hesitated before answering. "Surely, you two must have guessed by now." His piercing glance provoked Will to stammer and admit he and Adam had speculated about it.

"And what did you conclude?"

"That you are recruiting spies for when the British land on the Island."

"It is somewhat more than that," Van Hooten said. "I have found those who will recruit and pay others to gather information. I have left substantial sums with people we have met in whom I have confidence. They in turn will create an expanded network of contacts- farmers, wagoners, tradespeople- those who can freely enter and leave the British army camps. It is natural they will see and hear things that may be of value to our cause." Van Hooten turned to see if Adam was listening in the back of the wagon. Adam removed his slouch hat and sat up.

"But for what end," Adam said. "The battle will not be here. General Howe will attack Manhattan from the Hudson River on the west and from the East River north of the city. Their fleet provides them with superiority we cannot defend against. They simply have to wait for favorable winds and tides and trap the army in Manhattan."

"What say you Will?" Van Hooten asked.

He thought how to reply to the question. He sensed Van Hooten was testing him, gauging his abilities since they had driven up Brooklyn

Heights. "Military strategy is beyond me, sir and Adam certainly knows more about the sea than I. But, they say General Howe has more than 20,000 troops. He will find more provisions here to feed them than on Staten Island. I believe at least some of their army will land here and threaten our forts."

Adam grunted. "One conclusion to draw from what you say my friend is the British will move quickly against Manhattan before they deplete the food supplies on Staten Island. You and I will be away from the battles, idly traveling over the turnpikes of Long Island. I would rather be of use somewhere else and you should be too as an artillery man." He slumped back down against the sideboard and pulled his slouch hat down over his face, indicating he would say no more on the subject.

"He does not like playing the role of a servant and being mistaken for a slave," Will said to explain his friend's behavior.

Van Hooten contemplated the sullen stocky figure slouched on the floorboards of the wagon. "Whatever the British battle plan, we must have sound intelligence," he said gruffly to Adam, whose face was still hidden by his hat. "To provide the means to obtain it is our mission. Tomorrow, we will venture to the middle of Long Island and discern the sentiments of the people there."

The flat farm fields, bordered by low hedges, gave way to wooded hills on both sides of the road. As their host of the previous night had informed them, the inn was just beyond the break in the woods.

The Rising Sun Tavern was a solid, two-story stone building with a pair of tall chimneys at the rear of the pitched shingled roof. It stood at the intersection of the King's Highway and Jamaica Road.[1] They arrived sweaty and sore from the constant jarring of the rutted road. It was late in the hot July afternoon, but still early enough to secure comfortable lodgings. One room for Van Hooten and Will to share, and a less desirable place for Adam in the servants' quarters. Will unhitched Big Red from the wagon and watered him at the trough behind the stable. Adam followed Van Hooten into the Tavern, carrying his haversack up to the room. When they came down the stairs, there were three British Cavalry officers in the dining room, together with a civilian. They were seated at a long table, drinking from tankards. The owner, a curly haired, ruddy-faced man hovered nervously near their table, uncomfortable in their presence.

"What is your name landlord?" one of the officers asked, stretching his feet on the bench.

"I am Everts Howard, and this is my son," he said placing a hand on the shoulder of the young boy who had carried out the tankards.

"So this is Howard's Half Way House," the officer said. "It is named after you but then why the sign out there," he said pointing to the window with his crop, "The Rising Sun? Are you trying to confuse us?" One of the other officers laughed.

"We face due east and catch the sun rise in the morning," Howard replied nervously. "Some people call it after me as we are halfway between Jamaica and Brooklyn Village. Others prefer the name for the position of the sun. And who do I have the honor of addressing and serving," he asked, wiping the sweat from his face with his apron and placing his broad hands protectively on his son's shoulders.

The officer waited before answering, increasing Howard's discomfort. "I am Lieutenant Chatsworth of His Majesty's 16th Dragoons." He introduced the other officers. "And our other companion is from the Loyal American Associators, John Stoner, aide to General Timothy Ruggles."

Chatsworth turned his attention to Van Hooten who had come into the barroom, Adam trailing behind him.

"Do not Negroes take their hats off in the presence of gentlemen in this country?" he said with an edge in his voice.

Van Hooten raised his hand to Adam, who immediately removed the slouch hat.

"And who are you, sir?" Chatsworth asked.

"I am Lukyens Van Hooten, from Albany. May I join you," he asked, pleasantly. Chatsworth removed his feet from the bench and gestured for Van Hooten to sit down. Adam had the presence of mind to move forward quickly and use his sleeve to wipe the bench of the mud that had dislodged from Chatsworth's boots. He retreated and sat on the lower step in sight of the table.

"If you are from Albany, perhaps you know my father, Thomas Stoner," John said. "He frequently went there to sell his wheat."

Van Hooten studied John's face as if he were trying to recognize his features as those of his father. "I deal with many farmers," Van Hooten said dismissively. "Neither the name nor your face are familiar."

"Oh, I have been in Boston for many years," John replied quickly, uncomfortable dwelling on his background as the son of a farmer.

"You are Dutch," Chatsworth asked Van Hooten. It was more of a statement than a question. "We have found the Dutch on the Island to be supporters of the rebels rather than loyal to His Majesty."

Van Hooten smiled over the rim of his tankard and stood up. "To His Majesty, King George. Long may he reign." There was a clatter of scraping furniture and stomping of boots as Chatsworth and the others rose and repeated the toast.

"True, I am of Dutch origin as are many in the Albany area," Van Hooten continued as he resumed his seat on the bench. "If you were to visit you would find us steadfast supporters of the Crown. I grow and buy wheat from farmers, mill the grain into flour, ship it down the Hudson on my own vessels for transport to England. My livelihood depends on our continued ties to our mother country. I have no desire for all this rebel talk of independence."

He took another sip from his tankard, his dark eyes studying John.

"And you sir. Is your father Dutch?"

"No," John said quickly, not wanting Chatsworth and the others to think he was anything other than English.

Van Hooten nodded, absorbing that information. Adam sitting on the step coughed to attract his attention. They must prevent Will from coming into the tavern. Van Hooten turned as if remembering Adam was still there.

"Adam. Go to the wagon and bring me my pistol. I want to show these officers what fine gunsmiths we have in Albany." He turned back to Chatsworth. "I am sure you will appreciate the craftsmanship." Adam effected a bow and walked quickly out the front door. He heard Chatsworth angrily commenting that Negro servants should leave by the servants' entrance, and Van Hooten making some excuse for his man's indiscretion. Adam estimated they had been inside for no more than ten minutes.

He walked quickly behind the back of the tavern and past the low framed wood shed and smoke house. Three more cavalry men came down the Jamaica Road from the east. Adam hid in the shadows of the stable as they tied their mounts to the railing in front of the inn. He dashed past the empty stalls and out the rear door into the pasture. Will was halfway up the hill loosely holding Big Red's reins as the horse grazed contently.

"Lie down in the grass. Out of sight," he said rushing up to Will. "Do it," he hissed, as Will, confused, hesitated. Adam took Big Red's reins and stood there, not looking down. Quickly he related who was inside The Rising Sun.

"My brother," Will said incredulously staring up at Adam. "Johan is here?"

"He calls himself John Stoner now. He is some kind of aide to General Ruggles, the same loyalist from Boston. Worse for us, there are now six British dragoons with him." He glanced up at the July sky just beginning to turn deep blue as the light from the sun faded. It would not be completely dark for another few hours.

"You have to stay out of sight. I will go back inside. I have to get Mr. Van Hooten his pistol. It was an excuse to get me out of the inn."

Will thought quickly. He couldn't stay hidden forever. The landlord and his son had seen him. He was supposed to be sharing a room with Van Hooten. What if the landlord asked Elisabeth's father, in front of the British, where his nephew was? No, they would have to leave now. And risk being pursued. It was only twelve miles to the ferry, and closer to the forts. They would have to leave the wagon. They could not out run the cavalry with it.

Adam led Big Red down the hill toward the stable. Will kept the horse between him and the tavern until they were safely inside.

The simple solution was for him to disappear before being seen by Johan. He could hide in the woods overnight and wait until the British left.

"Tell Elisabeth's father I will be in the woods down the Jamaica Road. You can find me in the morning."

"No," Adam said. "You must remain here until I talk to Van Hooten. Find a hiding place in the stable and wait for my return."

Adam slipped back into the tavern through the servants' door, quietly went upstairs to the room, removed the pistol from the haversack, wrapped it in a cloth, and came back into the inn through the kitchen. In the brief time he had been gone, the barroom had filled with travelers and farmers as well as the additional cavalry troopers. Van Hooten waved at Adam.

"What took you so long?" he said angrily, grabbing the pistol and dismissing Adam with a wave of his hand. "Look at this, Lieutenant. Do you not agree it is a fine example of the gun maker's craft?"

John studied Adam's muscular shoulders as he retreated around the corner. He had taken a dislike to the Negro. He was too confident, carrying himself almost with an air of equality, he thought. The way he walked was peculiar. Not like a house servant or even a field hand. He couldn't quiet place the gait. He mulled over the image. It would come to him, he thought as he drank down the last of his second tankard of ale. He decided to use a portion of Ruggles' money to pay for the food and lodging tonight. He would forge a few receipts from inns for the times they had been guests of the landed gentry. Might as well make a few pounds on the side from this trip.

Will waited nervously, squatting down in the shadows at the back of Big Red's stall. The familiar smell of the horses, even the pungent odor of the urine drenched straw calmed him. He heard several farmers boisterously enter the stable, leading their horses.

One walked further back into the darkness and tied his animal to a ring outside Big Red's stall.

"This is a large horse," he said, leaning against an upright beam, admiring Big Red. "At least 17 hands, maybe more." He took a step into the stall. "He must be a wonder behind a plow."

"Come, Ephraim," another farmer called. "We want to eat and drink and get some sleep before we leave for the ferry in the early morning. You may admire horses another time."

Will held his breath and watched the man reluctantly turn and follow his friends. He stood up to flex his legs and stroked Big Red's neck.

Inside the inn, Adam sat nervously on the steps leading to the servants' quarters, a low ceiling room with a long sloping overhang of a roof. He hoped Van Hooten would leave the British officers and talk to him alone. They needed a plan. If Will left on his own and something went wrong, the troopers would hunt him down like a hare.

"Adam," Van Hooten shouted over the noisy crowd in the barroom. He was still seated on the bench surrounded by the British cavalry men. Adam noticed John Stoner was not there. It was hot in the room and the officers' faces were flushed, almost as red as their scarlet coats, which they had removed and thrown carelessly across the benches.

"Take my pistol back to my saddlebag and then help the landlord's son feed and water these officers' horses." Adam nodded and holding the pistol tightly in his hand backed away, remembering to turn toward the servants' quarters to leave the inn. Van Hooten caught up with him as he squeezed past a crowded table of farmers.

He leaned closer to Adam and said in Dutch, "Tell Will to be ready to leave after dark. Take the musket and your haversack and have three horses ready. We will have to leave the wagon. Do you understand?" Adam nodded and turned to see John Stoner brush past behind Van Hooten, who was oblivious to his presence. He tried to warn Van Hooten Stoner had passed behind him, but Elisabeth's father had already started back to the dining room.

John sat down with the officers, thinking over what he had just witnessed. He was returning from taking a piss behind the tavern. He deliberately chose to walk behind Van Hooten to hear what he was saying to his servant. He didn't understand but he knew the words were Dutch. Why would Van Hooten speak Dutch to his servant and how could a Negro learn Dutch? There was more to this amiable Albany merchant than he was letting on. He would find out by dealing with the black first and then confront Van Hooten. He smiled, thinking how his cleverness would impress Chatsworth and further ingratiate him to the Lieutenant. In the meantime, it wouldn't hurt to have another tankard and some food.

Adam and the landlord's son, each leading two of the cavalry horses, walked them slowly past the low stone wall, through the rectangular wood gate and into the stable. Adam sent the boy back for two more. Quickly he moved back to Big Red's stall and while tying up one of the horses related Van Hooten's plan to Will. "Stay hidden," Adam cautioned. "The boy will be in and out until the horses are fed and watered."

"What is your name," the landlord's son asked as he and Adam poured oats from a barrel into wooden feed buckets and carried them to the horses' stall.

"My name is Adam. What is yours?

"I am Ethan. Where is the other man who came with you?"

"He is not feeling well. He is lying upstairs in my master's room."

Ethan nodded. "My father is afraid of the soldiers. He told me to stay away from them. May I remain here with you in the stables?"

Adam needed time alone with Will, to plan what to do and to wait for Van Hooten to come.

"Is there not a safe place for you in the inn?" he asked.

Ethan looked at him with disappointment showing in his eyes and shook his head.

"Very well. Go back to the kitchen, get some cheese, bread, butter and some cider and bring it back here. I am very hungry so get enough for two. Ethan. Do not let anyone see you carrying the food and come back here. You can stay the night with me in the loft."

The boy smiled and dashed out the stable door.

"Will," Adam said softly standing outside Big Red's stall. "You will have to pick out two other horses and get them ready. I will take the musket and our haversacks from the wagon and leave it in this stall."

"The dragoons mounts are far better than the farmers' plow horses," Will replied. "We will take two of them and their saddles. Help me remove the others from the racks and hide them about the barn. Then, cut the cinch straps all the way through." He slipped past Adam and disappeared into another stall near the stable entrance.

Adam moved quickly. He returned the pistol to the saddlebag and left their belongings from the wagon outside Big Red's stall, the musket leaning against a post. He made two trips to the loft, carrying one saddle at a time, thinking the cavalrymen would spend a long time searching the stable before they looked there. He carried two more through the side door to the manure pile, found a pitchfork and covered them.

He was bending over to pick up another saddle when he heard a sound behind him. "Ethan," he called. "I am over here."

"I can see you Negro," Johan said. He stood in the middle of the entrance, a metal candle lantern in one hand and an unsheathed sword in his other. "It is time we find out the truth about you and your Master Van Hooten."

Adam backed further in the stable, crouching lower as if in fear, looking for the pitchfork he had used earlier. The candlelight reflected off the bright steel of the sword that Johan waved menacingly in front of him.

"What did Van Hooten say to you in Dutch, you black bastard? Tell me or I'll cut off your arm." He stepped forward and swung the sword back for the strike.

"Johan," Will called, stepping out of a stall behind his brother.

Johan turned and held up the lantern, lowering the sword to his side. In the yellow light, Will saw his brother had changed. It had been three years since their father had apprenticed Johan to a Boston merchant, leaving Will to assume his brother's tasks on the farm and bear their father's wrath alone. When they were growing up, he remembered Johan as quick to smile, to tease Will, and proud when his younger brother learned some skill Johan had taught him. Now, Johan's eyes were sly and feral, like a predator ready to take advantage of weakness but fearful of being attacked by a stronger animal. He had the pinched and mean look of a man constantly seeking to get the better of another, by force if he could, but preferring trickery because it was less risky. Just like their father, Will realized. Will saw he now was taller and broader across the shoulders than his older brother.

"Willem? Is that you?" Johan said raising the lantern higher. "What are you doing here?" he said, his eyes widening with surprise.

Adam hit him on the back of his head with the pistol butt and Johan collapsed without a sound. Adam quickly grabbed the lantern from the straw covered floor, snuffed out the flame and poured some water from a wooden bucket on the spot where it had fallen. He grabbed Johan by his boots and dragged him into a stall.

"Is he dead?" Will asked, looking down at Johan lying still against the wooden slats, a horse standing skittishly next to him. Even now, he did not wish his brother dead.

"I do not think so," Adam said bending over him and feeling his throat. "No, he is not. For some reason, I did not use all my strength."

There was a rustling of straw, Will tried to hide but it was too late. Ethan stood at the entrance of the stall, the pockets of his shirt bulging with bread and cheese. He held a crock in his small hands. He looked at John's body and stared at Will.

"Do not be scared, Ethan." Adam said. "This man tried to harm us. Come with me and bring the food. We will go to the rear, away from the entrance." Adam found a place where he and Ethan could sit on clean hay and Will could crouch behind them, ready to hide if someone came in.

"Ethan. You must be quiet and not say a word to anyone." The boy nodded his head and chewed on a piece of bread.

"With Johan here," Will said, gesturing with his head toward the stall," no one in the tavern knows me. "I will go back and stay with Mr. Van Hooten."

"No," Adam said. "They know me as a servant, I can move around the tavern without arousing suspicion. You must do what Mr. Van Hooten told us. Ready the horses and wait for us. Ethan. You stay with Will."

"Why do you need horses?" the boy asked, looking up at Adam.

"Because we will have to leave in haste," Adam replied.

"You promised I could stay with you."

"That was before my friend's brother came into the stable. You will be all right with your father," Adam said gruffly, hurrying into the night

After Adam left, Will crept around the stable sizing up the horses. He selected two of the cavalry mounts which seemed the most fit and rested. Will steadied each horse, while he saddled and bridled them. He readied Big Red and led the three horses outside, tying them to the hay rick behind the stable. Adam had not cut any of the cinches before Johan had surprised him. Maybe there was time for Will to do it. When he came back inside, he found Ethan sitting in the stall, looking at Johan's body.

"He is my brother," Will said quietly. "I wish he had turned out differently and we could be friends." He was relieved Johan was alive. "I wonder," he said softly to Ethan, "if he would think the same of me. Or would he kill me without hesitation." He shook his head. "I hope to never find out."

The boy's eyes were fixed on the motionless figure on the floor. "He lies so still. You have killed him instead."

"No, Ethan, my brother is. . ."

"Will. Where are you?" Van Hooten whispered loudly. Will stood up. "The horses are out back," Will said pointing outside. Adam grabbed the musket and saddlebags. Van Hooten followed them carrying his haversack. "There is no alarm inside. I thought to scatter the horses but the noise would attract attention. Leave them be, Will," Van Hooten said.

Will saw the small dark shadow of Ethan running toward the tavern. "Hurry," he hissed to Adam who was still trying to mount the horse. "I do not know how to ride," his friend replied, helplessly hopping around on one foot, the other stuck in the stirrup. The horse kept turning and now was facing toward the rear of The Rising Sun. Van Hooten impatiently trotted his mount back and forth, eager to be off. Will moved Big Red toward Adam, who dropped his foot out of the stirrup and grabbed at the reins to steady the horse.

The door to the smokehouse burst open, a bright shaft of light poured out, and then it was obscured by the dark figures of men pushing through the narrow low door. Will heard someone shout, "There they are," followed by the flash of powder and a pistol shot. He reached down, grabbed Adam by his arm and hoisted him up behind him and turned Big Red west down Jamaica Road. Van Hooten was ahead of him, his horse going at a gallop. Will nudged Big Red with his knees and felt the huge horse's strength as he surged into a lengthened stride. They had left only one horse saddled, the one Adam couldn't ride. One pursuer would be better than seven, but he could not fight off even one cavalryman brandishing his sword, with Big Red carrying double. Van Hooten had the pistols and the musket. Will urged Big Red on and they closed the distance to Elisabeth's father. The night sky was cloudy. Without any moonlight, the thickly wooded hills on either side made the road darker and more perilous at full gallop. Van Hooten apparently had realized this too and had slowed his mount to a canter. Will caught up with him at a slight bend in the road.

"You have to reach the safety of Bedford" Will shouted. "There should be some patrols from the forts. Give me a pistol and musket. You take Adam on your horse and I will wait here."

"No," Adam objected. "Mr. Van Hooten is the prize they want. He must ride on alone. You and I will delay the dragoons."

They were riding side by side having slowed to a trot. Van Hooten handed Adam his two pistols, powder horn and shot. Will took the musket from him.

"If we do not rejoin you by noon, proceed on to the Ferry," Will said. Van Hooten leaned across his saddle and grasped Will and then Adam by the forearm. "I hope to see you both in Bedford," he said before spurring his horse down the road.

Will and Adam listened in the darkness. It was too early for farm wagons to be out. The only sound of horses would be the British cavalrymen. It would take some time for them to find the saddles and mount the remaining horses. He tied Big Red to a tree. He and Adam fumbled about in the woods, working more by touch than sight. They grabbed fallen tree trunks, dead limbs, anything that they could pull loose and dragged them down to the road. It took them several trips clambering back and forth through the underbrush before they created a low barrier that extended from one side of the road to the other. Will hoped in the darkness it would be enough to either throw a rider or cripple his horse. They retreated down the road one hundred or so yards, stopped, found more fallen trees and branches and hastily pulled them on to the turnpike. There was still no sound of pursuit.

"We may have time for one more," Will said, hoisting Adam up behind him. Big Red easily carried the two of them and stood patiently amongst the trees as they scurried about the woods dragged fallen debris, dead branches and stones to the edge and rolled them down the sloping embankment. Adam put his ear to the road and shook his head. The thick clouds that had obscured the moon were dissipating and the glimmer of moonlight revealed a few tall twisted trees, the tops of their dead branches pointing like crooked fingers upward to the night sky. They rode back up the road toward the second barrier, found a densely wooded area and settled in where they had a view of the pike.

Will loaded the musket, biting off the end of the paper cartridge, pouring a little powder on the flashpan and emptying the rest down the barrel. He dropped the lead ball in and rammed it home. He would only get off one shot and as much as he hated to do so, he would aim for the horse. In the darkness, he had more chance of hitting it than the rider. Adam had loaded and cocked both pistols and rested them against a log. Will's sweaty shirt clung to him. He shivered as the cool night breeze blew across his back.

Big Red stood tied loosely to a tree behind them. He raised his head, his ears pricked forward in the direction of the tavern, his nostrils quivering. The horse made a low snuffling noise. Will nudged Adam and motioned for him to take his pistols in hand. He pulled the hammer of the musket back to full cock. There was the shrill neighing of a horse, a man's cry and other voices yelling. They had run into the first barrier. He tried to discern how many voices he had heard. Three maybe four, counting the man who had cried out. He wasn't certain.

Three men on horses came down the road more carefully and slower, at a trot now rather than a gallop. From the way they sat on their mounts, Will knew they were cavalrymen. They came to the fallen trees across the road and paused.

"Tricky rebel bastards," one of them said.

Will's finger tightened on the trigger. He braced himself for the ignition of the black powder in the flashpan close to his eye, aimed at the dark mass of the lead horse's chest and fired. The horse reared up screaming and the rider fell to the ground. Will was unsure whether he had hit the horse or the dragoon. It didn't matter. Adam fired both pistols and the two of them fled to Big Red. Will jumped up first and pulled Adam up behind him. He eased the horse down the slope to the road, loosened the reins and urged him into a gallop. Adam turned his head to look back. "There is one behind us. He is coming up fast."

"Hold on," Will commanded and felt Adam's arms tighten around his chest. He nudged Big Red with his knees and felt the horse's power. He had to gauge this right or he and Adam would both be dead. In the sparse light, cast by the sliver of the moon through the clouds, he spied one of the upright trees with the tall twisted gnarled branch he had marked as his point of recognition. He counted off Big Red's strides, leaned forward on his neck and kicked him with his heels. Big Red sailed over the last barrier they had made, landed without missing a stride and galloped down the pike. Their lone pursuer hit the last log barrier at full speed, his horse went down with a neighing cry of agony, the rider tumbling off. In the darkness, Adam, looking back, could not see whether either the horse or man got up.

Will eased up on the reins and slowed Big Red to a trot. No sense wearing him out carrying a double load. "When I reached down to pull you up I dropped the musket."

"I would prefer you not return to find it," Adam said, relaxing his grip around Will's chest.

They approached the crossroads settlement of Bedford well before dawn. They were challenged by a few irritable, drunk militiamen, rousted from their revelries at the town's one tavern, who escorted them into town.

"Thank God you are safe," Elisabeth's father said, pushing his chair back from in front of the fireplace and embracing them both. He scowled at the militiamen who followed Will and Adam into the tavern's main room.

"I had to pay them to stand guard," Van Hooten said, disgustedly. "Although I did not expect Lieutenant Chatsworth and his troopers to ride into Bedford. And now these derelict excuses for soldiers think their duty is done and they return to spend my money on drink." Will and Adam hungrily devoured the stew, bread and cheese Van Hooten ordered for them. Between mouthfuls, Will told Van Hooten of how they had delayed pursuit and of losing the musket.

Van Hooten studied the two of them in the dull lamplight of the inn. "It is good you both are unharmed. I would have had a difficult time of it with my dear daughter, if you had not returned," he said, smiling warmly at Will. "As for you, Adam, I was well served by your coolness at The Rising Sun and will genuinely thank your Colonel for recommending your participation in this mission."

Will felt a flush of happiness, and was transported to the last time he had seen Elisabeth, in Mrs. Knox's sitting room that peaceful sunny afternoon. How foolish it had been of him to plan a ride and picnic and a week long frolic. He was an enlisted soldier and the British fleet's arrival had brought the war to New York.

He thought about Johan, looking at him with surprised recognition and then lying on the stable floor. He had wanted to confront Johan and give him a chance to explain his conduct against patriotic families in Boston. Now, that would be impossible. There could be no bond between them after The Rising Sun. Still he was his brother and it was strange to know Johan was here and perhaps, they would face each other again, when the British landed in force on Long Island.

He kept these thoughts to himself as they rode out of Bedford and joined the caravan of farmers and wagons heading down the turnpike for the Brooklyn ferry boats that left at dawn.

Chapter 5 - Skirmish at Flatbush Pass

Private Georg Friedrich Engelhard stood on the deck of the H.M.S. Good Intent waiting, along with the rest of the Knyphausen Regiment, to climb down the rope ladder to the landing barge rising and falling below. Reveille had been at five. They had struck their tents, and marched in the grey light of early dawn to the ferries that took them to their assigned transports. Now, at nine a.m. he was eager to set foot on the Long Island.

Georg, conscripted at age seventeen, had been with the Regiment for three years. As the third son of a poor peasant farmer, with no possibility of inheriting his father's small land holding and without a trade or craft of his own, he had been classified as "dispensable" by the district authorities of his cantonment. Upon entering service as a private, he earned eight pence a day, barely enough to satisfy his minimal needs after deductions from his pay for his recruitment costs, uniform and unspecified medical services. Nevertheless, he had authorized ten percent of his remaining pay to be allocated to his family.[1]

At six feet two, he satisfied the Regiment's height requirements. The officers took pride that the soldiers, generally of a uniform height appeared more formidable on the battle-field and made a good impression on the parade grounds. Georg had never been in combat but had learned the Hessian's creed well. It had been beaten in to him. Obedience to orders first and above everything, then discipline and finally honor. His closest friends were two of his tent mates, Christoph Weber and Andreas Felsenheim, strong young farm boys like himself, who took to the rough life and harsh treatment like the stolid suffering oxen they had whipped to plow the fields back home. The three had been assigned to the same company, commanded by Captain Otto Seckendorf. Like all the soldiers of the Regiment, they curled and powdered their hair, tied their tails neatly with a dark ribbon and waxed their mustaches.

This time Georg was not so afraid of the sea but he still felt uneasy on open water. However, he reasoned, he could almost touch Staten Island on his right, and to his left, across the bay he could see their destination, the flat sandy beach of Long Island. Neither he nor any of his fellow soldiers could swim. Even if he could, he thought he would sink like a stone, weighted down by his powder blue woolen uniform and his knee-high black gaiters. His British-issued Brown Bess musket alone was eleven pounds, more with its seventeen-inch-long bayonet, affixed and gleaming in the early morning sun. Not to mention the extra cartridges and rations they carried. Georg touched his high peaked brass cap for luck, running his fingers over the embossed Hessian lion and along the monogram of the reigning Friedrich Wilhelm. His Landgraf, his most gracious and hereditary Prince and Lord, he thought proudly. He knew the crossing would not be a matter of luck. He placed his trust in the sixteen British sailors waiting below to row him and his comrades to the other shore.[2]

As the barge pushed away from the Good Intent, Georg sat rigidly on the bench, one of fifty Hessians, tightly wedged in, his musket at sloped arms, concentrating first on the blue and white Regimental Colors fluttering from the pike held by Sergeant Wochler, the words "For Prince and Fatherland," visible when the banner unfurled in the light breeze. Christoph was further down the bench and Andreas was seated more toward the prow. To calm his fear of the water, Georg listened to the helmsman calling the cadence for the men rowing them across the bay.

Georg's first sea voyage, from Dordrecht in Holland across the North Sea to Portsmouth, England had been relatively short but very rough. It was nothing like the terror of the fifty-eight day voyage across the Great Ocean. More than two hundred of them had been crammed into the Good Intent. Instead of hammocks, six men were packed into narrow wooden bunks, sleeping on their sides on lice infested straw sacks, covered with thin blankets and shivering from both cold and fear. No amount of washing or disinfecting the hold with steaming vinegar could rid that dark, dank place of the awful stench of urine, feces, vomit, and stagnant sea water.

A severe storm had struck their convoy when they were only three days out of sight of land. Mountainous waves, higher than the mast, broke over the decks and terrified them all, including their officers. They had stood in the hold, ankle-deep in filth and water, singing their Lutheran psalms and praying, as the English sailors, manning the pumps, laughed at the Hessians' religious fervor. Like the others, Georg had been seasick, vomiting constantly. The sailors' promise there were even more ferocious storms to come and this had been but a little one, did nothing to quell their fear of drowning. In anticipation of worse storms, the Regiment's chaplain reminded them of the saying-'He who does not know how to pray should go aboard ship.' Georg prayed harder than he ever had in his life to survive the crossing.

After a week or so, they learned to drink small amounts of seawater daily, both to calm their stomachs and to combat rotting of their teeth and gums, a disease the English sailors called scurvy. They subsisted on a monotonous diet of bacon, peas, porridge and peeled barley. The salted beef and biscuits were so infested with worms as to disgust even the hardiest of soldiers from eating them.

When the weather was calm, they cleaned their equipment and drilled on deck in small numbers. Up on deck, with time off, they were permitted to enjoy the smoking tobacco their Landgraf had generously purchased for them as a farewell gift. Below deck, smoking was not allowed. The British sailors were petrified of fire on board and made clear, by shouted threats and raised clenched fists, they should not light their pipes in the hold.

The men of the Knyphausen Regiment had been chosen not only for their height but their strength. Yet, men around Georg died of coughing, the cold, the damp smelly stuffiness of the hold, and the dreaded bloody flux. Others just succumbed as they became weaker from the constant seasickness and vomiting. As Georg learned on the fearsome voyage across the Atlantic, bravery in battle did not translate into courage at sea. The lieutenants, sergeants and corporals, who had seen action on the Continent, cowered in their bunks during the fiercest storms, along with the lowly privates. Nor did obedience and discipline save the ones who became ill. Nine men from their two companies died before the Good Intent sailed into the broad bay below New York City. At least forty were so sick they were not fit for duty for weeks.

Their first few days on land convinced the men they had arrived in the Garden of Eden. The sandy shores were populated by huge flocks of brilliantly feathered ducks and long legged cranes solemnly stalking small, silver fish in the shallows. The water teemed with all manner of fish and eels could be caught by hand. Inland, there were herds of deer grazing on thick vegetation. Rabbits were everywhere. Foxes cautiously prowled around their campgrounds at night, as did a curious grey creature, with two small forepaws, rounded hindquarters and a black masked face.

Just being able to lie in the sun on the grassy fields of Staten Island, to climb a tree and pluck an apple or pear and eat it, to have the fresh sweet juice drip down their arms and faces was paradise. Even the familiar drills and cleaning of their uniforms, whiting their cross straps with clay, blackening their boots, and polishing their equipment and brass caps and buttons, had been pleasurable. As Company Seckendorf drilled and marched with their Regiment on wide shaded dusty country roads to regain their land legs after their lengthy time at sea, they forgot the miserable voyage and, in full throated joy, sang once again their marching songs of getting rich in America with "silver, gold and money."[3] From everything Georg observed, the words in their songs were true- the abundance of animals, the fertile soil and bountiful crops, the fruit orchards, the magnificent homes, rivaling those of even the nobles of Hesse-Cassel and Waldeck, the numerous cattle, sheep and swine, fat from grazing, the plump geese in the well tended farmyards, horses roaming free in the meadows and tame enough to pet. It was only a matter of defeating this rebel army and capturing New York, one of the largest cities in the colonies.

He was dreaming of the prize money and plunder when the landing craft jolted him into the present as it hit the white sands of Long Island. Georg stood and marched with his Company down the wooden ramp and formed up with the rest of the Regiment on the level grassy ground beyond the beach. In the midday sun, they proceeded on to the King's Highway. Except for the cannon fire in the distance, their landing might as well have been a parade dress drill. Not a shot had been fired against them. They marched for two hours before turning west on a broad road cutting through flat countryside. In the distance, he saw spirals of grey smoke rising from the cultivated fields ahead of them. Georg wondered whether the fires had been caused by the fast moving Jaeger reconnaissance patrols sent out ahead of their marching columns, or by the rebels destroying the forage before the advancing army.

The Regiment passed through a small village, which did not seem to Georg to offer much in the way of plunder and pitched their tents beyond it in a luxuriant green field. George's Company was sent to investigate a cluster of three stone houses. In each home, it was obvious the residents had fled in haste. Food was still cooking in the hearth. In the kitchen, fat carrots and large onions freshly pulled from the ground with the dirt still on them, waited to be washed and cut. Ahead, on their left, the road stretched west. In front of them a stone wall bisected two cleared fields, the farthest one abutting up to thickly wooded hills. Several squads were sent forward as pickets. The rest of the Regiment turned back the way they had come and pitched their tents for the night.

The following morning, Georg was awakened by the sound of rifle fire, followed by the familiar drum beat calling the Regiment to arms. They marched over the crest of the gently sloping hill and up to the stone houses. The bodies of several Hessian pickets lay where they had been picked off, the tops of their heads shot away or their throats a bloody pulp. Georg heard the whispered message passed through the ranks- Rebeller riflemen had done this. Georg shuddered and kept his eyes on the neatly tied tail protruding from the back of the head of the man in front of him.

The drums and high-pitched oboes signaled to advance. The

Regiment moved in perfect order across the fields adjacent to the road and halted about one hundred and fifty yards from the woods. There, Georg came under fire for the first time. Sporadic shots, marked by puffs of white smoke came from the line of trees. Here and there men in the ranks fell. It is the dreaded Rebeller riflemen, Georg thought. Captain Seckendorf had told them the riflemen carried tomahawks and would give no quarter. Among his fellow soldiers, there were rumors these riflemen were cannibals.[4]

On command, his Company fixed bayonets and marched rapidly forward, clambered in good order over the stone wall and proceeded in lines three deep through the knee high grass. They pushed forward into the woods. The first line fired their muskets from the hip and knelt down to reload while the second line passed through them, fired and reloaded while the third line passed through them. The wind was behind them and the smoke from their powder blew forward toward the Rebels, making visibility in the woods even worse. Georg, now in the first line, thought he caught a glimpse of a brown shirted man, darting from tree to tree, his long rifle held loosely in his hand. The drummer struck the beat signaling fall back and they retreated to the stone wall where they formed a line, facing the impenetrable woods. There was a shout of rage from the ranks, very unusual in their disciplined Regiment. Georg looked up and saw two lean men in nut-brown shirts retreating from the field closest to the woods, carrying a dead Hessian soldier by his shoulders and legs. He uttered a cry of fury and dismay, adding his voice to the roaring animal anger of the men around him. To his surprise, no officer ordered them to be silent.[5]

Georg did not like this fighting amidst the menacing shadows of the trees. The Regiment was trained for attacking across open ground, firing while marching and then charging with their bayonets. This warfare in which a ball could come from the dank gloom of the forest with unerring accuracy was terrifying. He was filled with a savage desire to close with the hidden enemy and drive his bayonet deep into their bowels. Only his training and discipline kept Georg from rushing forward in frustration to avenge the sacrilege of the Rebellers stealing a dead comrade's body.

All morning they alternated between waiting behind the wall

or marching forward into the woods, discharging volleys of musket fire as they attempted to overrun the Rebels' positions in the brief pause in firing when the brown-shirted riflemen reloaded. By noon, with the hot August sun beating down on them, the soldiers of Company Seckendorf were no further than they had been earlier in the morning, holding the three buildings and the stone wall as their forward perimeter. Suddenly, the volume of rifle fire increased, as if the Rebels had been reinforced. Georg heard the drum signal form up and retreat. Relieved but dispirited, they marched rapidly back toward the village reaching their camp, not too far ahead of the skirmishers left behind as a rear guard. They lay down over the crest of a hill, hidden from the Rebels who had now taken possession of the three stone houses. They were ordered to rest. Georg found himself lying on the warm grass next to his friends.

"Can they really be cannibals?" Christoph asked him. "I saw one with a short axe in his belt."

"They are like the red savages," Georg responded. "And cowards for all their hiding behind trees," Andreas added. The conversation of the three friends spread along the line of men, lying on their backs in the sun. One speculated they must eat human flesh raw because there was no time to cook it. Another claimed a friend of his in the Lossberg Regiment had heard General Howe himself confirm to General von Heister these backwoods riflemen were uncivilized animals who drank the blood of their enemies.

"Silence in the ranks," Sergeant Wochler ordered. "Even cannibals are men who can be killed," he said loud enough for others around them to hear. "They have sworn to give no quarter and bear a special hatred of us. When we catch them in the open, we will spit them like a hare on a skewer. Now, make use of the break. I want you fresh for the next assault. We will recapture those three houses," he said. Georg understood their Sergeant's words to be a command.

—⁂—

Will squeezed his knees against Big Red, urging the horse to keep up with Lieutenant Hadley as they hastily left Fort Greene and headed east on the Flatbush Road. Big Red easily pulled the large-wheeled field artillery carriage and the brass twelve-pounder with its fully loaded side boxes. Behind him, another horse towed a lighter nine-pounder, followed by a wagon driven by Sergeant Otis, with Sergeant Merriam beside him. The two gun crews sat on the planked floor, bouncing up and down as the wagon clattered over the rutted mud road. Less than thirty minutes ago a messenger had arrived at the Fort with orders for Lieutenant Hadley. Now they were mounted and moving the two field guns to support Colonel Hand's Pennsylvania Riflemen who were engaging the Hessians somewhere ahead on the Flatbush Road.

It took them the better part of an hour to cover the three miles from Ft.Greene to the outskirts of Flatbush. The road was crowded with locals from near Gravesend, where the British Army had landed. Fearful of being caught between the two armies. they drove their cattle and sheep ahead of their wagons, piled high with whatever food stores and furnishings they had time to save. The fat, slow, black-and-white cows stood stupidly in the road, blocking the artillery. Lieutenant Hadley drove them off using the flat of his sword and crop. Flocks of frightened sheep bolted into the adjacent fields to nibble on the grass. The farmers shouted angrily at the passing gun crews as their wives left the small comfort of the wagons and dashed with their children after their scattered animals.

As the sound of rifle fire became louder, Hadley halted and told them to wait. He rode his horse into the woods, threaded between the trees along a deer trail and disappeared in the foliage. Sergeant Merriam sent several men forward as pickets. Will remained mounted. Big Red, still hitched to the cannon, stood calmly despite the noise of volleyed musket fire. He lifted his massive head, his nostrils flaring at the strong smell of gunpowder that blew towards them.

Will had caught Hadley's enthusiasm for battle. On the ride forward, he had not thought about being afraid. Now, waiting on the side of the road, with the sounds of a battle ahead, he had time to think and his fears returned. Would he have the courage to stand in the face of enemy fire? They would be engaging the hated Hessians. He had heard the talk among the four Connecticut militiamen assigned to their gun crews. The Hessian Grenadiers were the ones with the long triangle- shaped bayonets. They were said to be so strong, they could spear a man and lift him off the ground and toss him over their shoulders, like a farmer flinging a pitchfork of hay. Although the August sun was warm, Will felt a chill on his back from the light breeze. He turned in the saddle and saw Private Oliver Strong and the other three Connecticut militiamen standing behind the wagon. None of them held a musket. They looked like rabbits ready to flee.

Lieutenant Hadley returned with several Pennsylvania riflemen who loped easily through the woods, keeping pace with the Lieutenant's grey mare. They were tall and leathery, like the soldiers of Morgan's Rifles who started the fight with the Mariners at General Washington's Cambridge headquarters. Will remembered his part in the brawl, the outnumbered Mariners surrounded by swarms of brown shirted riflemen, trying to maim Adam and the other black freedmen of the Regiment, and the battle cry Will had answered, "Marblehead Mariners to me!"

Hand's Pennsylvanians neither smiled nor greeted the Massachusetts Artillery men but waited until the gun crews unhitched the horses from the carriages. Together, the riflemen and the gun crews wrestled the two cannons up the grassy slope and into the woods. Once away from the road, the ground leveled off but was soft from the violent summer storm of two days ago. The gunners grabbed their handspikes. The iron-coated six-foot long wooden poles jammed between the spokes gave them greater leverage against the thick clinging mud that enveloped the wheels. At one place where the terrain dipped into a muddy ditch they had to laboriously remove the side boxes and struggle to haul the cannons up the ravine's steep and slippery opposite side. Then, they re-attached the side boxes and slowly, pushing and pulling the cannons, reached the rear lines of the riflemen's position. Will's blue jacket and britches were coated with mud. His knuckles and palms were bleeding from holding on to the handspike and the rough wooden spokes of the carriage wheels. Ahead of them, at the edge of the woods, Will saw many riflemen, their dark brown shirts and breeches blending into the shadows of the trees, lying behind fallen logs, awaiting orders.

Hadley went to confer with Colonel Hand and two of his officers.

They stood in the shade of a wide branched oak. The Colonel a tall balding man, welcomed the Lieutenant with a clap on his back. He drew a diagram in the dirt with the point of his sword. Hadley nodded and walked briskly back to the gun crews.

"The Hessians are in three stone houses at the end of the farthest field," Lieutenant Hadley said. "We are going to support the Pennsylvanians' attack to force them out and drive these Hessians all the way back to the Bay." His face was flushed with excitement.

Will strained with the rest of the crew to pull the twelve-pounder into position at the edge of the woods. Across the two fields, he saw the mass of Hessians grouped between the houses with a line of pickets at the stone wall midway to the woods. It would be the pickets who would fire at them first, he thought. The others at the stone houses were too far away. Simeon Webb sponged the cannon. Will took a canvas charge from Oliver Strong, who had been relegated to standing by the powder box. It was the position where he could least disrupt them. Will ran forward, handing the charge to Corporal Tyler. Tyler slid it down the barrel and Webb rammed the powder home, followed by the twelve-pound cannon ball. Sergeant Merriam pricked the powder bag, slid a quill with powder into the touch hole and shouted "primed." Almost instantly, Lieutenant Hadley yelled "give fire." A heartbeat after the match ignited the powder in the quill, both cannons roared simultaneously. Will saw one ball strike the corner of the forward-most building, the other splinter the wooden center door. At the same time, he was aware of the whistle of musket balls shredding the leaves and striking the trees around him. He waited until Tyler had wormed the barrel and Webb had thrust the sponge down and retracted it, before handing him the fresh charge. Both cannons fired another round, doing more damage to the building shielding the Hessian troops.

The Hessians, emerged from behind the houses, formed up into lines and marched quickly across the first field, as Colonel Hand's riflemen took up positions at the edge of the woods and began picking them off. The Hessians clambered over the stone wall, redressed their ranks and advanced, muskets level, the first line firing from the hip and kneeling to let the second line pass through, fire and kneel in turn.

The sun was behind Will, glaring off the brass caps of the advancing Grenadiers.

"Load with grape shot," Lieutenant Hadley ordered. Will turned to take a canvas charge of gunpowder from Oliver Strong but the Connecticut militiaman was gone. Will bent down, lifted the charge and ran forward with it, gave it to Tyler and raced over to the side box. He grabbed the bag of lead balls and pulled the cord at the top to shape the bulging sack to fit down the muzzle. Webb rammed the shot home and Sergeant Merriam shouted primed. Will waited for the order. Lieutenant Hadley stood between the two cannons, his sword held aloft in his raised arm as the Hessians came closer. The deadly noise of musket balls zipping through the woods around them increased in volume. They made a dull thunk as they struck the tree trunks and a sinister hissing sound as they ripped through the low, leafy branches.

"Give fire," Hadley shouted. There was a loud roar and Will saw gaps torn in the ranks of the advancing Hessians, who hesitated. The riflemen held their fire, waiting for the grape shot to decimate the enemy's ranks. A split second later they let loose a concerted volley and more Hessians fell. The Pennsylvanians, led by their Colonel rose from their positions and charged from the woods, screaming and yelling, driving the Hessians back beyond the houses, down the slope and over the ridge on the nearby hill.

"Move the cannons up," Lieutenant Hadley ordered. He joined Will's gun crew pushing the larger gun forward. Will rushed forward with Tyler to the stone wall. Webb had already wrestled a massive stone off, his thick neck bulging from the exertion. Together the three of them flung stones to the side, creating a large enough breach in the wall for the cannons to get through. Ahead of them, the riflemen had reached the stone houses. Puffs of white smoke rose from their new line as they fired at the retreating Hessians.

The field sloped slightly downward. Will felt his arms wrenched from their sockets as the wheel suddenly turned the handspike he was holding. Tyler and Webb grabbed the iron pole and the three of them prevented the field cannon from rolling away from them. Hadley directed both pieces be placed on the far right side of the smallest stone house. This gave them a field of fire on the Flatbush road, should the Hessians attempt to flank them. The riflemen were spread out on either side of the houses. A few took up positions at the upper floor windows.

Hadley sent Will, along with two others, back through the woods for the horses and the wagon. They had to cross the field and into the tree line where the Pennsylvanians had begun their assault. A few wounded Hessians lay moaning in agony. He did not understand German but recognized one soldier, his chest soaked in blood was begging for water. "Vasser. Vasser. Bitte. Vasser." Will could not stop to help him or any one of them now.

"They all have mustaches," one of the men said. "At least those who still have heads," the other replied, smirking. Will looked away, fighting the feeling in his stomach to throw up. Iridescent green flies buzzed in pools of blood of a dead Hessian whose legs had been blown off. He lay on the grass his blue, sightless eyes open and staring at the bright sky. Will gagged, bent over and dry heaved on the trampled grass. Embarrassed, he ran to catch up with the other two as they made their way through the dense woods to the road.

He returned riding Big Red, thankful he did not have to tread on foot again across the field with the dead Hessians. In the partial shade before the stone wall, some of the Pennsylvanians were tending to their wounded. A rifleman struggled against the strong hands holding him down and screamed as one of his comrades attempted to wrap torn white strips of a shirt around the man's shattered arm, bone splinters protruded from the bloody pulp of flesh. Will stared down at the gore and quickly turned his head away and dry heaved again.

Gratefully, he rejoined his gun crew and let Big Red graze in the small pasture adjacent to the nearest stone building. None of his friends had been wounded, although Lieutenant Hadley was fingering a musket ball hole in the red facing of his coat.

"Look to your tri-corn, sir," Corporal Tyler said, pointing at the Lieutenant's hat. Hadley removed it and put his index finger through a black seared hole next to his red cockade. A few inches lower, it would have struck Hadley in the head.

"It was either an errant shot or the Hessians have their own marksmen to pick off our officers," Tyler observed.

"We are all unscathed today for which we must thank Providence," Merriam said, motioning for the men to take off their hats. They formed a small circle around the twelve-pounder as he led them in prayer. Sergeant Otis' crew joined them.

"With Divine Providence watching over us, there was no need for our new Connecticut recruits to flee," Webb said, wiping the sweat dripping from his beak of a nose. "Perhaps you could also beseech our Maker for a cooler day," he said, unbuttoning his coat.

"No need to mock Providence and tempt your fate," Merriam replied.

Baldwin, who had slouched down next to Webb, made a show of moving away from him. "I do not wish to be smitten by mistake if a bolt should strike Simeon," he said, struggling to remove the leather vent thumbstall. He smiled innocently at Merriam, who turned his back and walked away grumbling to himself.

Several of the riflemen wandered over to inspect the cannons up close. Hadley went to confer again with Colonel Hand. Will leaned up against the thick oak tiller, next to Isaiah Chandler and soaked up the afternoon sun. He felt calm, relieved and exuberant all at the same time. The rush of emotions confused and disquieted him. This had been his first time under fire. He had not panicked nor run. He had done his duty as part of the crew. He was more shaken by the bloody aftermath of the battle and walking among the mangled bodies than being shot at.

"Do you think," he asked Isaiah, "if one is not afraid in his first battle, he will not be afraid in the others to come."

Chandler looked thoughtfully at a biscuit he had pulled from his knapsack, as if deciding whether or not it was edible. "I cannot speak for others. My fear is always there each time. I try not to think too much about the enemy soldiers. I concentrate on worming and loading. If I let my mind digress too much and do not search the piece for all of the spent cartridge, the cannon will explode and I will be as dead as if bayoneted by a Hessian. And all my comrades would be blown to bits." He gnawed tentatively on the biscuit. "This is hard enough to break the teeth of a rat," he observed. "My advice to you Will is to do your job, which is something you can control and not worry about things best left to officers and Providence."

Will thought this over. He had functioned as he had been drilled from the beginning. Maybe that was the reason for all the repetition and the endless practice. To train him to do his duty under fire and not to flee. That would also explain the difference between the regular Continental Army Regiments and the fresh militia units. But the Pennsylvania Riflemen this day had not fled from the field and they certainly did not drill or practice. There was more to this business of fear and fighting than he understood. But he thought to himself proudly, he had done his duty, stood by his crew and not embarrassed himself. That was enough for this day.

Several of the riflemen had begun to drift back toward the woods. Hadley ordered the gun crews to hitch up the two cannons and wagon. They were leaving the field and returning to Fort Greene. They loaded several wounded Pennsylvanians on the wagon, along with captured muskets and cartridge boxes. Will thought he would take one of the muskets with a bayonet. To replace the one he had lost on the Jamaica Road. The gun crews walked alongside, holding on to the side-boards. The wounded lay on the wagon floor, crying out or moaning as the wagon jolted slowly through the meadow until it reached the Flatbush Road. On a rise, Will stood up in the stirrups and looked east down the road. In the far distance, were the orderly rows and rows of the clean white tents of the British Army. Rumors were 8,000 British soldiers had landed on Long Island. This afternoon was but a minor skirmish. Will knew a major battle was yet to come.

Chapter 6- The Hessian Bayonet

Georg's Regiment formed up in the early morning hours. The Rall and Lossberg Regiments fell in as well. Ahead of them, he could hear the woody sound of the haut pipes above the steady beating of the drums, as two other Hessian brigades proceeded west on the Flatbush Road, their flags waving. The Scottish Highlanders were on their right flank, soldiers as tall as the troops in the Knyphausen Regiment, armed with huge broad swords and led by bagpipers. Georg found their marital music strange and not as inspiring as the rhythmic beat of his Regiment's drummers.[1] Behind them, the tents of the British regulars stood empty. It was strange they had left their campfires burning, he thought. He supposed the regulars had marched north of the Highlanders on the right flank.

They were moving in force and while he was not supposed to think, Georg knew today was the day of a big battle. Last night, in camp, Sergeant Wochler had reminded them they should give no quarter and use their bayonets to good advantage.

They marched beyond the now abandoned small town of Flatbush and spread out into the woods on both sides of the road. Flatbush Pass was ahead. The Knyphausen Regiment halted at a tangle of brambles and bushes on the edge of the woods. Orders went through the ranks to unbutton their wool regimental coats and remove their short sabres from their hips and sling them across their chests. Georg liked the easier access to his sabre. Now, his scabbard would not get caught in the thick underbrush. However, he intended to favor his bayonet and keep the sabre in reserve.[2]

This time, he was not afraid of the dark woods. He was eager to enter them, find the Rebellers and spear them with all his strength so the triangular blade would come out their backs. He was well disciplined and trained to obediently follow orders but he understood from Colonel von Borck, their regimental commander, their Company commander, Captain Seckendorf down through the Lieutenants to Sergeant Wochler, they were under no constraints once they closed with the enemy.

Several cannons on both sides of the road were engaged in an artillery duel with the Rebellers' guns. The booming from their side was almost incessant. Georg hoped the barrage would not drive the enemy from the front. He eagerly wanted to fight. He could sense the same impatience among his companions, standing with shouldered arms, waiting for orders. He couldn't calculate how long they waited. The sun, in the east warmed his back. Sweat dripped down his neck. His dark brown hair, powdered white, was slick under his brass cap. There was a rustling in the ranks to Georg's left. Orders were relayed down the line. The drums struck up the beat of forward march. Company Seckendorf was first, advancing three deep following the flag bearers into the thick brush and woods. Puffs of white smoke appeared ahead of them. Between the trees, Georg could see Rebeller riflemen firing from behind an earthen redoubt. The Hessians increased their pace.

Georg, in the front line, heard the drum beat pick up and the men surged forward toward the low dirt wall. They leaped it in a bound. Fifty or sixty of the Rebellers were in front of them. Georg saw one lean, dirty haired Rebel hastily trying to reload his long rifle, plunging the ramrod down the barrel. Charging forward, he lunged and felt his bayonet thrust through soft flesh between the man's ribs. He pulled it out as the Rebel collapsed, blood gushing from the large wound in his side. They pursued the fleeing soldiers who turned in a futile effort to regroup, using their long rifles as clubs. Georg was incensed by the sight of these men, refusing to surrender, their evil looking hand axes hanging on a loop from their belts. He waited for the Rebel in front of him to commit by swinging his rifle, dropped down on one knee as the stock made a whishing sound over his head and drove his bayonet deep into the man's stomach. He twisted it out sideways so the exit wound was a wider gash than the initial stabbing. He watched with satisfaction as the Rebel fell to the ground, his fingers grasping to retain his slippery, grey, rope-like intestines.

Sergeant Wochler shouted to reform their lines as they ran through the brush, pushing aside the low branches with their bayonets. Ahead in a clearing, a group of riflemen, stood with their backs against the trees, their long rifles pointed barrel down. Suddenly, a shot rang out and a Grenadier pitched backwards, blood bubbling from his throat. With the simultaneous roar of a wounded beast, Georg's forward line fell on the remaining riflemen.[3] Georg thrust his bayonet so hard into the chest of one of them, it emerged alongside the rebel's spine and stuck in the tree trunk. He put his foot on the man's stomach and pulled the bayonet out. The Rebel screamed in agony, the blood gushing from his mouth.

They swept out of the woods and into open fields. Before them panic-stricken Rebels were fleeing everywhere. Good, Georg thought. We have pushed them back through the pass. The rebels were running toward a fort in the distance, pursued by Light Dragoons and the green-coated Jaegers. Just ahead, he recognized the regimental flags of the Rall Grenadiers who were mopping up after the Dragoons and Jaegers. They surrounded the isolated pockets of Rebels in the fields. The Grenadiers formed a circle their bayonets pointing to the center and closed in.

Georg's Company reformed its lines. They had lost only a few men. Christoph, grinned exuberantly at him, his bayonet stained with Rebel blood. Andreas nodded soberly to Georg indicating he was unscathed. Georg, caught up in the exhilaration of battle didn't care whether Andreas was somber from having faced death or from having killed the enemy. He simply raised his musket in a slight salute.

The sun was almost overhead. Georg looked back. In the distance, to their right, a huge tidal wave of British Redcoats were advancing across pastures and roads, driving a large body of panic-stricken Rebels fleeing helter-skelter in great disorder before them. Hearing the drums and shouted commands Georg's company reformed their ranks. He faced forward, smiling. Soon, he thought, they would be in New York City and then there would be plunder. The Knyphausen Regiment marched through the field to the road and headed toward the sound of cannon and musket fire on their left.

Will and the two gun crews of the Massachusetts Artillery were positioned, on a small steep hill, in a copse of trees to the right of the Shore Road. Three cannons manned by New York State militia completed their battery. They had been engaged since early morning by a large force of British troops supported by cannons and mortars attempting to force the Shore Road. It had mostly been an artillery duel up to now, with the British firing twice as frequently as the Americans.

Will was confident they would hold their position. The American troops blocking the British advance were well equipped Regulars, Haslet's Delaware Regiment in their short blue jackets and high peaked round caps of black leather with the motto "Liberty and Independence," and Smallwood's Marylanders, in their tan hunting frocks and black tri-corns. Both regiments had fixed bayonets and were under orders not to fire until the British came within 50 yards, a distance at which massed musket fire would be effective. All morning the enemy had relied upon their artillery and plentiful ammunition to harass the Americans, the troops advancing no closer than 300 yards. One mortar bomb had burst over the New Yorker's nine-pounder, blowing off the head of their Captain and wounding three of the gun crew. Lieutenant Hadley had taken charge of the New Yorker's cannons, and left Sergeants Merriam and Otis to command the fire of the two Massachusetts guns.

"Will," Merriam shouted over the roar of incoming fire. The British cannon balls and shells were falling short of them or sailing over the guns to land among the Delaware and Maryland troops. "We need both artillery buckets refilled." The smoke was blowing away from their cannons. He would be in clear view of the enemy. Will knew there was a small stream below the bare knoll that curved around the American's position. He dashed down the side of the hill, a bucket in each hand, hoping there were no British skirmishers ahead of their line of troops. He scooped up two buckets of the swampy brackish water and ran back up the hill, trying not to spill them. He tensed for the musket ball in his back but it never came. When he reached the redoubt he breathed a sigh of relief.

"Good man," Simeon Webb said dipping the sheepskin-covered sponge into the murky water and ramming it down the barrel. Sergeant Merriam adjusted the tillers of both nine-pounders, aiming them at one of the British mortars. Webb levered the breech with a handspike as Merriam forced another wooden wedge under it for elevation. He did the same at the other cannon and on his command, both guns fired and a cheer went up from the Marylanders followed by a shout from the gun crews. One cannon ball had struck the mortar itself, upending it and the other had plowed into several of the mortar's crew before continuing to bound on into a line of Redcoats. Throughout the morning, the American soldiers had stoically endured the British artillery fire, standing their ground and occasionally losing men, their legs taken off by the force of cannonballs or suffering head wounds from bursting mortar shells. Now it was their turn to cheer as their own artillery wreaked havoc among the enemy, although the cheering seemed less loud than before.

Will turned to see Smallwood's Marylanders led by their Major running in good order up the Gowanus Road toward their left, away from their positions. He was conscious of the noise of musket fire and he could see the blue haze of smoke hanging over the woods and fields to the north. Lieutenant Hadley rushed up. "Follow the Marylanders. Move those two nine-pounders," he yelled. "Quickly, men." Confused, Will helped turn one of the cannons around and push it down the rear of the slope and on to the Gowanus Road. The soil was sandy and the cannon, with its side boxes loaded with powder charges and cannonballs, bogged down almost to the wheel hub. Webb, the muscles in his thick bull neck straining, lifted the axle as the rest of them pushed until the cannon was freed. They moved it along with handspikes, the gun crews on each side of the carriage, leaning against the poles to turn the wooden spokes.

"Lend a hand here," Sergeant Merriam called as a group of militia fled out of a field on their right. They ignored him and continued across the road toward Gowanus Creek. Will was astounded by the number of men fleeing, many without muskets or hats, wide-eyed with terror. The woods seemed full of desperate militia, officers and men running with one purpose- to escape from whoever was pursuing them. He caught fragments of their desperate cries about the Hessians hot on their heels. Lieutenant Hadley, his sword drawn tried to rally them, commanded them to stop and then, in desperation swiped at them with the flat of the blade. They simply ran further to the side before resuming their headlong flight, as if Hadley were a natural obstacle, like a boulder or large tree, to be circumvented in their mad scramble to safety.

"Cowardly scum," Hadley shouted, recognizing their fear was so great he could not stop their flight. Ahead, they heard heavier musket and cannon fire and the air was thick with the smell of gunpowder. They struggled all the harder. Fortunately as they advanced, the road surface became more compact. With all of the crew pushing they were able to roll the nine-pounder along at a good pace. The dust from the road coated Will's mouth and the heat from the sun, now overhead, baked his head. He had lost his tri-corn. He saw the Hessian musket with its long bayonet he had taken from the wagon at Flatbush Pass. It was strapped to the wormer. He felt better having a weapon with him, although he hoped no Redcoat would get close enough to the cannon for him to have to use it.

The Marylanders were ahead of them in the woods to the right of the Gowanus Road. Lieutenant Hadley disappeared into the trees as they waited on the road. Will heard, above the constant volleying of muskets, drums and the high pitch of the fifes. He looked at Simeon for an explanation.

"It sounds as if the entire British Army is in front of us," Webb said, taking a drink from his canteen.

"Save your water," Merriam commanded. "We may yet need it to sponge the cannons."

"It would be a waste of watered rum," Webb said, capping his wooden canteen and winking at Will. Merriam scowled at the tall rammer and then, reluctantly smiled, acknowledging the joke.

Suddenly, Hadley burst from the woods. "The British are massing at a stone farmhouse commanding the field. If we do not hold them, they will sweep down the Road and trap the men behind us. Quickly now, move these cannons over there." He pointed with his arm toward to a grove of trees.

Will and the others manhandled the guns up a slope and to the forward edge of the trees, as more American troops continued to rush through the underbrush in their panic stricken flight. The ground was littered with muskets, knapsacks, coats, hats, flasks, cartridge boxes, canteens, all cast aside by the terrified soldiers.

"May God grant them a clear conscience," Merriam said, as he watched in disbelief as a group of forty or more men, struggled through the thickets around them and dashed down toward the road and into the swampy salt meadows beyond. "It is for them the Marylanders are holding the line." And us too, Will thought. This time he was afraid. The panic of so many around him was infectious. When they reached the edge of the woods, his fear increased. In front of them, in the distance, it seemed as if the entire American army had been defeated and was fleeing, pursued by lines of Red coats, wave upon wave, coming over the grassy hills. To his right, he saw the cause of the panic of the men who had run across the Shore Road. The Hessian regiments, distinguished by their blue coats, were coming swiftly through the fields in orderly ranks, driving before them a mob of screaming men, who had once constituted rifle and militia units.

Directly in front of the Marylanders was an apple orchard and a large stone house. British troops massed at the house, while two field pieces discharged grape shot at the Americans fleeing down the Gowanus Road and struggling through the muck of the swampy millponds beyond. Will guessed there were at least a thousand Redcoats ready to push forward and he could see more coming up from the rear. And the Hessians were approaching from to their right. Smallwood's Marylanders numbered less than three hundred.[4]

"Over there. Position the cannons over there," Hadley shouted, pointing with his sword just beyond the edge of the woods. "Support the Marylanders, men. Load and fire at will."

Sergeant Merriam adjusted the tiller, and they swiftly loaded the cannon. The first shot was wide of the British gun but the ball cut a swath through the troops behind it. The British gunners were still concentrating their fire on the fleeing Americans. The Regulars, however, took notice of the American artillery. In response, musket balls whizzed through the trees and showered them with leaves and branches. Will heard several cries behind him. He turned quickly and saw the British fire was striking remnants of the American troops fleeing through the woods. Merriam shouted "Give Fire." Their second shot hit the edge of the house, wounding the British gunners with stone fragments. The nine-pound ball from Sergeant Otis' cannon shattered the wheel of one of the British gun carriages, and ricocheted beyond, smashing the legs of soldiers in the ranks.

Smallwood's Marylanders emerged from the woods and led by their Major, moved rapidly in two orderly but sparse lines through the orchard. They took the first volley from the British line and then discharged their muskets. Instead of reloading, they charged the stone house with their bayonets. By the time Will had brought the canvas charge forward, he could see the Marylanders had been driven back. They retreated in good order through the orchard. Hadley shouted for the battery to open up on the British troops. Will worked in a blur, carrying first the powder charge and then the ball, waiting for the deafening roar of the cannon and then carrying a new charge forward through the acrid blue smoke. Almost in a detached way, he thought the powder smelled too much of horse urine. Sergeant Merriam had once explained it meant the powder was of lesser quality, although he had forgotten why that was so. He would have to ask him afterwards.

The air around him was alive with musket fire, aimed not only at them, but the diminishing ranks of Smallwood's Regiment. He lost count of how many times the Marylanders formed up and assaulted the stone house only to be beaten back by the sheer numbers and firepower of the ever-increasing ranks of Redcoats. Their dead and dying filled the orchard. This was the end, Will thought. The gun crews were running low on powder and ball. Smallwood's men must be almost out of ammunition and their numbers were too few to make another bayonet charge. Will felt his resolve to fight on ebbing and with it, his courage as well.

Lieutenant Hadley rushed over. "General Stirling orders us to disperse and save yourselves. Spike the cannons first." Will looked for Simeon who was in charge of the spike. Webb was sitting on the ground among a carpet of leaves and twigs knocked down by the intense musket fire. He had puzzled look in his eyes, as he raised one hand to his cheek feeling for something missing. His chin had been blown away by a musket ball. Blood poured down his waistcoat and pooled in his lap. Merriam was frantically searching Simeon's haversack for the spike and hammer. The musket fire from the British increased. Balls pinged off the brass gun and viciously ricocheted around them. Will grabbed his musket and pulled the bayonet from the end of the barrel. He stuck it in the touchhole and hammered it home with the stock. When it was tightly wedged in, he grabbed the musket by the barrel and swung at the protruding part of the bayonet with all his might. It broke just above the top of the touchhole.

"Come on, Will," Isaiah shouted at him as the gun crews disappeared into the woods. Will looked back at Simeon. The big man was leaning to his side, his back against a tree, his head sunk into his chest. Will ran down the hill and caught up with Sergeant Merriam who was limping into the marsh on the other side of the road. The Sergeant had lost his tri-corn and his balding head glistened with sweat. His face was contorted with the pain of each step on his right side.

"It is my ankle," he said, grunting in pain.

"Lean on us," Isaiah Chandler said, motioning Will to move to Merriam's other side. With his arms on their shoulders, the three of them stumbled into the swampy warm mud around the millponds and the salt meadows off Gowanus Creek. Crowds of men raced up the road and threw themselves into the deeper water of the creek in an attempt to escape the onrushing British. Several of them immediately went under, their hands frantically thrashing in the water.

Merriam shook his head. "The tide is high and coming in. There is a rough current in the middle," he said, looking across to the far bank. Will guessed it was eighty yards wide in front of them.

Merriam pointed to Hadley and others from their battery, who were attempting to cross where the tidal marsh was the narrowest. "Follow the Lieutenant," he shouted.

"I cannot swim," Will said in desperation. Chandler grabbed him by the arm and pulled him into the muddy water. "We can," he said simply. Merriam, no longer having to put weight on his foot, paddled alongside, lifting Will's shoulder to keep his head above water. Musket balls splattered around them, making soft plopping sounds, as the British, no longer delayed by the Marylanders fired at the fleeing troops. A militia man ahead of them, cried out and sank, leaving a bloody pool in the water. Will frantically tried to touch bottom. He couldn't. His legs were pulled sideways by the current. For a brief moment his mouth was under water. He choked, gagged and thrashed to free his arms from Chandler and Merriam.

"Keep your head up, you young fool, and your feet out behind you," Merriam snarled. "Do not fight us. Let us tow you along," Chandler said on Will's left. Will tried to do what they told him but all around them he could see men drowning, crying out for help and being swept under by the current. His mind screamed at him he would be next to be pulled down into the dark murky water, to breathe his last breath, to see nothing and to be no more and no one would care. No, he shouted, Elisabeth would care, Elisabeth would mourn for him.

"Stop shouting Elisabeth and help a tired old man get up this muddy shore," Merriam said to him. Chandler looked at Will with a bemused smile on his face. They were knee deep in the mire on the west bank of Gowanus Creek. Will put Merriam's arm over his shoulder and helped the Sergeant limp up the embankment.

They found Lieutenant Hadley and the others, covered with drying muck and lying on the far side of a slope that hid them from the British. The men lay on the warm grass, too exhausted to even wave away the swarming clouds of mudflies, gnats and mosquitos. Miraculously, Will thought, their two gun crews had suffered no casualties other than Simeon. At this thought Will sank down onto the matted grass, the foul taste of the creek water still in his mouth. Isaiah tapped him on the shoulder. Will opened his eyes and took the proffered canteen.

"We only have this one for all of us. Take a small taste and pass it on." Will swished the watered rum around in his mouth, making it last before swallowing it. He passed the canteen to Tyler, whose damp scraggly grey hair and long nose made him appear more like a drowned rat than a human being. Mosquitos buzzed around his wispy hair and ears.

Exhausted groups of soldiers and militia, officers and Continentals, indistinguishable in their mud-covered uniforms, lay all around them. The only motion was the occasional waving of a hand to swat at the omnipresent insects.

Lieutenant Hadley stood up and shouted in a loud voice, " I am Lieutenant Samuel Hadley of Colonel Knox's Massachusetts Artillery. My men and I are going to march to Fort Box. If there are other officers here, they should form up their units. If you men have no unit, fall in with us."

A few bedraggled men stood up, smoothing their waterlogged and mud stained coats, called out their rank and unit and waited. Some men obeyed, others just remained where they were in a weary daze in the late afternoon sun, all semblance of discipline and order gone.

"All you men, listen to me," Hadley yelled. "The entire British army is on the Shore Road across the Gowanus. He pointed back across the creek. You may wait here for them to come and imprison you before dinner, or you may follow me to the Heights, to Fort Box and beyond."

The thought of being safe within the American line of forts, protected by fresh troops, and the fear of the British prisons and Hessian bayonets had the effect Hadley desired. The defeated men struggled to their feet, some trying to find their companions and officers. Others simply formed in ragged groups behind the Massachusetts men and waited to march out.

It was early dusk, when they approached Fort Box, fatigued, hungry and thirsty. They were greeted first by cheers and then stunned silence as the troops manning the fort saw how few were returning and their condition. Will felt he could sleep standing up. The gnawing hunger could wait. Numbly, as if in a fog, he went through the motions of eating the hard biscuits which had been distributed and fell asleep against an earthen wall, not caring whether the British assaulted the fort or not.

He dreamed he was on the battlefield, in the orchard in front of the stone house. Elisabeth was walking slowly among the bodies of fallen soldiers, all lying without a wound showing, as if they were sleeping. She was searching for him. There was no gunfire, no smoke, not even British troops. All was quiet and he was screaming for her, running toward her, a dwarf on the bloody stumps of his legs, yelling he was alive but without legs.

He awoke, shivering. It was almost dawn. He drew his mud-covered coat around his chest and looked around confused. The men he had crossed the Gowanus with were still asleep, sprawled around the inside of the fort. The parapets were fully manned by soldiers, tense and tired from having been up all night waiting for the British to attack. Will recognized Hadley standing near the gate with two saddled horses. The Lieutenant had managed to get some of the dried mud out of his hair. The mud embedded in the red facings of his uniform made them almost as dark as the blue of his coat.

"Ah, Will," he said, seeing him approach. "I wait for Major Gist of the Marylanders. We ride to Fort Greene where we hope to meet Colonels Knox and Smallwood and report on yesterday's battle. I have instructed Sergeants Merriam and Otis to begin marching our men toward Fort Greene. I will send wagons if they are available."[5] He mounted, waited as sentries swung the heavy wooden gate open and rode off with the Major.

As the sounds of the horses hooves diminished, Will became aware of another noise, metallic and rhythmic with a steady menace too it. It came from beyond the Fort's outer defenses. Puzzled, he climbed the parapet, wondering why soldiers from the Fort would be digging the outer trenches deeper. In the early light of dawn, he saw the trenches closest to the Fort occupied by militia. Beyond them, about a half a mile away and well out of musket range, the British were digging their own trenches and assault assembly areas. Riflemen from the Fort, already in position ahead of the American trenches, kept up a harassing fire at the British work parties.

Will felt a sense of despair and helplessness. He had no musket or any weapon other than his knife and a hatchet in his haversack that, by some miracle, he had not lost in the Gowanus. They were a gun crew without a gun. The cannons at the Fort were manned by men from New York City, looking crisp in their relatively clean uniforms. Despondently, he formed up with the remaining men of the two gun crews, and without breakfast, marched out of the Fort. They headed north on an interior road which Will knew linked all the forts from Red Hook below where the Gowanus emptied into the bay above the Narrows, to Fort Putnam just south of Wallabout Bay. Sergeant Merriam, refused any assistance from Tyler and Will. He used his musket as a crutch with the stock under his armpit. The barrel made peculiar round circles in the dirt with each step. They passed small groups of men lying or squatting on both sides of the road, listlessly waiting for orders or officers. In the fields beyond the road Will saw clusters of militia walking toward the Heights away from any potential combat, or collapsed from exhaustion under bushes or low-branched fruit trees.

As they marched toward Fort Greene, they met fresh troops, two brigades of the New Jersey Militia, clean white flags emblazoned with the word "Liberty" heading toward Fort Box, the American lines and beyond to the Gowanus Canal. The militia stared as they passed the artillery men. Will sensed the men from New Jersey lumped them together with all the other stragglers and deserters they had passed on the road.

The gun crews were dirty and hatless, their uniforms encrusted with mud. Sergeant Merriam ordered them to form ranks, two lines of five each, he and Sergeant Otis in the lead, and to march smartly. "We are not some militia who fled the field," he said loud enough for the New Jersey men to hear. "We fought bravely, supported the Marylanders, killed the enemy and left the field when ordered to do so and not a moment before. Hold your heads up, men. We are Colonel Knox's own. March like the proud Massachusetts patriots you are."

At this, Will and the others stiffened their posture and moved more briskly, brushing pieces of dried mud from their sleeves, as they walked. When they rested he thought he would take off his jacket and beat it with some branches to get more of the mud off. His thoughts drifted back to the furious battle at the orchard. Sergeant Merriam had not mentioned it, no one had, but they all knew that Simeon

Webb lay dead and unburied in the woods near the stone house. Will remembered his raptor like beak of a nose, his small eyes and mottled skin, smiling at him through brown teeth when Merriam had ordered them to save their canteen water.

As they marched, Will heard musket fire and the occasional boom of a cannon ahead. They reached Fort Greene by midafternoon as the skies darkened and the wind blew the smell of gunpowder from the northeast. They learned Lieutenant Hadley and Major Gist had ridden on to Fort Putnam. Their orders were for the crews to remain at Fort Greene. From the parapets, Will could see the American lines extending a little more than a mile and a half to the Ring Fort. Between the two Forts, the British were probing with small groups of skirmishers and field guns. American riflemen, protected by the earthen wall and fascines of brushwood, kept up an accurate fire, picking off the occasional officer or gunner who mistakenly thought he was out of range. Behind the skirmishers, British troops were energetically digging their own trenches. Beyond them, about two miles back, in the open fields, stood rows and rows of clean white tents. Will guessed there were several thousand British troops arrayed against this part of the American defenses alone.

The sky darkened and Will scampered down the parapet ladder as the hail and rainstorm struck. There was little protection other than to huddle against the interior walls of the Fort and pull their muddy coats over their heads. Without tents or cooking pots, and unable to start cooking fires anyway, Will and the men of the Massachusetts Artillery ate the meager rations of biscuits and cold bitter pickled pork, given them from the Fort's provisions. They fell asleep, grouped together more for companionship than warmth, among the pools of water and muddy ground beneath the parapets. The storm continued through the night and into the morning. The dawn was clammy with a chill and the winds, although abated a bit, continued to bluster from the northeast. Will recalled how hot he had been during the battle. With nothing to do, he pulled the coat over his head and climbed the ladder. The interior roads, behind their lines were filled with troops, slogging ankle deep in the mud, fresh troops he thought, coming from the Brooklyn Ferry.[6] Isaiah Chandler joined him, as the bedraggled troops on the parapets cheered the reinforcements.

"It will be a different story when the British attack our fortifications," he said. "The Militia cannot turn and run and our Regulars will more than hold their own." He pointed through the rain to the open fields before Fort Greene and the twisted barricade of fascines below the walls. "The Redcoats will be entangled down there and slaughtered. You wait and see."

The gates were opened and two wet brigades of New York Militia marched in, their rain soaked flags blowing in the strong winds. Will wondered how either side would be able to keep their powder dry if the storm continued throughout the morning.

Around noon, Lieutenant Hadley arrived on horseback. He had ridden through the mud from Fort Putnam where Colonel Knox had been earlier that morning with General Washington. Their orders were to stay at Fort Greene. Two twelve-pounders were being ferried across the East River and, if the rain let up, could be at the Fort by nightfall. General Howe's army, with most of the British troops, was opposite them. Hadley said General Washington expected the main Redcoat thrust to be at Fort Greene, an attempt to smash the center of the American fortifications, get on the interior roads, roll up the line and trap the Americans between the fortifications and the river.[7]

"Lieutenant," Tyler asked, the water dripping off his long hair and nose. "If the twelve-pounders do not arrive before the British attack. What are we to do?"

"I will talk to the commander of the New York artillery. Surely he will find some use for battle tested experienced gunners as we are," he said poking Tyler in the shoulder. "I have brought some rum and biscuits." He patted the two bulging leather saddle bags and handed them to Sergeant Merriam. "We will share that and hope the rain ceases and our baggage train arrives before we all float away." The two gun crews followed Sergeant Merriam to a relatively dry place under the east parapet, holding out the few canteens they had and parceling out the handfuls of biscuits.

"Will, a word with you," Hadley said. Will moved away from the others and followed the Lieutenant. He wrinkled his nose at the foul smell. They were standing near one of the Fort's vaults. Hadley looked as if he had not slept in three days. The dark bags under his eyes blended into the stubble on his unshaven cheeks. His damp brown curly hair stuck out under the front of his tri-corn. Somehow, he seemed to have cleaned his coat enough so one could see the blue color with the red facing and now dull brass buttons.

"The Colonel has received a letter from his wife. She and the baby are well and in Fairfield. She wrote her husband to tell you Elisabeth is safe with her father and they are to return overland to Albany. You are reminded by Mrs. Knox herself, to write Elisabeth."

"Sir," Will said, after thanking him for the message. He looked around hopelessly at the incessant rain, the lack of shelter and the mud everywhere. "When and where am I . . ."

"All in due course. I too must respond to my sister who has written me our mother is ill. I would prefer to leave here and visit Boston to see her, but" he pointed toward the front of the Fort, "we first must deal with General Howe and his minions." Will thought of Mrs. Hadley, sitting in front of the hearth, shortening a shirt and her kindness while he was recovering from the savage beating. He would include her in his prayers at Sabbath services in three days. He forced the unspoken thought from his mind. . . "if he were still alive by Sunday."

Chapter 7- Retreat Across the River

Adam, together with Jeremiah Fisk and Solomon Vining rapidly rowed the heavy square-prowed boat away from shore. Still shielded by the southern tip of Blackwell's Island, they were not yet in the strong current of the East River. The rain beat down on their backs. In the early evening darkness, made more impenetrable by the storm, Adam could barely discern the figures of the militiamen on shore restraining the owner of the boat. It is a bad business to take a fisherman's boat, he thought. But the orders were to bring everything that floated down to the ferry on the New York side.

"These are good oars, well made and shaped," Jeremiah said, pulling hard. Adam grunted. He kept an eye out for any darker outline on the water. They were without lanterns. The only light they would see on this dreary night would be at the ferry boat landing. All along the Manhattan shore, Marblehead Mariners were manning boats seized from their owners by force, without even a receipt being given, and steering them down the East River. Ahead, he caught sight of white water, the wake of a ship and the dull gray of a low square sail. The boat was most likely one that had been confiscated. There were no reports of British sloops upriver and none could enter from the Bay with the northeast wind against them. Unless of course they were attempting to row against the current. Adam gauged the current rushing them along and thought that impossible. Still, if the orders were to be believed, the Mariners were about to attempt the impossible. Transport before daylight the entire American army, cannons, horses and wagons across the East River, in a storm, to the safety of New York City. With British warships sitting just below the Battery and Governour's Island, waiting for the wind to shift.[1]

The sailing vessel had slowed, decreasing the distance between them. He sensed rather than saw the canvas being hauled in. They were nearing the ferry landing. It was slightly after eight p.m. He and Jeremiah compensated for Solomon who had ceased rowing and taken the tiller. Deftly, Vining steered the boat toward the shore as the two other Mariners backwatered to slow them down. The wind whipped the spray ahead of them as they scraped bottom on the mudflats adjacent to the wharf. The area was crowded with all kinds of craft: wide flat-bottomed ferries with railings instead of gunnels, ketches, sturdy dories, some with a mast and a cabin, most without, light sloops, oyster fishers, narrow and low to the water, and one packet. It must have been above The Battery and beyond reach of the British fleet, Adam thought.

The men sheltered in the lee of a building, huddling against the gusts of rain. "We will not be able to use sail to get across to Brooklyn," Jeremiah said, his short blue jacket buttoned up to his neck, the collar turned up and his dark blue round hat pulled down tight on to his head. "Not with this wind," Adam agreed. They would be rowing all night, he thought.

"I did not know they had nor'easter's in New York," Vining said. "I have seen worse than this off Salem. Why once, I think it was in '73. . ." Adam signaled him to be quiet. Colonel Glover emerged with the Regiment's officers from the Ferry Landing Tavern, a snug building of stone, built back from the wharf. The Mariners assembled in front of the Tavern, less than four hundred of them, awaiting orders. As Glover shouted to be heard over the storm, Adam sensed a change in the wind. The strong northeastern gusts were subsiding. The others, all experienced fishermen, noted it too. The drenching rain turned into a fine drizzle, wet and cold but bearable.

Colonel Glover said that after the battle of two days ago, there were less than 9,000 soldiers facing a British army of at least twice that number. He acknowledged the now light southwesterly breeze. "We have the advantage of darkness and surprise, if no longer the wind. The troops have been instructed to withdraw in orderly silence. The British will not discover we have left our lines until dawn. It is our task to rescue all of them from harm's way before sunrise." He looked over the Mariners standing in the gloom up to their ankles in mud. "Those of you in dories will bring the sick and wounded over first. The ferries will carry cannons and supplies."

Lieutenant Holmes divided the men of his company into crews. Adam, Solomon, Jeremiah, together with the Lieutenant and six others manned one of the ferries. It was shortly after nine p.m. They had to fight a strong ebb tide to cross the mile-wide river. Even with the ten of them pulling with all their strength it was a struggle to prevent the flat-bottomed thirty-foot craft from drifting down river below the Brooklyn Ferry landing. The landing itself was a silent scene of masses of defeated men, soaked and shivering in the night chill, waiting to get on a boat, any boat to safety. Supply wagons were axle deep in the churned muddy road leading to the wharf. The Mariners secured their oars in the rag covered oar-locks and firmly tied the ferry to the pier. They joined the militiamen on shore struggling to push the wagons out of the mud and on to the ferry.

Returning was not much easier. The ferry, carrying four wagons, with their teams of nervous horses, was less maneuverable and rode lower in the water. Initially, they rowed upriver until they were away from shore and let the tide bear them down stream, rowing hard to make headway across the swirling current. They dared not shout warnings to the other boats in the water and there were many of them. All they could do was rely upon their own skill to steer clear of the dories, skiffs and ketches in the river around them, loaded down with wounded and dark masses of men huddled together, the water washing over the gunnels and soaking the soldiers even more.

By the third trip, Adam and the crew had learned to gauge the weight of the wagons and supplies on the ferry and the strength of the ebb tide, how far to row up river, where to pull hard to get through the current and the place close to the Manhattan shore where the tidal pull slackened. At that point they rowed with the steady back- bending rhythm that was as natural to them as breathing, and brought the ferry boat alongside the wooden planked wharf.

Adam knew he could row all night through the fog if necessary. He feared there simply would not be enough hours before morning's light to bring the Army across. Each time they crossed, the Brooklyn landing seemed more crowded with men. The line of wagons waiting to be ferried across extended up into the blackness of the road from the wharf. And the artillery had not yet arrived.

Will rode hunched down on Big Red, pulling the last of the twelve-pounders from Fort Putnam on one of the inner roads toward the Brooklyn ferry. It was an eerie sight, ranks of troops marching in complete silence with their heads bent into the light rain, as Sergeants and Corporals conveyed orders in whispers. The only constant sound was of the sucking of the ankle deep mud as it reluctantly released the retreating soldiers' feet. The troops moved quietly into the wet grass and brush on the side of the road, to permit Will to pass. He guided Big Red so one of the gun carriage's studded wheels, muffled by rags, was on the relatively firm crown of the road.

He had been in the saddle for at least five hours. Ever since Lieutenant Hadley had arrived with horses and the orders to move all the cannons down to the Brooklyn Ferry. He and some of the other artillery men began at Fort Putnam on the north end of the defensive fortifications. Others, were at Fort Box on the extreme right of the line. The field artillery were the priority. The eighteen-pounders and mortars would have to be spiked and left behind. It would take too many horses to pull them. In this mud, they would never arrive at the landing in time.

Will stopped alongside a line of wagons, their horses standing patiently in traces, waiting to be driven down the sloping hill. What a waste, he thought. Once across the East River the horses would be useless for the evacuation effort. Why didn't they emulate the example of the Massachusetts Artillery. These horses were needed back at the Forts to bring the remaining cannon balls and powder, food and supplies.

Slowly he threaded his way toward the landing until he recognized the men of his Regiment ahead. He waved and they came to him, quickly unhitched the gun carriage and handed Will the worn and muddy leather straps. As he turned Big Red back toward Brooklyn Heights, he saw them struggling to push the cannon through the muck toward the landing.

Will headed to the Ring Fort, closer to the British lines and further away from the Ferry. This inner road, like the others was clogged with troops. He felt like a fish swimming against this tide of men. As he approached the Fort, he was aware of another sound. It was noise of digging, of many men putting shovels to earth. The British were digging their trenches closer to the Fort. The contrast between the silent troops retreating on the dark roads and the light and noise of the Fort was stark. As he rode in, he noticed the parapets were manned by a mere handful of Regulars. They talked loudly among themselves to give the impression of a full garrison. Cooking fires sent smoke wafting into the air, although the wind was now blowing it away from the British lines and toward the River.

He dismounted, stretched his legs and rubbed the insides of his thighs, trying to separate his wet breeches from his chaffed skin. There were several field cannon waiting for him and others on the Fort's parade grounds. Here, away from the river and the fog, a three quarter moon and the occasional star intermittently peeped out from between large swaths of clouds smeared across the sky.

"I was hoping you would get here before I left," Lieutenant Hadley said, walking over. His buff colored breeches and dark blue cloak were both splattered with mud. "Others will haul these," he said waving at the cannons on the Fort's parade grounds. We must get the ones from Fort Greene." Will looked at Hadley, waiting for the order he did not want to hear. It was getting lighter and the rain had abated somewhat. He guessed dawn was less than three hours away.

"It has taken longer than I thought to bring the guns to this point. The riders who are not from our Regiment seem to have shrewdly estimated the time so as to be far enough along the road to continue on to the Ferry but too late to be sent back for the remaining artillery."

Will looked down at his boots, thankful for the darkness that hid his face. He was exhausted and sensed Hadley's anger at those who had abandoned the effort to save the artillery. Will also had made the same calculation. He had thought to bring one more cannon from the Ring Fort. That would be his last trip. Then, he would wait at the ferry landing, help push the artillery and supplies on board, and be crossing the river to safety around dawn. Now, Hadley was sending him further down the American lines.

"My mare is still fresh, but then she has not been hauling guns all night. How is your horse?"

Will patted Big Red's neck. "He has the stamina to carry on," Will said, a tinge of bravado in his voice. The horse did not know to be afraid. But I am, he thought. I know there are more British troops closer to Fort Greene who might attack at dawn or capture me before I reach the Ferry. He saw himself a prisoner, stripped of his uniform, standing shivering in his shirt in the cold rain, with his hands bound behind him, turned over to the Hessians, or worse to his brother and the Loyalist Militia.

"Good," Hadley said. "We ride together as we did on Dorchester Heights." He smiled at Will and patted him on the back. "I have something for you." He pulled a crumpled tri-corn from under his cloak, handed it to Will and mounted. "I took it from a supply wagon carrying what the militia in their haste to flee had thrown away."

Will jammed the hat on to his head, put his foot in the stirrup and hoisted himself in to the saddle. He followed Hadley out of the Ring Fort. Just outside the perimeter, they passed orderly ranks of men marching silently in the darkness. Will recognized the high peaked black hats of Haslet's Delaware Regiment. The best troops had been holding the lines further down, he thought, until the militias, the artillery and supplies had been evacuated. Now that it was their turn, it meant the fortifications were almost unmanned and the withdrawal was nearly complete.

When they arrived at Fort Greene it was as he suspected. There was only a rearguard of Haslet's troops at Fort Greene. He and Lieutenant Hadley attached the traces to the tillers on two nine-pounders. There was no time to cover the wheels with cloth. Besides,

Will thought, with the muddy roads, getting bogged down was more of a danger than the studded wheels making noise and alerting the British. Hadley motioned for Will to follow him and they mounted the parapets. In the darkness beyond, they heard the steady sound of the British digging their trenches. The three a.m. gun sounded, the small three-pounder, emitting a barely visible puff of smoke on the east wall. Another sign of the garrison's regular routine, Will thought, hoping the British would not probe the ever thinning American lines.

There were four eighteen-pounders facing the Redcoats' lines. The few soldiers around them moved from place to place, talking and occasionally banging a canteen or musket to simulate the usual night noises of troops.

"T'is a pity to leave them, but there is nothing to be done for it," Hadley whispered, caressing the cold iron of the nearest cannon. He took a spike and hammer from his haversack, placed the spike down the touchhole, wound a strip of cloth around the head of the hammer and wrapped another strip on the top of the spike. He hit it once with all his might, driving it down flush with the top of the cannon. To Will, the noise seemed deafening. Hadley did the same with the other three guns, each time driving the spike into the touchhole with one blow. "You and I cannot be captured now," Hadley said, grinning and pleased with himself. "I have no more spikes for the nine-pounders."

Haslet's rearguard formed up quietly and marched out of the Fort. They stepped to the sides as Hadley and Will rode by, pulling the two cannons. Will felt ashamed. On horseback, he and the Lieutenant would reach the landing long before these men, and they were not panicked. He shivered, whether from fear or wetness, he didn't know. The mud seemed to grab at the wheels and hold them fast. It was a tough hard slog, even for Big Red. Twice, the nine-pounder sank in the mud to the axle hub. Without orders, the marching troops stopped, lay down their muskets, swarmed around the cannon and pushed it through the muck to firmer ground. Then, they resumed their soundless march toward the ferry, in disciplined, determined, ranks, their muskets at shoulder arms.

There were far fewer troops at the landing when Will had last been there. It seemed to him like hours ago. The remaining soldiers sat wearily on both sides of the road, waiting to be rowed across the river. A few officers on horseback quietly gave orders to others, who assembled their units and marched them down to the landing.

"There you are, sir," Sergeant Merriam said, limping toward them through the gloom. "I was hoping you and Will would arrive before we embarked." Will dismounted and exhausted, leaned against Big Red. He stroked the horse's muscled neck. Big Red raised his head and Will scratched his jaw, feeling the prickly whiskers of his chin.

Seeing Merriam, Tyler, and Baldwin gave him comfort. If they were captured, he at least would be with his companions.

He stood there, almost asleep on his feet, vaguely aware of the voices around him. The sky began to lighten as the orders were given to embark.

"No need to unhitch these guns," Hadley said. "The horses are coming across with us." Will mounted and touched Big Red lightly with his heels. The horse slowly pulled the cannon down the slope with Merriam and the others riding on the carriage to the edge of the wooden ramp of the waiting ferry. The boat's center was clear for the horses and gun carriages. Some of Haslet's black-capped troops lined the railings. Will dismounted and led Big Red on to the wooden platform.

"You troops back away and give our men room to row."

Will recognized the voice. "Nat, is that you?" he called out.

"He is in command of this ferry," a voice nearer to him said, "and Titus, Solomon and Jeremiah are here too."

"Adam. Where are you?" Will dropped the reins and pushed through some soldiers to find his friend sitting on a narrow piece of wood, the handle of a long oar in his hands.

"You are in one piece, I see," Adam said, smiling and looking up at him. "And your big horse? You have brought him to make the ferry heavier and our task harder?" Will nodded and felt the boat lurch away from the shore. Adam and the other rowers on the downstream side, pulled strongly against the ebb tide. The square prow of the ferry slowly turned up river.

Although it was dawn, they were enveloped in a thick fog. Will standing next to Big Red could hardly see the forms of the soldiers at the front of the ferry, less then six yards away. There was a strange, yellowish light, as if the sun was trying to break through the blanket of mist but could not penetrate it.[2] They were out in the river now, encased in an eerie glow unable to see ahead of them. The danger now was swamping the smaller dories on the river carrying other soldiers across, or being struck themselves by another ferry.

"Did you see the General?" a soldier near Will asked his companion, in a low voice.

"I saw him. Sitting on his white horse above the landing. Setting an example of calmness now that he has lost the battle."

"It would have turned out differently if General Lee had been in charge," a third voice said. "General Washington was appointed by Congress. Our defeat and this retreat is proof political generals do not make good field commanders."[3]

Will listened to their comments. He did not understand why Haslet's men were so critical of General Washington. The Americans had been outnumbered and overwhelmed by a superior force. They were escaping and would beat the British in Manhattan, he thought.

When they landed on the far shore, Will pulled the cannon off onto dry land and looked back. The thick fog and yellow diffused light began twenty yards out on the River. On the New York side, it was as clear as a normal morning. This was just like the fog that had aided them in the taking of Dorchester Heights, he thought. Sergeant Merriam would attribute this fog on the river to Providence. Corporal Chandler would challenge Will to think. If it was the hand of Providence protecting their escape, why did not the same hand give them a victory in Brooklyn, he would ask. It was too confusing for him. And he was too tired to think it through. Will dismounted and slogged through the mud back to the ferry. Nat was untying the boat in preparation for another crossing.

"Nat," Will called out. "I am pleased that you are safe and well."

"And you too, Will. There is no time now. We must go back for the remainder of General Mifflin's rear guard. Pray the fog holds for one more trip," he said, waving to Will and lithely jumping on to the ferry.[4] Will watched until Nat's figure and the square prowed ferry disappeared into the mist.

He did not remember riding Big Red to the Regiment's barracks. He must have led the horse into the stables and watered and fed him. The last he remembered was sitting on an empty cot in the barracks, Isaiah Chandler already asleep next to him, and Sergeant Merriam groaning as he lifted his wet, dirty stocking feet onto the straw filled bedding. Will pulled off his boots, thinking from the beginning of the battle till now, he had slept perhaps four out of the last seventy-two hours. He lay down. He heard a loud sigh, which might have been his own.

—␣␣—

Georg and Christoph walked from their camp, past the Rebeller prisoners digging mass graves for their dead. He looked at them with pity, almost one hundred of them, guarded by fewer than ten Hessians. He recognized Andreas in the guard detail and waved to his friend. Andreas removed the handkerchief covering his mouth and nose to protect against the stench of rotting bodies and acknowledged Georg and Christoph. These Rebels were peasants, Georg thought, with no more fighting spirit than a herd of sheep. They were dressed in patched and mismatched jackets, trousers and breeches, a rabble that had run at the first charge.

The two friends reached the fortification the Rebels had named Fort Greene and climbed the parapet. The brilliant warm mid-morning sun was a welcome change to the storm and cold rains of the two days following the battle. The men of the Knyphausen Regiment had set up their tents, cleaned their equipment and now had been granted rest. Many of them crowded the vantage point on the west side of the fort to get their first close view of New York. Georg absent-mindedly ran his hand over a large cannon and counted three more. These guns, plus the supplies and muskets, uniforms and equipment that had been captured were all part of the booty. Each soldier would get his share.

They could see the brick buildings of New York and the Battery. The cannons there, the powder, anything in the armory, the baggage train with its tents, cots and bedding, all would be spoils of war to be shared among the men of his Regiment. Many of the homes were three storied and three gabled with multiple chimneys. The city looked calm and peaceful. And prosperous, Georg thought. Their Officers told them there would be opportunity for plunder. Georg relished the idea.

The Rebeller army had been defeated. They had escaped but there was no fight left in them. The war was over. With his share of the booty and any plunder taken in New York, he would return to their small family farm outside of Hofgeismar, with more money than he had ever dreamed of. Surely more than 400 Thaler needed to buy a 30 Acker plot of fertile farmland. He would buy his father one new milk cow. No. He would buy two, one also for his oldest brother and family. And find himself a wife. The village girls would throw themselves at him. Perhaps, he would build his own house, near his parents. Maybe Count Freidrich Wilhelm would even give them land. They would be home by Christmas. If he worked diligently, the house could be finished and ready for he and his new wife by early summer the latest.

Chapter 8 - A Fortuitous Fire

As the English sailors pushed off from the Brooklyn shore, Georg once again stood packed on the rectangular landing craft with men from Company Seckendorf, his musket with bayonet at shoulder arms. Ahead of them was Manhattan Island, hidden temporarily from view by the line of five British men of war in the middle of the East River. He was afraid, and sensed the rising fear among the men around him, helpless and exposed in the flimsy, flat-bottomed landing barges. The Regimental Chaplain, who was in their boat, shouted the number of a psalm and they began to sing. The familiar words asking for God's protection provided Georg with some comfort. He thought the British soldiers on an adjacent landing craft had joined in, until he realized it was one of their drinking songs. He understood a little English and heard the refrain "God damn their eyes." He shivered at the blasphemy, fearful that God's wrath would be visited on the Knyphausen Regiment as well. It was bad enough they were engaging in battle on the Sabbath.

Their barges had almost reached the line of men of war, when the British ships let loose their broadsides at the redoubts and fortifications of the Rebellers on the far shore. The thunderous cannonade drowned out the Hessians' fervent singing. Georg stood mouthing the words of the psalm although he could no longer even hear his voice in his own head. The acrid smoke from the cannons blew back over the soldiers in the boats, bobbing gently in the tide line. And then the broadsides ceased and they were being rapidly rowed through the line of the men of war and heading toward a broad beach and landing. "Favor your bayonets," Sergeant Wochler shouted as the ramp was lowered and they embarked onto the wet sand. The Company quickly formed and led by their Captain and two Lieutenants, with the drummers and haut boys on the flanks, marched up the gentle slope toward an earthen redoubt blasted apart by the ships' cannon fire. Outside of sporadic musket fire, they met little resistance. As he topped the first earthen works, Georg saw swarms of Rebellers fleeing across a field, throwing their muskets aside as they ran. On a shouted order, the men increased their pace, a solid, implacable powder blue uniformed wall, bayonets lowered and glinting in the mid-September sun. It was just like the battle at Flatbush Pass, Georg thought, grinning in anticipation.

—⁂—

In the days following the Rebels' flight from their fortifications, John was like a man possessed. He roamed the prison pens on the fields of Brooklyn Heights, searching for Will among the ragged stinking Rebels, living exposed to the elements, beaten, frightened and starving. He was disappointed not to find him.

He was obsessed with finding his younger brother. Not to free him, if he were a prisoner, or to provide him with proper care if he were wounded. He wanted to ensure Will was duly punished for daring to take up arms against the Crown. By tracking down his own brother, he would further prove his loyalty. Perhaps, Lieutenant Chatsworth would mention his actions to his commander, Lt. Colonel Harcourt, who always seemed to be in the company of General Howe.

When the British and Hessians landed at Kips Bay and chased the Rebel army across open fields toward the craggy hills in the middle of Manhattan Island, John followed with Ruggles' American Loyalist Associators. While the main army and the Associators pivoted north in pursuit of the Rebel troops, John wheedled an assignment from General Ruggles to accompany the garrison troops into newly abandoned New York City and restore loyal Tories to their rightful homes while protecting their property from looting by overzealous troops.

The brigade of British troops were welcomed by joyous throngs, celebrating the end of Rebel rule. Large crowds cheered the soldiers as they marched down Broadway to the Battery, the pretty young girls waving and smiling flirtatiously. John reveled in the attention. When he walked the streets, even though he was in civilian clothes, leading a small squad of British soldiers, he acknowledged with a restrained nod, the greetings of men of means, their wives and daughters, as if he personally had been responsible for their liberation. He zealously carried out his responsibility for seizing the fine brick buildings of recently departed patriots as quarters for British officers, directing a soldier to paint GR, for George Rex, in bold white letters on the doors, signifying it was the King's property. He took advantage of the opportunities afforded by inspecting the homes, to purloin for himself valuables left behind- dining ware silver, a lady's hand mirror, an engraved pocket pistol hidden in a desk drawer and forgotten in haste by its Rebel owner- anything portable that could easily be carried in the saddle bag he had slung over his shoulder.

The Rebels had fled New York City on the Hudson River side. John expected General Howe to cut off their retreat at the northern tip of Manhattan Island, if not lower down, while the British Navy would prevent any escape to New Jersey. Then it would all be over. In the meantime, John prowled the Common, just north of St. Paul's Church, where there was a makeshift open-air prison for Rebels captured at Kip's Bay. He held a handkerchief across his nose and mouth, a fine embroidered linen one he had taken that morning while inspecting an abandoned home near the Battery, to ward off the stench of human waste and evil vapors emanating from the miserable mass of men lying in the mud and trampled grass. The British Sergeant in charge of the guard detail told him the prisoners were mostly levies from Connecticut who had fled at the first naval barrage and been found cowering under shrubs and bushes like partridges for the taking. Those who had not been bayoneted by the Hessians, as they deserved, the Sergeant added with a laugh.

John looked only at the young, more fit among them, without deigning to speak or question any one. They were beneath him, riffraff, farm boys, ignorant common laborers, uneducated, undernourished and undisciplined, without a spark of military spirit.

It was possible he thought, Will had escaped and was still with the traitors fleeing north. No matter. He would have ample opportunity to survey the prisoners after the next and final battle. If he did not find him, he would assume Will had been killed. That would be a pity. His younger brother's death on the battlefield would deprive John of the prospect of further exhibiting his loyalty to the Crown. But, he still had the gratitude of Lieutenant Chatsworth for saving his life by killing that Negro in North Hempstead.

Unconsciously, he fingered the slight bump on the top of his head. There was another score to settle with the Dutchman's black servant who had been with Will that night at the Inn. He ardently hoped Van Hooten was still with the Rebel army in Manhattan. Capture the Dutchman and John would have his Negro servant.

It was late afternoon when the men of Knox's Artillery Regiment arrived at a makeshift camp in Harlem Heights. They had ridden in wagons piled high with the supplies they had hurriedly loaded, the tents and blankets covering side boxes of shot and powder. The men sat on top, silent and subdued as they passed American troops despondently trudging north on the Bloomingdale Road, after abandoning New York City. The woods to their east shielded them from the battle they all heard- cannons followed by volleys of musket fire. These sounds served to hurry all of the retreating troops along, fearful the green-coated Jaegers with their short hunting rifles would burst from the tree line at every turn in the road.

In the darkness, they erected their tents and unloaded the cots and the few heavy cooking pots they had brought with them. Fires dotted the hillside where they were camped and their Regiment made do with whatever food supplies they had managed to carry.

"It is strange to me," Corporal Levi Tyler said, moving to the edge of his cot. "We were able to secure our equipment and baggage from Brooklyn Heights to Manhattan, across the East River, and yet we hastily abandon these precious supplies in New York. Better to have started a day earlier and brought more of our cannons with us, I say." The dust and dirt from the road covered his face and neck, and powdered his long narrow nose.

Isaiah Chandler looked up from stitching a patch above the pocket on his blue coat. "Perhaps the British navy precipitated our sudden departure." He spat on a brass button and wiped it with his hand, examined the shine and resumed sewing. "Remember how the good citizens of the city greeted us when we arrived across the East River. There was enough gloom and wailing to cause the entire army to despair. Instead of encouragement and willingness to sacrifice and enlist, I could sense every whore's son of them calculating how to escape or profit from the entry of the British. I, for one, am glad to be rid of them and their city. My only regret is we did not burn it to the ground before leaving."

"No need to curse them," Sergeant Merriam said, rubbing his aching ankle with both hands, "though I agree many of them are a godless lot. Remember, it was Divine Providence that intervened on our behalf with the dense fog. And it will be by a providential hand we defeat our enemies."

"I suppose we should give thanks this Sabbath for this cold pickled pork covered with slime and watery soup we enjoy, while the British feast on the meat and bread and vegetables we have left behind," Tyler said with bitterness. He stared at Merriam, challenging him to respond. "This is unfit to eat. One could break a tooth trying." He hurled his hard biscuit out the tent flap in disgust.

"If you did and had less than four good teeth left in that scraggly head of yours, you would no longer be able to bite off the end of the paper cartridge and fire a musket," Chandler said. "Then you could go home and we would be done with your complaining."[1]

Tyler jumped up. "I have never shirked my duty and never will," he said, advancing toward Chandler, who remained seated on his cot.

"No one said you did," Merriam said, groaning as he stood to come between them. "It is the militiamen who run and line up before their doctors to be declared unfit for service." He sat down and nursed his swollen ankle.

"I meant no insult to you, Levi," Chandler said calmly. "I am distraught at the lack of patriotic fervor from the good citizens of New

York. They welcomed us well enough when we arrived in April and cheered us on until they saw the size of the British fleet and the number of troops they had brought with them. And now, after Brooklyn, when we need every able-bodied man, the New York and New Jersey militias march back home, declaring their term of service up."

Will listened, too unsure of himself to join the conversation. He had seen entire militia units leaving to return to their farms and towns, their officers riding in front as proud as if they had done their duty, the clatter of wagons bringing up the rear, drowning out the moans and cries of their wounded and sick fellow soldiers. On the one hand, he knew the militias were the ones who had fled at the first shot or sign of the Hessians. They were worthless to the army and good riddance to them, he thought. On the other hand, the number of men on the line decreased every day. The British seemed to draw on endless fresh replacements from Staten Island, and Loyalist recruits from New Jersey. Will was infected with a sense of hopelessness. Why continue to fight on? He would never desert his friends, he assured himself. But if they and a few others were all that was left of the American Army, how could they possibly prevail?

"It is still the Sabbath" Merriam intoned solemnly "We must give thanks for whatever we have to share on the Sabbath and on any day, and we pray for our continued safety and remember those we lost in battle." The men fell silent. Will thought of Simeon Webb and those he had seen shot and drowned in Gowanus Creek and the dead of Smallwood's Regiment after their valiant charges against overwhelming numbers. If only the soldiers were more like those men, he thought, the army would not have to retreat.

The next morning, Will and the others heard the sounds of battle to the south. From the sloping hill of the camp, Will saw a group of officers galloping down the road in the direction of the firing. The musket fire seemed to be heavier. After a while, although the intensity was the same, it sounded as if the battle had moved farther away. Lieutenant Hadley walked through the camp and told the men to see to their muskets and procure extra cartridges from the supply tent.

"Are we to ready the field cannons?" Tyler asked him.

"No orders yet. We may be used as infantry today," Hadley replied.

They waited, first lining up by companies and then being dismissed to sit in the shade until further orders. By midday, Lieutenant Hadley left them, riding south toward the continuing sounds of fighting. In the late afternoon, as the air became cooler, promising a fresh and pleasant September night, a body of officers came back up the road at a trot, their horses kicking up clouds of dust. Will thought he recognized the bulky figure of Colonel Knox. The mounted group continued north on the road past their camp. Soon Lieutenant Hadley rode into their camp, grinning broadly. Will ran up and took the reins of his horse.

"Sergeants," Hadley shouted. "Assemble the men. I have good news." Hadley mounted an empty sidebox as the fifty some men of the Company formed up in lines before him. Other troops from nearby units drifted over to hear the news.

"Today, we have taught the British a lesson and twisted the royal lion's tail," Hadley shouted exuberantly. "They attacked this morning, driving some ill disciplined militia before them. The redcoats chased them across the fields and then, contemptuously their buglers blew the fox hunting call. This so enraged our regulars they waited for the British advance, rose up to fire a volley at them and then charged with their bayonets. Those fox hunting redcoats turned tail at the sight of real soldiers and ran for their lives." The men yelled a loud roar of approval.

"The British now cower behind their defensive lines across the Bloomingdale Road, beyond the big apple orchard we passed yesterday noon." Again the men cheered. "I heard this account from Colonel Knox, who urges us to be of high spirits and tasked me to remind you this is what free men can accomplish." The men spontaneously gave three cheers for their Colonel and then three more for General Washington.

That night the pickled pork and hard biscuits did not taste as bitter or stale, while the men speculated on what would happen next. Will had no opinion but leaned toward those among the Massachusetts men who thought they would defend Fort Constitution on the heights beyond Harlem. The British army would be decimated by a bloody frontal assault just as at Bunker Hill.[2]

On the fourth night of the army's encampment above the Harlem plains, Will was on sentry duty from midnight to six a.m. There had been rumors of a night attack and talk of the possibility of a mass assault with Hessians and Highlanders coming out of the woods in the early morning mist. Pickets had been posted along the road to the south. Hand's riflemen were scattered in the woods on either of the Bloomingdale Road, hiding Indian fashion, waiting to pick off the enemy's officers. Nevertheless, Will remained alert, peering into the darkness below him and listening intently. All seemed normal. He heard the usual night sounds of crickets and cicadas, a hoot from the occasional owl and the distant barking of a farm dog. It reminded him of the countersign- foxhound. A good one he thought, appropriately commemorating the Redcoat's retreat several days ago.

With his concentration focused on the terrain immediately in front of him, he almost missed seeing the dull red glow to the southwest. Fire, he thought. It must be huge to be seen from their camp. He ran back to awaken Lieutenant Hadley.

—⚊⚊—

John Stoner awoke to the boom of an alarm cannon and cries of "Fire!" "Fire!" from the street. He had secured a comfortable room for himself in a fine three-story brick building, once the home of one Alexander McDougall, a prominent Rebel known as an abuser of New York merchants loyal to the Crown. There were no church bells to ring, all having been taken by the Rebels to be cast as cannons. Together with Lieutenant Chatsworth, and troopers of the 16th Light Dragoons, John raced out of the McDougall Mansion on lower Broadway. The west side of the city was ablaze. Cinders and bits of fiery flakes of wooden shingles, like orange darts, flew above them on the strong southwest wind. The air was thick with acrid smoke and gritty dust. It burned his throat and clogged his nostrils. Charred bits of clothing, paper and fabric, whirled by. Soldiers milled about, uncertain whether to answer the windborne threat of the fire spreading to as yet unburnt areas in lower Manhattan, or to race toward the inferno and fight the fire there. A column of sailors and marines, led by naval officers ran past them toward the fire and the North River.

In the streets, all was confusion and chaos. Residents of houses nearer to the fire, fled past John and the Dragoons, carrying bedding, linen and whatever else they could rescue, running for refuge toward any grassy area clear of the buildings. People looked frantically up at the roofs nearest to them, screaming in alarm as the flames jumped from one building to another, starting first as a small glowing flicker on the dry shingles and then bursting into a searing sheet of fire.

Chatsworth led his men west from Broadway, heading toward where the fires raged the fiercest. John kept close to the Dragoons, anxiously glancing up at the burning buildings, afraid he would be hit by falling fiery beams or other debris. He coughed continuously, despite the damp handkerchief he held across his mouth and nose. The closer they got, the more intense the heat. The steep roof of Trinity Church was a roaring inferno, the large pyramid frame of the tower's beams exposed and pointing like a fiery arrow toward the night sky. John was surprised at how loud the noise was, not just from the crash as roof beams fell and brick walls collapsed into the street, but the fire itself. The flames emitted a roaring intense sound, sucking up the air around it and throwing off a searing heat. His face felt red and tight as if his skin had been burned and roasted.

At the intersection of Lumber and Stone Streets, a squad of Marines had surrounded a young man in a dark brown, patched coat and were beating him with their musket butts. He lay curled up on the cobblestones, his breeches torn at the knees, protecting his head from their blows and screaming for mercy. Other Marines hurried from a three story brick building on the far corner, its roof and top story ablaze, carrying trunks, rolling barrels or bent double under the weight of makeshift sacks made of bed linen.

"You there, Sergeant," Chatsworth yelled. "What is the meaning of this," he said, pointing to the Marines emerging from the building.

"We caught this one skulking around and up to no good," he said, signaling his men to cease hitting the man on the ground. "The others are rescuing goods which would only feed the flames," he replied smirking. "There is no fire fighting equipment, to speak of, sir," he said, adding the "sir" almost as an afterthought.

"Where is your commanding officer? Bring me to him."

"He is ahead of us, sir. I will lead you to him."

The Marine Sergeant pointed up Lumber Street and as Chatsworth and the Dragoons followed the Marine, John ducked into a shop that caught his eye. The door had been battered in. The low ceiling room was filled with smoke. John could hear the crackling of the fire on the roof. Still it was worth the risk, he thought. It was a silver smith's shop with a front counter, stripped of whatever goods had been on display for sale. He pushed aside a curtain and found himself in a small storeroom. His eyes burned from the smoke and his throat was dry and scratchy. He felt his way along the wall and bumped into a chest on the floor. It was too heavy for him to lift, let alone carry by himself. It was locked. He took the small pocket pistol he carried, primed it, stepped back and fired directly at the padlock. The ball shattered the catch mechanism. Quickly, he pried the lock off with his dirk and lifted the lid. A pair of intricately worked silver spice containers lay on a velvet tray. He wrapped them in their cloth and stuffed them in his coat pocket. The roof groaned and creaked. He heard part of it collapse and a whooshing sound as the night air entered the third floor. He could sense the flames fanned by the wind spreading above him. A hardwood box, almost half yard long, lay at the bottom of the trunk. Without opening it, he grabbed it and clutching it to his chest, dashed from the storeroom, through the smoke filled entrance of the shop and out onto the street. He coughed and hacked as he headed north on Lumber Street hoping to find Chatsworth again. He glanced apprehensively at the flames shooting out of the second story windows of the buildings around him. The roof of one had collapsed and he could see the fire devouring the wooden furniture within.

"You there, halt," someone yelled behind him. John kept walking praying Chatsworth and the Dragoons would appear.

"I said Halt!" the voice shouted again, this time closer.

John stopped and turned around. He was confronted by a Corporal and six Regulars, their bayonet tipped muskets pointed at him. In their red uniforms with the glow of the flames from nearby buildings lighting up their faces, John thought they resembled a squad of Satan's minions from Hell.

"Yes, Corporal," John replied, hoping his voice did not betray his fear. He wished he had a uniform instead of his long black walking coat. Self-consciously, he brushed cinders and ash from his shoulders and smoothed his yellow linen waistcoat.

"Who are you and what are you doing here," the Corporal said. He held his musket loosely in his right hand, the point of the bayonet less than two feet from John's groin.

"My name is John Stoner. I am adjutant to General Timothy Ruggles of the Loyalist Associators. I am safeguarding Crown property and ensuring the security of Loyalist citizens."

"It looks to me, you are more of a looter. Maybe even a Rebel arsonist," the Corporal responded, looking at the bulge in John's coat and the hard wood case he held in his hand.

"You are mistaken, my good man," John replied with as much confidence as he could muster. "I was on patrol with Lieutenant Chatsworth of the 16th Dragoons and we have become separated. I would appreciate your escorting me up Lumber Street where I was going to find him."

"My orders are to stay in this vicinity and prevent looting, which is what I am doing."

John heard a scream from down the street. Another patrol of soldiers had formed a U around a man in civilian clothes and with their bayonets were forcing him back into a burning building. The man fell to his knees begging them, but they began pricking him with their bayonets. John could see the blood from the cuts as he backed crying and screaming into the doorway.

"That is the proper way to deal with looters and arsonists," the Corporal said, grinning to reveal a mouth of brown worn teeth. "However, before we commit you to the flames, I will relieve you of this wooden case and whatever is the bulge of your Rebel coat pocket."

"Please," John pleaded. "I can prove who I am. You must not do this."

"Must I now," the Corporal replied. There was an edge in his voice as he placed the point of his bayonet on John's testicles. "You do not seem to be the man you claim to be."

John almost fell to his knees in fear. He heard the clumping of boots on the cobblestones behind him.

"What is this?" he heard Chatsworth call out. "Why are you holding this man?" Chatsworth and the Dragoons strode up and the Corporal moved back a respectful distance. "This man is with me," Chatsworth said. "I am sure he explained who he is. John. Do you wish to bring the Corporal up on report for his offensive conduct?"

"No, Lieutenant," John said quietly. "No, he was merely performing his duty," he said regaining his confidence. "We want the King's troops to be zealous in apprehending looters and arsonists," he said more loudly addressing the Corporal and his men.

"The entire city north and west of here at least as far as Cortlandt is ablaze," Chatsworth said, putting his arm around John's shoulder. "There is nothing we can do there. The fire will simply have to burn itself out. We will be more useful preventing cinders from falling on the unburned buildings that house our troops."

He walked next to Chatsworth, regaining his composure with each step south on Lumber Street away from the Corporal.

Even though the heat from the fire was intense, he shivered involuntarily at the thought of the Corporal's bayonet piercing his balls.

John labored with the Dragoons for the remainder of the night, filling buckets, running up stairs and dousing the roofs of their barracks and adjacent buildings. The wind had carried the fire south almost to the East River, before shifting again, blowing burning fragments back toward the Hudson. The fine brick building John had selected for the Dragoons and himself, and their neighborhood in the lower part of the city, survived the night. In the morning, although the fire still raged on the west side, it was clear the worst was over.[3]

Exhausted, John sat on the wooden spindle chair in his room, his shirt and breeches covered in soot and ash. The dark wooden case was next to him, on the desk, unopened. He took no pleasure in the upholstered chair or the desk with its brass fittings, both of which he had confiscated from a Patriot's home, although at the time, he had thought them fine pieces. Now, they reminded him of how close he had come to being killed by his greed. His throat was dry, from the pervasive ash and cinders and smoke in the air, but also from the fear still with him. He saw the predatory look of the Corporal and subconsciously moved his hand from the wooden case to his groin to protect himself. He did not like being thought of as prey. John started at the knock on his door.

Chatsworth came in, without waiting for his reply. John rose and offered him the chair and moved to sit on the edge of his bed. "You should not stray too far from us in the future, John," the Lieutenant admonished. "You are useful to me and I do not want to see you come to any harm." John nodded and mumbled his thanks. Chatsworth sat with his elbow on one of the chair arms, his hand rubbing his chin. John anticipated there was more. "Gentlemen do not engage in looting, John. It is demeaning. If you intend to make something of yourself you must end this practice."

John thought of the night in North Hempstead, the Lieutenant and he and some of the troopers, taking turns with Onderack's wife and daughters. "Do gentlemen do that?" he thought, but held his tongue. The lesson was that gentlemen did whatever they could get away with. He had been caught by lower-class men, a Corporal and his squad. That had been his offense.

John nodded. He picked up the wooden box and handed it to Chatsworth. "It is for you." He had no idea what was inside but hoped it would something fine and well crafted.

Chatsworth took the box from him, lifted the carved metal latch and opened it. His face broke into a broad grin. "John you have outdone yourself. I will be the envy of every officer in the Army."

He turned the open box toward John. Inside were a matched pair of pistols, with highly polished dark wood handles, inlaid with intricately carved silver from the firing pan to the end of the muzzle. Two large silver ovals decorated the pistol butts. "I shall have my initials engraved in their center," Chatsworth said excitedly, lightly caressing the graceful leaf pattern that curled around the oval. He removed one pistol and then the other, turning them over in his hand and weighing their balance. Reluctantly, he returned them to their case and tucked the box under his arm.

"This brace of pistols is a most wonderous gift, John. I appreciate you took a risk for me. No more about the events of tonight." He patted John on the shoulder. "My men will keep their silence and the Corporal will count himself lucky not to have been court martialed and broken in rank." Chatsworth left a little hastily, eager to show off his new pistols to the other officers.

I could have sold them for a fine price, John thought. Now they are just another payment for Lieutenant Chatsworth's good graces and with his help, perhaps a position in London. The pistols may turn out to be a good investment, after all, he thought as he lay down, forcing the terrifying events of the night from his mind.

Georg had never felt prouder. General von Knyphausen himself had reviewed the Regiment. Newly arrived with 7,000 fresh Hessian troops, he referred to the Regiment that bore his name as his "battle-tested men," distinguishing them from those who had accompanied him across the ocean. Georg, Christoph and Andreas, along with the rest of their Company, had spent a day brushing the campaign's dirt from their light blue coats, buffing the buttons and polishing their high brass caps until they shone like mirrors. They applied whiting to their cross straps and, just before the parade, powdered their hair and waxed their mustaches. Their finely honed bayonets glinted lethally in the noonday sun. Still, their uniforms looked worn and more used than the newcomers. Georg sensed the men wore them with an added sense of pride, a sign they had been under fire, done their duty and chased the Rebellers out of Brooklyn and driven them from New York City. He smiled to himself recalling the militiamen fleeing before them like rabbits.

After four days of drilling and rest, well fed with roasted beef, green vegetables and freshly baked loaves of bread purchased by the Quartermaster from the farmers of Brooklyn, and led by their General they once again embarked on the flat bottomed British landing craft. It was a crisp fall October day. This time Georg knew they would annihilate the Rebeller army retreating somewhere in the middle of the island they called Manhattan. This time, he saw, there were more than one hundred British naval vessels on the East River, forming a mighty line of cannons pointing to the far shore. This time, he was not afraid. There was no need to sing psalms or to pray. With their overwhelming numbers of such finely equipped and disciplined troops, nothing could withstand their onslaught. As if to give proof to Georg's optimism, their landing was unopposed.

—◆—

Will was excited. He was back among the Marblehead Mariners. Lieutenant Hadley and four gun crews with two nine and twelve-pounders, were supporting the 14th Continentals under Colonel Glover. The four hundred or so Mariners, together with a few regiments of Massachusetts militia, were stationed near a village called Eastchester. Will hurried from the hastily formed gun emplacements where they had placed the cannons the night before. The morning was his first chance to spend time with Lt. Nathaniel Holmes, Adam and the others with whom he had shared a barracks at Cambridge, so many months ago. He found Adam, Solomon and Jeremiah around their breakfast cooking fire. Adam was the first to recognize him. He jumped up and gave Will a bear hug, lifting him off the ground.

"You look different in a uniform," Jeremiah said, shaking his hand. "In the fog and dark on the East River, I had no opportunity to see you fully."

"And I would recognize you anywhere," Will replied, "from your snaggle-toothed grin."

Jeremiah covered the right side of his mouth with his hand. "I never did find a silversmith to grind down my stubs. I still hope to though."

Solomon stood next to Jeremiah, his long arms and big boned hands dangling at his sides. He shook Will's hand and put his own on Will's shoulder.

"You have grown," he said, measuring Will with his eyes. "A few inches at least."

"Where is Nat, I mean Lieutenant Holmes," Will asked, glancing around the tent area.

"He is with the Colonel," Adam said, pointing toward a nearby hill. An officer with a dark blue coat was facing toward the East River, a telescope to his eye. Will could make out Colonel Glover's red hair beneath his tri-corn. Nat stood next to him, staring in the same direction. Abruptly, the two of them turned and ran down the hill. Nat came up to them as the Colonel continued into camp, shouting for all officers to report to him immediately.

Nat embraced Will quickly and catching his breath, ordered the men to grab their muskets and fall in.

"There are at least one hundred sail on the East River and Regulars and Hessians are landing by the thousands. Their vanguard is a mile from the river shore already, marching down Split Rock Road toward us." He pointed at the road that ran to the left of their camp and continued west to the Hudson. "May Providence protect you today and God willing we will meet later," he said quickly, grabbing Will's shoulders.

"You too, Nat. All of you," Will said. He turned and raced back to the gun emplacements, already thinking they would have to move the cannons to cover the road better. He took his place with his crew. Sergeant Merriam ordered them to load the side boxes with grape shot. When the powder boxes were filled with canvas bag charges they stood impatiently waiting for orders. Will wondered whether he should get Big Red and hitch him up to one of the twelve-pounders to be ready.

He glanced at Sergeant Merriam, hoping he would give him orders but the Sergeant was looking at Colonel Glover's command tent.

"We will be in the thick of it soon enough," Levi Tyler said, grunting as he sat down, leaning his back against the gun carriage wheel and stretching his long legs in front of him.

The Officers emerged from the tent, running toward their companies. Lieutenant Hadley waved to them with his tri-corn and Sergeant Merriam ordered Tyler, Will and Baldwin to go.

"The Colonel needs every available man," Hadley said, setting his tri-corn back on his head. "His plan does not involve field artillery. Go to the supply tent and bring back a musket, bayonet and cartridges for every one of the gun crews. We are fighting alongside Lt. Holmes' company."

The gun crews, forty some odd men, trooped to where the Mariners and the Massachusetts Militias had assembled in roughly two hundred man units. The entire body marched double time east down the narrow Split Rock Road, spaced apart at fifty-yard intervals. Will was with the lead group. Ahead he saw Adam and the tall figure of Solomon, and the sea of dark blue jackets of the Mariners. He had no idea what the plan was or what he was supposed to do, other than fire his musket when ordered. They were being led by Lieutenants Hadley and Holmes and he assumed the Colonel knew better than to have their small unit run head on into an advancing combined British Hessian force of thousands.

A scout loped down the road coming from the direction of the East River and conferred briefly with Lieutenant Holmes. The two Lieutenants took off their hats and waved the men to climb the stone wall on the right of the road. Will nimbly clambered over. The companies to their rear scaled the stone wall on the left side and disappeared behind the rocks about fifty yards behind them.

Will crouched down, next to Levi and checked his musket for the first time. It was a Brown Bess, probably taken after a battle, whether from a Patriot or Redcoat, he did not know. He bit off the end of the paper cartridge, poured a little powder into the firing pan and rammed the paper tube with the remainder of the powder down the barrel, followed by the lead ball. Grasping the hilt of the bayonet, he made sure it was firmly seated, and waited. Lieutenant Hadley scuttled toward them in a crouch, stopping at each group of ten or fifteen men before moving on.

When he reached Will and Levi, he beckoned for the Mariners nearby to come closer.

"We are the most forward unit. When the British column is within thirty yards, either I or Lieutenant Holmes will give the order to fire. We will hit them with a volley that will send them reeling. Reload and wait for the order to fire. No scattered shots. We must strike with all of our firepower. Aim low and reload quickly." He smiled reassuringly. Will wished he had Hadley's calm. *What happens after we fire several volleys, and the British and Hessians keep coming,* he thought, but was too ashamed to ask. Hadley answered as if he had read Will's mind.

"The Colonel's plan is for us to fall back and let the enemy proceed down the road. Another company on the other side will give them what for and then it will be our turn again. Wait for the command to withdraw. We must do it in good order."

"Good thing he added the last part about withdrawing," Levi muttered to no one in particular. "I was wondering if we were going to ask the British gentlemen for permission to take their leave."

"You may have to learn German," one of the Mariners whispered. "I hear the Hessians are leading the column."

Will felt in his cartridge box and fingered the paper packets. He ran the tips of his fingers over the lead balls, sitting snug in their holes in a wooden block, nailed to the bottom of the leather case. He counted twenty of them. He counted the balls again. It helped steady him. He was ten to fifteen feet from the corner of the double stonewall lining the road. Ahead, at the corner where the road wall met the narrower wall on his right, he could see Mariners behind the stones for thirty or forty feet in from the angle.

Will took comfort in the numbers of blue-jacketed Mariners around him. He heard the steady beat of drums from the road, the high-pitched wooden instruments the Hessians used and the rhythmic menacing sound of marching men. Here they come, he thought. All along the line there was the noise of hammers being pulled back ready to strike and ignite the powder in the firing pans. Will waited, his throat dry. The drumming and marching were like a buzzing in his ears. He saw Nat rise up from a crouch and wave his hat as he heard the command to fire.

Two hundred men rose almost as one. Will held the musket to his shoulder pointing it slightly downward and pulled the trigger. There was a pause and then simultaneously an explosion in his ears and puff of smoke from the firing pan. He saw the column of Hessians in their light-blue uniforms, squeezed in and forced together by the narrow road. Individual soldiers fell, bright red stains blossoming on their white waistcoats and breeches. Those still standing fired on command. The balls bounced harmlessly off the stones of the wall, as

Will knelt along with the others and reloaded. He went through the routine automatically- bite the cartridge, pour some powder in the pan and close the pan cover, half cock the hammer, empty the rest of the powder down the barrel, ram the paper and ball home, reset the ramrod, pull the flint back to full cock and ready.

"Fire." He heard the command, stood up and there was a tremendous roar as their second volley tore into what remained of the Hessian vanguard. More of them fell and then, in confusion, they retreated back down the road, toward the main body.

The Hessian wounded lay in the hot sun on the narrow road, some lying on top of others, others calling for help or water. On the near side, lying in a ditch, Will saw a young boy, a drummer, maybe ten or eleven, cut in two by their musket fire, his entire middle a thick band of red blood. Will could not say whether his ball had hit any Hessian. But he knew the effect a volley of musket fire could have on a mass of soldiers, closely packed together as the Hessians had been. He swallowed hard thinking perhaps his ball had struck the boy.

He reloaded and waited. The taste of black powder was on his tongue and in his nostrils. His eyebrows were singed from errant flashes of powder. Lieutenant Hadley came down the line again.

"They will be back. This time, we will not let them get too close. We want to draw them on. Wait for the command. Remember to aim low and reload quickly. Do not retreat until the order is given."

The enemy announced their renewed attack with an artillery barrage. Will and the others clung closely to the wall as cannon balls flew overheard and crashed harmlessly in the field or struck the stone wall, sending slivers of stone and metal slicing through the air. Will waited and looked to his right for Nat to give the command. When he rose to fire, the Hessians were fifty yards away, further than before but close enough for the volley to still have a devastating impact on their tightly massed columns. The narrow road pressed them together so there were few men in their front line but the column was deep. The first line of Hessians, dropped down on one knee and those standing immediately behind them simultaneously loosed a volley. Will heard the balls whizz by him or strike the stone wall in front of him.

Will was not sure but he thought he fired two more volleys before he heard the shouted command to fall back. He ran in a crouch close to the wall, following the men in front of him. He jumped over the body of a Mariner, part of his head torn off, lying on his back, one open eye gazing skyward. Behind him, he heard the panting of other men. There was no panic, just the sound of steady scampering until they reached the wall separating their field from the next. He was aware of the silence. The enemy troops on the road had not fired a shot to impede their withdrawal.

Without an order they clambered over the stones, dropped down in the slender band of shade provided and rested against the coolness of the wall. Merriam was among the last to reach the wall. He collapsed to the ground with a groan, took off his tri-corn, his face sweaty and red from the exertion. He opened his canteen and took a long drink, his Adam's apple bobbing up and down with each swallow.

"Not here," Nat shouted as he came over the wall. "Across this field and on to the next. Regroup, position yourselves as before." They ran, this time more slowly through the knee-high grass. Will estimated the field was more than one hundred yards long. He dropped back and helped Merriam limp along, his arm draped over Will's shoulder. When they reached the other end, they found the men spread out from the corner point along both stone walls, the one that was perpendicular to and the one paralleling Split Rock Road. Will waited for the pounding in his temples to subside. He was sweating profusely, his shirt clinging to his body under his uniform jacket. He reloaded first and then opened his canteen and swallowed the warm water. He glanced around and realized, with relief, they had suffered very few casualties. The next time may be different. The enemy would know what to expect.

—⁂—

Georg waited as the British gun crews brought their light field artillery into position on the road. His company had been the second in line. He had heard the volleys and seen the men in front stand and return fire, before being compelled to retreat. His unit had been too far back to bring their muskets to bear. Why not charge with their bayonets, as before, he thought. He looked at Captain Seckendorf and

Second Lieutenant Reuter, standing impatiently on the side of the road. Georg admired them. They led from the front, as did all their officers, but the Captain in particular exuded an air of casual courage which inspired the troops. Seckendorf casually raised his hand and his batman rushed forward and handed him a silver flask. He took a drink and passed it to Lieutenant Reuter as they studied the retreating men, passing through their ranks toward the rear. Good, Georg thought. It would now be their turn and they would deal with the Rebellers as they had done before. Show them the steel of the bayonet and they would run.

Georg shifted from foot to foot impatiently, eager for the British cannon barrage to cease. Finally, the drums struck up the beat for forward march, the haute boys added their reedy wooden sound from their oboes to the rhythm and they proceeded down the road, their muskets at shoulder arms. Georg felt the cadence hesitate slightly as they walked past their dead comrades. Trails of darkened bloodstains marked how they had been dragged to the side of the road to make a passage for the rest of the army. Georg felt a deep anger and hatred for the men who had done this. These Rebellers did not stand and fight in open battle. They hid and skulked behind stone walls, shooting at those like he and his comrades who bravely confronted them and then they turned tail and ran like scared rabbits. This time, he would show no mercy when he caught up with them.

They marched past the field where the cowardly Rebellers had lain in wait. The stone walls had been blasted by the British cannon. Ahead, Georg could see the fields on both sides of the road, neatly demarked by waist high walls of stone. He would like nothing better than to race through the tall grass, bayonet held low with the rabble fleeing before them, until they were brought up short at the end of the field. He would skewer them against the wall, careful not to break the tip of his bayonet on the stones.

Georg heard a shout, saw a wall of uniformed men rise up on his right from behind a stone fence, then a cloud of smoke and the roar of a volley of musket fire rolled toward him. Almost simultaneously, the soldier next to him let out a cry, more of surprise than pain, looked at the bright red circle of blood spreading into an irregular pattern on his thigh, and collapsed to the ground.

Sergeant Wochler shouted the command to kneel and fire. The first line knelt and the two lines loosed a volley at the Rebellers. Methodically, he began to reload. He sensed the second line, kneeling and reloading behind him, as the third and fourth lines squeezed forward through their ranks and fired another volley. The smoke swirled around him, his ears rang from the explosions of muskets, and his head ached from the sun beating down on his brass hat. He saw Christoph and Andreas, further down the row unhurt, waiting for the command to advance.

Now it was their turn. They brushed past the ranks of the two lines that were kneeling and reloading. Several of men in Georg's line were unable to get through. Georg knelt and those in the second line stood behind them. Lieutenant Reuter gave the command to fire a split second after the Rebellers stood from behind the stone wall and let loose their volley. Georg sensed some in his line toppling forward. A soldier behind him fell on to his shoulder. Georg groaned involuntarily under the sudden weight and at the same time lowered his right shoulder so the wounded man slid off him to the ground. The man's arm was shattered and part of his chest was a bloody pulp. Georg automatically reloaded, trying to avoid the wounded man's frightened look and his pleas for help. He stood up, noticing there were fewer men in his line, now the third of four. He lost count of how many volleys there were, how many times he knelt, fired and reloaded, stood and stepped through the kneeling ranks in front of him. He heard the shouted commands and the beat of the drum ordering them to retreat. He reacted not first to those signals, which seemed to come from a long distance inside his head, but to the sight of Captain Seckendorf, cooly waving his sword directing them to fall back. They turned, leaving a small rear guard and many blue-jacketed Hessians lying in the road, and marched back toward the main force, their ranks noticeably thinned.

—ɯ—

Will heard the cannons and then the musket fire ahead, this time from his left on the road. Now, he understood Colonel Glover's battle plan. The two, hundred-man units were spaced on alternate sides of Split Rock Road, hidden behind stone walls. The British and Hessians could only bring a small part of their force to bear, because of the constricted road. After firing several volleys, the men withdrew on the same side of the road one field beyond where they had been, leapfrogging past another unit hidden on the opposite side of the road. They would be able to do this, Will thought, as long as there were fields and stone walls. He knew the fields ended at a shallow creek. Beyond that was their camp where they had left the cannons early in the morning. He wished they had brought the artillery with them to duel with the British guns.

It was silent again. Will imagined the forward regiment that had just engaged the British and Hessians, running back through the fields to the one past where he and the Mariners waited on the other side of the road.

"It will be our turn again soon enough," Sergeant Merriam observed.

"Better to drink up now before it gets hot and heavy again," Levi Tyler said, mopping the sweat from his brow on his sleeve.

Will looked up and down the line and spotted Adam, leaning with his back against the stone wall, his musket across his lap. Will waved and Adam raised his hand in recognition. Anxiously, he scanned the faces of the Mariners he could see. None of them he knew were missing. Lieutenants Hadley and Holmes were creeping along the perimeter, stopping to talk to small groups of men. Nat reached Will's part of the wall, holding his sword hilt so the blade was parallel with the ground.

"Get down as low as you can. They will give us an artillery barrage, hoping to drive us out. Wait for the order to fire. It is the hated Hessians still in the lead, so give them a warm Massachusetts welcome."

May we all get through unscathed, Will thought as Nat moved down the line. They would hold them and inflict casualties, but could they withstand a charge at their positions? Wouldn't they be overwhelmed by the enemy's sheer numbers? Will forced the thought from his mind and counted the paper cartridges in his box. There were twelve left, plus one ball in his musket.

Here they come, Will said to himself, as the drums and sound of marching feet on the dirt road became louder. They were less than fifty yards away when Lieutenant Hadley rose up and gave the order to fire. Will saw the Hessian line advancing before it crumpled and recoiled as the musket fire hit home. Quickly, he reloaded, heard the order to fire and when he stood up the Hessians were closer than before, although there were fewer of them. The second volley decimated the compacted crowd of men and more of the blue uniformed soldiers lay on the road. By the third volley, Will saw they were retreating, but in good order. He reloaded, reseated his ramrod, and waited for the command to either fire or withdraw. He heard the boom of field cannons and the wall to his right, separating the two fields, exploded in stone fragments. A cannon ball, a twelve-pounder he guessed, ricocheted into the air above the wall and bounded harmlessly into the field. Will burrowed down with his back curved against the warm irregular stones as an endless bombardment continued. His ears resonated from the sound of a ball striking the double stone wall near him, the space between the rocks serving as an echo chamber to magnify the noise of impact.

Will did not hear the command to fire but rather sensed it. His ears rang and sounds, even musket fire, seemed dull and far away. He rose up and pulled the trigger, aiming low at the lines of Hessians advancing in ranks down the road toward the corner of the stone wall. The volley of roughly two hundred muskets sent them reeling. Will saw one soldier throw up his hands and pitch backwards, his shiny brass helmet falling from his head to the ground. Kneel down and reload, he told himself. He took another cartridge from the box, bit off the paper end, rested the stock against a flat stone and rammed the paper and ball down the barrel. At the command to fire, when he stood up, more Hessians were jammed on the road methodically pushing forward toward them. He fired, wondering whether he had remembered to aim low, and dropped down to reload. When the order came to withdraw, Will felt in his cartridge box and found only three left. Had they really stood and exchanged ten rounds with the Hessians? He had lost all sense of time and even place. At the battle at the Old Stone House he had seen much of the entire battlefield. Here his vision was limited to a portion of the narrow road and the enemy troops he saw when he stood up to fire. It was as if he was looking at the battle through a sliver of a window. His only view though the thick clouds of smoke from the musket volleys, was of the road choked with soldiers, living and dead.

Led by the two Lieutenants, the Americans withdrew without panic or haste. Prudently, they kept low, and crouched close to the wall. When they climbed the stones separating the field where Will expected they would again make a stand, they found the space occupied by one of the Massachusetts militia regiments. The men of Knox's artillery and the Mariners were ordered back to Hutchinson Creek to demolish the wooden bridge, ford the creek and man the four field pieces on the hillside which commanded the crossing. They marched west on Split Rock Road in good order, led by Lieutenants Hadley and Holmes, proud of what they had accomplished, standing up to the Hessians and stopping the enemy advance. A company of the Mariners were left at the wooden bridge to dismantle it. The artillery men, still in disciplined ranks, returned to camp.

Will walked to where the horses were kept. Big Red turned his large head and pricked up his ears as he approached. Will took a moment to rub the white blaze on his nose and muttered an apology to the horse for not bringing him something to nibble. He quickly saddled up and rode to the artillery emplacement. He heard volleys of musket fire from across the creek, Will knew Hessians must be approaching the last field before the bridge.

With the help of Tyler and Baldwin, he hitched up one of the twelve-pounders. The two men clung to each side of the carriage as Big Red pulled it up the hill where Will had first seen Nat and Colonel Glover that morning. It was now late afternoon. Below him, he could see the long line of British and Hessian troops, baggage train, supply wagons and artillery, clogging the road for several miles to the east, their advance blocked by the Massachusetts Militia.

He turned Big Red around and galloped down the hill. The cool air rushing past and the familiar feel of the horse beneath him made him forget the dead and wounded he had seen this morning and his fear bordering on panic as the Hessians approached. When he returned to the hill with the second twelve-pounder, the lighter nine- pounders were already in place and the rest of the Massachusetts artillery men were ready for action.

"Once our militia are away from that field, we can play a tune with our cannons to make the Hessians dance," Sergeant Merriam said. Even with his pronounced limp, he seemed more energetic now that he was manning a field piece instead of firing a musket. As they watched from their hilltop vantage point, there was one more concentrated volley from the militia. The front of the Hessian column visibly recoiled, like a snake's head being threatened by a burning torch. The Massachusetts militia's officers had their men fall in and they marched as precisely as if they were on parade, down the short stretch of Split Rock Road where they splashed across the creek to the cheers of the Americans on the west side.

"Sight the guns to aim where the road reaches the creek," Lieutenant Hadley ordered. With their cannon loaded and primed, Will watched as the enemy column, the Hessians still in the lead, passed the part of the road where they had last encountered the Americans and came on as methodically as before.

"Fire," Lieutenant Hadley shouted, dropping his sword arm dramatically. All four guns roared. One cannon ball from the nine-pounder fell short and skipped harmlessly across the creek and into a field to the right of the road. Another landed at the correct distance but wide to the left. The two twelve-pound balls struck the road and smashed through the troops in the front lines. A red-coated British officer on horseback rode along the stalled column and before the gun crews could reload, the column turned and quickly retreated back out of range.

In the distance, the disciplined columns of Hessian and British troops marching west parted to let the horses drawing the gun carriages pass and move toward the front. They stopped well back from the creek. Redcoats began tearing down a section of the stone wall lining Split Rock Road.

"They intend to move their cannons into the field so as to bring more of them into play," Lieutenant Hadley observed, looking through his telescope. "They have many more cannons further down the road."

He snapped the scope shut and returned it to the worn leather case.

"Aim for the cannons," he said. "As more guns come up, aim for the horses." Will shuddered, thinking of the British targeting Big Red. Hadley must have seen the look of horror on his face. "A wounded panic stricken horse, thrashing in the traces, causes more delay in maneuvering the gun into position," he said brusquely.

For the next hour, as the late afternoon sun sank lower and dusk approached, the Massachusetts guns engaged the British in an artillery duel. At first, it went in their favor. They had the range and their cannon balls disrupted the enemy's efforts to bring their cannons into position. As the battle wore on, the British resorted to tearing down stone walls further back on the road, and driving their cannons through the fields below the hilltop. By the time it was almost dark, they had succeeded in placing eight twelve- pounders in four well-spaced batteries, protected by the stones they had removed from the wall, and were beginning to find the range.[1]

Will was relieved when Lieutenant Hadley commanded them to cease fire. The British fired one more salvo, an ominous warning of the re-engagement to come in the morning and then all was quiet. The silence felt like a warm blanket draped over his shoulders. He had been engaged in battle since early morning. There was a ringing in his ears and the voices of those nearby seemed to come from far away. Will opened and closed his jaws rapidly. He was tired, thirsty and hungry. He had long since emptied his canteen, as had the others in his crew. He was not so thirsty as to drink the water in the artillery bucket. Impulsively, he dipped his two hands into the bucket and threw the dirty water, smelling of gunpowder on his face.

"Now you look the real powder monkey," Nat said giving Will a rag. "Here, wipe your face. Colonel Glover is up there conferring with Lieutenant Hadley. I must go." Will saw Nat join the two officers, Hadley bent slightly listening to the Colonel and nodding. They came toward the gun emplacements.

"Sergeants. Ready the cannons for transport. Will, I need a word with you." Hadley beckoned him to join the Colonel and Nat. Will wiped his face with the back of his hand, hoping much of the residue from the cannon's sponge was already gone and he was not smearing it further.

"We are retiring to join our army moving north and west of here. We must move quickly. We lack enough horses to pull the cannons and supplies. I told the Colonel, Big Red is able to do the work of two."

"He most certainly can. If we rig a hitch for a wagon, he could pull that and a cannon behind," Will said confidently.

"One wagon must carry our wounded," Colonel Glover said. "Could your horse pull that with a nine-pounder behind?"

"He could do it with a twelve-pounder," Will replied without hesitation. The Colonel studied Will's soot covered face and dirty uniform. Involuntarily, Will straightened his back and stood taller.

"Will was with us at General Washington's Cambridge headquarters during the fight with Morgan's Rifles," Nat said, by way of explanation. "Before he enlisted in Colonel Knox's artillery."

"Ahh," Glover exclaimed. "Lieutenant Holmes brought you to the dinner with Colonel and Mrs. Knox. I thought I had seen you before although you are much changed since March of earlier this year."

"Yes sir."

"Well. Let us begin and rejoin our army," Glover said. He walked briskly down the hill to where his Regiment and the militias were camped.

By the time Will had ridden Big Red down from the hilltop pulling the second of the twelve-pounders, the wagon, loaded with the dozen or so wounded men was waiting. Will tried to ignore the groaning coming from the men in the wagon. He avoided looking at the bloody stumps of feet, the torn shirts wrapped around wounds which seeped blood, and the deathly pallor of some of the men. He knelt at the rear of the wagon and examined the makeshift hitch. It would do, he thought. He and the gun crew, using handspikes, maneuvered the cannon until the carriage shafts aligned with the hitch. Satisfied, it was secure, Will walked around the wagon and stopped. One of the wounded, a man wearing a Marblehead Mariner's uniform, struggled to sit up. His midriff was wrapped in a white cloth. Fresh red blood stained a swath from one side of his body to the other.

"Water," he pleaded. "For the love of God, give me some water." He reached out to grab Will. Will stopped and took his hand, holding it tightly, not knowing what to do.

"I will ride with them," Sergeant Merriam said to Will, taking the wounded soldier's hand in his. He poured some water from his canteen onto his hand and let it drip onto the man's lips. "You cannot give liquids to a soldier with a stomach wound. And nothing to eat until a surgeon has seen him."

"If I ride Big Red, there is more room on the wagon seat," Will said. This meant more weight for the horse to pull but Will knew he could do it. Sergeant Otis and Baldwin joined Merriam on the wagon. "We will take turns with the wounded," Merriam said to no one in particular. Will shortened the reins and mounted the horse. They joined a long line of weary but proud men, marching quietly in the dark, parting for the occasional horse drawn wagon or artillery piece or officers on horseback, proceeding up the column. Will, lost in his own thoughts, reconstructed the day's events. Every battle scene from the daylong firing from behind stone walls to the evening's artillery duel, ended for him with the same vision- the little Hessian drummer boy torn in half by their musket fire.

—w—

Georg bent forward in the cool dark, leaning on his short handled shovel. The dead Hessians lay in rows in the unused part of the little cemetery. He had counted more than one hundred of them. There were no rebel prisoners to do this dirty work. He and the rest of the men of his company were burying their dead in the graveyard of a small stone church with a low wooden black-shingled steeple. Their mood was somber. They all were exhausted from the battle. Georg kept his back to the blue clad corpses, some of whose arms were grotesquely pointing toward the night sky.

Andreas grunted as he threw a shovel full of earth to the side. "Think about this," he said to Georg and Christoph. "Why do these ill-trained militias of farmers and tradespeople fight so hard against us? They have fertile land and prosperous towns, a good life, far better than our own families back home. Why do they rebel against their king?"

"Be quiet," Christoph hissed. "Sergeant Wochler will hear you. Do you want to run the gauntlet?"

"I do not care why they fight," Georg said loudly. "All I want to do is kill them and return home with our share of the booty and plunder. With that and our pay and we will have a good life of our own."

He angrily stepped on his shovel, driving its square blade into the sod. He was confused by what Andreas had said. If they were rabble led by mechanics and shop keepers instead of real officers with military training, why were there so many Hessian soldiers, lying dead against the church wall. He shuddered as the scream of one of wounded inside the church pierced the quiet of the graveyard. Yellow light from the church's own candles flickered through the thick paned windows of the narthex. The regimental surgeon and his assistants were inside doing their bloody, necessary work. Georg sensed the battle had gone badly for them. They had found no dead or wounded Rebellers and had taken none prisoner. He did not like to think his Regiment's toll was greater than the enemy's. He knew nothing of grand strategy. It was the simple arithmetic of dead and wounded that determined for him if they had won or not.

Georg resumed his somber work. His back ached. The short handled shovel was meant for digging trenches not graves. He consoled himself with the thought at least the Hessian fallen would have individual resting places instead of the mass pits for the dead Rebellers the prisoners had dug in the fields around Flatbush Pass. It was an honor, Georg told himself, to dig graves for a fallen comrade in arms, in this pleasant tree shrouded cemetery. He just wished there were not so many of them.[2]

Part Two
Retreat Through The Jerseys

Chapter 10 – Assault Up The Cliffs

The men of the Massachusetts Artillery Regiment were among the last to cross to the west side of the Hudson at Peekskill. The early morning frost of the mid-November day glistened on the grass by the side of the deeply rutted road that disappeared into the forests stretching to the south. They were part of a 2,000 man force, led by General Washington heading toward Fort Lee. They left behind two Regiments of New York militias, to guard Peekskill. A larger body, under General Lee, formed up at reveille to begin a quick march in an easterly direction.

Sergeant Merriam and Corporal Chandler, sitting on the wagon next to Will, looked back wistfully as the mills of Peekskill disappeared behind the sloping terrain. The wagon was loaded with barrels of gunpowder, flour and hard cider, as well as new leather harnesses, reins and stirrups, all purchased with sterling and Spanish dollars from the local factories. Behind them, were the wagons carrying Colonel Knox's baggage, the Regiment's tents, cooking pots, cots and other supplies.

"It would have been more comfortable if we had loaded this wagon with sacks of grain instead of these barrels," Levi Tyler grumbled from the back of the wagon.

"Well, do not come crowding me," Baldwin called in mock offense. "Besides, no one commanded you to ride. You can march along with the Regulars, if this carriage is not to your liking. Or dispute with others on the more crowded wagons behind us."

Tyler spat over the side. "I have done my share of marching up from the tip of New York Island thirty miles to here and now fully intend to ride back down. All this to and fro with nothing to show for it."

"You have your hide intact to show for it," Baldwin responded. "General Washington has avoided a pitched battle and bloodied the Crown's nose. That is no small accomplishment."

Sergeant Merriam turned to look back at the two men, wedged in a narrow space between the barrels, and Sergeant Otis, blissfully dozing, curled up in a ball on the rough plank floor, like a cat in a creamery.

He started to say something about the abandonment of New York City, thought better of it and picked up the thread of his thought of moving south.

"I wish my tannery was as busy as these at Peekskill," Merriam said. "Better yet, I desire to be with my wife and little girls and away from this terrible war. These merchants have turned a fine profit. At the end of the day they are in the bosom of their families before a warm and safe hearth, while we, having left our own homes in April and been in battles since, are now marching to engage the vicious Hessians and British Regulars once again."

"If you were safe at home, you would not be Sergeant Merriam," Chandler observed, chewing on a piece of fresh bread covered with a dark red jam. "And what kind of life can your little girls expect if it is under British tyranny, or worse, the Hessian boot?" He poked Merriam in the arm. "My bindery suffers too. There is no great demand for books in Boston, unless they are to be used for fuel in the coming winter. And my nephew, whom I left in charge is likeable enough but dull as a froe." He shook his head, remembering some incident involving the young man that substantiated his assessment.

"It would be good to have news from my wife," Merriam said sadly. "I worry constantly about the pox marring the sweet faces of my little girls. Or worse, their being inoculated, contracting the 'speckled monster' and God forbid, succumbing to the disease in my absence." He closed his eyes, his lips moving in prayer. Chandler waited until Merriam seemed to have concluded.

"Is there no one to help with your tannery?" he asked

"Perhaps my fence-sitting brother-in-law could be persuaded to restart the tannery and make supplies for our army," Merriam replied, mulling over the idea. "Though he is so afraid the British will return to Boston, he will not risk a nose hair in any enterprise they would deem to aid our cause."

Will hesitated to join in the older men's conversation. After a pause, he decided they would take no offense. "My father, who has no love for patriots, is moved more by his desire to make money."

Chandler finished the bread and licked the residue of jam from his fingers. "The lad makes a good point," he said. "You should appeal to your brother-in-law's sense of greed. It is a weakness in men who have no political principles."

"I will have to offer him some share of the profits, at least while I am still at this bloody business. My dear wife has a good head on her shoulders and is shrewd with numbers. She can watch out for our interests and cleverly, without seeming too forward, guide her younger brother in the right direction." Merriam smiled at the thought. "When we get to Fort Lee, I will pen a letter to her with some instructions."

Will hoped he too would have time to write Elisabeth. He had written her one letter since the abandonment of New York City and received none in reply. He was unsure how his letter would reach her in Albany or if she had even arrived safely home with her father. He listened as Merriam and Chandler talked of how Fort Washington, newly renamed for His Excellency, could hold out against the enemy. Merriam was of the opinion General Howe would not dare another direct frontal attack, after their heavy casualties at Bunker Hill. Maybe the men of the Massachusetts Artillery would be ferried across the Hudson to reinforce the garrison under General Greene. That would be risky if the winds were favorable for the British fleet. Better to worry about that later, Will thought, clicking his teeth and lightly hitting the reins against Big Red's broad flanks.

On the second day, they reached Fort Lee late in the afternoon and set up their tents in a flat field a hundred yards from the sheer rock palisade overlooking the Hudson and within the shadow of the Fort. In the distance, Will could see Fort Washington at the southern end of the fingerlike two hundred foot high plateau of Mount Washington, surrounded by ramparts and breastworks. Viewed through Lieutenant Hadley's telescope, it looked impregnable to him. The northern end of the rocky promontory, less than a mile from the Fort, was manned by numerous riflemen who had erected earthen works among the natural protection of the rocky cliffs.

"It will be a repeat of Bunker Hill," Hadley observed as Will handed back his telescope.

"Sir. Will we be sent over as reinforcements?" he asked, hoping his voice did not betray his fear of being caught by the British fleet as they crossed the Hudson.

"I doubt it, Will. There are at least 2,000 of our troops defending the Fort. They have almost seventy cannon, including field pieces. I am not privy to General Washington's thinking, but I seriously disbelieve he will commit more troops or that we are needed to carry the day." Hadley put his arm around Will's shoulder and led him back to the cooking fires. "I understand Sergeant Otis has bartered some of our supplies for freshly killed deer. Once we have dined on roast venison, I have some paper for you. Find a drumhead for a desk and write to your Elisabeth. Colonel Knox mentioned there is a dispatch rider leaving for Albany in a few days."

After the past months of constructing fortifications, the tension of sentry duty, periods of brief, intense combat, with the ever present fear of being killed or captured, followed by hasty marches pursued by a numerically superior force, Will enjoyed having time to write, to wash and mend his uniform and, for the first time in many weeks, not suffer the gnawing hunger in his stomach for days on end. The next two days were the kind of fall weather he had enjoyed as a boy in Schoharie. Chilly at night and pleasantly warm by late morning. The ominous occasional boom of a cannon and the sight of frigates on the Hudson reminded him the British were nearby.

—⁄∿⁄—

They started before dawn, led by their drummers and haute boys, the familiar woody tones of the oboe mingling with the steady tramp of their marching feet. By seven in the morning, with their regimental flags fluttering in the light breeze, the men of the Knyphausen Regiment were in sight of Mount Washington and the Rebel redoubts at the top of the cliffs. Georg heard the heavy cannonade from both the west and east. He assumed it was coming from the British warships on the two rivers that surrounded Manhattan. The men waited in the early morning sun, clustered together in ranks, until the orders came to stand down and rest. The Knyphausen Regiment disbursed on the east side of the road, while Colonel Rall's Regiment were hidden in the thick woods on the west side.

Georg stared silently at the towering, precipitous rocks above them. He could make out an earthen work lower down, another part the way up, and the outline of a third one just below the summit. In between, the Rebellers had constructed obstacles of felled evergreens, the needles on the thick branches still green, as if a forest had taken root horizontally, instead of pointing toward the sky as God intended.

"It will be slow going up," Christoph said, following his gaze. "If the Rebeller riflemen are there, they will pick us off at their leisure."

"At least our death will be quick," Georg replied, with more bravado then he felt. "They aim for the head so there will be no pain for us." Andreas smiled grimly, as if visualizing a rifle ball to his forehead. "That comforting thought does not make me less fearful of climbing these rocks," he said.

Georg regretted he had not spoken to their regimental chaplain when they were camped north of King's Bridge above the Harlem River. He would have liked to hear his words of comfort and confirm his pay and share of plunder and booty would be sent to his parents. He thought to remove his brass cap but they were under orders not to. Georg bowed his head and prayed for God in Heaven to preserve him in the coming battle. When he finished, he looked up and noticed many of his fellow soldiers were either praying or looking fearfully up at the heights they would be ordered to scale. He hoped he had beseeched the Almighty God fervently enough.

There was a stirring on the road behind them and General Wilhelm von Knyphausen himself rode up with his staff. He waited for his orderly to take the reins and dismounted. The men hastened to their feet and stood at attention even before the echo of the orders had dissipated in the dense forest. Georg had never been so close to the General. He was a tall man, over sixty but still slim for his age, with a high forehead, close set eyes and a long scar running from his left cheek below the eye to the corner of his mouth. The brass buttons and gold braid on his blue coat gleamed in the sunlight. He strode along the front lines of the Regiment, followed by Colonel von Borck, and Major Heckmann. The General was as calm, Georg thought, as if he were inspecting the men on a parade ground. When he had walked the front line of the five companies, he remounted and sat silently surveying the ranks of the more than eight hundred men.

"We have been given the privilege, by General Howe of making the main attack on this Fort. I will lead you. I expect this Regiment to fight bravely for our honor and for our Gracious Landgrave." His brief comments were relayed through the ranks by Captains, Lieutenants and Second Lieutenants and then the Sergeants. The men remained standing motionless in the shade. The General crossed the road where he was met by Colonel Rall before disappearing into the woods.

Georg was aware the barrage of cannon fire had ceased. He glanced up at the sun through the trees and thought it was but an hour to noon. A solitary cannon boomed followed by silence. Then, he heard shouted orders, the drum beat and the high pitched notes of the haute boy players. The men of Company Seckendorf moved forward out of the cool protection of the forest and into a swampy flatland at the base of the cliff. Georg was aware of sporadic rifle fire, coming from the first breastwork. On command, the front line fired and knelt, followed by Georg's line. He reloaded and ran forward, the mud grabbing at his shoes and spattering his leggings. They were now onto the lower slope, exposed to the fire of the Rebellers behind their earthworks. He only heard the boom of a small cannon before the grapeshot cut through the ranks in front of him, men falling, screaming, bright red stains appearing like roses blooming on arms, shoulders, chests and stomachs. He heard himself shouting as they charged up the slope, bayonets lowered, scrambling through the low brush, until they jumped over the dirt barrier, driving the few remaining Rebel troops before them back up the slope.

The brush gave way to big boulders, interspersed with a few small trees and large bushes that served as handholds. Georg held his musket tightly in his right hand and used his left to grab a root or trunk and haul himself up. Above him, was a barrier made of a tangle of trees and branches. Behind that, Georg saw the second earthen work. Musket fire and shrapnel filled the air around him. As men fell with horrible wounds, Georg resisted the urge to hide behind a boulder and forced himself to advance. Suddenly, he heard the cry to his left, "Follow our General! Follow our General!" Through the smoke of gunpowder ahead he saw General von Knyphausen tearing at one of the trees obstructing their way, as if he were a common soldier. Georg surged upward, clambering over the branches of a fallen tree and rushing further uphill toward the second earthwork. Others in his Company ran with him. He heard Sergeant Wochler shout an order, he dropped automatically to one knee, fired at the Rebels hiding behind the dirt wall, and then charged forward, leaping the low wall and bayoneting a soldier sprawled on the ground before him, before realizing the man was already dead. They regrouped with the earth wall to their back, exposed to musket and rifle fire from above, watching their own artillery balls strike the third and last redoubt just below the summit.

"Move on, move on," Captain Seckendorf shouted urgently. "See there is our General." Georg looked up at the rocky cliff. General von Kynphausen, surrounded by powder blue coats from another company was darting from rock to rock, waving the men on. Georg felt the energy in his legs as he took long strides, grasping any handhold he could find to pull himself up the steep slope. He and others from his Company were even with the General now. Georg's feet slid on the loose stones. He struggled for more solid footing, placing his right foot on an exposed tree root and vaulted up. He found a narrow gap among the rocks just as grapeshot from a Rebel cannon above, depressed to fire down at them, spattered a boulder next to him. A sharp stab in his left shoulder almost made him lose his hold on the thin beech tree trunk he had grabbed. He flexed his fingers and found they worked. Then, General von Knyphausen himself was near him, shouting to the men to assault the summit.

Georg pushed forward, his eyes scanning the rocky cliff for ways to the top. He saw a cleft in between two boulders and suddenly there was a dirt path opening and he was vaulting over the last Rebel barrier and stood on the summit. The Rebels had abandoned their last redoubt and were running across the flat land of the plateau toward Fort Washington less than a mile away.

"They run like rabbits," the General shouted. "After them, my brave soldiers! Chase them down before they reach the fort." Georg, who had stopped for a moment to catch his breath, looked around for others of his company. He saw Christoph, grinning triumphantly, his teeth bared, yelling madly. Without waiting for any command to form up, the two of them sprinted after the fleeing Rebels. Together with almost a dozen others Georg rushed forward shouting loudly, his bayonet pointing straight ahead. It occurred to him if the Americans were to turn and fire, he and his companions who had reached the summit first were outnumbered. He rushed on exhilarated by the wild freedom of running through unobstructed flat terrain and the realization, in the bright afternoon sunshine, he had survived and was alive.

They were within one hundred yards of the fort when the drums signaled for them to form ranks. Georg was disappointed. He was certain they could have caught the Rebellers and either captured or bayoneted them. The men of the Knyphausen Regiment, those who had made it through the hail of grapeshot, musket and rifle fire, retired to assemble just below the lip of the plateau. There they were shielded from the Fort's cannons. They collapsed amidst the rocks, as a few balls sailed harmlessly overhead and bounced down the rocky slopes below, dislodging a clattering shower of stones before coming to rest in the shrubs and woods at the bottom.[1]

Georg looked around. Captain Seckendorf stood calmly under a tree in conversation with Lieutenant Reuter. Andreas, seated on a tree stump, was binding a bloody gash on the back of his hand. He signaled to Georg that it was of no consequence. Of their Company, almost one quarter were not there. Georg removed his brass hat, lowered his head and prayed they were not dead or mortally wounded. He drank thirstily from his wooden canteen, almost emptying it in long gulping swallows. He fingered the tear in the sleeve at the shoulder and saw the shrapnel of rock had barely sliced the skin. He would have to mend the fabric however. Sergeant Wochler would not tolerate a torn uniform, regardless of the reason.

They fell in behind a solid squat storage house made of the same kind of rocky granite stones the Regiment had clambered over to reach the summit. General von Knyphausen had established his headquarters here, about one hundred and fifty yards from the fort. The gaps in the Regiment's ranks were obvious. Georg muttered another prayer for the welfare of his comrades lying on the slopes below. Colonel Rall's Regiment stood further forward from the makeshift headquarters on the west side of the plateau. Georg watched as one of the Captain's of Rall's Regiment, a white flag flying from his raised musket barrel, accompanied only by a drummer boy, walked slowly toward the Fort. Georg recognized the beat, a universal call to parley. Puffs of bluish smoke appeared on the wall as muskets were fired at the approaching pair, drawing an angry murmur from the ranks. The shots continued until the Captain and drummer reached a barrier of pointed tree trunks and branches. There, they were met by three Rebellers who made a show of turning them back to face the direction they had come from, tied white blindfolds around their eyes and led them through the barrier and into the fort. They reappeared within ten minutes and marched slowly back, the drummer boy keeping a steady beat for the two of them, until the Captain signaled him to stop and walked by himself to the General's temporary headquarters.

"Do you think they will surrender?" Christoph whispered. Georg shrugged not willing to draw the attention of Sergeant Wochler by speaking. Georg thought the earthen works, which formed the northern wall of the fort, was not particularly high. There also did not seem to be any ditches or other defensive obstacles, other than the tangle of trees to block their advance. Still, they would have to advance more than one hundred yards, exposed to rifle fire from the moment they started, and then volleys from muskets and grapeshot from cannons as they got closer. It would be a bloody business, but he thought his chances were better now, having survived the ascent of the cliffs.

General von Knyphausen himself, holding a large ornate pocket watch, emerged from the storage building and gestured vehemently to the Captain. The Captain nodded and once again, holding his musket with the white cloth, advanced on the fort, accompanied by the drummer boy. This time, there were no puffs of smoke from the earthen wall. In a few minutes, the Captain and drummer emerged from the tree barrier, accompanied by a Rebeller Officer who, although shorter, matched the Captain's step, stride for stride. Georg was in the front rank and he stared with curiosity at the enemy officer. The man wore high black leather boots, which encased his tan britches just below the knee. He had a blue coat with red facing and a sword in a black leather scabbard on his right side. The two officers approached General von Kynphausen who stood waiting in front of the stone building. The Captain apparently could understand English because he waited for the General to speak then turned to the Rebeller Officer and back to the General. At the end of a brief exchange, the enemy officer unbuckled his sword, bowed slightly and handed it to General Knyphausen. Georg suppressed a shout of victory but could not keep from smiling. Up and down the ranks, the men obediently remained motionless in rank, their faces showing the relief they felt at not having to make a frontal assault on the fort.

They did not relax for long. Lieutenant Reuter shouted an order to the Company. As the Regiment marched toward the fort, Colonel Rall's Regiment proceeded in the same direction until the two were lined up facing each other on the flat approach to Fort Washington. The Rebel garrison came out, straggling in ragged groups between the Hessian troops.

Georg stared in fascination at the Rebellers. They were an odd bunch, he thought, some very young, some grizzled, gray haired and stooped, all of them filthy, with torn shirts and coats, some with leggings, others with shoes with buckles, some with one boot and one shoe, and even some barefoot. Discipline in the ranks relaxed as the Hessian soldiers laughed out loud and hooted and pointed out a particularly miserable looking specimen or one who seemed especially ill suited to be a soldier. Their mockery continued and grew in volume as the long line of enemy soldiers filed past. Midway down the column they were made to drop their muskets and whatever other weapons they carried. One proud Rebel officer tried to maintain his dignity by marching erect but, surrounded by such a crowd of misfits, this only served to make the Hessians shout and call out all the more. The ridicule increased once they were disarmed and turned over to a prison guard detail that led this odd collection of defeated, shuffling men off the plateau.

The parade of the Americans had taken more than an hour. Georg estimated at least 2,000 men had surrendered, maybe more. He found it hard to believe this rabble had held back their two Regiments for even a moment, or that they had the prowess and courage to hold positions and kill his comrades.[2] He wondered what Andreas would say now they had been victorious and had seen up close what kind of miserable creatures comprised the Rebellers' army.

—⁂—

It was past three in the afternoon. Will stood disconsolate with a small knot of artillerymen, looking across the river at the two long light blue uniformed lines of Hessians on the plateau north of Fort Washington. Their bayonets and brass caps caught the sun and glinted mockingly at the Americans across the River, demanding those on the Jersey side accept the fall of Fort Washington. Will had long since lost his eagerness to look through Lieutenant Hadley's telescope. He had watched the beginning of the American troops' surrender and declined further use of it. He preferred to see their shame in defeat in less detail. It could have been him, he thought, captured, paraded before the hated Hessians, stripped of his clothes and meager possessions, and imprisoned, trapped without hope, waiting for his brother to find and torment him. He wondered what the group of mounted American officers on the heights between Fort Lee and the river thought.[3] The militia men around Will sullenly dispersed, muttering about the foolishness of Generals who had decided to defend Fort Washington, forgetting they themselves had regarded the Fort as impregnable.

"Our term expires in less than twenty days," one said loudly. "I can only pray God grant our Generals the sense to keep me from being captured by the British until the end of the month. Then I am back to

Maryland and done with this soldiering." His opinion was seconded by a chorus from his companions, including their Captain who urged the men only to honor their commitment and promised a swift march home.

That night around their campfires, Lieutenant Hadley brought the only good news of the day. Colonel Knox had told him dispatches had been sent to General Lee urging him to rapidly march south and join the Army.

"We can defend the rocky palisades with far fewer men and they will have a hard time scaling these natural obstacles against our determined troops," Lieutenant Hadley said. "Once they do, they will be trapped between us and General Lee's forces." Will took confidence from his words. The next morning, the Massachusetts Artillery Regiment moved their tents and baggage wagons to the south side of Fort Lee, adjacent to a roughly constructed earthen rampart. After setting up the tents and unloading the wagons of the cots and cooking pots, they took up their positions in the gun emplacements on the east side of the Fort, facing the Hudson. Below the ramparts, on the palisades high above the river, the men of the New York Artillery manned the large twenty-four pounders and stubby iron black mortars that protected the fort against an amphibious attack.

—⋙—

Three days after the capture of Fort Washington, renamed Fort Knyphausen to the delight and pride of the men of his Regiment, Georg stood on a flat boat in a cold pouring rain, being rowed by British sailors across the North River to the Jersey shore. The Hessians had boarded at four in the morning, just as the rain increased in intensity. He knew his powder was wet and would never fire. They formed ranks on a small beach of round, smooth and slime-covered stones. The rain slick slabs of the rocky palisades loomed ominously over them. Word was passed through the ranks to march to the base of the cliffs and form a single column. Georg and Christoph were second and third in line. Lieutenant Reuter who spoke a little English, was ahead of them, following three local men from New Jersey to guide them up a narrow rocky path to the top of the cliffs.

Stunted trees closed in on both sides and the four foot wide path was slippery and treacherous. Georg, who had been trained not to think, succumbed to his fears because he was thinking. What if the three Loyalists were in fact traitors, leading them into a trap? The Regiment stretched behind them, constricted by the narrow path. There was no way they could bring any fire-power to bear. Their muskets with wet powder were useless anyway. How could they charge uphill one behind the other? He remembered the Rebellers he had seen at the surrender at Fort Knyphausen. True, they were merely a dirty, ragged rabble but even undisciplined militia could lever boulders down the path crushing the Hessians struggling below and causing panic in the ranks. Even small round stones, like the ones on the beach, would be enough to knock their feet from under them, sending them tumbling back on the bayonets of their comrades behind. It would be strange he thought, if he died by Andreas' or Christoph's bayonet in his spine. Or the stones would break his leg in such a way, the surgeons would have to amputate and he would return to his home a useless cripple, unable to work in farm or field. Feeling trapped and desperate, Georg almost cried out. Damn these Rebellers, he muttered. He remembered the fine summer day in Brooklyn, on the ramparts of the Rebels' fort when he had dreamed of being home by Christmas. He thought angrily that he would be fortunate to be on a British transport heading home by Christmas even if they finished this peasant army off here and now.

Georg could barely see beyond their Loyalist guides. Rain dripped onto his nose and mustache from the brass front of his cap. The cap's red cloth top and back were soaked through. The soles of his shoes, worn thin and smooth from marching, gave him no traction and every sharp stone jabbed the bottom of his feet. Behind him, the men of his Company moved silently followed by the remainder of the Regiment, and then Colonel Rall's Regiment and British Regulars. He guessed they were half way to the top when the precipitous path veered sharply to the left, continuing up at a steep angle. Now was a time for an ambush, with much of the two Regiments committed to the ascent. He peered ahead into the grey gloom. Nothing.

The three guides climbed ahead with Lieutenant Reuter slightly behind, moving methodically and silently, toward the top. Below

Georg heard a loud clang. Someone had dropped a shovel or some metal implement. The guides halted and Reuter held up his hand signaling for the company to stand still. Georg had been in mid-stride but thought he could at least lower his raised foot despite the Lieutenant's signal. Each man in line relayed the hand signal down the narrow path. Georg remained motionless, listening to his own heavy breathing and the steady patter of the rain on the leaves and the rush of rivulets of runoff, seeking the path of least resistance down to the stony beach below. His senses were alert for any unusual sound that might indicate the enemy waited above them. He glanced over his shoulder at Christoph who shook his head imperceptibly. Good old Christoph, George thought. His presence was reassuring.

The guides resumed their climb upward. Ahead, Georg saw the beginning of a line of grey sky above the gloom of the trees and cliffs. They emerged onto a heavily wooded flat plateau that seemed in the darkness to stretch in all directions. Lieutenant Reuter and Sergeant Wochler had the company form up into their usual ranks, as the rain continued to beat down on them. More men emerged from the break in cliffs. Soon both Hessian Regiments and the British Regulars were on the summit. They took shelter and rested in the woods of evergreens, maples and oaks. Georg quietly muttered a prayer of thanks as he sank down on the faded dull orange and red leaves covering a bed of older, fallen brown pine needles. The pounding in his head decreased. He breathed in the fresh evergreen scent and let out a sigh.[4]

"Were you afraid?" Christoph asked him.

"Were you?"

"I do not like the darkness of the woods. I think of goblins! And unnatural beings and such,"Christoph confessed.

"I was afraid of either being crushed by a rock thrown from above or falling back on Andreas' bayonet behind me."

"I would have nimbly stepped aside and let you crash into someone else," Andreas said with a grin.

"Well, we are still here in whole body," Christoph concluded, offering Georg and Andreas a bite of cold salted pork.

Georg bit off a piece and handed it to Andreas. "And with God's protection, we will take this other fort as we did a few days ago, accept the surrender of their Generals and finish this business."

—⁂—

Will walked in the light rain and mist to the copse of trees where the artillery horses were tethered. He ran his hand along Big Red's neck, scraping the water off with his cupped hand. The horse turned its head towards him and nuzzled his shoulder with its upper lip. Will responded by rubbing the horse's nose with his knuckles feeling the coarseness of the hair underneath his hand. The horse's coat was thickening for the winter ahead. If the sun came out later, Will thought he would groom his mount and untangle some of the knots in his mane. He stayed with Big Red for a while, feeling the calming presence of the horse, before returning to the fort.

The usual gun drills, postponed because of the rain, began mid-morning as the sun struggled to break through the grey overcast sky. Will felt his stiff muscles loosen up. He welcomed the physical effort. It warmed his body against the damp chill in the air. They had just finished a dry firing when a courier coming from the west galloped up to General Greene's headquarters tent, his horse lathered and heaving from its strenuous ride.

Sergeant Merriam, as curious as the others as to the courier's message, motioned for them to rest.

"I guess there are urgent orders for some of us," Levi Tyler said.

Merriam sat on the tongue of the gun carriage and rubbed his ankle.

"Does it ache more in this weather," Will asked.

"It hurts in warm weather, in cold, in dry and in wet. Otherwise, it does not trouble me," Merriam replied with a tight smile, massaging the ankle with both hands.

Will looked up as Colonel Knox rode into the camp and headed straight for their battery. At the same time, he heard the drums signal for the troops to fall in and saw officers racing from General Greene's tent to their companies.

"The British are on the Palisades less than six miles away," Colonel

Knox shouted, his booming voice carrying to anyone within earshot. "Leave the heavy guns and mortars, hitch up as many of the artillery pieces as you can and retreat down the road toward Hackensack."

Will raced to the grove of trees, quickly threw his saddle on Big Red, mounted and led three of the artillery horses the short distance back to camp. Sergeants Merriam and Otis and the crews had pulled the twelve-pounders from the emplacements. Will backed Big Red up to one of the wagons, and while the crew attached the hitch to the horse's traces, he ducked into his nearby tent, grabbed his haversack, with the precious uncompleted letter to Elisabeth, his quill pen and ink, and his musket. Then, he helped the crew maneuver a twelve-pounder into position behind the wagon. Levi ran leather straps from the rear wagon axle to the cross piece of the gun carriage, creating a makeshift hitch and signaled it was secure. Together, Will, Levi, Baldwin and Merriam struggled to lift the extra side and powder boxes onto the wagon.

"Leave the tents," Colonel Knox commanded as the gun crews started to strike them. The men grabbed their haversacks and muskets and piled into the wagon. Will stood up in the stirrups, and when he was certain all of the crew were settled, nudged Big Red with his knees. The horse strained, the wheels of the wagon and the gun carriage bounced over the ruts. Will followed Lieutenant Hadley who rode his mare in tandem with another, pulling a twelve-pounder. Behind them, the rest of their artillery regiment, four hundred or so men, left Fort Lee in good order, most marching in ranks with some crowded into wagons or precariously balanced on gun carriages.

All around them, the camp was in a panic. Colonel Knox and General Greene had succeeded in forming the regular Continental Army regiments and some of the militias into columns and marching them west toward the DeGroots Road and Liberty Pole. Will saw members of a New York militia, having used the butts of their muskets to stave in hogsheads of rum in the suttler's supply tents, filling their canteens and cups, and then running through the field to catch up with the retreating columns. Others, despite orders to the contrary, remained in the camp at their cooking fires, eating breakfast and drinking copious amounts of rum and cider. Some Militia were looting the abandoned tents of the personal effects of the Regulars. One soldier had audaciously grabbed General Greene's field desk and was running with it over his head. Another, the pockets of his country coat stuffed with freshly baked loaves of bread, was pushing a wheelbarrow with two unbroken casks down the road. Will saw a mounted officer hit the man with the flat of his sword, forcing him to leave the barrow and fall into line. When the officer rode ahead, the soldier deserted the marching troops and returned to retrieve the wheelbarrow with its precious cargo.

The column of horse drawn artillery, numbering no more than twenty guns, ploughed down the muddy road as the Regulars moved off to the sides to let them pass. After they had turned north on the DeGroots Road, they encountered a group of officers riding hard toward them. Will recognized General Washington, his face grim, his lips tight as the General and his aides galloped past them, in the direction of Fort Lee.[5]

The Regiment with its artillery passed through Liberty Pole and crossed the Hackensack River at New Bridge. It was four in the afternoon and already getting dark. Below the bridge, several low one-masted river transports were tied up. The column halted in front of the large Dutch sandstone mansion house on the west side of the landing. Will left Big Red standing in the drizzle, walked into the barn next to the grist mill and found a barrel of oats. He put some in his coat pocket for later and more in a wooden bucket that he brought outside for Big Red to eat.

Lieutenant Hadley and the gun crews had taken shelter from the rain on the mansion's porch. A man in a miller's apron was filling their canteens with apple cider. Will passed his canteen forward.

"This miller tells us the owner, a well known Loyalist, fled this place when the first of our troops arrived," Lieutenant Hadley said to Will. "We are not far from Hackensack where the owner's brother has opened his home to General Washington."

"If we retreat from Hackensack, that brother will suffer when the British arrive, and this one will thrive," Levi muttered, handing Will a full canteen.

"At the least, this wretched Tory's brother will provide food and drink for our Army as it passes through," Baldwin said, holding up a large chunk of hard cheese on the point of his knife.

As they headed south on the Hackensack Road, which followed the river, Will saw some of the troops from Fort Lee, marching into New Bridge. They were Haslet's Delaware Blues, the Regiment easily distinguished by their black-jacked leather hats with the high peak in the front. Tired and wet as they were, they came in good order, four abreast across the wooden bridge, before disbursing in front of the landing.

"If all our troops were like those," Tyler said, "we would not have to retreat."

"Or as the men of Smallwood's Regiment," Chandler added. "So many good men lost and nothing to show for it," he said loudly enough for the others to hear as he climbed on to the wagon. Will saw Simeon Webb, dying under the trees, a look of surprise in his eyes, watching his blood flow from his shattered jaw and throat. He did not know the men in Smallwood's Regiment, although he recognized their brave sacrifice. It was harder for him to accept the death of one of their own, a man he knew from the campfires and gun drills, one he had shared rations with and even drunk from his canteen. It could as easily have been him or any of the others, Merriam, Chandler, Baldwin or Tyler, wounded and dying in the woods near the cannon. Why had Webb been the one? Was it random bad luck or the hand of Providence? He shook his head as if these thoughts were too heavy to carry on the retreat, lifted his knee high to get his boot into the stirrup and vaulted himself into the saddle. Once set, he leaned forward and patted Big Red's neck, watching the warm air from the horse's nostrils form clouds of steam that disappeared immediately. Like my life, he thought. It could be snuffed out in a moment.

The artillery made good time, stopping only once to push the wagon out of a deep hole, hidden in the darkness by the rain filled puddles. The flat farmland, mostly devoid of forests, and stone walls, seemed inauspicious terrain to make a stand against the pursuing British and Hessian forces. At the battle on Split Rock Road their vastly outnumbered force had held the Hessian columns with concentrated musket fire leapfrogging from one stone walled field to another. That had been an orderly withdrawal. This was a full-scale retreat, a flight from Fort Lee where they had been surprised by the enemy. And it seemed to Will, they would keep running south before the British Army until they reached some natural barrier of which they could take advantage.

In Hackensack, they headed towards the candlelight of the large stone mansion that had been taken over by General Washington's staff. They were directed to quarter in the adjacent barns. The gun crews and horses bedded down together, where it was dry inside. Will was awakened in the middle of the night by the sounds of troops crowding into the barn for shelter. When he awoke in the morning, they were surrounded by cold, tired and wet soldiers. Some had blankets, others had covered themselves with straw and hay. Outside, more troops from different militias lay on the ground, under the eaves of the barn and alongside the stone walled mansion, seeking shelter from the cold November rain. Some shivered uncontrollably, having left their blankets, tents and entrenching tools behind when they fled Fort Lee. They had enlisted in July and had only thin shirts and coats, worn even thinner by the campaign. Their frayed clothing offered little protection against the late November cold. Some of them were barefoot.

The small column of artillery left Hackensack in the early morning, retreating south west to Aquackanonk Landing and safely crossing the rain-swollen Passaic river. They arrived in Newark, twenty miles to the south of Hackensack just before dark. The road out of Newark was choked with people from the town fleeing with their wagons laden down with bundles of clothing, bedding and whatever furniture they had been able to load.

Some Patriots remained, whether to protect their homes and property or to help the retreating Army, Will could not say. He was exhausted, cold and hungry. He knew the ride had been worse for the eighteen men in the wagon, exposed to the constant rain and bounced about on the rough roads. And harder still for the men of the Regiment retreating on foot in the rainy darkness. Sergeant Merriam ordered them to halt before a solid stone house near the Common. It was empty and shuttered.

Baldwin and Tyler helped Merriam down from the wagon seat.

The Sergeant winced as he put weight on his right ankle.

"Should we inquire of the locals if the owner is a Loyalist, or should we assume it is just and fair for us to enter?" Baldwin asked.

"We can make inquiries later," Merriam answered irritably. "Let us first get inside and dry, light a fire and see about provisions." He nodded to Tyler, who removed a handspike from the gun carriage, stepped forward with the long iron covered pole in hand and easily pried the wooden door open. Inside, they found candles on the mantle, lit them using a flint starter, and soon had a large fire burning in the front room and kitchen. The men stripped down, hanging their dirty wet clothing everywhere around the two fireplaces.

"You present a fine military appearance," Lieutenant Hadley cried in mock surprise when he came through the askew front door. "I have never seen such a collection of skinny shanks and bony arms," he said, surveying the crowded room.

"Nor such a shapely thigh," Chandler said, raising his long shirt almost to his hip. Several men hooted.

Merriam scowled. "We took the opportunity to dry off our clothes and to clean ourselves. Not to prance about in lewd displays," he admonished. "We discovered a tub of soap in the cellar and have taken turns washing," he said to Hadley. "There is a pot of soup in the hearth with potatoes, turnips and cured meat we also found. Otherwise, we have not harmed the house, not knowing whether it belongs to a true Patriot or a Tory."

Hadley acknowledged Merriam's report, nodding approvingly at the state of the room. "I am told this home belongs to a disaffected landowner who has fled in the direction we have come. Still, it is good you did not use the owner's furniture for firewood and loot the cupboards. We are not Hessians. The taking of food to satisfy our own hunger is permitted."

"Not to mention, Lieutenant, the hard cider we discovered to slake our thirst," Chandler added, hoisting his cup to his lips and toasting Hadley.

"Well, since provisions are well in hand here, and I have not been invited to dine with our Colonel, who is still between here and Hackensack with General Washington, urging our troops on, I would be honored to share a meal with you."

By early morning, the remnants of the Army had arrived and were bedded down in whatever shelter they could find. Will found them crammed into the barn with the horses, the stench of unwashed men and human waste far surpassing the ammonia smell of horse urine. He pitied Big Red and the other horses in their stalls as he walked out in the light drizzle.

Lieutenant Hadley emerged, together with a few officers from a stone house on the other side of the Common and walked through the mud toward the barn. His cloak was wrapped around his shoulders and his tri-corn was pulled down low over his brow to keep the rain off. He was unshaven and looked haggard. He motioned for Will to move away from the barn. They stood under a broad oak on the near side of the Common.

"I have been up since four attending a meeting with the Colonel. General Washington has issued orders to divide again. All the sick and wounded will go west in wagons to Morristown. They are slowing our retreat and in danger of being captured." Hadley took off his tri-corn and shook the water from it. "We must use our own wagons. The good inhabitants of Newark have fled with their belongings and taken every usable wagon and conveyance with them. There is not even a wheelbarrow to be found," he said with disgust. "The able bodied in the army, together with the artillery will remain here, unless forced to retreat further, which Colonel Knox anticipates will occur once the British regroup in Hackensack and follow us in force."

"How many of them are there?" Will asked, hoping the Lieutenant had not heard the tremor in his voice.

"We estimate more than ten thousand, including Hessians and cavalry."

Hadley put his hand on Will's shoulder. "The Colonel has charged me to proceed with the wounded to Morristown. There is a powder mill there and we are in dire short supply. My orders are to obtain as many barrels of gunpowder and charges as we can and rejoin the army here or further south." Hadley turned to face Will. "You could stay here and pull a cannon south with the army when the time comes. Or haul a wagon of our sick and wounded and bring our precious cargo of gunpowder back to wherever the army is. We cannot spare any troops as escort and we will be traveling, certainly on the return trip through a countryside infested with Loyalists and British cavalry."[6]

Will heard himself agreeing to go with the Lieutenant. He wondered why he had said the words without thought or reason. A train of slow-moving, heavily laden wagons would be no match for Loyalist militias or British cavalry. He knew Hadley would have been disappointed had he answered he preferred to stay with the gun crews and rest, snug and dry in the house they had commandeered. He felt it in the firmness of the Lieutenant's grasp of his shoulder, the muttered "Good lad," and the glint of excitement in his eyes. Poor Merriam, Will thought, as they walked back to the house. If the army retreated from Newark, he would have to walk on his swollen ankle.

"I would like to complete my letter to Elisabeth. Would the Colonel accept it to be sent when it can?"

"I am certain he will do so. Finish it quickly and help the men load the wounded on to your wagon. We must leave as soon as possible," Hadley said.

Will nodded somberly, thinking of how to write Elisabeth without conveying his fear he may never see her again.

Chapter 11- The Powder Mill at Morristown

John Stoner was pleased with himself. Very pleased indeed. Lieutenant Chatsworth had told him of his appointment even before John had met with General Ruggles. John had listened impatiently as the pompous old man had run on, the white ruffles around his hand waving about, almost as much as his flapping lips. He went on, sometimes pausing to find the right flowery word or phrase, how John's service had been invaluable to him as his aide but John had come to the attention of men in the regular British Army and reluctantly the General had agreed, even though John had performed admirably in Boston and New York, to permit John to be assigned elsewhere. He suppressed a smirk as Ruggles informed him he must hold the rank of an officer before being transferred and therefore, Ruggles was promoting him to First Lieutenant in the Loyal Associators. Of course, Ruggles said, this required a uniform and knowing of John's modest circumstances, the General would himself generously provide an allowance for the purchase of a suitable uniform as a farewell gift to his loyal aide. The old fool, John had thought. If he only knew "his loyal aide" had accumulated enough gold and silver to buy his own uniform three times over.

John's official role was to serve as liaison with the 16th Light Dragoons, ensuring the protection of the property of loyal Jersey Tories and the seizure of farms, animals and goods belonging to those properly identified as Rebels or Rebel sympathizers. He intended to use his position to enrich himself and confiscate enough to keep the troops supplied with food and an adequate share of booty. He would ingratiate himself further with Lieutenant Chatsworth and perhaps even his commander, Colonel Harcourt.

He felt smart in his new uniform, a well-tailored bright redcoat with dark green facing, shiny brass buttons, complimented by tan breeches and a short sword. His high black boots ended just below his knees. The change in the way others dealt with him was instantaneous. When he had visited the custom building and non-Anglican churches in New York City, where the wretched Rebel prisoners were being warehoused, prison guards snapped to attention. Warders followed obsequiously behind him, waiting on his every question. It had been a rewarding experience and he was amazed at how quickly he had grown accustomed to his new role.

But he had not found his brother. After the fall of Fort Washington, there were more than 2,500 new prisoners. He had concentrated on those from New York State Militias, reasoning Willem would have enlisted with the local farmers and tradespeople. None of the prisoners from upstate New York had heard of him. The rumors in camp were the bulk of the New York militia men were with the rebel General Charles Lee to the north, although some units were said to still be with General Washington in New Jersey. No matter, he thought. He would find Willem and make an example of him, proving by his brother's punishment his own loyalty to the Crown.

It was his good luck the 16th Light Dragoons were assigned to General Cornwallis' army, instead of remaining in New York or on Staten Island. They crossed the Hudson and arrived once the Rebels had been driven from New Bridge. After staying one night in a solid stone home, confiscated from a prominent local Rebel, John enjoyed riding with the Dragoons on the wet jaunt from New Bridge to Hackensack. They entered the town close behind the British and Hessian troops who were engaged in an orgy of plundering Tory and Rebel homes alike. Fortunately for the Loyalist owner of a fine three story manor, Lieutenant Chatsworth had quickly spied the place as likely lodging for the night, instead of camping on the village green. Once occupied by the Dragoons, the property was off limits to the hungry, rampaging

Hessians and British troops. The owner knew how lucky he was and spared nothing in his larder. The cavalrymen and John ate very well that night and slept in real beds, warm and dry under fine goose down comforters, their horses, fed and sheltered in the adjacent barn.

The weather broke the last few days of November. On a crisp fall day, John rode with Lieutenant Chatsworth and twelve Dragoons through the flat rich farmlands of New Jersey, east of a gentle sloping mountain range. They were accompanied by two Loyalists from Hackensack, a father and his fourteen year old son. The father said he had promised his neighbor, a Rebel who had fled the town prior to the British troops' arrival, he would mingle their cattle with his to protect them from being seized by the British.

"Fat chance of my harboring that traitorous Whig's herd," the Tory farmer had said when he had responded to the British command's call for supplies to feed the troops. Now the man was guiding the Dragoons to a field, near the town where the cattle had been driven. John harbored a suspicion this could be a trap. The man could be leading them into an ambush with militia crouching in the woods, waiting to shoot them out of their saddles.

It was hard to trust any of the locals, he thought. Some, the most wealthy among them, were obviously solid supporters of the Crown. They told hair-raising tales of the harassment and threats they had endured from the Committees of Liberty. Night-time visits of mobs of armed men, alternately threatening to seize their property or put a torch to it and kill all who resisted or failed to take an oath of allegiance to their rabble-run provincial congress. Others, John thought were simply opportunists, expressing loyalty to the Crown because British troops now occupied their town.

Under General Howe's new orders, letters of protection were issued to any who took a loyalty oath to the King. These promised that even those who had been patriots and taken up arms in the past would have their lives held safe and their property sheltered. Still, one could rely upon the good Loyalists to help ferret out those among them who had supported the rebellion. Even with letters of protection, an accusation of continued rebel support could forfeit a home and the things within, as well as valuable land holdings. It was a good thing men were greedy, ready to avenge a slight or settle an old score, John mused. He knew how to manipulate such emotions and could turn such a situation to his advantage.

They found the cattle, almost thirty of them, fat and glossy, grazing placidly in a field. The animals looked at the mounted men with soft, curious brown eyes and continued chewing their cud, as if inviting the troopers to dismount and enjoy the bucolic afternoon. The farmer removed two railings and they rode in. "The ones further up the hill are mine"

John nervously scanned the sparse woods bordering the meadow. Nothing moved. No sound other than a few birds calling to each other from the trees. At an order from Chatsworth, the Dragoons boisterously rode forward shouting, to roust the somnolent beasts and drive them back through the open railing toward the road. The cattle reluctantly left their grazing. Surrounded by shouting troopers they moved hesitantly down the road. As they approached the town, John found himself riding next to the farmer.

"We are rewarding you as though these cattle are a gift but these animals," John said, gesturing with his riding crop to the herd ahead of them, "they were there for the taking. Unclaimed livestock in a field are proper booty of war."

The farmer looked at John, uncertain how to respond. "I led you to them," he said. "With a herd this size, your troops will have fresh meat for weeks. That is worth something."

"Perhaps and perhaps not. With our cavalry scouring the countryside, we would have found this herd. The fresh meat was waiting to be seized."

The farmer looked at John, his eyes narrowing. "The Colonel I spoke to was most appreciative of my information. I do not see any reason to offer further explanations to you."

"Do not be impudent with me," John snapped. "I can cause you much trouble, if I wish to bother to make the effort," he said, striking the right tone between threat and a gentleman's disdain for a lower class person.

"What do you want?" the farmer asked, his voice betraying his nervousness.

"The thought occurred to me if your Rebel neighbor thought you worthy enough of his trust to mingle his herd with yours, he may have entrusted you with more of his wealth than you have revealed to us. Perhaps, you intend to keep it for yourself."

"No, no," the farmer replied quickly. "He gave me nothing else. Nothing at all."

"Yet, when we claimed his house for the Crown, no valuables were found there. No coins, no silverware, no plate, no jewelry. Just a few large pieces of furniture, some linen and worn clothing. And you said he fled in haste," John said, his voice quiet and reasonable. "Why do you suppose the house was empty of all such things?"

The farmer took off his stained black hat and wiped his forehead with the back of his hand. "He did not leave me anything, nothing at all," he stammered. "He may have hidden it and, since he was a neighbor, I could guess at where that might be."

"You do that," John said. "Guess well, find it and bring it to your home, if it is not already there."

"No. No. I told you he did not leave any of his valuables with me. I swear it."

"I place little value on oaths of liars. I will visit your house tonight. Depending on what we shall say you 'found,' I am authorized to give you a small reward for your surrendering Rebel property to the Crown. If you withhold a single coin, I will return in the morning with the Dragoons and we will confiscate your own property."

They were almost to the outskirts of Hackensack. "I will have everything for you," the farmer said. "Everything. I promise."

"I am sure you will," John answered pleasantly. There was a small risk of going alone to the farmer's home. But with the town occupied by the British Army, the farmer was neither courageous nor stupid enough to attack a British officer. Nevertheless, John decided he would carry a pistol for protection. He would give the farmer just enough of a reward to satisfy his greed. As for the rest of the valuables, he was interested only in the coins and the silver he could carry in his saddlebags. This had been a very agreeable and prosperous day, John thought as he returned to their temporary quarters. Chatsworth hailed him as John gave his horse to an orderly.

"The news from Rebel deserters is their army, numbering no more than few thousand, is encamped in Newark. We are leaving early tomorrow morning to scout the countryside in preparation for our advance." He clasped John by the shoulder. "You shall ride with us tomorrow. Perhaps we will enjoy some Loyalist hospitality along the way, or give some young Rebel girls a manly flourish. Sabres for the Rebels and a different kind of sword to prick the women's flesh. Eh, John. Are you up for that?" He grinned and nudged John in the ribs.

John smirked but he was not thinking of wenches. He congratulated himself for arranging to meet the farmer tonight instead of the morrow.

—m—

The slow train of more than seven hundred sick and wounded soldiers, led by Lieutenant Hadley took two days to cover the eighteen miles from Newark to Morristown. The men suffered terribly, lying almost twenty to a wagon on hard planked floors. They had stopped numerous times, both before and after they had passed through the low wooded mountains, to bury those who had succumbed to their wounds. The only able-bodied men, soldiers like Will, quickly dug shallow, unmarked graves for the deceased. The roadside grave services were just long enough to be respectful but short enough not to unduly delay them. Along the way, they passed small bands of militia, deserters heading home for the winter, or families fleeing the oncoming British and Hessian troops. Will found this mournful journey worse than the retreat with the army. At least there he had the companionship of the others from Boston. Here, he had no one to talk to and was alone with his somber and morbid thoughts. He dreaded each stop, the carrying of a still warm body to the roadside. Much as he tried, he could not avoid looking at the dead soldier's face, and imagining it was he who had passed in agony and alone. As he drove the wagon, the only sounds came from the moaning of the men in the back, interrupted by the occasional cough, vomiting, or the noise he feared the most, a gurgle that presaged a soldier's death.

They reached Morristown in the early evening. Lieutenant Hadley, at the head of the wagon train, had sent a rider ahead to alert the residents. In the bone-chilling mist, they were directed to the two churches in town, one Presbyterian, with its thin narrow spire, the other Dutch Reformed, recognizable by its stubby round shape and squat steeple. Candlelight glowed from within the two makeshift hospitals. Several young boys ran down the main street, carrying thin straw mattresses on their heads and disappeared into the nearest church. Others pushed wheelbarrows, loaded with linens, hay and straw. Will stopped his wagon at the side of the Presbyterian church. As he dismounted, he heard a woman's voice call clearly from the side door.

"I need men to assist in bringing the wounded inside."

Will unhinged the sides of the wagon and motioned to a wounded soldier with a gangrenous wound from a musket ball in the flesh of his upper thigh. He hoisted him on his back, and walked bent, up the two wooden steps and into the church. The soldier clasped Will tightly around the chest and lowered his grizzled face into Will's ear to avoid banging against the low lintel beam. The smell of the man's decaying leg overwhelmed his bad breath.

Inside, the wounded men were arranged in rows of mattresses on the wooden floor. Will was about to lower the soldier onto one, when the woman who had spoken earlier directed him to the pallets of straw along the far wall.

"The mattresses are for the more seriously wounded," she said, pointing toward the wall.

Will grunted and lowered the soldier as gently as he could on to his good leg, and then holding him by the waist, eased him on to the straw. This will have to do, he thought. The large high-ceilinged room was cold. Churches had no fireplaces. At least it was dry, although a pool of water on the floor attested to a leak somewhere in the spire. Several of the women of the town were already moving among the soldiers, covering them with blankets and offering ladles of water.

Will turned to leave and saw a slim, young woman, in a brown homespun cloak, her head covered with a white cap, efficiently directing where the wounded should be placed. She had a high forehead, slightly arched eyebrows over deep piercing brown eyes, and a thin mouth over a narrow chin. Her skin was luminescent. The candlelight gave her face an angelic appearance although her entire manner was of one of command.

Will ducked back out the door. Men from the town were helping the wounded from his wagon. He ran down the muddy street, calling for the oncoming wagons to alternate between the two churches. By the time most of the soldiers had been carried inside, the churches were full and there were more wounded to be sheltered. Will was at a loss what to do. The woman emerged from the Church holding a lantern. Lieutenant Hadley, and several townspeople followed her into the street. Hadley recognized Will and motioned to him.

"Have the remaining wagons follow us to the courthouse."

There, the wounded had to wait in the cold drizzle while the men inside moved the desks and chairs to the sides, creating an empty space for the soldiers to be bedded down. Once that was accomplished, they were quickly brought inside by the townsmen who had finished their work at the churches and gathered at the courthouse.

Lieutenant Hadley emerged from the building and called for the thirty or so troops who had driven the wagons from Newark. Once assembled he ordered them to divide up, tend to the horses and seek lodging in Morristown's two taverns and the farms on the outskirts of town.

"We will not depart in the morn but be prepared to load your wagons and leave by nightfall. Assemble at the taverns by noon and I will have further orders for you."

Hadley motioned for Will to remain behind.

"We are staying, at the invitation of Miss Mercy Buskirk Ford, at her father's home near to the very powder mill whose contents we have been sent to procure. Bring your wagon round and follow me."

Will returned to the Presbyterian Church, untied Big Red from the railing and rode him bareback pulling the wagon behind. He had sat for too long on the hard wooden seat, now wet from the rain and he had no desire to see the blood stains on the wagon's floor or recall the last gasps of some of the poor souls he had carted from Newark. He waited while Hadley offered his hand to Miss Mercy and saw she was the slim young woman Will had first seen in the church. As they drove slowly down the main street, the still lit lantern bobbing in the young lady's hand, Will recalled a different ride, crossing the frozen Hudson at Albany with Elisabeth nestled under his right arm. That had been almost a year ago, he thought sadly.

The Ford home was a solid stone saltbox, longer across the front than it was deep, with a broad columned porch. It had two white dormers above and three side windows which Will assumed provided air to the garret on the second floor. Miss Mercy alighted at the steps leading to the door and handed her lantern to Lieutenant Hadley. Will followed the yellow glow of the candle into a large stone barn. He and Hadley unhitched the wagons. Will led Big Red and the Lieutenant's grey mare into adjacent stalls. Hadley took two wooden feed buckets from the stall of a well-groomed matching pair of chestnut mares and found some oats and hay while Will filled the water trough. As he followed Hadley toward the house, Will realized how hungry and weary he was.

They scraped their boots on the iron stand before Hadley knocked on the door and waited. Miss Mercy herself opened it, with a friendly smile for the Lieutenant. Inside, the light from the candles and the large fireplace in the family room to the right of the wide center hall, cast a warm welcoming glow. A long polished wood table had been hastily set for a late meal. Delicious aromas flowed from the adjacent kitchen. After two days of short rations of hard biscuits and dried pieces of cheese, the odors of meats and roasting chickens were overpowering. The servants must have commenced cooking when the first of the wagons arrived.

"Forgive my manners, Miss Mercy," Hadley said slightly clicking the heels of his boots together. "This is a member of my company, Private Will Stoner, a good soldier and friend." Will blushed at the compliment and bowed slightly. As they followed her into the family room, Will had a better opportunity to observe her. She had a slender but wiry figure. Her walk was feminine and purposeful at the same time. The paleness of her skin gave her a delicate look, belied by her air of firmness and decisiveness. He guessed she was older than his Elisabeth, maybe eighteen years of age although to him, she seemed more mature than that.

"My father will join us soon," she said gesturing for them to sit near the fireplace. Will took off his blue coat, aware it smelled of wet wool and sweat. He had not washed it since their chaotic flight from Fort Lee. He hung it across the back of a worn maple chair, unbuttoned his waistcoat, which was equally filthy and gratefully sat down, pointing his soaking wet boots toward the fire. Hadley remained standing. He was at least a foot and half taller than Miss Mercy. She stood near the hearth, unabashedly intent on the Lieutenant without any affectation of demure feminine deference.

"Are you the only female of the house," Hadley inquired.

Mercy laughed lightly. "Our home is full of women, Lieutenant. We have my mother's relatives who have fled Bergen County due to our uncle's support of the Crown." Hadley looked surprised.

"The Van Buskirks are Loyalists. My uncle, a physician of some renown in New Bridge, resigned from the Provincial Congress and was persecuted for his principles by the Bergen County Committee of Safety. He sent my aunt and nieces to live with us in relative safety."[1]

"And what does your uncle do now?" Hadley asked.

"I suppose, with our Army in full retreat, he will come out of hiding and offer his services to the British," she replied matter-of-factly.

"'Tis a pity," Hadley said, leaning against the mantle and taking in more of the warmth of the fire. "We need good surgeons in our cause. What does your father say to his brother-in-law serving the Crown?"

Before Mercy could answer, there was a sound of a side door slamming. "You may ask him yourself, Lieutenant," she said, turning toward the kitchen.

"Ah, I see we have guests." Benjamin Ford threw his cloak on a hook and stamped his boots on the red brick kitchen floor before coming toward the fire to warm his hands. "Welcome, gentlemen. Welcome indeed." Will rose from his chair but did not have time to put on his coat, before Mercy introduced them. Self-consciously, he smoothed his unbuttoned waistcoat.

"I understand you brought the wounded from New Ark," he said lifting his coat tails and turning his large rear to the fire. He was a big man, as tall as Hadley but heavier and with a more robust and thicker torso. His sandy hair was tied back in a tail with darker brown ribbon.

A horse-like jaw accentuated his long pale cheeks bare of stubble, and his eyes were deep brown with a hint of worry and tiredness in them. Will saw that Mercy had her father's eyes and complexion but fortunately seemed to have received her looks from her mother.

They sat down at the long dinner table. Mercy went into the adjoining kitchen and soon dishes of meat were delivered by two of her nieces, young girls of eleven and twelve, who after placing the platters on the table, gave their uncle a hug and curtseyed to Hadley and Will.

"Your daughter informs me your brother-in-law will become a surgeon for the Crown," Hadley said, glancing at Mercy who brought a pitcher of cider and sat down across from him and next to her father.

"Yes," Ford acknowledged. "He has his views and I have mine. He believes that whatever grievances we have can be settled amicably with the King and Parliament. This talk of independence and rebellion comes only from those who seek power and to profit from discontent."

"Surely, he does not include you and Miss Mercy with such condemnation."

"No, Lieutenant. He thinks we are misguided and duped. Unfortunately, Dr. Van Buskirk cannot recognize that a Royal Sovereign is still a man who like any other is capable of committing injustice and brutality and inflicting this cruel occupation and war upon us."

"And where are your good wife and sister-in-law?"

"They are visiting the wife of a neighbor in childbirth," Ford answered.

"They both have a decent working knowledge of medicine which we sorely need with all of these poor wounded soldiers," Mercy added.

Will was almost in a swoon from the smells of the food on the table, roast chicken and beef, preserved plums to go with it, boiled potatoes, bread with butter and cheese, turnip greens. He waited for Ford and Hadley to help themselves and then, restraining himself, speared one thick slice of roast beef with his knife, and cut himself a modest slice from the chicken.

"We are here," Hadley said, between bites, "on orders from General Washington, to procure gunpowder and rejoin the Army with the most haste. I understand Sir, you are the owner of the powder mill."

Ford nodded. "And a Whig and strong patriot as well, despite having a brother-in- law on the other side," he said waving his fork in the direction of the kitchen.

"Father. We are not the only family at odds with themselves," Mercy said. "All of the Jerseys are divided in their loyalties."

"Precisely correct my daughter. These are dangerous times in which one cannot tell friend from foe, Whig from Loyalist, patriot from poultroon, unless they wear a uniform."

Will glanced around the table and helped himself to what he thought was another modest portion and filled his tankard with more cider. He noted the two young nieces in the kitchen doorway giggling and staring at him.

"I will sell you the powder at a fair price," Ford continued. "However, it will be risky to transport it from Morristown to wherever the Army is. The countryside is filled with armed men, some bandits and common robbers who loot and pillage the defenseless and do worse that I will not say because of the young ones present." He turned and smiled at his nieces peering from the doorway. "And of course, Loyalist militias who do all their evil in the name of the Crown."

Dulled by fatigue and the large meal, Will listened with half an ear. Ford reported he had just come from a meeting of the Captains of the militia companies raised in Morris County. They were woefully undermanned. Only three companies had their full complement of eighty men, the other seven somewhere between forty and fifty, depending on the time of day one called the roll. While everyone who had enlisted had a musket or firelock, some were nothing more than fowling pieces. Cartridges were in plentiful supply, but bayonets were scarce. Ford chortled, describing the swords the volunteers had worn, often ornamental, or so rusted as to be useless.

"No, sir. It is both a pity and the truth. Our county is unable to provide a well-equipped, eight-hundred man Regiment to defend our own part of New Jersey."

"Nevertheless, Father," Mercy said, "I have seen them drill and they are eager to fight and spirited as well."

"With all due respect to your assessment of their fighting quality," Hadley said, "we have had poor experience with State militias who flee at the appearance of the first Hessian. They compromised our lines at Flatbush and on Manhattan Island, as well as at the battles of Harlem Heights, White Plains and Fort Washington. Not to mention their despicable behavior in the presence of Generals Washington and Greene at Fort Lee. Why, when commanded to retreat in orderly ranks, they became a mob of looters and deserters." Hadley caught himself before he rushed on and offended Mercy who seemed taken aback by his vehemence.

"I believe," Ford said quickly, "some units of the Morris County militia will prove steadfast and courageous. All are eager to join General Washington's army." He paused and nodded toward Will. "Your young Private seems to have succumbed to a warm fire and full belly." Hadley coughed loudly. Will jerked his head up. "Go lad," Ford said. "There is a staircase in the back to the garret. Sleep in one of those beds." Will mumbled good night, remembering to thank Ford for the meal and shelter. As he left the room, he heard Hadley and Ford discussing how much gunpowder was to be had and whether canvas charges for nine and twelve-pounders were available.

Will awoke to the cock's crow in the yard below. He sat up in bed, immediately aware of the low ceiling beams and the grey light in the room. Hadley was sitting in a roughly hewn chair by the thick glass window.

"Have you been awake for long?" Will asked, swinging his bare feet from under the coverlet and pulling his stockings on.

"I have not slept at all," Hadley replied. "I have never met such an intelligent and personable, well informed and enchanting young lady," he said, turning away from the garret window. "Her father and I stayed late into the night discussing the amount of powder we need. It is of very high quality. They get their saltpeter from nearby niter caves.[2] Did you know all of Ford's children, including Miss Mercy as a young girl, helped to harvest it?" He paused, apparently reflecting on the image of Miss Mercy as a child, bravely crawling into the dark bat-infested cave, torch in one hand, and a bucket with a small shovel in the other.

He rubbed his cheeks covered with a heavy three-day stubble.

"Once we had set a fair price and he discovered the Spanish silver dollars I am carrying are not nearly enough to cover the purchase, Mr. Ford agreed to accept Continental paper or even General Washington's word for future payment." He smiled at the thought of Ford's generosity.

"Miss Mercy contributed to the discussion and her fervor in our cause and certainty of the successful outcome inspired me. She is well educated. Why, she knows how to read and write, do sums, and she speaks French," Hadley added with astonishment. "Her father obviously values her opinions. She is in correspondence on political issues with women in Boston, New York and Philadelphia." He rubbed his neck to ease a crick. "We stayed up into the wee hours of the morning, at that table, talking about the actions of our Congress. My God, Will, I would give my soul to be able to spend my life in the constant company of such a woman as Mercy Buskirk Ford."

Will pulled on his breeches and his boots that were dry for once. He was embarrassed by the Lieutenant's extravagant praise of Miss Mercy. The man he had observed as so suave and polished in his conversations with women seemed smitten like a young boy. Like himself, Will thought, the way he described Elisabeth.

"I will feed and water Big Red and your horse," he said, waiting for Hadley to come out of his reverie.

"And I will find hot water and shave my unsightly face and hope Miss Mercy will find favor with what lies beneath."

Will waited in silence, uncomfortable by Hadley's distracted air.

"Oh yes, Will," said Hadley, remembering he was not alone with his thoughts. "Come back to the house after seeing to the horses. We will breakfast here and then meet the drivers at the taverns. Some of them are artillery men. We will take them with us to the powder mill and make canvas charges today. Load them and the barrels of powder, and some flints Mr. Ford will provide, and be ready to leave early tomorrow morning."

Outside, a thick white mantle of frost clung to the withered grass. The puddles he had stomped through last night on the path from the barn were now covered by a thin sheet of ice. The ruts in the road were frozen hard as rocks. Will thought with winter coming, the horses would have a difficult time pulling cannons and wagons.

At breakfast, Will devoured food as if he had not eaten his fill the night before. When Ford mentioned his horse was at the blacksmith's, Will stopped mopping up his porridge with a chunk of bread.

"May I take my horse and the Lieutenant's to be reshod, sir. They both have worn shoes and there may not be another opportunity." He left unsaid, that once they rejoined the Army in retreat, who knew how far they would have to flee with the British in pursuit.

After breakfast, Hadley and Ford went to the taverns to assemble the men and bring the wagons to the powder mill by the stream. Will slowly rode Big Red and led Hadley's mare to the blacksmith's shop on the road leading east out of Morristown. He carefully watched the man shoeing a horse and seeing his skill and attention, he knew he could trust him with their horses.

"Can you make cleated shoes for these two," Will asked when the man had finished nailing the shoe and straightened up, arching his back to rid himself of the stiffness.

The blacksmith looked from Will's worn uniform to the two horses. "It will take longer. If you stay, help me with the bellows and tell me news from across the Passaic River and how our Army fares, I will make the cleats and charge as if they were regular shoes."

"Fair enough," replied Will, taking off his coat and hanging it on a wooden peg protruding from a worn beam. The blacksmith pushed a straight piece of flat iron into the forge with a pair of long-handled blackened tongs. He watched as the fire glowed from Will working the bellows, and when he was satisfied it was ready, put it on the anvil and drove nails into it. The sparks flew as he worked the iron to the thickness of a horseshoe.

"My helper has gone for drilling with the militia," he said between hammer blows. "He makes more money, a sterling shilling a day, marching up and down, than I pay him for his labors. There is a provincial decree for the recruitment of all able-bodied men and I cannot object." He nodded to Will who grabbed the handles on either side of the arrow shaped bellows and pulled it down to his knees and up again. He kept at it, the exertion warming his body, his muscles across his broad shoulders pushing against the resistance of the creaking black leather folds. The fire in the forge roared to life.

As the blacksmith hammered the shoes on the anvil, he peppered Will with questions about the loss of Fort Lee and the crossing at New Bridge, both of which he had heard about. Will found his story telling voice and recounted the valor of Smallwood's Marylanders at the Old Stone House, the successful escape across the fog bound East River, and the Marblehead Mariners' battle against the Hessians on Split Rock Road.

"These are all events I witnessed," Will concluded as the blacksmith nipped off the last nail head with pincers and filed it to a rough point, leaving a two inch spike sticking out. He held up the shoe to the light, examining his handiwork, turning it this way and that with a short handled tongs.

These cleats will serve your horse well," he said, bending down and clicking his tongue for Big Red to lift his left front leg.

Late in the afternoon, with a chill wind beginning to blow, Will returned to the Ford's barn, stabled the two horses and went into the house. He found Lieutenant Hadley and Ford sitting at the dining table with a third man, dressed in a dark blue uniform coat. He was stocky and thick-bodied, with a round face, and fleshy cheeks framing a nose with prominent bulbous nostrils. His blue eyes, lighter than his uniform by several shades, were sharp and inquisitive, set above pouched bags of loose skin. He assessed Will as if appraising a recruit.

"Ah, Will," Hadley said, welcoming him with a smile. "May I introduce Captain Henry Van Allen of the Morristown Regiment.[3] He and a company of his men will escort the powder train to Newark. This is Private Will Stoner of the Massachusetts Artillery and a veteran of the battles I have described to you gentlemen." The Captain nodded and Will thought he detected a glimmer of respect regardless of their differences in age and rank. Will had never thought of himself as a veteran before. He pulled a stool closer to the fire, warmed his hands and listened to the conversation.

Captain Van Allen's company of sixty-four men, two Lieutenants and one Ensign had been hand picked from among the ten Morris County companies raised so far. The Captain had spent the day interviewing each man, looking for those who were likely to be of stout heart, cool under fire and who would follow orders. Most of the men he had selected were young, capable of a forced march and eager to fight. Some were good marksmen, armed with Pennsylvania rifles instead of muskets.

Hadley was impatient to rejoin the Army. While he welcomed the addition of Van Allen's company, he did not accept the Captain's suggestion to take the roads to the south. He favored a forced march to Newark. Ford argued the powder was too precious to risk by marching back toward the British Army.

"Newark or the surrounding countryside could be swarming with British cavalry and Loyalist militia and spies." Ford said. "Morristown, while solidly Whig, has its Tory sympathizers," he added, "who may have already sent messages about your presence and mission. Even the Captain's company and your own men would not be a match for a large body of British troops."

"My men are ready for any eventuality," Van Allen said confidently. "However, I do agree with Mr. Ford. Prudence dictates we should proceed south. The route to Brunswick is through the mountains, steeper than to Newark and longer, but more secure."

Hadley, torn between his fervent desire to deliver the powder to the Army as quickly as possible and the danger of being attacked and losing the precious barrels of gunpowder, could not decide. He pushed his chair back and stood before the fire, staring into the flames.

"This is a vexatious question," he said out loud.

"I believe Father is right," Mercy said firmly. "And Captain Van Allen too." Will had not seen her enter the room.

The Captain scowled at her for speaking out. He looked at Ford to reprimand his daughter. The miller seemed not to notice and nodded approvingly to his daughter to continue.

"If our Army is to the north of Brunswick," she said in her clear voice, "then Lieutenant could you not urge your horses and wagons forward at great speed, at that point unencumbered by the Captain's men on foot? And if it is to the south, then the British Army would not be between you." Mercy cocked her head and smiled at Hadley.

To Will's surprise, Hadley blushed and returned the smile. He bowed slightly to Miss Mercy and turned to the Captain and Ford.

"The southern route it is," he said. "Can your men be ready to march at midnight?"

Van Allen nodded. "They will be ready when you are."

"Then it is settled. We leave for Brunswick at midnight. And Captain Van Allen, tell your men it will be a quick march. I intend to be in Brunswick by tomorrow before dark."

Chapter 12 - With the Rearguard at the Raritan River

The train of more than thirty wagons left slightly after midnight, delayed by a last minute decision by Hadley to rearrange their precious cargo. The canvas charges for the nine and twelve-pounders had been unloaded and stored in wooden crates, boxes, barrels and any other container found in Ford's mills and barns. These were then placed on three wagons. Will rode on the first one, toward the front of the train. Hadley had instructed him and the other two drivers, if the Army was engaged in battle when they arrived, they were to break from the train and ride forward quickly, find the artillery and unload the containers.

They were a long way from rejoining the Army, Will thought, as they moved in silence on the broad deeply rutted road through the flat farmlands to the west of the Watchung Mountains. Captain Van Allen had sent scouts ahead of the train. The plan was to cross the Passaic River and reach the Hobart-Milburn gap that ran between the first and second mountain ridges shortly before dawn. They should be through the gap and on the eastern side of the mountains by early morning. Van Allen said that would position them less than ten miles north and west from Brunswick, but in open countryside. If the British Army had moved south from Newark, it was likely the train would encounter cavalry and light infantry once they were east of the mountains. As long as the British force was not too numerous, Will thought they would be able to fight their way through and rejoin the Americans.

To make better time, the men of Van Allen's company rode on the wagon seats with the drivers. There was little likelihood of running into British troops and Loyalist militias west of the Watchung Range. Will's companions as they left Morristown were a young ferret-faced farm boy, with abnormally small curled ears, protruding like a tree fungus from under his stained slouch hat. He was of slight build, with short dark bristly hair, roughly cut. The long rifle he carried seemed too heavy for him. A large hunting knife with a crudely carved bone handle was strapped to his thigh, along with his powder horn. In his ill-fitting hunting frock, with a wide leather strap across his narrow chest, dirty breeches and worn moccasins, he looked more like a boy dressed as a militiaman than a soldier. He said his name was Peter Bant.

The other, seated next to Will, gave his name as Jacobus Brouwer. He was older than Bant, perhaps twenty or so and was a carpenter and joiner by trade. He had on a country coat over his dark waistcoat and buttoned gaiters that covered his shins down to his black shoes with buckles. He too had a long rifle placed in the wagon on top of a crate just behind the seat, next to Will's own musket. He pressed himself closer to Will to avoid being prodded by Bant's knife handle and powder horn. Will held the reins loosely but with his right elbow out to move the carpenter further away.

Both the young boy and Brouwer had attempted conversation with Will about the battles he had been in. "Have you killed any Redcoats?" the farm boy had asked. Will silenced him with a glare and when Brouwer followed with an inquiry as to whether the Hessians bayoneted their prisoners, Will gruffly grunted yes. He pulled his collar higher around his neck as much to ward off any further questions as the cold night air. He watched Big Red's breath condense in front of his nostrils in puffs that quickly dissipated, vanishing into the darkness ahead of them. The coldness reminded him he had no scarf for his throat and his thoughts wandered to Elisabeth and the red scarf she had given him and her promise to make him a new one. It would do no good to let his mind dawdle on such thoughts. He wondered if Lieutenant Hadley was similarly daydreaming about Miss Mercy. Just before departing, he had seen Hadley, framed in the light of the Ford's doorway, bowing and kissing Miss Mercy's hand before he climbed onto his mare and led the column out of Morristown. Will shook his head to clear his mind of all thoughts of Elisabeth. The image of her face looking up at him that warm summer day at Colonel Knox's headquarters in New York City remained.

At the Passaic River, Captain Van Allen rode across to the eastern bank and sent scouts down the road toward the gap. The rest of the company waded through the cold water with much groaning and complaining. Once across they fanned out on the opposite side, and disappeared into the woods. Lieutenant Hadley on his mare preceded the wagons, carefully choosing a route across the shallow rocky ford before signalling for Will and the other drivers to follow. The crossing was slow but uneventful. In the early dawn, Will saw the outline of two ridges. He had imagined the mountains were like the Berkshires and anticipated a steep climb through a rocky pass. Instead, the ridges were maybe four to five hundred feet high, notched by a flat road between them at their base, heading east toward what Captain Allen called the Hobart Milburn Gap. The wagons lined up on the road and waited. In the growing light, Will saw grey layers of clouds. It would be a cold day but he hoped one without sleet or snow. That would delay their progress and expose the powder to moisture.

When the scouts returned, Captain Van Allen and Lieutenant Hadley conferred in a clearing among the bare maples and oaks. The soldiers had found no sign of enemy forces, only a few local farmers and solitary riders on the road ahead, returning from whatever ordinary business had kept them out at night. Nevertheless, Captain Van Allen increased the number of scouts and ordered the rest of his militia to ride the wagons through the gap. Once through, they stopped again. Van Allen formed his men into marching columns on either side of the wagon train, with a ten-man contingent at the rear.

They made good time through flat open countryside, moving through the small settlement of Bound Brook, and accepting stale bread, hard cheese and much appreciated cider from the locals who handed it to the troops as they marched by. Brouwer, on foot with the other militia men, caught up with Will's wagon and passed him a loaf and canteen. Will nodded in gratitude. They continued on without break until they reached the Raritan River. A string of small settlements dotted the valley downriver. Here, the Raritan was narrow and the water shallow, flowing gently over rounded stones and gravel. Hadley and Van Allen again conferred. Will watched the two men sitting on their horses, engaged in animated conversation.

Hadley abruptly turned his mare and rode up to Will's wagon. "Captain Van Allen advises we are less than five miles from Brunswick, which is situated on the south bank of the Raritan. He recommends we cross here so that if the army has retreated to Brunswick and is using the river as a natural barrier, we will not be on the wrong side." And trapped on the same side with the British, Will thought. A more likely possibility if the Americans had destroyed any bridge across from Brunswick. "It is just before noon. Once over on the other side, I want you and the other two wagons with powder charges to lead the train. When we arrive, if our cannons are engaged, you are to ride as if chased by the furies for our positions and deliver the charges." Will nodded.

They crossed the Raritan and Will guided Big Red to the front of the train. He stood up on the wagon seat. The land ahead was relatively flat. To the southeast, past where the road wound through the trees, he saw a line of people leading heavily loaded ox-drawn wagons and hand carts. Van Allen and Hadley saw them as well and rode forward. The carts and wagons were piled high with furniture, large black cast iron cooking pots, wooden chests and bulging sacks. The men walked alongside their oxen, the women sat dejectedly on the wagon seats, their children clinging precariously to perches on the goods in the back. They were from Brunswick and settlements to the north.

Van Allen ordered the civilians to move off to the side and let the powder train pass. A few resisted but under threat of force from Van Allen's company, reluctantly did so, cursing them, although not too loudly, in the process. A company of militia followed the fleeing civilians.

"What unit are you," Van Allen called from his horse as they approached. "We understand the battle is ahead."

"You understand well," a tall soldier answered, not bothering to stop or slow his pace.. "We are of the Sussex militia. It is December 1ˢᵗ and our term is up. We are going home."[1] He turned his back on Van Allen and continued up the road.

"Surely you are not abandoning our army with the British hot on their heels," Van Allen sputtered in disbelief.

"We surely are," another man replied as his unit continued marching past. "We signed up, served our four months and now it is home before winter sets in." They plodded on, ignoring the shocked stares and angry looks from Van Allen's men.

"Well," Van Allen called to his own men, but loudly enough for the Sussex militia to hear. "March on. It is clear we will be needed to fill the ranks of those who have abandoned our cause so quickly."

"Good luck to you Captain. And your men," one of the militia in the rear called out with a smirk on his face. "General Howe is coming with ten thousand soldiers. There will be more than enough for each of you."

Will sensed unease and a diminution of some of the swagger among the Morris County militia. There was much muttering as they continued their quick march towards Brunswick. There were fewer civilians on the road, only the occasional farmer's cart, pulled by a team of slow oxen. The dull brown grass on both sides of the road marked fields that had been harvested earlier in the season. Approaching a low rise, Will saw one of the scouts standing in the road, waving his hat and gesturing. Captain Van Allen and Hadley rode forward and conferred briefly with scout. Van Allen suddenly wheeled his horse and gallop back to the train.

"There are British cavalry in the field beyond those trees. Riflemen follow me. Close up the wagons. Lieutenant," he shouted, to one of his officers. "Bring up the company and stay on the road but keep out of sight."

If the cavalry are on the southern side of the Raritan, the wagon train was too late, Will thought. They would not have crossed the river that far ahead of the British Army. The Americans must be below Brunswick. They were cut off and would be captured and their vital cargo lost. He wondered how long it would take him to sever the traces and escape with Big Red. The riflemen had run down the road and disappeared into the woods. The rest of the militia formed up in front of the wagon train. Will felt hemmed in and trapped. He loaded his musket and waited nervously.

—⁓—

John Stoner's anxiety had turned into outright fear that he suppressed with great difficulty. The Light Dragoon's mission had changed in the past few days. Before it had been a leisurely ride into prosperous settlements, enjoying the abundant hospitality of grateful Tories and gathering information about Rebel supporters. Now, with General Cornwallis in close pursuit of the Rebel Army, it was a full-fledged reconnaissance mission. As long as he could see the columns of British troops or know they were a short ride away, he had felt reasonably safe. He cursed Chatsworth's bravado when he and the troopers had crossed the Raritan "to scout behind the American army," as the Lieutenant had put it. "We may surprise some of these riffraff of Rebel soldiers and teach them a lesson," Chatsworth had explained. At the risk of my life, John had thought but remained silent. The rest of these troopers were equally fools, he thought. Playing the brave and gallant cavalry men to the young daughters of their Tory hosts, and then fulfilling their roles by riding across open fields when there could be Rebel marksmen behind every tree. He let his horse slow so that he was more in the middle of the group rather than up front.

John saw the puff of bluish smoke from the trees ahead at the same time as the throat of the trooper ahead of him exploded in a cloud of red froth. The sound of the rifle shot reached him as he heard a high-pitched scream. It was his own voice. Chatsworth and the others milled about, uncertain in which direction to turn. The trooper lay on the ground, his horse standing placidly next to his rider's twitching body. A band of militia emerged from the woods and formed into two compact lines, their muskets at the ready.

John had seen enough. There were only eleven of the troopers and more than thirty of the Rebels. If Chatsworth decided to charge them, he, John, would not follow. The Rebels would have other riflemen hidden in the woods as well. And more troops coming up behind them. Chatsworth made the decision to retreat, a moment before John turned to flee. They slung the body of their dead comrade over his saddle and left the field in haste. John felt a great sense of relief as they headed in the direction of the main body of British troops.

—◊—

The militia returned from the woods and rejoined the wagon train. Captain Van Allen was furious. "My orders were to hold fire," he shouted. "We are lucky there was no light infantry with those Dragoons. We do not want a pitched battle. Our purpose is to get this powder to the Army." Will learned it was the ferret-faced farm boy who had shot the trooper. Bant was boasting about it to his comrades as they continued marching down the road. Despite their Captain's reprimand, the militia were buoyed by the cheap victory of having driven the cavalry away. The swagger was back in their step.

"Silence on the march," Van Allen called. His orders were echoed by the Company's two Lieutenants. After a quarter of an hour, they heard the boom of cannons and the sound of musket volleys in the distance. It came from the direction of Brunswick.

Hadley rode back to Will. "Follow me," he ordered, gesturing for the three wagons with the canvas charges to move out of line. "Captain Allen. Have your men mount the other wagons and bring the rest of the train as fast as possible."

Will urged Big Red forward and the wagon jolted and bounced over the frozen muddy road. The sharp crack of sporadic rifle fire interspersed with the deep boom of artillery became louder as they approached Brunswick. They clattered up a slight rise. The town was less than a mile away, a cluster of red brick and stone buildings. The tree- lined road to the south was choked with marching soldiers. The American Army in retreat, Will thought. A narrower road forked to the left, north toward the Raritan. A cloud of smoke marked the Americans' rear guard positions on the bank closest to Brunswick.

A group of officers clustered at the fork facing the river. Will recognized Colonel Knox by his size and girth, mounted on a large dappled New England saddle horse. He thought he saw General Greene and then, in the center of their circle, sitting calmly on his white horse, his cloak falling loosely over the rear of his saddle, General Washington. Hadley rode ahead of the wagons to report to Knox, whose broad fleshy face broke into a grin upon seeing the Lieutenant. Knox pointed to the river and Hadley dashed back to the wagons.

"Captain Hamilton's New York State Artillery is engaged to prevent the British from crossing. The Colonel has ordered us to bring the charges forward." Will directed Big Red on to the road through the trees toward the river, followed by the other two wagons. As they passed the fork, Knox recognized Will and greeted him in a very unmilitary fashion, "Halloo Will. Forward lads. Hurry. Hamilton needs you."

Will glanced down the road toward the town and saw ranks of troops marching south. He recognized Haslet's Delaware Blues, with their distinctive black jacked peaked caps, standing in ranks. He felt better knowing they were the rearguard troops covering the artillery's retreat.

Once through the trees, Will had a clearer view of the battle. Across the river, the British guns were spread out in a quarter mile arc, on both sides of the road. Wisps of blue white smoke came from the windows of the few stone houses along the river where British infantry were firing in support of their artillery. Will counted eleven of Hamilton's cannons, widely spaced apart, situated in an open field, back from the Raritan, but within easy range of the British guns. A wooden bridge, its brace beams and king posts charred, smoldering and partially collapsed, spanned the river. American riflemen, hidden in the buildings along the southern bank on either side of the bridge, were firing at the British light infantry and Hessian Jaegers across the river. The New Yorkers' cannons were engaged in an artillery duel with the British guns, which had been brought up to support their infantry's efforts to capture the bridge.[2]

Will drove Big Red forward toward the nearest battery. Ten yards behind the cannon, he saw several empty side boxes. He leaped from the wagon seat. Unable to carry the full boxes of charges by himself from the wagon, Will pried one open with his hatchet, grabbed a charge and carried the canvas bag to an empty side box. Big Red stood calmly in his traces, trained not to be spooked by cannon fire. Hadley had directed the other two wagons to the left and right emplacements, leaving Will to manage for the guns in the center. After filling the side boxes at one emplacement, Will drove to the next, feverishly running back and forth from the wagon to the side boxes, fearful a British cannon ball or rifle shot would hit Big Red. He remembered when Lieutenant Hadley had ordered them to aim for the British horses bringing up the cannons on Split Rock Road. He hoped no British gun commander was of the same intent.

When the wagon was empty, he rode it well back behind the lines, tied Big Red to a tree that seemed safely out of range and grabbing his musket ran back toward the cannons.

"Help us with this," one of the gun crew shouted to him. Will gasped for breath carrying the heavy powder box, loaded with charges forward to the nine-pounder. The crew loaded a ball and stood back as the gun commander shouted "Give Fire." Will saw a wheel on the gun carriage of a British twelve-pounder shatter and the ball careen past harmlessly. The noise of all the batteries firing was continuous. The crew stepped forward and quickly went through the worming and swabbing before the gun commander noticed Will.

"Go two guns down," he said gesturing with his hand to the left. "They have wounded and need help." Will could barely hear his words over the booming of all the cannons. He was unclear whether they needed him to remove the wounded or to be part of the gun crew. He hunched down and ran toward the next cannon, barely twenty yards away. Halfway there, there was a loud explosion behind him, strong enough to throw him to the ground. He got up deafened, dazed and unsure in which direction to turn. Through the smoke, he heard a high-pitched scream of pain and shock. The gun commander, who a moment ago had ordered him to another cannon, lay next to the cannon, his arm and shoulder gone, the blood spurting out onto his buff colored breeches. The broken bodies of two of the crew lay forward of the cannon, their backs blown away. Wisps of dark smoke drifted lazily up from their burned blue jackets. Will smelled the acrid odor of gunpowder. Behind them, a charred black patch in the grass marked where the powder box had been before it exploded.

He turned away from the grisly scene and ran in a crouch to where the gun commander had pointed, only seconds ago. There were three privates and a Lieutenant, short-handed and slowly working the gun.

"I am from the Massachusetts Artillery Regiment," Will shouted to make himself heard. "Colonel Knox's Regiment," he added by way of explanation, feeling silly after saying it.

"I do not care if you are from The Holy Ground," the Lieutenant barked, referring to the brothel area of New York City. "Do you know how to worm a cannon?" Will nodded thinking of Isaiah Chandler's calmness under fire with the lives of the rest of the crew in his hands.

"Poor Ephraim had his leg blown off. He is bleeding to death back in the grass."

"If he is not dead already," one of the crew said, ramming a charge down the barrel and rolling a nine pound ball after it. He was a short stocky man, his face and blue jacket black with powder burns and smudges. He stuck the rammer into the barrel and leaned on it with his weight. The Lieutenant, serving as both gun commander and firer, pricked the powder charge, pulled a quill from his pocket and stuck it in the touchhole. He shouted "primed." Will grabbed the long-handled worm and moved away and slightly behind the barrel's mouth. The Lieutenant put a slow match to the quill while yelling "Give Fire." Will tensed until there was the familiar loud boom and he was enveloped in a cloud of smoke, unable to see the effect of their shot. He leaped forward and stuck the spiral metal coil down into the barrel. He felt it strike the breech at the end, beyond the touchhole. He twisted the pole as he had seen Isaiah Chandler do many times, and pulled it out. Small pieces of charred canvas clung to the worm, burning his fingers as he tore them off and plunged the worm down a second time.

"Hurry, lad. This is not a drill," the Lieutenant said. Will turned the pole a full revolution and pulled it out again. This time it came out clean. He stepped back as one of the gun crew stuck the sponge down the barrel. The Lieutenant, acting as vent tender, placed his thumb, encased in a leather pad, over the vent hole. One of the crew dropped a charge down the brass barrel, rammed it home, and followed it with the cannon ball. The Lieutenant, pricked the powder bag through the touchhole, primed it with the quill, and shouted "Give Fire." Will, on the right side of the cannon, saw the flash of flame from the barrel, heard the sound of the explosion and was again enveloped in a haze of acrid smoke.

His ears rang and he thought he would be stone deaf by the end of the day. "If I am still alive," he mumbled to himself.

He was aware of the sound of explosions up and down the line and the constant sharper crack of rifle fire from the American side The riflemen were shooting from the relative safety of stone houses along the river, trying to pick off the British officers directing the field artillery. Several of the British cannon were concentrating their fire on the houses, which gave the New Yorkers a brief respite from the artillery duel. The Lieutenant ordered the men to re-position the cannon, aiming at one of the British heavier guns. Will wormed the cannon twice, despite the Lieutenant shouting at him to hurry. The ball was rammed home, the charge primed, and Will's eardrums throbbed with the clap of the explosion. In what seemed far away in the distance, he heard a cheer and saw the rest of his gun crew smiling and yelling. Their shot had been a direct hit on the British gun, a twelve-pounder that had been sideways to them to blast at one of the stone houses. Redcoats lay amidst the charred wood and twisted metal of the British emplacement.

"Hurry," the Lieutenant yelled, urging Will forward to worm the cannon again. Will lost all sense of time. He did not count how many rounds they fired. He concentrated on worming properly, following Isaiah's example, oblivious to the battle going on around him. Each time, when he ran to the still-smoking barrel and rammed the worm down, he focused on twisting it full circle, searching the barrel carefully for remnants of the canvas cartridge casing. He stopped only when he felt a hand on his shoulder, restraining him from rushing up to worm once again.

"Captain Hamilton has ordered us to withdraw," the Lieutenant said. He pointed to a young, slender man on a dappled grey riding calmly behind the batteries. Will stood still, exhausted, and watched the Captain directing the cannons to be pulled back and hitched up to horses.

Across the Raritan, the British had withdrawn from the field sloping down to the banks of the river. Behind them, on the road to the north, Will saw the late afternoon sun glinting on the brass plated hats and bayonets of the British Army coming down the road toward Brunswick. Their ranks extended as far as he could see.

He found his musket lying next to a side box and loped back to the trees where he had left Big Red. He stood, leaning up against the horse, feeling the warmth of his neck, and vigorously scratching the dark red hair under his large jaw. Slowly, the pounding in his ears receded.

"You there, we need that wagon for the wounded." Will turned and saw a Lieutenant from the New Yorkers, mounted on a small, jittery brown horse. "Down by the houses. Be quick about it and get on the Brunswick Road. You do not want to be behind the rear guard."

Outside the first house the wounded were lying among the remnants of a vegetable garden, soaking the rough clods of brown soil with their blood. The riflemen who were uninjured, carried the wounded and laid them out head to foot, across the width of the wagon. Many had bandages around their heads, having been cut by stone slivers, sharp as knives, when the British cannon balls had struck the building.

Will steadied Big Red with a word and went into the battered stone house. Inside, there were several dead riflemen. Trails of dried blood on the floor, pointed like crimson arrows to where they had fallen at their firing positions at the open windows, before being dragged to the back of the house. Will recognized Bant, leaning over a man with a huge gash in his chest that had been bound with cloth but was still oozing fresh blood. It was Brouwer, the carpenter from Morristown. The farm boy was holding the carpenter's hand.

"We must get him to the wagon outside," Will said. The boy didn't move. "Before there is no more room," Will said, placing his hand on Bant's shoulder. Bant nodded. "You carry his feet. I will take his shoulders. Steady now," he said to Brouwer who gritted his teeth in anticipation of being lifted. "It is this or being bayoneted by the Hessians when they arrive," Will said, regretting his statement immediately. Brouwer screamed as they lifted him and then his head fell to one side as they carried him outside into the dusk of early evening. Will thought they may be carrying a dead man, but he saw Brouwer's chest rising and falling in shallow breaths as they placed him in the wagon and secured the L shaped iron bolts of the side panel. Bant climbed on to the wagon seat, squeezing himself next to three other riflemen.

Ahead, dark orange flames from a huge bonfire sent fiery fragments floating into the dark sky, like so many burning leaves. The men of Haslet's Regiment were throwing new white canvas tents on to the fire. Big Red shied away and Will felt the heat sear his face as they passed by. The flames illuminated the gilt on the soldiers' high peaked caps that now seemed incongruous with their footwear. Once they had worn smart black canvas gaiters and square-toed shoes. Now, some were in stocking feet and others had tied cloth around their worn leather soles to hold them together. They looked much different than the smart troops who had escaped across the East River at the end of August.[3]

Will joined a few other wagons, following the New Yorkers' horse drawn artillery south out of Brunswick. The road was clogged with tired soldiers, marching in as good order as exhausted men could muster. "One more forced march to escape the oncoming British Army," he thought.

By eight in the evening, they reached Kingston where the rest of the army had camped for the night. Will was directed to a small tent that served as a one of the field hospitals. He brought his wagon to a halt on the road afraid, if he went to the sides, he would crush the helpless wounded lying on the ground. The area was already filled with injured men lying in the open, exposed to the cold night air, unattended except by an occasional companion, and untreated by the overworked surgeons.

Will and Bant carried Brouwer from the wagon and found a space closer to the road in the damp grass. The carpenter groaned weakly. Bant disappeared and returned miraculously with a candle. In the light, Will could see Brouwer was close to death. He realized with sadness, he had seen enough men die to recognize it when their time came. Brouwer's eyes were sinking into his head, and in the dim light, his cheeks and the skin around his eye sockets were turning brown.

The carpenter feebly raised his hand. They both leaned closer, to hear him over the moaning and cries for water from the wounded around them.

"I never was more than twenty miles from home. I thought I would fight to defend Philadelphia." The name of the capital escaped his lips as a soft sigh. It was the last sound he made. His mouth remained open and his eyes stared sightlessly toward the dark sky. Bant, sobbing quietly, continued to clasp the carpenter's hand. Will stood up and put his palm on Bant's shoulder. Slowly the boy rose and together they carried the dead carpenter back to the empty wagon. They drove past the cluster of houses that made up the town until Will saw the dim outline of a church spire. They carried the body to an area beyond the sparse line of low tombstones. Brouwer seemed heavier in death than when they had brought him still breathing to the field below the surgeon's tent. Will and Bant took turns using the one shovel Will had in the wagon.

With the candle at the head, they were both in the grave, alternately digging when they heard a rustle in the grass. Looking over the lip of the ground, Will saw two thin and graceful women, their gray hair loosely tied, clutching shawls tightly around their shoulders. Each one held a lit candle in front of her waist, giving their faces a ghostly appearance. Will and Bant stared at the women as they sorrowfully looked at Brouwer's corpse. Will continued digging, careful not to throw the dirt towards the two women. When they finished, they climbed out of the grave and self-consciously brushed the loose soil off their hands and pants. The women said nothing but watched, with a compassionate look on their faces as Will and Bant lowered the carpenter into the ground. Will thought they might be sisters but was not sure. Bant jumped into the open grave, careful not to step on Brouwer and arranged the dead man's arms so his hands crossed in the middle of his chest, as if to hide the horrific wound he had suffered. He nimbly climbed out and stood next to Will, uncertain what to do next.

The two women approached the edge of the grave. They both bent down, lowering their candles in the process. Stooped over, each with an arm draped across the other's neck, Will thought they looked like two swans in repose. The one closest to him turned slightly. The yellow glow of candle-light gave her a sad yet peaceful countenance.

"Do you intend to shield his naked face before covering him with earth?" she asked.

Will shook his head. He did not speak for fear of disturbing their solemn, mournful countenance.

The other drew a white lace handkerchief from her sleeve and held it out. Bant took it from her, knelt at the head of the grave, and let the handkerchief float gently down on to Brouwer's face. He took the shovel from Will, stabbed it into the mound of freshly dug dirt and rhythmically began dropping shovel loads into the grave. Will, shivering from the chill air on his sweat-drenched body, waited until Bant had half- filled the grave, took the shovel from him and completed the task. The two ladies watched until it was done and then turned and silently walked back up the path beyond the church, their skirts rustling in the still night, the disappearing light from their candles the only sign they had been there.[4]

It was close to midnight when Will and Bant returned to town. The General Officers and staff occupied the solid houses. The exhausted soldiers of the retreating army slept where they had collapsed, filling the fields on either side of the road. It was a cold night and Will wished the two sisters had offered them shelter and food. He had no wish to be near the surgeons' tent so he halted at the southern end of Kingston, unhitched Big Red and tied him to a tree by the side of the road. As much as he disliked the idea, he preferred sleeping in the wagon with the blood of the wounded soldiers staining the floorboards, than on the cold damp ground. He and Bant slept curled up against each other for warmth. Will fell asleep drained and weary, his empty stomach noisily complaining, but not enough to keep him awake.

Chapter 13- Plunder and Revenge

"I hear this town is called Brunswick. A German name," Andreas said excitedly.[1] "Someone here must speak our language." Georg and Christoph, nervously looked around for Sergeant Wochler to silence their talking in the ranks. Their Sergeant was several files ahead.

"What does it matter if they speak German?" Christoph asked.

"We can communicate. I want to learn more about these people," Andreas replied as if it were obvious.

Georg kept silent. He was not going to risk being disciplined for such silly talk. He wanted his plunder. The most efficient method would be to wrap what he could take in a blanket or linen. The camp followers and carters assigned to the Knyphausen Regiment were not far behind. The Company's carters at least would protect a soldier's plunder from being taken by others.

Company Seckendorf was in the advance guard marching into Brunswick. The Light Dragoons and Jaegers had already scouted the town. The reports were the Rebellers had fled again and Brunswick was theirs for the taking. About twenty men from the town, guarded by a few Jaegers, stood anxiously in front of the wall of an imposing stone building. No need to take the time to sort them out, Georg thought, as they marched past. Better to treat all of them as Rebellers.

The troops were excited at the prospect of plunder and booty. Their officers encouraged them to get there ahead of the British regulars. They had been in the vanguard of the fighting, used as shock troops by the British so why should they not have the first opportunity to pillage this town. They quickened their pace and, on the command to search all homes, broke into a run. Soldiers pounded on doors with rifle butts, and when the doors were not opened quickly enough to their liking, broke them down and stormed inside. Georg heard the terrified screams of women and the sounds of shattered glass and dishes. It served to spur him on to find his own place to loot.

"Follow me," he shouted to Christoph and Andreas as they ran ahead of their comrades to a two story stone house with green shutters, all closed against them. He peered through the heart shaped design in the shutters. Through the glass behind it, he saw drapes, and beyond them rich, dark brown furniture with many shining brass handles.

"It must be a wealthy family who lives here," Christoph said, "to bar their home so securely."

"Hurry. Help me force open this window. If we are first inside, we get the pick of their furnishings." Georg grunted as he forced his bayonet through the slit between the double shutters. Christoph stuck his musket in the opening and using it as a pry bar, snapped the shutter open. It fell askew on its hinges. Georg smashed the glass window behind it, cleared the jagged shards from the frame with the barrel of his musket, and climbed in. Christoph and Andreas quickly clambered through the broken window. They looked around the parlor. Georg grabbed two silver candlesticks from the round cherry wood candle stand, pulled the white linen cloth off a table, threw it on the floor and dropped the candlesticks on to it. A good start for his loot bag, he thought.

In the center hall, Andreas was removing the two thick pieces of planed wood that were set snugly into iron brackets, double-barring the door. Georg cursed him for his generosity as Andreas threw open the doors, letting in light and several more Hessians who had been futilely battering against the door.

Georg gathered up the four corners of the cloth to form a sack. He pulled open a cabinet door, found nothing but dishes stacked vertically behind thin wooden strips. The other cabinet had good pewter plates, mugs and forks and spoons. He had no need for them but could trade

with the other soldiers. Two Hessians were smashing the dining room
table to get at the inlaid mahogany centerboard. Another was pulling
down an ornate chandelier, ripping it out of the ceiling. Neither was
worth his time, Georg thought. He dropped his sack on the floor and
tossed the pewter and utensils on top of the candlesticks and grabbed
the corners again before rushing into the next room.

It was like a treasure hunt, he thought to himself. He could take
anything he wanted, as long as he could carry it. One Hessian had a
tall floor clock hoisted on his shoulder and was trying to maneuver
through the doorway. Fool, Georg thought. That is all he will be able
to manage.

The next room was the kitchen. Nothing but pots and pans there.
Let others grab those. Several of the Hessians were doing just that,
piling pots inside each other and then lugging them outside. Others
hauled away chairs, the spindles made of a dark mahogany, the seat of
ash or maybe some other lighter colored wood.

Georg took the stairs two at time, hoping to find some clothing
before the other soldiers ransacked the rooms. In one room, larger than
the others, a soldier was busily prying the brass handles off a six drawer
high cherry wood armoire. He had successfully dug out two, leaving
white scars on the dark wood drawer. A large poster bed with its heavy
ribbed striped cotton hangings and blue, grey and white patterned
bed rug stood in the center of the room. The bed coverlet would come
in handy Georg thought, and serve as a stronger sack for his loot. He
grabbed it and quickly ran his hand under the thin mattress, searching
for hidden valuables but found nothing.

The soldier, having finished extracting the brass handles, ripped
down the dark green curtains covering the windows and slashed
the cushioned window seats with his short sabre. Georg was more
interested in looting than random destruction. A wooden chest in the
corner, partially hidden by the fallen green curtains caught his eye.
He forced it open with his bayonet and found two woolen blankets,
a white mattress cover, and under them, men and women's shirts, all
made of fine linen and several pairs of women's white cotton stockings.
The men's shirts he would wear, he thought and the rest he would
either sell, barter or keep. By now, his makeshift sack was bulging and

he had yet to find any shoes or boots. The Rebeller probably took them with him. Georg needed new shoes. His were worn through from constant marching. If the Rebel army stood and fought, like men, he muttered to himself, his shoes would not be worn out and his feet sore and bloody in their thin leather sheathing. Downstairs in the center hall, he pushed his way around several soldiers who had discovered bottles of wine and port. They were guzzling away, smashing the empty bottles against the pale green painted walls. Georg stepped carefully over the broken glass. Good, he thought. If more of his comrades were drunk and preoccupied with searching for brandy, rum and wine, he would have more time to ransack other homes.

Outside, on the road, the carters and camp followers had arrived. Georg had no use for these women, dirty, coarse and to his eyes, ugly. They caused trouble among the men and were a burden on any march. Still they cooked, and for a small price would do your laundry or polish your belts and boots. Now that he had goods to barter with, he could get these tasks done without parting with any coins. He took a piece of charcoal from his knapsack that he usually used for blackening, marked his sack with his initials and made sure the carter knew it was his.

The street was filled with Hessians carrying chairs, small tables, cabinets, desks, fine wood wainscoting pried from interior walls, bulging sacks of who knew what treasures, and odd knickknacks, here a broken mirror in a gilt frame, there a crib. A woman fled from a house, her woolen black cloak wrapped around her thin body. Two camp followers pursued her, one knocking her to the ground and tearing off her cloak, while the other pulled off her shoes and stockings. The woman tried to go back into the house she had come from, but the Hessian women barred her way. Barefoot and with only a thin frock to protect her from the cold, she staggered down the frozen road sobbing.

Two Hessians emerged from a low shed. One held a pair of flapping chickens in both hands, the other grasped a fat, squealing piglet under his arm. They stood in the street as the woman limped toward them, oblivious of their presence, her head down, her arms crossed in front of her, both for modesty and warmth. The soldiers looked at each other and grinned. The one with the chickens grabbed each of the birds by their heads and swung them around until their necks broke. The other took his short sabre from its sheath and hacked at the piglet's throat. Blood spurted out. The soldier, holding the squirming piglet in front of his groin, directed the red stream toward the woman. Then, handing the still bleeding pig to his companion, he strode forward, grabbed the barefoot woman by the arm and pulled her forcefully back toward the shed. She screamed and he hit her hard across the face, forcing her before him and disappeared into the shed. His companion, carrying the dead chickens and piglet followed.

Georg, aroused by the scene, was tempted to join in. Fortunate for him, he thought, the house he had ransacked had no women inside to delay him. Otherwise, he might have been distracted. There would be time enough for that later, he thought. If he got enough coins, silver and pewter, he could buy some time with an unattached camp follower, or even better, pay for or take a young Rebel woman in Brunswick. The road through town was filled with Hessians some already drunk, while others like him were intent on finding more goods. Camp followers fought over dresses and bolts of cloth, drapes and coverlets, quilts and linen, ripping their prizes apart and dragging them over the frozen ground. Ox-drawn carts laden down with beds, cabinets and pieces of broken furniture, lumbered past the looted buildings. All the homes behind them had been broken into as evidenced by the splintered doors and smashed windows. Boxes and chests, desks, cabinets and armoires, stood in piles in front of many of the buildings, their contents strewn on the street.

Some Hessians had discovered the barns and sheds behind the houses on the road that ran through Brunswick. Several men were pulling a wagon, followed by a drunken soldier who pretended to whip them to move faster. Saddles and harnesses, sides of leather, tanned calf skins, shovels, long and short handled hammers, axes, adzes, chisels, planes, scythes, and other tools formed a pile of loot, almost up to the sides. Georg looked enviously at the leather hides and skins, thinking how useful they would be in repairing his shoes, or making new ones. He would have to barter later for some leather.

The only place there was order was in front of a fine two-story stone house. The Regiment's officers had taken it as their quarters.

Two sentries stood smartly before the closed dark red double doors, the officers dining and loudly carousing within, while their men continued the pillaging unabated outside. Women huddled in broken door frames, frightened and horror-stricken as their household goods, furniture, food and even pots and cooking utensils were taken from them. It was time for Georg to find another house, perhaps one with a store cellar with barrels of salted butter, wheels of cheese, dried fruits and smoked meats, waiting for him. He could taste the food in his mouth. Ducking down a muddy lane between two houses, he saw two camp followers guarding a stove, frying pans and griddles by a side door. They watched Georg with suspicion as he walked past, fearful he would steal some of their loot. A Hessian staggered out of the door, holding a baby's crib loaded with wine bottles. Groaning from exertion, he lifted it on to the iron stove, held one bottle up to Georg in salute and shouted, his speech already slurred, "Rebel good for Hesse man. Yah." Inside, Georg heard a woman scream as he hurried past.

That night, when his Company had finished their huge meal of roast beef, from freshly killed cattle, whole pigs on spits, plump chickens whose fat made the cooking fires hiss as the rich yellow globules dripped into the flames, cheese, bread thickly slavered with butter, all manner of preserves in glass jars sealed with thick circles of beeswax, and had drunk their fill of rum, cider, wine and brandy from bottles shared by all, Georg realized Andreas was missing. His first thought was his friend had been stabbed to death by a treacherous Rebeller, lurking behind some door. No, Andreas would have been found by now, he reasoned. "Has he deserted?" Georg asked himself. "What for?" These miserable people had nothing to offer. The rumors were the desertions from the Rebeller Army were so great, there were less than two thousand of them south of Brunswick. The British had offered protection to those who took a new oath of loyalty to their King.[2] They had issued papers to those who came in and signed the oath. The joke among the Hessian troops was they were lucky they could not read English. If the soldiers wanted to plunder a home, a man waving a paper in their faces would not stop them. They would treat the home-owner roughly but not bayonet him. Just in case he had protection from the Crown.

At reveille the next morning, Andreas still had not returned. The Company fell in for roll call in front of their tents. Sergeant Wochler noted and reported his absence to Lieutenant Reuter who reported it to Captain Seckendorf. The Captain was personally reprimanded by Colonel Von Borck because Andreas was the only man missing from the entire Regiment. Georg had heard of desertions from other companies. They usually occurred before or after a battle when men disappeared and hoped their absence would be attributed to death on the field. The talk among the soldiers was the deserters walked west into the province called Pennsylvania, where they say the people spoke some kind of German, but no one knew for sure.

They spent the day cleaning their uniforms, whitening their cross straps and polishing their brass hats, buttons and buckles and sharpening their bayonets. They told stories of the treasure they had found, the women they had raped, and traded goods they had plundered. Georg gave a camp follower one pewter fork to wash his white linen breeches, blue coat and red waistcoat. He took inventory of the goods he had seized from the day before. He had been lucky in finding valuables hastily hidden in a root cellar while looking for food- a silver watch, several forks and silver tea spoons, five Spanish dollars and assorted brass and silver shoe buckles. He had decided to turn in the linen mattress covers and tablecloths to the Regiment's Payroll Officer and be credited for their value. They would be hard to dispose of and were bothersome to carry. He would keep the rest, including the women's cotton stockings, which he might use to his advantage to exchange for a female favor or two, at the right time.

Georg was sitting on his cot, in his coarse linen overalls, polishing his brass metal cap, noting the threadbare nature of the frayed red pompom at its peak, when Andreas simply pushed back the flaps and came in. He was dirty, unshaven and looked like he had not slept, but his eyes shone with excitement.

"Where have you been?" Georg asked as Christoph and a few other men crowded around.

"Where is your loot, or is it all gold and silver coins hidden in the pouch around your waist," Christoph said, playfully patting Andreas.

"I have better than coins and money," Andreas said pulling off his shoes and rubbing his big toe that protruded through the thin dirty stocking. "I have information. I found a family, hiding in the woods and they spoke enough German for us to communicate. We talked all night."

"You let an opportunity to plunder pass just to talk to some dirty Rebellers?" one of the men said in disbelief. "This river air around Brunswick must have addled your brain." He waved his hand in disgust and moved away having no interest in hearing anything more Andreas had to say. The others, hoping he had booty to trade or share and finding that was not the case, drifted back to their cots to continue their own talk.

Alone with Georg and Christoph, Andreas described how he had found this family fleeing the town, pushing a wheelbarrow of their meager possessions, a few cooking pots and some blankets. The man, afraid he was going to assault his wife and two young boys, begged him in German not to harm them. They had nothing, he said. The man spoke German like the Dutch people they met travelling from Hesse to Dordrecht, Andreas explained. He had asked the family if he could walk with them. At first, they were afraid, but by his gestures and demeanor, Andreas said, he won their trust.

"For what," Georg asked. "For what gain."

"For the information as to how to get land, like the rich farmlands we see around us," Andreas said, beaming, as if he had opened a sack of gold coins in front of the two of them. "Do you know," he said excitedly, "one can clear and work the Province's land and after seven years, it is yours. Or, as this family has done, they bought their land from the landholder, and paid him a pittance for it in return for a promise to give him a portion of their crop each year for five years. They grind their flour at his mill and pay for it with bags of flour. They keep and sell the rest," he exclaimed, throwing up his hands. "With good land, a man can become a rich landholder in a decade. And no one may take his land away."

"We just did," Georg observed brusquely, tiring of his friend's exuberant monologue.

Andreas waved the objection aside. "Of course one cannot plan for war. But if there is no war, the land is yours and your children inherit it. At home our fathers farm small plots of land that are barely sufficient to grow enough food to keep one step ahead of starvation. And we," he said gesturing to the soldiers in the tent, "second and third sons cannot inherit the land and are sent off to war. We are so poor we have no exemptions from the Regimental draft. And after twenty years service, if we live and are not maimed? What will we have? He waved his hands enthusiastically. "Here, there is plenty of land and the only limit is how much you can clear, plow and plant. Now I know why these people fight us so fiercely.

"Pray tell us," Georg replied sarcastically. "Perhaps you can report your findings to General Von Knyphausen himself."

"They are fighting, not because they enjoy prosperity but to preserve their opportunity to acquire it," Andreas explained. "They are fearful the British King will take their land away from them. They are fighting to protect what they have made with their own labor. They. . ."

Georg interrupted him, annoyed by his naïve enthusiasm.

"We are earning our share of plunder and booty. Soon, I will have enough to buy my own farm in Hesse."

"Perhaps you will accumulate enough, say 300 or even 500 Thaler," Andreas conceded. "What good will that do you? You will own a piece of land barely able to support yourself, your wife and children. And your sons, only the oldest will inherit that land when you die. Your other boys, will be like you, a soldier in the army of our Landsgraf, serving in the same Regiment as their father, unable to . . ."

Sergeant Wochler stormed through the open tent flaps and cuffed Andreas with his big meaty hand, knocking him off his cot. He grabbed him by the collar and reaching under his coat, held on to Andreas' belt and quickly frog-marched him outside. They heard the Sergeant's rough curses and promises of severe punishment for his desertion.

That evening, before watch, the Company lined up in ranks, their uniforms clean, their brass caps shining, their muskets at shoulder arms. The Chaplain announced the names of those who had died in the Regimental hospital, one Corporal after having both legs amputated, and two privates, one of wounds, the other of small pox. The Chaplain offered a prayer for their souls.

Sergeant Wochler led Andreas forward and Lieutenant Reuter read the charges against him. The Colonel, recognizing that Private Andreas Felsenheim had voluntarily returned to the Regiment, sentenced him to receive fifteen blows with a broad sword across his back, delivered by Sergeant Wochler.

Andreas is lucky, Georg thought. If it had been up to Captain Seckendorf, Andreas would have been punished much more severely. The Colonel, known to be a strict disciplinarian himself, had subjected others to running the gauntlet of the entire Company, sometimes as many as twenty times. Georg had seen men, toward the end, barely able to stagger down the lines of soldiers armed with cudgels. They were unfit for duty for weeks. Perhaps, the Colonel preferred to have Andreas ready to chase the Rebellers than be in hospital. He watched as his friend was forced to kneel half-naked as Sergeant Wochler hit him repeatedly on his shoulders and spine until the thick red welts broke open and Andreas' blood oozed in wide horizontal stripes against his pale white flesh.

It was after midnight when Georg returned to their tent from sentry duty. He found Andreas lying on his stomach shivering, his back covered with a coarse blanket. Georg went to his chest, took the blue, grey and white bed rug he had looted, and gently placed it on his friend's back. The overlapping pattern was like the scales of a river trout. In the dim candlelight, Andreas, lying beneath it with his arms by his side, looked like a fish swimming upstream on the frothy white foam of his cot. Georg added the rough blanket to further shield his friend from the cold.

Andreas turned his head and smiled. "Think of the land, Georg. How much one could own and leave to our sons to farm forever," he said, before drifting off into a troubled sleep.

—〰—

The British regulars, to their chagrin, found little left to plunder. The Hessians had been thorough, sacking Loyalist and rebel homes alike, driving all from their households without any distinction. For John Stoner, it was no longer as simple as wandering around New York City, having a soldier paint "GR" on a front door, based on the word of a known Loyalist. He sat in the main room of the Brunswick Town Hall, listening to complaints of pillage and destruction from upstanding citizens, claiming to have suffered for their loyalty when the Rebel Committees of Safety had held sway. He preferred this duty. It suited him, to judge a man's demeanor and measure whether he could be made to pay to get his own property back. One Loyalist, agreed to give him sterling for John's help in having a Captain von Muenchhausen, who spoke some English, hear his complaint. The poor fellow, who claimed he had always supported the Crown, was confined to one room with his wife, while his large home was occupied by Hessian Officers, servants and carters. He listened to the situations, involving violation of Loyalist women by Hessians, asking politely for the salacious details which excited him, and then, his voice full of regret and compassion, referred the outraged husband or father to the British High Command.

He did not miss riding with Lieutenant Chatsworth and his Light Dragoons. John had noticed the Lieutenant was a changed person after the rifleman had shot one of his troopers. He lived only for revenge. He talked about it constantly. His mission was to seek out the militia and destroy them. Burn their farms and drive the vermin and their families into the woods where they could live like the animals they were. Armed with General Howe's recent order authorizing the immediate hanging without trial of any armed band firing upon soldiers, he had equipped each of his troopers with a stout rope that they prominently carried across their pommels.[3]

Let him scour the countryside for Rebel militia. John wanted no part of the risk involved. He was stung, however, at how quickly Chatsworth had accepted his excuse of sorting out property in Brunswick as the reason why he could not join them in their scouting forays.

"Perhaps, another occasion," Chatsworth had said, patting him on the back. John had seen the smirks of the other troopers as they mounted and rode southwest out of Brunswick that morning. He consoled himself with the power he exercised over these prosperous Loyalists who, less than a year ago, would not have deigned to even invite him into their kitchens to eat with their servants.

—𝔴—

Peter Bant awoke in the cold darkness, and gathering up his
few possessions, left the American Army camp at Kingston before
dawn. If he was stopped on the road, he would tell the sentries he
had permission to return to Morristown and join another company
that was being formed. He had heard the black-capped soldiers from
Delaware and their officers talking about leaving. They were close
enough to Delaware to be home within the week. The pull was too
strong. If they were abandoning the army, Bant saw no purpose in his
staying.

He had shot the cavalryman in the throat at more than 150
yards. He was sure he had killed at least two Jaegers, picking them off
as they raised their heads in the second story windows of those houses
across the Raritan. With Brouwer dead, and others from Van Allen's
company openly discussing leaving in the face of ten thousand rapidly
approaching British troops, Bant decided it was time for him to go.
He did not think of it as desertion, but more of returning home after
having done his part.

He was not alone, as he discovered when daylight came. There
were small groups of militia, here two or three, then eight or ten,
slogging along the hard frozen roads to the west. His joined up with
a group, carrying his rifle and Brouwer's as well, one in each hand,
the barrels extending out in front of him. The men he met were part
of the Somerset Flying Camp Militia. They had served less than the
four months required, but by the end of December, they said the army
would no longer exist. It made no sense for them to wait for the harsh
winter to set in before returning home. They intended to walk due
west toward Rocky Hill and then on a northerly route skirting the end
of the Watchung Mountains. Bant thought that would bring him close
enough to Bound Brook. He would find his way home from there.

Normally, he was not talkative. However, when he discovered
his companions had not seen any action, he described escorting the
gunpowder wagons from Morristown, his killing the cavalryman and
the rearguard action at the Raritan. Somehow, words slipped from
his mouth. He told them he killed more than the two Jaegers he had

been certain of, and his shot at the mounted trooper was now, in his retelling, just over two hundred yards. The men he was traveling with embellished his original story as they fell in with others. By close to noon, when they were a band of more than twenty, his reputation was of a keen eyed rifleman, who had, almost singlehandedly, halted the Hessian advance across the Raritan. He was the only rifleman in the group. The rest of the militia with their odd assortment of muskets and fowling pieces, old swords and sharpened spikes for bayonets, respected him for the prowess they did not possess.

They were in a cheerful mood and in no hurry when the band stopped before a bend in the road to rest. The men spread out, small clusters sitting in the flattened dead brown grass, rubbing sore feet and chatting amiably about how far they had come and the welcome they expected when they returned home. A few pried some rocks out of the frozen ground and formed them into a circle. Others gathered twigs, bark and dead branches from the nearby stand of elm, sycamore and oak trees. Soon there was a lively fire burning brightly under a battered pot filled with a mixture of ground acorns, hickory nuts and a pinch of real coffee.

The ground was cold and hard. Bant scraped together a few remaining dead leaves which had fallen from the nearby trees, and made a pile under his thin breeches. The leaves, already damp, gave him little comfort. He took a swallow of water from his canteen and laid it down next to the two rifles. He hoped some of the men knew where to find water. His was almost gone. Bant felt the wetness on his butt. If they were going to stay here a while, he might as well be comfortable. He rose and walked several yards off the road to a grove of evergreens and began to gather fallen pine branches.

He heard a shot, the cry of "Cavalry!" cut short by a piercing scream. A troop of near two dozen red-coated riders galloped around the bend. The militia scrambled to their feet and ran in every direction, some down the road, others into the adjacent fields. Bant watched in horror as the mounted troopers slashed the fleeing men with their sabres and began herding the frightened survivors who had surrendered, back toward the road.

For an instant, he thought to run, but knew that would be futile.

Quickly, he climbed one of the cedars. He flattened himself along a thick limb, about twenty five feet up, and peered through the foliage. He was facing the road. He would have been better protected if he had been on the far side of the tree. It was too late to move. He lay frozen in position, the horn handle of his hunting knife digging uncomfortably into his ribs.

Below him, he counted twelve terrified militiamen standing in a circle, surrounded by the troopers with drawn swords, many already stained with blood. "You Rebel scum. By order of General Howe you will be hanged without trial," their officer said. Some of the men sobbed and fell to their knees begging for mercy.

"Please, Your Excellency. We are deserters. We never fired a shot against the Crown," one cried. "There was one man with us, a rifleman. He claimed to have killed cavalry and Hessians. He is the one you want."

Bant flattened himself closer to the tree branch and tried to control his breathing. If they hung the men from the cedar trees, a trooper would look up and he would be seen for certain.

"Who is this man?" the Lieutenant asked eagerly. "Where is he? Point him out to me." The militiamen looked at each other, searching for Bant.

"He is none of us, Your Excellency. Maybe your men already killed him."

"I saw him run into the fields," another offered hopefully, pointing down the road. Several others chimed in with their opinions as to where they had last seen Bant. A few troopers trotted their horses purposefully into the bare fields below the bend. They returned shortly, empty-handed.

The Lieutenant sat grimly on his horse, listening to the desperate babbling of the militiamen, competing to offer information as to Bant's whereabouts. "Silence," he shouted. "Perhaps there never was such a man among you and you think to bargain for your miserable lives with some false story."

"No, no," several of them cried at once. "He was here."

The officer leaned forward on his horse and looked at the men cowering before him. "One of your band fired on my men when we approached. We cut him down where he stood. General Howe's order applies." He looked around and pointed with his sabre to the bare limbed elms close to the road. "There is a good place to show all who come this way, the punishment that awaits those who rebel against their King."

Bant peered through the cedar boughs as the militiamen were prodded by sabre point to the grove of elms where they were forced to their knees. The troopers threw ropes over several low branches and then slipped the nooses over three of the kneeling men's heads. None too gently they stuck them, forcing the men to reluctantly stand up. The three looked uncertain what was going to happen next.

Bant watched horrified as two troopers stepped forward and without hesitating, grabbed the end of the rope dangling from the branch and hoisted one militiaman off the ground. He kicked and frantically clawed with his fingers at the noose tightening around his throat. His face turned red, his eyes bulged until blood oozed from the corners, his tongue protruded from his mouth and his legs moved spasmodically until his body went limp. The two troopers gave the rope an extra tug and let go. The body fell to the hard ground with a sickening thud. One of the men with a noose around his neck, fainted. The other, whimpering, cried out for mercy. Both were quickly hoisted up to their fate, one still unconscious, the other pleading until the rope cut off his words.

The remaining captives were hung in the same manner. Their screams, sobs, pleas and begging to no avail. After the first three, Bant closed his eyes and caught himself mumbling a prayer out loud. He quickly stopped, although there was little chance the troopers could hear him.

After it was all over, one of the troopers stood on his saddle, while another steadied his horse. They tied the ropes of the three men they had hung last tightly to a thick branch. The troopers left their bodies to swing and dragged the corpses of the other nine to the base of the elm.

"What a stench they make," a cavalryman said, waving his hand in front of his nose. The Lieutenant raised his arm in a command and the troop rode off in the direction of Brunswick.

Bant lay perfectly still, clutching the branch as if it were his dearest possession. He was numbed by the horror of what he had witnessed. He began to sob, at first softly and then in deep, gasping breaths. If he had not wandered off to find some pine needles he would have been hung. If he had surrendered, perhaps his death may have saved the others. No, he muttered to himself. The troopers' ruthlessness indicated otherwise. He remained stretched out along the length of the cedar branch for a long time.

As the afternoon sun set he shivered from the cold. Gingerly, he flexed his fingers, his arms and then his feet, loosening his stiff muscles. When feeling returned, he slowly climbed down the tree. Steadying himself for a moment against the soft bark of the cedar trunk, he limped over to the base of the hanging tree. It smelled like a foul latrine. The victims had released their bowels as their life's breath was choked out of them. Bant had no shovel and even if he did, it would take too long to bury twelve men. He knelt away from the tree, beyond the overhanging branch bending from its burden of the hanging dead men, and said a prayer. He struggled to his feet. His knees ached and his calf muscles were cramped from grasping the limb he had clung to.

In the fading light, he stepped over the bodies, deliberately not looking at their faces distorted by the slow agony of being choked. He took out his hunting knife. Laboriously, he carved into the elm tree's trunk- "MURDURD BY BRITISH SOLGERS." It was dark when he finished.

With difficulty on the moonless night, he retraced his steps to where he had been sitting before the cavalry had attacked. He couldn't find his hat. He must have lost it climbing the cedar. It was too dark and he did not want to leave the road to look for it. He picked up a discarded tri-corn near the cooking fire that had long since gone out. A dried goldenrod stuck out from the left side as a makeshift cockade. It fit snug and better around his bristly hair than the slouch hat he had lost.

Bant found the two rifles, his and Brouwer's. Carrying one in each hand, he moved slowly down the road toward Kingston. Even walking at this pace, he thought, he could rejoin his company by midnight.

Chapter 14 - On the Water Once Again

Colonel Glover dismounted and walked with the men of the Marblehead Mariners through the town of Trenton. They went past the stone homes grouped around the large Episcopal church and on to the road descending to the Delaware River and the ferry. The Mariners were tired, having marched with the rest of the Army from Brunswick to Princeton. After staying one night, sleeping on the hard, wide-planked pine wood floor of the College Library, they were ordered to proceed as quickly as possible to Trenton, twelve miles away. They were the first units of the retreating Army to arrive.

The Regiment, reduced in numbers from those who had ferried the Army across the East River and fought in the battles in New York, were now slightly less than three hundred men. They had left Princeton while the frost was still on the fields and reached Trenton by early afternoon. This was the first time they had rested since departing. The men collapsed on the ground, lying on sodden leaves covering the hard ground and awaited orders.

"It is good to see water again, even if tis only a river," Solomon Vining said, laying down his musket and voicing a sentiment all of them felt. He eased his haversack from his shoulders and stretched his long thin legs out before him. He slid his shoes off and rubbed his bleeding feet through the threadbare stockings. "If we were only on a ship, this shoe leather would not wear down. All this marching. Any more of this and we will wear the flesh off our feet down to our bones."

Jeremiah Fisk shielded his eyes from the winter sun shining low through the trees on the far bank. "It is a thousand yards wide, if not more." He continued watching the river. "The current is strong and the depth, at least a few feet higher than the tallest Hessian. What say you Adam?"

Adam Cooper grunted, scanning the Delaware from where he was sitting. "We are not across yet. And how are we and the Army to reach the other side? There are no boats," he said disgustedly. He was in a bad mood and had been since encountering slaves in the households of some of the patriots in Princeton. Most were manservants in the household or scullery maids, doing the hard washing and scouring in the kitchen. He disliked being around them. It reminded him of his parents before they were free. On the march from Princeton he had turned the thought over in his mind- the British, whom he despised, and would fight to his last breath, were offering freedom to slaves if they would desert and join their Army. The Americans offered them nothing but continued slavery. Only a few freedmen, like himself were in the ranks.[1]

There was a shout and the men closest to downriver stood and pointed south. Four long flat bottomed boats, resembling black centipedes, propelled by two banks of rowers, their oars rhythmically dipping in the water like long pairs of legs, appeared around the bend in the river. Two triangular sails billowed from slender masts, fore and aft. Adam and the others stood and watched as one of river craft, the name Camden, clear in red letters on the bow, swiftly approached the ferry dock. It was armed with thirty-two pounders fore and aft, and six guns, elevated above the gunwales, on each side of the deck.[2] Colonel Glover waited on the dock as the first boat took in its sails. The rowers raised their oars and the boat drifted into the pier. Before it was tied up, the Colonel jumped on board, followed by the Regiments' officers.

"What do you make of them?" Solomon asked no one in particular, staring at the three other black-hulled craft holding position mid-river. He propped his back against a tree trunk and resumed massaging his bloody toes and feet.

"If they are that heavily armed, they have the men to man the guns. Maybe they need us to row," Jeremiah said, appraising the vessels standing off from the dock.

Adam shook his head. "We will find out soon enough from the Colonel. I doubt we were ordered to double march to Trenton to relieve these rowers." He took out his canteen and shook it, measuring by the sound, the little remaining watered cider left in the wooden container. "Whatever our orders, I hope they include provision for food and drink."

By the time Colonel Glover and the officers emerged from the deck cabin, three more of the black boats had arrived. Lieutenant Holmes strode toward his company of men and mounted a tree stump. The men fell in loosely. Holmes knew they were tired and saw no need to require them to form ranks.

"These are the galleys of the Pennsylvania Navy, Captain Thomas Houston in command. Their orders, from General Washington, are to scour the eastern shore of the Delaware south of Trenton for any usable craft. North of here, right above the falls, New Jersey militia have hidden several sloops and skiffs. We are to take them in hand and search the Jersey shore as far as Coryell's ferry, a distance of fifteen miles. When found, we are to seize all usable craft and bring them to McConkey's Ferry landing. Anything else that floats is to be destroyed."

The men shifted their feet, some to keep warm, others from uneasiness over the orders.

"I had an aversion to taking of a fisherman's livelihood when we did so at the East River and I loathe it here as well," Jeremiah said to those near him.

"Hold your tongue," Adam hissed. "I like it no better than you. But now it is us and the Army retreating on the road to Trenton with the Redcoats in close pursuit, or the boat owners. There is no choice."

"Our Company is to go north of the Falls," Holmes continued. "The rest of the Regiment will board the galleys and go south. Ours is a two mile march. We must move quickly to find the boats before dark."

The men groaned at the prospect of trudging on the hard rutted road with their worn shoes but the thought of being on the water again, gave them incentive. Instead of taking the wagon road, Holmes followed a guide from the Camden who led them along a narrow, worn trail through the woods, closely paralleling the river. Behind them, the remainder of the Regiment, lined up on the pier in the diminishing light to board the Camden and the other galleys waiting to approach the ferry.

The sixty or so Mariners moved rapidly through the woods, in more of a trot than a walk, toward the sound of the wide rushing waterfall. Within twenty minutes, they stood beyond the rapids of the Lower Falls, looking down on a small inlet. Two thirty- foot river sloops and one long, low skiff were tied up, guarded by several militiamen. Holmes halted the men and sent their guide and three scouts forward to alert the militia to their presence. Once the signal was given, the entire Company broke into a run and milled around on the pier, grinning at the boats, like young boys after church services. Their spirits soared when the militiamen opened barrels containing dried salt fish, biscuits without the usual mealy worms, and a keg of hard cider.

Eagerly, each man grabbed their rations, refilled their canteens and boarded the boats. They cast off and rowed up river, until Lieutenant Holmes found another inlet where they put in for the night. Their exhilaration of being on small craft on the water was tempered by the chill early December wind on the river. They spent the cold night in the woods beyond where they moored the boats on a sandy spit, with only small fires to warm them.

They were up at dawn and by noon, they were past McConkey's ferry and half way the distance to Coryell's landing. They had seized several skiffs, two more river sloops, one a slim, well-made thirty three foot long craft, and several ungainly flat-bottomed river transports. Each time, Holmes assigned a few of the Mariners to row, pole or sail the craft down river to McConkey's. The river transports had required six men to man the poles. By early afternoon, there were less than a dozen Mariners remaining, divided among the original two sloops, and one leaky fishing skiff.

Together, the little flotilla moved slowly upstream, peering into the dense foliage for inlets and streams and scanning the open fields for any sign of farms or cottages. Two inlets appeared promising. Each time, Adam, Solomon and Jeremiah in the leaky skiff rowed ashore, explored the narrow creeks and found nothing. It took time and they were aware that in a few hours, darkness would end their efforts for the day.

A thin wisp of blue smoke above the tree line indicated an isolated farm, although they could not see a building.

"Perhaps it is only troops, theirs or ours, and their cooking fire is what we see," Solomon said.

"No," replied Adam, pointing to a wooden pier and a long green skiff tied to one of the posts. They could make out nets and conical cane fish traps at the far end of the jetty. Adam turned and watched Lieutenant Holmes studying the decrepit dock through his telescope. He snapped it closed and waved for Adam and the others to go ashore.

When they came alongside the pier, Solomon jumped aboard the skiff and found a pair of oars. He was standing up to untie the skiff when they were startled by the sound of a gunshot. Solomon threw himself down banging his head on an oarlock and soaking his stomach in the slimy water in the bottom of the hull. The three of them froze their muskets ready, unsure where the shot had come from. Adam stood up, peering through the trees.

"I do not think it was aimed at us," he whispered. Solomon put his musket down and rubbed his bruised forehead. "I cannot say I heard the whistle of a ball, a sound I am fair familiar with."

Suddenly, there was a woman's scream followed by another shot. Adam jumped from the boat into the shallow water and started for shore.

"Adam. No. Our orders are to take the boats," Jeremiah said.

Adam looked over his shoulder at them. "I will go alone if necessary. Come with me if you will." He took off his tri-corn and waved it to Lieutenant Holmes standing near the prow of the sloop. Then he ran across the clearing at the pier landing and disappeared into the brush. Solomon and Jeremiah followed. They climbed uphill on a well-used narrow path, their wet stocking feet squishing in their worn shoes. The squawking of chickens alerted them they were close. The three Mariners crept forward.

A small wooden house stood in the middle of a clearing. It door hung askew on one hinge. The two windows on either side of the door were covered with opaque thick glass. Smoke swirled from a chimney at one end of the moss-covered cedar-shingled roof. The other end adjoined a low barn. It was more of a shed, with a pine plank door attached by leather straps at the roofline. A dead cow lay in a pool of fresh blood at the corner of the yard with a large chunk of its hindquarter cut off. A few scraggly chickens pecked around the dirt in front of the barn. A low stone wall surrounded the two buildings, with an opening for the path leading toward the house.

Adam, Solomon and Jeremiah ran in a crouch to the stone wall. Inside they could hear men's voices. "They are drunk," Adam said. "Listen." Two or three voices attempted a song and two others were engaged in some sort of argument, angrily shouting at each other. "Unlikely they are the men of this place," Solomon said, after listening carefully. "They may be armed." Adam nodded and the three Mariners made sure their muskets were loaded and primed. They walked quickly across the yard, paused for a moment and then rushed into the room with Adam in the lead.

To the left of the door, against the far wall, seven men sat on benches around a long plank table warming themselves in front of the fireplace. The table was littered with overturned empty cider crocks, pewter mugs, bread and a round of cheese. Slabs of meat, cut from the cow lying in the yard, were roasting on musket ramrods over the fire.

"Who are you dick weasels to barge in on us," one of the men said angrily. "You fancy-pants deserters. We found this place first. Do your God-damned looting somewhere else," he said, mistaking the Mariners for deserters and taking courage there were only three of them. He wore an old dirty grey wool hat on his head, tied down with a yellow strip of cloth. His frayed blue coat, too short to have been his originally, was unbuttoned revealing a greasy hunting shirt. He pointed to the door with his mug, directing them to leave. "Yeah," another chimed in, waving his hunting knife with a piece of cheese on the point. "Move your dirty asses out of here before I carve a new hole for your bloody flux to shit from." He stuck the cheese in his mouth, wiped the blade on his yellow breeches and hissed at them, as if he were shooing geese.

Adam said nothing and looked around the one room, taking in the empty loft above them and the windowless rear wall. A small thin woman in a plain linen dress, her arms protectively around a young girl, who appeared to be no more than ten, stood shivering in the far corner. There was a red bruise on woman's cheek and a thin line of dried blood at the corner of her mouth. A skinny black slave woman, her boney hands clutching the cloth of her apron, was slightly to her left.

"I saw how you looked at the slave woman, you thieving black bastard," the man in the wool cap said to Adam. "She is mine. Now, get out and take the other two pocky scum with you." He rose from the table but was hemmed in by the other men. "Get up and throw their God-damned asses out of here," he ordered.

Adam turned and hit the man sitting immediately in front of him with his musket butt. He caught him on the back of his head before he had even turned around. He swung the stock viciously and hit the next man, just starting to get up, below the left temple, crushing his eye. Solomon had doubled one up with a vicious poke of his musket barrel to the stomach, and brought it up sharply under his chin, knocking out a few teeth. Adam went straight for the leader in the wool cap. He overturned the table, forcing the man back into the fireplace. Wool cap screamed as the hot rods burned through his pants. Adam was on him instantly, pulling him out of the hearth. He lifted him by his throat, banged his head against the stones of the chimney, and tightened his grip on the man's windpipe.

"Adam," Jeremiah shouted. "Enough. It is over." Adam released his hold and the man slumped against the wall, spittle drooling from his mouth. Adam righted the overturned table and benches. Solomon and Jeremiah walked among the deserters taking their knives and tomahawks. "We need some rope," Solomon said to no one in particular. The slave woman opened a Dutch door behind her, ran into the attached barn and returned with a few coils of rope. They tied the men's hands behind their backs. "They have not washed in months, judging by their smell," Solomon said, tying a knot around a man's filthy wrists, none to gently. Jeremiah wrinkled his nose in agreement. "Where are your menfolk," Adam asked the woman.

"They are with the militia somewhere along the river," she said waving her hand vaguely toward the water. "My husband and two sons left three days ago. Then these blaspheming devils arrived," she said, dabbing at her bruised cheek with a wet cloth the slave woman had brought her. "Her man," she said gesturing at the woman with her head, "left as soon as my husband was out of sight and not a moment later. He could not wait to find the British and become free. You will see how free he will be," she said nastily to the slave woman, who bowed her head. "They will make him labor for them, with little food and a chance to get killed. I pray to God my husband or sons find him first and shoot him down. Imagine him leaving me and my poor daughter alone and defenseless for the likes of them." She spat on the floor at the nearest tied up looter.

Adam turned away in disgust and went outside. As soon as he appeared in the doorway, Lieutenant Holmes with three other Mariners, all armed stood up from behind the stone wall.

"I see you are safe and well," Holmes said smiling and coming forward. Adam nodded, thinking about the harsh words the woman they had rescued had said. That woman would rather her former slave be dead than free. He grimaced and controlled his anger. "There are seven deserters tied and bound inside. Most can walk but one or two may need to be carried."

They loaded the two skiffs and transported their prisoners back to the sloop. Whether the deserters became rowers on a galley of the Pennsylvania Navy or were thrown in prison and made an example to the Army, did not matter to Adam. The entire incident had spoiled his joy of being back on the water. He simply wanted to return to Marblehead, where he was recognized and treated as the free man he was. Perhaps he could ship out on a privateer and gain some prize money. "That will have to wait until the entire Army is safely across," he thought.

Thinking of rowing the troops, he realized something was not right. Seizing all of these boats north of the Lower Falls and bringing them to McConkey's landing, would not help the Army cross the

Delaware. Were they taking the craft to deprive the British of being able to pursue them across the river? Or was there some plan to bring the army back north of Trenton? He had no idea. He did know, the Mariners' term of service ended on December 31st. He and the others would soon be going home. That thought cheered him. He sat in the stern as Jeremiah hoisted the sail on the skiff and held the rudder firmly for the Pennsylvania shore.

—✳—

By nine in the morning Will, with Sergeant Merriam next to him on the wagon seat and a squad of men armed with muskets in back, had been to three homes on the edge of Princeton. Their orders were to collect wagons and horses urgently needed for the retreat south. Two farms were already abandoned, the shed doors left open, the few pigs in the yard evidence of the owners' hasty departures. At the third place, a neat, one story house with real glass in the windows and a porch extending the length of the front, a man sat in the dirt yard on a spindle backed chair next to a pile of furniture, a blanket wrapped around his shoulders for warmth. A wooden bed frame stood on its headboard leaning against a wagon with two missing wheels. Desks, a dining room table and a several chairs and benches were arranged in front and in back of the wagon, as if inviting bystanders to come, sit down and view the wagon's lop-sideness. Chests, small ornate side tables and a few copper pots still on the wagon, leaned at a precarious angle against the side boards.

Sergeant Merriam approached the man, who without being asked said brusquely, "The wagon wheels broke. I have sent my son with our horse to a neighbor for fixing."

Merriam looked at the man skeptically. "Both wheels broken at the same time?" He walked around the wagon. "You appear to be a careful man who suitably maintains his material goods." He ran his hand along the well-greased hinge of the rear board.

The man acknowledged the compliment with a proud smile. "I do. That is true. Usually, my wagon is not loaded with this heavy a burden. My wife insisted we leave before the Hessians arrive and we take our possessions with us. She has relatives," he gestured somewhere toward the northwest, "and who knows when it will be safe to return."

"Strange though," Levi Tyler observed, "it is two of the wheels which broke instead of the axle. That is the piece which bears the great weight."

"We are prepared to pay for a wagon and a horse," Merriam said, studying the man.

"Money does not help us escape from the Hessians," the man answered quickly. "If they find us here, they will plunder our possessions and steal the money as well. So I profit nothing by selling you what I need for my own and my family. Besides, my wife is set on leaving." He paused, stood up pulling the brown blanket more closely around his shoulders, and nervously eyed the Sergeant and the armed soldiers. "How much sterling were you prepared to pay?" he asked slyly.

"Sterling is out of the question. We will pay in Continental currency, authorized by the Congress in Philadelphia," Merriam answered.

The man spat on the ground. "My spit is worth more than a Continental," he said contemptuously. "There is nothing here for you. No wagon and no horse. Now be on your way and leave me to my waiting for my son to return."

"It is the likes of you who lift not a finger to help us when we are fighting for your benefit," Merriam said, losing his temper. "I have half a mind to search the woods behind your home where I am certain I will find the rest of your family, your son and horse and two solid wagon wheels."

The blood drained from the man's face but he maintained his bluster. "Search the entire God-damned forest if you wish. In the meantime the King's troops come closer. You and the rest of you sorry excuses for an army had best be on your way before a Hessian bayonet splits your foul gut. And remember this. If my family is here when the Hessians arrive, we will suffer whether we are Whig or Tory." He waved his arms angrily. "Your Godforsaken army has not protected us. You will get no help or thanks from us. God damn you for bringing these plundering rapists to Princeton."[3]

Merriam ordered Will and Levi to search the barn. "Some fodder is all there is," Levi reported. "We will take that for our artillery horses," the Sergeant said, as the men loaded the bundles of hay on the wagon. "Since you have such a low opinion of Continental currency, I will not insult you by offering to pay for it."

After fruitlessly searching several other homes they returned to the artillery camp, with nothing more than the sheaves of hay to show for their morning's work. The same was true for the other squads. The people of Princeton, fearful of the approach of the enemy and well aware the Army was retreating, had taken to the roads in the dark of night, by wagon and on horseback, abandoning their homes.[4] Only those who did not have the means to flee, and nothing to give to the Army, remained.

Shortly after noon, Will rode Big Red slowly down the road, pulling one of the twelve- pounders. Reluctantly they had given up the wagon to carry munitions, the few provisions remaining and whatever else the Army could take with it. He was jammed up against the pommel by Sergeant Merriam bouncing behind him, his arms clasped around Will's chest. The warmth of the Sergeant's body was welcome. It kept the chill wind off his back.

Their Regiment retreated bringing thirty-eight cannons in all. Every artillery horse carried two riders, a few men clung precariously to the tongues of the gun carriages or the side boxes. The rest of the Regiment, like the Army, had to march.

Captain Hamilton's New York Artillery, with a few remaining field pieces, were part of the rear guard. It was said General Washington himself was there, bolstering the morale of the troops.

"The rumor is we will cross the Delaware and make a stand on the western side. Do you think we can hold the British?" Will asked Merriam.

"With the grace of God, we will," he said. He leaned forward until his mouth was close to Will's ear. "I pray for Providence to turn our men's hearts to their duty," he said softly. "If any more desert we will be too few to fortify the shore and hold a line strong enough to withstand our enemies."

Will thought of the men of the Army retreating ahead of them and those bringing up the rear. Some were barefoot, many were sick with coughs or dysentery. Most companies and regiments were well under strength and no new troops had come to bolster them. He knew, following the arrival of Van Allen's company at Brunswick, no others from Morris County had joined their ranks. And once on the Pennsylvania side of the Delaware, the Army was safe only until the river froze and the British and Hessians could cross it. It was still the first week of December. Will had no idea of how harsh the winters were in Jersey and Pennsylvania. Perhaps, they had until mid-January before the Delaware became a bridge of ice. If the Army did not hold on the western shore, the British were a mere day's march away from Philadelphia. Will thought of Brouwer's last word, gasping out the city's name, the glimmer in his sunken eyes simultaneously going out with his breath.

He was shaken from his morose thoughts by a thud, a cry of surprise followed by a loud scream of pain. The artillery train stopped. Sergeant Merriam slid off Big Red, landing inadvertently on his bad ankle, grunted and limped down the road toward the noise. Will stood up in the stirrups. The cold wind penetrated his breeches and froze the sweat to the back of his thighs.

A crowd of men clustered around one of the gun carriages ahead. Big Red pawed the hard dirt, snuffled and stood still, his ears perked forward. After a while, Sergeant Merriam returned and Will dismounted. The Sergeant used Will's knee as a step and launched himself from the stirrup into the saddle. Will hoisted himself behind him and held the reins around his Sergeant's plump body.

"A Private. His name is Jonathan Chambers. I believe from Cambridge. He used to be in Sergeant Otis' gun crew." Merriam twisted his head around toward Will. Will smelled Merriam's stale dry breath. The Sergeant's face was unshaven. Sparse black hairs grew from his ears and his long hair, unwashed for so many weeks, stuck out in uncombed, dirty strands, flecked with grey.

"The poor man fell off the tongue and the wheel rolled over his leg crushing both flesh and bone."

They passed Chambers lying by the side of the road, another soldier bent over him. "They will have to wait for a wagon to carry him on. Hopefully, once we get to the other shore, there will be surgeons and a hospital," Merriam said. Will shivered, both from the wind now on his back, and the thought of the iron studded gun carriage wheel supporting close to one thousand pounds smashing Chambers' leg to a bloody pulp.

"This would not have happened if we had proper wagons for transporting our men and supplies," Merriam said bitterly. "To refuse to help the Army defending one against the hated Hessians is sinful. But to blaspheme and use such scandalous words against the very God who made them, is beyond my comprehension." He began muttering to himself. Will could not tell whether he was praying or recalling the encounter earlier in the day with the farmer and his disabled wagon. Will could sympathize with the man. There were many rumors of Hessians raping women in the towns from New Bridge to Brunswick. The tales were frightening. Neither the elderly, the pregnant nor the very young were safe. Other than fleeing, how could the man have protected his wife and children. He thought it better not to argue with Sergeant Merriam, who was still deep in recollection or prayer.

Once in Trenton, they proceeded west out of town. Bands of weary soldiers, some with remnants of uniforms, others with torn and shredded jackets, some in frayed shirts with only a blanket as an overcoat, lay on the hillside or leaned against trees, asleep or so starved and weak they barely moved. Here and there, groups of gaunt, hollow eyed, bearded men huddled around small fires, cooking whatever meager supplies they had. Most simply had collapsed from fatigue and were waiting to be taken across, like a herd of cows docilely lying in pasture before being led to the shelter of their barn at the end of the day.

At the top of the sloping road toward the ferry landing, Merriam dismounted and the soldiers who had been riding the gun carriage got off. Will pulled hard on the reins and leaned back in the saddle as Big Red strained to slow the twelve-pounder behind him. They cautiously inched down the hard, compacted dirt incline. The horse's muscular haunches bulged as he used his rear legs to restrain the cannon from running over them. At the bottom, the men unhitched the cannon and Will stood up in the stirrups and stretched his back. Three flat-bottomed galleys stood midstream. There was a constant flow of a fleet of mismatched sloops, skiffs, river transports, fishing vessels, rowboats and rafts plying back and forth between the ferry landing on the Trenton side and the pier across the river.

They were taking the troops first, at least on the smaller boats. The artillery would have to wait until the galleys docked at the ferry. Will walked Big Red into a copse of trees, letting the horse wander where he wished. The December ground yielded nothing in the way of grass and Will had no handful of oats to offer him. If the horse couldn't eat, he wouldn't have the strength to pull a cannon. The same was true for the pitiful men Will had seen on the road outside Trenton. Weak from all manner of disease, reeking of filth, unwashed, and barely clothed and starving, how could they fight, he thought. His last good meal had been in Brunswick, three days ago. Since then, it had been nothing but hard biscuits and watered cider. His stomach shrunk as his hunger grew. He knew if he kept busy his mind would not dwell on his empty belly. He led Big Red back toward the ferry road, mindful of the exhausted men strewn around him, seeking any shelter from the chill air and coming darkness.

Lieutenant Hadley was at the landing, supervising the men wrestling the cannons onto a roughly hewn ramp attached to the stern of one of the galleys. His face was thinner and covered with dark stubble, just beginning to form into an unwanted beard. Will unconsciously felt his own chin, rubbing the stubby bristles on his cheeks and chin. He tied Big Red next to the Lieutenant's horse and joined in, putting his shoulder to the carriage wheel, as two of the gun crew heaved on the long handspike. The twelve- pounder rolled slowly up the incline.

"Careful men, do not let it come back on you," Hadley cried. Will thought of Chambers and his crushed leg. It would be better to be dead than to have only one leg to walk on, he thought. The cannon rolled over the lip of the ramp and onto the galley whose stern immediately sank lower in the water.

"Move it along to mid-ships," Hadley shouted. "Balance the load and snug it down tightly. No leeway in the ropes, men. We cannot afford to sink the boat at least until we get to the other shore." Tired as the men were, they chuckled and worked to secure the big cannon.

Hadley crossed the deck to Will. "Stay on this shore for now. Our scouts tell us the British have stopped in Princeton, less than a day's march behind us. Colonel Knox is forming work parties. We will keep the boats going all night. For that we need bonfires to light the way."

Will nodded, anticipating what Hadley would say. "There are a few axes but enough for those experienced and strong enough to work. Find some rope or chains for Big Red to haul the timber. I will mark off where the bonfires can best cast the light for embarkation."

In the gathering darkness, Will and teams of men chopped down the tall pines, maples and oaks. They used small pine boughs and dry, leafless branches as kindling to start the fires. Next, they cut the tops of the trees and laid the tall trunks in triangles to create huge roaring bonfires. The pitch pine branches served as torches in the darkness for the work parties. As the night wore on and it became colder, the hardest part for Will was the time spent hauling the logs from the woods to the bonfires. His body, sweating and warm from the wielding of his axe, froze in the chill night air, as he sat motionless on Big Red. Once he arrived at one of the giant fires, he warmed himself for a brief moment. Then it was back to the woods, the brisk December wind in his face, to get his blood flowing again with the strong, steady rhythm of his strokes, his axe blade sending chips flying as it bit deeply into the trunk.

He guessed it was well after midnight. They had been feeding the fires with trees for several hours. The sparks rose up seeking their starry comrades in the sky above. Will found the crackling of the burning wood comforting. It reminded him of the winters at home, when his mother was alive, with a fire in the hearth and a stew bubbling in the black cast iron pot on the hook over the flames. He licked his lips at the thought of hot food.

Beyond the lines of tired men marching down toward the river, Will recognized Sergeant Merriam watching the flames consume the fresh pyramid of logs. Will moved away from the fire and approached Merriam who seemed mesmerized by the massive bonfire.

"It is a large fire," Will said amiably, proud to have helped fuel it this many hours.

Merriam pointed at the soldiers shuffling by. "Look at those poor souls. They make no sound. These men have no shoes. That man, over there, his uniform is a blanket wrapped around his gaunt flesh. Look closely at them, Will. The light shows their ill kempt hair and beards, their open sores, their bound-up wounds and bloody bandages. They are marching past 'the unquenchable fires of Hell,'" Merriam said, raising his hand as if he were preaching to Lieutenant Hadley's Company on Sunday. He shook his head sorrowfully. "They are the damned, the fearful, the unbelievers, the blasphemers and whoremongers among us. I tell you Will, this is as it will be at the end of the world. 'The Son of man shall cast them into a furnace of fire,'" he shouted. A few soldiers looked at him as they passed slowly by, their faces illuminated by the flames.

"Yea it is written, Matthew 13:40," he yelled at them, waving his arms as if beseeching God above. In the shadows cast by the bonfires, with his hair untied and standing out from his grimy tri-corn, he seemed like a wrathful Old Testament prophet, enraged at the sin and immorality around him.[5]

Will took his Sergeant's arm, fearful he would do something to the poor wretches, who only sought to reach the boats that would carry them to safety and end the misery of their long retreat. He led him away from the road, supporting Merriam on his right side as he limped along.

"We have been on the march since early this morning. I saw you hurt your ankle when you dismounted, when Chambers, . ." Will could not bring himself to describe the crushed leg. "Was injured," he added. "Your ankle must be throbbing. Let me fashion a crutch for you. I have an axe and there are plenty of branches around." He helped Merriam lean against a tree and ease himself down on the ground. Will ran back to the bonfire, selected one of the pine branches in the pile of kindling, lopped it off just above the crotch in the branch, and brought it back to Merriam. The Sergeant sat with his head back, his lips moving in silent prayer. At Will's touch, he struggled to stand. Will measured the length from Merriam's armpit to the ground, trimmed the bottom of the branch and fitted it under his arm. The Sergeant nodded in appreciation.

"I am all right now, lad. I believe I had a spiritual vision. Perhaps, Providence intended for me to see the 'unquenchable lake of fire', so that I will be prepared for what is to come."

Will shivered at his words. He didn't know whether the Sergeant meant they were all going to hell or that Providence intended to favor their rescue and lead them to prevail against the British. He walked with Merriam down to the ferry. Across the impenetrably dark ribbon of the Delaware, he saw equally huge bonfires marking the ferry on the Pennsylvania side, their safe haven.

—⁓—

Bant stood in the small skiff with some of the men of Captain Van Allen's company. They were in jovial mood, eager to cross to the security of the far shore. Bant was furious, seething, barely able to control himself. The Captain had made him surrender Brouwer's rifle. He said some other member of the militia needed the weapon. Who could use it better than him? Bant thought. He could keep both loaded and could kill two British soldiers before the man who got Brouwer's rifle would even aim it.

Van Allen had it in for him. Bant was convinced of it. Because he had shot that Dragoon out of the saddle. Against orders. An order not to kill the enemy made no sense to him. Now, they were retreating across the river. The Company should stay on the New Jersey side, hide in the woods, harass the Redcoats and strike them when they left their camps.

He had not had an hour's peaceful sleep since he rejoining his Company south of Kingston. His dreams were always nightmares, populated by stranger's faces swinging from hangmen's nooses, purpled, with bulging eyes. Asleep, he saw himself with great clarity, clinging to the cedar tree, silent and afraid to reveal his hiding place, saving his own skin and letting twelve innocent men hang. The smell of human shit, which had never before disgusted him, now made him gag as he recalled the released bowels of the hung men of the militia. When he was awake, he thought of nothing but how to kill British soldiers. This time, he would not aim for a clean shot at the head or throat. He wanted every Redcoat to die an agonizing death. He would shoot them in the stomach, well below the heart. He would not give them the blessing of a painless death.

Bant watched their progress toward the bonfires on the Pennsylvania shore. He was oblivious to the cold wind, the wet spray that chilled the other men and their boisterous talk of finding a shed, barn or house to sleep in. He would sleep fitfully tonight. And if Captain Van Allen would not lead the men back across the river, and instead, remain safe and secure in camp, tomorrow he would find some militia leader who would fight, or if necessary, he would steal a rowboat and go by himself. With that plan of action for the morning, he thought he would be able to make it through this night.

Chapter 15 - Death Along the Delaware

Will and his gun crew were in position, directly across the river from Trenton, slightly north of the ferry. Since early morning they had been moving the cannons along the road between their camp and Yardley's ferry, four miles up river, past the Lower Falls. Colonel Knox had concentrated most of the artillery one half a mile on either side of the Trenton Ferry landing, thirty-six guns in all, trained on the opposite bank. Behind them, the Continentals had thrown up barricades of earth and cut trees to form a line of defense if the British should successfully cross. From his hard riding that morning, Will knew there were similar defensive lines at every possible ford, manned by ragged and weary troops, fervently praying the British did not have the boats to cross and assault their positions.

By early afternoon it had become unseasonably warm. On the far shore, the smoldering pyres of the bonfires from the night before served as smoky signal beacons to mark the wide-open field above the sloping road from Trenton toward the water. The river curved north and on his right, Will now saw in the daylight a heavily wooded valley, the trees bare in this first week of December. The last boats ferrying the American rearguard were just passing the midway mark, when green-coated Hessians appeared on the opposite shore. There were a few puffs of smoke as the Jaegers fired at the retreating troops.

Merriam leaned on the twelve-pounder's carriage wheel. He had taken off his blue coat and stood in his soiled waistcoat and shirtsleeves, his paunch protruding over the top of his breeches which were stained with mud and soot, frayed and holed from wear and powder burns. Will looked at him carefully. The Sergeant seemed calm and in control, with none of the look of a mad man overcome by images of Hell, as the night before. Merriam caught Will staring at him.

"I am myself again, lad. It was nothing but fatigue and worry last night which led me to distraction." He pointed to the Hessians on the far shore. "The Jaegers are their advance infantry. The rest of their army is not far behind."

Levi Tyler, standing nearby, held up his hand for silence. They heard the sounds of a military band, drums, fifes and horns, and the high piercing wail of bagpipers. First came the Hessians, the sun, not yet low in the sky behind the Americans, glinting off their brass caps. They were followed by several companies of Redcoats, led by mounted officers. The troops lined up on the open bluff overlooking the ferry. Then, a group of officers followed and took position slightly forward of the infantry in the middle of the formation. Their uniforms were bright red, untouched by the dirt and grime of a campaign.

Lieutenant Hadley studied the officers through his telescope. He smiled broadly. "It is General Howe and his staff. Come to take a look at us, have they, sitting on their fine horses." He snapped the telescope shut.[1]

"Men," he shouted to the three nearest gun crews. "When the order to fire is given, aim for the King's General. Let them know we are free men and not a defeated rabble to be mocked by such an audacious display of contempt for our artillery."

The gun crews sprang into action and loaded the three twelve-pounders. Will wormed the piece and carried the twelve-pound ball to the muzzle. It rolled down the barrel with a deep smooth rumble and settled with a soft thud against the canvas charge.

Colonel Knox rode calmly by behind the gun positions. "Wait for the order to fire." His voice boomed out along the line of artillery.

Merriam stepped up to the touchhole, pricked the charge and inserted the quill. "Primed," he said loudly. "Watch where our ball goes. This is our ranging shot." Will looked across the river at the crowd of mounted officers. If they miss the British General Staff, the ball would plow into the ranks of soldiers. They will leave before we fire, he thought. They will not stay in the open and dare us to shoot.

"Fire," Colonel Knox shouted. "Give fire," Merriam yelled, a slight second afterwards. The cannon roared and Will was enveloped in the familiar smell of gunpowder and a cloud of white smoke, which blew away to his left. He thought the ball was to the right of the clump of officers. Several soldiers fell as the ball struck the ground and bounded through their ranks.

Without an order from Merriam, the gun crew shifted the cannon to the left and the Sergeant stuck a wooden wedge under the breech where it met the carriage. Will quickly wormed the cannon, carefully examining the spiral core after inserting it a second time to make sure it had come out clean. He was aware of the rolling fire of the cannons around him. Between the explosions he heard a collective shout of anger and defiance from the troops who stood on the newly constructed barricades and the occasional high-pitched scream of pain and agony from across the river. He took his position at the front left of the cannon, as Merriam shouted "Give fire." The smoke enveloped the twelve-pounder again as a shout went up from the crew. The ball had struck in front of the Officers, spraying them with clumps of dirt. One of the Officer's went down as his horse crumpled.

"The ball took off the horse's hind leg," Hadley said peering through the telescope. Will shuddered, thinking of Big Red under fire. "The Officer, Hessian I would say by his uniform, appears to be unharmed."

Merriam nodded. "We have the range. Load quickly men," he yelled, urging them on. Will peered across the river. The General and his staff were moving. They rode slowly along the line of their troops, making clear they were not afraid, and had nothing but disdain for the Rebel artillery. The cannons to Will's right opened up a concentrated fire on the staff, aiming for the bright red blotch on the opposite barren shore. The ground was soft and muddy, where the British staff halted. The heavy cannon balls fell in front of them and were entrapped in the muck. They did no damage to the surrounding troops.

—⚉—

Georg listened as their company stood on the field overlooking the Delaware. Andreas was talking openly in rank, which would earn him, and maybe them as well, harsh discipline, meted out by Sergeant Wochler.

"This is madness, foolish bravado," Andreas said. "I am as brave as any man in combat and will follow orders to charge or stand and hold ranks in the face of enemy cannons. But here, we are only targets. We cannot engage the enemy."

"Ssst," Georg hissed. "Be quiet," Christoph added.

"Are we supposed to walk on the river water then to attack the Rebellers?" Andreas asked. He shook his head in anger but remained silent.

Georg knew Andreas was right. They were standing in ranks simply as a show of force. Or as witnesses to the careless courage and honor of the General Staff. Massed together as they were, the Knyphausen Regiment was an easy target. The Rebel cannons were keeping up a steady fire and now the British General with his staff were riding this way. The Rebellers would concentrate their fire on them, and given the distance and their poor aim, the cannon balls were likely to land among the Hessians.

The General and his staff were closer now. Georg could feel the men tense, standing stiffer as if preparing to receive a blow from an unseen source. Lieutenant Reuter moved down the file toward the front. "Steady in the ranks," he commanded. Sergeant Wochler followed staring down the files of men. "Redress your line, there," he shouted at one unfortunate soldier, a half a pace behind.

Dear blessed God, Georg thought, do not let me die like this, standing helpless, unable to fight back. Please do not let me be maimed, he added as an afterthought. I need both my legs. I want to remain whole.

There was a whoosh, followed by agonizing screams. Several men were down on Georg's right, close to the British General and his staff. He saw the Hessian staff officer next to the General, fall from his horse as the animal, thrashed on the ground, neighing loudly in shock and pain. Blood gushed from high on the haunch where the leg had been severed from its body. The officer limped over, opened a saddle-bag, removed a pistol and shot the horse through the eye. The animal lay still. Georg had a vision of the officer approaching the wounded men of his Company, and shooting them as well, as they lay crumpled, their legs taken away by the cannon ball.

"Eyes front," Sergeant Wochler shouted. "Remain in ranks."

"This British General has no concern about Hessian lives," Andreas said loudly. Georg stole a glance at the General, sitting proudly on his white horse. Move on, he thought. I pray dear God, make him move away from us. The General was talking, laughing with an aide who nodded, both men sitting straight in the saddle, as if to present better targets. It is we who are the cannon fodder for you, Georg thought. He was afraid he had said it out loud, his thought was so clear. He must not have. Sergeant Wochler stood at the end of the file without reacting. When Georg looked to his right, the General was riding slowly by. Thank you gracious God, Georg prayed. He felt the men around him relax slightly. He stole a glance at Andreas. His face was grim and angry. Georg knew it was not directed at the Rebellers.

When the cannons began firing, Bant stood on the earthen wall he had helped build earlier that morning. The smoke from the artillery barrage obscured his vision and he moved forward with the intention of seeing what was happening. Across the river and slightly to the right of where he was, he saw mounted Redcoats on fine white horses. They were more than three hundred yards away. That did not matter to him. The hated enemy was in sight. He ran behind the line of cannons, looking for an appropriate place. He found a young maple tree with a low hanging branch. Carefully, he loaded his rifle, placed the barrel in the crook of the tree, steadied himself against the trunk and sighted across the river. He had never fired at such a distant target. Experience had taught him to aim higher because the ball would begin to fall over such a long range. He targeted the portly man in the middle of the troop, sitting upright on his white charger, resplendent even at three hundred plus yards in his bright red tunic covered with gold braid. Bant fired and stared intently across the river. The Officer remained upright on his horse. He had missed.

He took one more shot without any discernible results. As he was reloading, an artillery officer ordered him back to the trenches. "I cannot permit militia to be firing from behind my men," he said, before returning to the gun emplacement. Bant left, not because he was ordered to. It was too great a distance. He would have to get closer. Captain Van Allen had said the Morris County Militia would stay with the army on the Pennsylvania side. Bant had no intention of remaining. There were already rumors of New Jersey Militias harassing the enemy supply lines and foraging parties. Bant would seek out one of those bands.

—◆—

The following day, Sunday, after the Chaplain's sermon, Sergeant Merriam led a special service for those in Knox's Regiment who had died in battle or of their wounds. The latest was Private Chambers. The tourniquet had been unable to stop the bleeding from his crushed leg. Ferrying him across the Delaware had weakened him further and by the time he had reached the hastily erected field hospital on the Pennsylvania shore, he was in a coma. The amputation below the knee was too much of a shock. He had died alone on a straw pallet on the floor of the blacksmith's shed that served as poor shelter for those who had undergone the surgeon's saw. Merriam spoke quietly of God's love for those who suffered and now who suffered no more. There were tears in the men's eyes when he finished. They left the parade ground. Will had been on sentry duty during the night. He was eager to be inside, dry out his uniform and chase away the chill with some hot broth before a roaring fire.

Lieutenant Hadley's company was quartered in a Quaker miller's home and the adjacent mill itself. But for the winter and the war, their surroundings would have been pleasant enough. The miller's house had two large fireplaces, one at each end of a large room in which the family ate, worked and on very cold nights, slept. The miller and his family had been confined to three bedrooms upstairs, and the artillery men slept on the wide planked floor in the main room. The mill itself was a large barn like structure with a huge overshot water wheel powered by the stream which flowed from the hills behind it toward the Delaware.

Inside, huge oak beams supported the massive grinding stones and their carved wooden gears. The grinding and storage rooms served as quarters for both the men and their horses. The light field cannon, which had not been deployed on the banks of the Delaware, were lined up under the broad overhang of the mill's roof. Below the mill, was a small pond, surrounded by brown and withered cat-tails. Its shallow waters had frozen earlier, a harbinger of colder winter weather to come.

Will felt the warmth of the fires as he entered the main room. He smelled the wet wool of uniforms, drying on wooden racks in front of the blaze. There were several small pots of steaming water. Those soldiers who still had their kits, shaved and shared their soap and folding razors with others. Will longed for his chance to use one and shave off his itchy stubble. He had no razor because, until the Army had crossed the Hudson into New Jersey, he had no facial hair. He guessed because of the onset of winter his beard had started to come in. After all he thought, he would be seventeen in a few months. One man, sat on a stool, a copper pot with boiled water at his feet. He had a steel double-sided comb, which he ran through his long strands of hair. He looked curiously at the lice it had caught between its teeth, and then dipped it in the pot of hot water.

Sergeant Merriam was arguing with a plump, prosperous middle-aged man, Will took to be the miller. They faced off in front of the large fireplace. Merriam's ruddy complexion was redder than normal and his high bald forehead reflected the light from the flames.

"My orders are to obtain food for the men quartered here. We are to take no more than we need and pay for what we take," Merriam said angrily.

"And I tell you Sergeant, paying with Continental paper is no payment at all. You will not have a thimbleful of cider nor a crumb of bread until you pay sterling." The miller put his thick gnarled hands on his hips, contemplating Merriam. "I have a family to support and a livelihood to maintain," he added.

Will was astounded when Merriam, who was a peaceful soul, mindful, as he often said, of God's teachings that man must control his angry impulses, stepped forward and grabbed the miller by his shirt.

"These men have marched since April from their homes. They have fought from Brooklyn, up Manhattan Island and down the length of the Jerseys. They have not seen their families and loved ones in eight months. And you cannot spare them food for sustenance?" He released the miller, who looked apprehensively at the cannoneers in his main room.

"Do not talk to me of livelihood. All of us have a trade. I am a tanner. That one there," he said, pointing to Isaiah Chandler, "is a bookbinder. Our Colonel himself is a book seller. We have left our livelihoods to fight the British." He shook his head in disgust, the strands of his unwashed stringy hair, springing about his head like a dirty grey halo. "If I were not a religious man," Merriam said, waving his finger under the miller's nose, "I would order my men to smash your milling stones and destroy your precious livelihood, which blinds you to the hunger of these soldiers." The miller recoiled in horror, concerned the Sergeant was serious. Several of the men moved toward the door, as if to go to the mill.

"Stay," Merriam commanded, holding up his hand, palm facing outward. "For in Deuteronomy it is written 'No man shall take the nether or the upper millstone to pledge, for he taketh a man's life to pledge.'" Some of the artillery men looked confused.

"If he will not sell us food and you say we cannot smash his mill stones, what do we do?" one of the men asked. There were cries of "Let us take his food," "To the cellar," "To the larder," as fists were raised and the terrible din of shouting angry, hungry men filled the room. Will moved closer to Merriam prepared to do whatever the Sergeant asked, unsure whether it would be to restrain the men or plunder the home.

"Stop. All of you." Lieutenant Hadley ordered, slamming the door behind him to keep out the cold air. "Sergeant, what is this commotion about?" His uniform still showed the dirt and wear of the retreat but he was clean-shaven and washed. He took off his tricorn, tucked it under his arm and listened as Merriam explained the situation. Hadley's hair was combed and neatly tied back with a black ribbon. The miller, sensing an ally in Hadley, offered the Lieutenant a warm place near the polished walnut beam mantle. Hadley smiled graciously, removed his great coat and hung it and his hat on a peg.

"And you," he said to the miller smiling. "You are willing to sell us food and drink."

"Yes, sir," the miller responded. "But to purchase, your men must have sterling or Spanish colonials. The Rebel money printed in Philadelphia is of no value, as you must well know."

"Ah," Hadley replied, nodding his head as if he suddenly understood the miller's point. "But you call it Rebel money. It is not, sir. It is Continental currency. Our soldiers' wages." The smile vanished from Hadley's face and his voice became stern. "And where the Continental Army is, Continental money is the coin of the realm."

The miller shook his head to disagree but Hadley grabbed him by the arm. "I want four stout men to take our Tory miller down to the pond and give him a Boston sledding. It will cool his ardor for the Crown and perhaps warm his heart if not his rear, and incline him to sell us the food and drink we need." Several men who were still fully dressed, rushed forward and forced the miller, wearing only a shirt and breeches out into the cold December wind.

Hadley turned and warmed his hands over the fire. "Ah, there you are Will. Come dry yourself in front of the hearth." He looked him over. "You would not recognize yourself if you were standing in front of a mirror. Well, a good washing and brushing, and a shave as well, will certainly do you no harm. And we will have plenty to eat and drink in a short while."

Will looked at him quizzically. "Sir, what is a Boston sledding?"

"Oh, that," he said waving one hand to show it was of no consequence. "The miller will come to no harm, except to his dignity. They pull down his breeches and drag him along the ice on his bottom. Depending on how cold it is and how long he is dragged, it tends to bring one around to your point of view." He chuckled.

When the miller returned, his teeth were chattering and his face was red from the cold wind. He rushed to the fire, shivering as Lieutenant Hadley directed three men to take a candle and descend to the cellar, with orders to bring up what would feed the company that night, and no more. Soon, the long table in the main room was filled with rounds of cheeses, smoked venison and eel, salted shad, beef and cured hams, some good hard bread from the kitchen, a half barrel of salted butter, a crock of honey and several of cider.

"You may tell me miller, what is a fair charge for all of this, and if it is so, I will pay for it with good Continental paper," Hadley said, gesturing to the table as the men hungrily helped themselves.

"I will report this theft and outrage to your commanding officer," the miller replied. "No gentleman will condone such uncivilized behavior." The men hooted and shouted at the miller. Lieutenant Hadley held up his hand to silence them.

"Sir, our Colonel Knox is one of the finest gentlemen to walk on God's earth. He will receive you with courtesy and listen to your complaints with attention and render a fair decision. His headquarters are in the tavern at the ferry landing, well known to you I am sure." He smiled and inclined his head. "If you feel a need for an escort, I will be pleased to go with you." The miller looked suspiciously at Hadley.

"I will go by myself, sir and plead my case to the Colonel."

"As you wish," Hadley said. The miller fled upstairs to dress for his meeting and Hadley took a candle and went down to the cellar. When he returned, he beckoned to Will.

"There are several casks down there marked 'cider royal,' which I think the Colonel may enjoy. Take one of them, and a large ham and ride to headquarters. Present them to the Colonel with our Company's compliments and tell him what has transpired with the miller." He winked at Will conspiratorially. On the return trip, Will passed the miller, riding the short distance to Headquarters, wearing a fine great coat and a plumed hat on his head. Will pulled his tri-corn down over his forehead, to avoid being recognized.

Inside the miller's home, Will found the main room was almost too hot with the blaze of both fires. The men, cleaner, fed, warm and dry were in good spirits. Lieutenant Hadley was regaling them with stories of his encounters with Generals Washington, Greene and Sullivan. The somber mood following the morning's services was gone. The miller's wife and youngest daughter, a girl of around ten and a son of eight years or so, had joined them. Will noticed, those with families among the artillery men, who sorely missed their own children, paid special attention to the two young ones, joking or playing simple games with them. Their good mood seemed to feed on the children's voices and their innocent acceptance of the soldiers.

Just at dark, there was a loud pounding on the door. The men became silent. Two uniformed sentries from the Colonel's Headquarters escorted the miller in. The man looked defeated, so shrunken in his great coat and ridiculous in his white plumed hat, Will actually felt sorry for him. From the few questions the Colonel had asked when Will had delivered the cider and ham, Will knew what the outcome of the interview would be.

"Lieutenant Hadley, sir," one of the sentries called. Hadley stood up. "Yes, Private."

"With the Colonel's compliments sir. This Tory rascal, under threat of being sent to the main guard house, is to sell you provisions for your Company's daily rations, to be paid for in Continental currency." The gunners cheered, causing the sentry to smile. He hurried on, having memorized the message and afraid he would forget it. "You and your men are directed to take no more than needed for your sustenance, to respect this man and his family, and to protect him and his property from all others."

"Tell Colonel Knox his orders have been received and understood," the Lieutenant replied. The much-chastised miller slunk upstairs, followed by his wife and children. Lieutenant Hadley thought it prudent to set sentries at the entrance to the cellar during the night, to secure the victuals and drink, now in their care.[2]

—⁓—

Bant impatiently remained with Captain Van Allen's Company for two days after the artillery barrage. Once he had confirmed the Captain intended to stay in camp at the landing across from Trenton, Bant simply walked away and attached himself to a New Jersey Militia from Hunterdon County, led by Captain Asa Horton. Bant heard they were headed to Coryell's Ferry up river before crossing to the Jersey shore. He marched along the muddy road with the sixty or so men, carrying his long rifle, walking grimly and talking to no one. When they camped for the night, and asked him, he told them he was from Morristown, had been in battle and wanted to do some more fighting. He said no more, convinced his bragging had brought the hangman's noose around the militiamen's necks, as if Bant had placed the ropes himself. He said nothing about the clash with the Dragoons or the action at the Raritan. The men saw the distant look in his eyes, assessed his unfriendly demeanor and decided against any further conversation. Bant responded by moving away from the circles they formed around the fires and curled up at the base of a tree, covering himself with a blanket he had stolen from one of Van Allen's militia. Apprehensively, he closed his eyes, knowing with certainty the visions that would come to him in sleep.

The next morning, before daybreak, Regulars of the Continental Army, rowed the Hunterdon Militia across the Delaware in narrow boats with rags tied around the oarlocks. They decided to avoid the well-used wagon road from the ferry running south toward Trenton. Several of the men came from the area and knew the forest well. Guided by these locals, the militia moved along old Indian and deer trails, keeping to the woods paralleling the river. Occasionally, they caught glimpses of open fields through the stands of trees. After a few miles of marching silently, strung out in single file, they turned away from the river and concealed themselves in dense brush, slightly more than one hundred yards from the road. Bant liked this countryside, thinking it was well suited for an ambush. If it took patience to kill Redcoats, he could wait. Captain Horton had positioned the several riflemen at the edge of the thicket. Behind them, in two lines were the rest of the militiamen, armed with muskets. The ground was cold and hard but Bant did not mind. From the soldiers' talk, he had learned this was the road from Trenton to Pennington and a supply line for the British garrison in the small town to the north. He glanced up at the sky and judged it to be about mid-morning.

The British wagon train came on slowly. Two columns of five Redcoats each, followed by eight baggage wagons and trailed by a small herd of cattle with two civilian drovers keeping them moving along the road. There were another ten soldiers for the rearguard.

"Wait until they are directly opposite us," Captain Horton whispered. "You riflemen, aim for the wagoneers. First line, a volley for the advance guard, second line the rear." Wait for my order."

Bant primed the pan of his rifle and snuggled his body down into the ground until he was comfortable. The other riflemen were all to his right. Bant pointed and held up one finger, signifying he would aim for the first driver. The rifleman next to him nodded and held up two fingers, turned to his right and passed the signal down the line. Bant sighted on the wagon driver. No chance of hitting him in the stomach. He would aim for the temple, slightly below where the tattered, worn plume joined his black cap. The driver slouched, his head leaning slightly forward, his shoulders bent, almost as if he were asleep. The wagon was almost even with him. Bant tightened his finger on the trigger and slowed his breathing.

At the command, he fired, feeling the comforting recoil to his right shoulder slightly after the hiss of the powder igniting in the pan. He saw the driver's head explode in a spray of red, blowing him off the wagon seat. The roar of musket fire sounded in his ears followed by a second volley. Quickly, he rolled over behind a tree and pulled out the long ramrod and began reloading his rifle. There was no need. Not a single Redcoat from the advance guard was standing. The driver of the last wagon dropped the reins and raised his hands. His musket lay unused next to him. The cattle, frightened by the musket fire, scattered on a run into the fields. The drovers stood facing the woods with their hands above their heads. No one paid them any attention. They were unarmed.

Captain Horton led the militia on to the road. Most of the Redcoats were dead, some were mortally wounded and only a few lucky ones had survived with minor injuries. Bant wondered whether they would kill them all and move on. Certainly, they could not take any prisoners with them. He would volunteer to finish them off. It would be fitting to use their own bayonets, he thought.

They stripped the dead and wounded of their muskets, cartridges, bayonets, knives and haversacks. Unfortunately, Bant thought, none of the Redcoats wore boots and their shoes were worse than his own. He unbuttoned a pair of spatter guards from a dead soldier and put them in his haversack. When the heavy snows came, they would at least keep his shins dry.

The Captain sent the eight baggage wagons, together with the captured weapons under light escort to the ferry. To Bant's disappointment, they left the wounded British to fend for themselves and sent the drovers and the remainder of their herd four miles south toward Trenton to deliver the news of the attack on the supply train. They crossed the road and headed northwest toward Pennington.[3]

Over the next few days, Bant won the respect of the men for his skill as a rifleman and his ice-like calm in the frequent skirmishes with the British. He still slept poorly, hearing his boastful words and revisiting over and over his cowardly hiding in the tree as twelve innocent men were hung. He had convinced himself he was to blame for their deaths. Awake or asleep, that thought was embedded in his mind like a cocklebur stuck in a horse's mane. He rose each morning feeling numb, tormented by guilt and apprehensive about the next night's sleep. However poorly he slept, he was eager for the day's ambushes and attacks, hoping that if he killed enough of the enemy, especially Dragoons, he could assuage his guilt. They went out in small bands of a dozen or so men, concealing themselves and waiting for the foraging parties to come out of Pennington, in search of fuel for their fires, fodder for their animals, and food for the troops. Bant would pick off the sergeant or officer in charge, and if the foraging party was small enough, the militia would reveal themselves and fire a volley at the soldiers. They would take the captured weapons and leave the wounded to be carried or stagger back to their camp in Pennington. If the foraging party was too large, they simply melted back into the woods.

One cold morning, they waited in the trees bordering a clearing near a small farmhouse. With their lines to Trenton cut, the British were desperate for supplies. They were attracted to the isolated farms and solitary settlements like wild turkey to overripe corn stalks. Bant waited silently, crouched behind a tree, watching the thin wisp of smoke emerge from the stone chimney. It would be snug in there by the fireplace he thought, rubbing his fingers together to keep them warm. He wondered if British officers wore gloves. A leather pair would serve him well.

The five Redcoats, led by their Sergeant walked arrogantly up the path from the fields, harvested more than a month ago. The men carried their muskets at shoulder arms, having nothing to fear from a lone farmhouse. Bant sighted on the Sergeant's white straps where they crossed his chest just below his ribcage. When he could, he would inflict a stomach wound. He fired and the Sergeant threw up his hands and fell backward. The militiamen behind him fired one volley and it was over. Six Redcoats lay, twisted in death or moaning in agony in the clearing in front of the pine planked house.

As they came out of the woods, a gaunt man, his face covered by a scraggly beard emerged from the door, his hands held up in surrender. A woman stood fearfully behind him, a thin shawl around her shoulders, peering at the soldiers on the ground. She put her hands to her mouth and her eyes showed her horror, as Bant and another bayoneted the wounded.

"No harm will come to you from us," one of the militia said. "If we may come inside for a moment to warm ourselves, and if you could spare us some bread and maybe salted meat or cheese, we will be on our way."

The man nodded. He was much older than his wife, but both were ragged and aged beyond their years by their hard life. The men warmed themselves by the fire, while the woman brought out a slab of cheese and some hard bread.

"If the Redcoats had entered, they would have taken everything you have. They would not have left you a morsel to eat. Cannot you not spare some meat for us?" one of the men asked. The farmer nodded to his wife and she silently walked to a rough hewn trap door, pulled it open with a grunt and disappeared below the floor. She emerged with a small ham, its reddish flesh blackened on the outside from smoking, with patches of pig bristles poking up like unwanted weeds. She handed it to her husband who offered it to one of the men.

As they left, the husband called out to them, "What will I do with the soldiers? If they are found here, they will kill me and burn my farm down."

"You will have to bury them in the woods," one of the men shouted back over his shoulder.

Bant thought to himself, if the British sent out patrols to find and bury their dead, it presented another opportunity for an ambush. He would suggest that to Captain Horton when they rejoined the main body farther south in a few days.

—〰—

The men of the Knyphausen Regiment in Trenton, welcomed the mid December hard frost. It meant the onset of winter, the freezing of the Delaware and a quick one day march to Philadelphia and decent winter quarters. Even their Colonel had been heard to describe Trenton as a "shitty place."[4]

Georg's Company occupied the top room of a three story stone U shaped barracks, built more than two decades ago. It was said to have been for troops in some war against the savage Indians. It appeared the buildings had long been unoccupied and neglected. The mortar had become brittle and turned into a chalky powder, which coated the wood floor. The wind blew through the large cracks between the stones and stirred up the fine particles of mortar until the men thought it was as natural to breathe dust as air. The one window on each floor, leaked so much cold, they might as well have been open.

Their only comfort had been the arrival, from Princeton, of their baggage train with their kits and cots, blankets and cooking pots. Even that was accompanied by the news the train had been attacked by the cowardly Rebellers hiding in the forest, and two soldiers from another Regiment had been killed outright and a few more wounded. The men felt more insecure knowing their supply route was vulnerable.

As cold as it was inside, going out on patrol and standing sentry duty was worse. It was frigid, a numbing, piercing, unrelenting cold which caused the men to shiver uncontrollably. It turned their lips blue and caused their teeth to chatter. Frost clung to their mustaches and eyelashes. The thin layer of hard pellets of snow, glistening on the ground like thousands of tiny pearls, worked their way into every shoe seam and froze a soldier's toes and feet within the first thirty minutes of a two-hour watch. The skin on their fingers split and their knuckles became raw. They endured this day after day, night after night, as the Colonel kept them in a constant state of high alert.

Georg, Christoph, Andreas, along with the other men from their patrol, huddled near the small fireplace in the picket house on the Pennington Road. Trenton lay less than a mile behind them. They had just returned, shortly after four in the morning, from two hours of standing sentry, one hundred and fifty yards beyond the picket house. There were fifteen soldiers and Sergeant Wochler in the house and fifteen more including a Corporal, currently on picket duty. The watches were two hours on, two hours off. It was all they could take of the cold at night and remain vigilant.

After feeling had returned to their hands and feet, Andreas announced he had to piss and signaled for Georg and Christoph to follow him outside. They moved away from the stone house and dropped their breeches. Their urine steamed as it melted through the light snow, leaving a yellow stained hole at the base of a tall pine.

"I tell you," Andreas whispered, "we are not going to Philadelphia. This is where we will stay all winter. Even if the Delaware freezes down to its river bed. I heard it from a friend in the Von Lossberg Regiment who escorted the baggage train from Princeton." Georg and Christoph moved closer, to hear him better. "Remember the British General who drew the cannon fire which killed some of our men." The two friends nodded. "He has retired to New York City for the winter. They say he has a mistress there, no doubt to keep him warm at night.[5] Most of the British troops are with him. We are out here on our own until spring. We are the front line while the British stay in comfort in the rear."

Georg considered what Andreas had said. Ever since the pompous General in his brilliant uniform, adorned with gold braid and ruffled lace, had pranced on his fine white charger along the banks of the Delaware, unconcerned that his presence drew artillery fire down on the Hessian regiment, he had come to understand the British would treat them as expendable. Georg recognized he was exhausted and probably not thinking clearly. He was worn down by the constant alarms, the cold, the lack of sleep, the meager rations and intermittent supplies. He thought of the British General, headquartered in New York with its substantial buildings, and plentiful supplies from the Loyalist farms on Staten Island and Brooklyn. He recalled the warm summer day when he and Christoph had walked the ramparts of the hastily abandoned Rebeller fort and he had foolishly thought they would be home by Christmas.

Andreas was right. They would spend the winter in Trenton. The events of the past week or so confirmed what he said. No British troops had come to reinforce them, although they had been under constant harassing attack by the Rebellers. Several small outposts had been overrun, the Hessians outnumbered by militia who emerged from the woods in the early dawn. Some men of the Regiment had been taken prisoner. The size of patrols had been increased, which meant the men got less and less rest. They were being ground down by their constant duties. Six nights ago, there had been a raid on the Jaeger position at the Trenton landing. The entire Regiment had been ordered to sleep with their weapons at the ready every night since.

Two days after that raid, in a dawn march only as far as the small ferry four miles beyond Trenton, they had come under harassing fire and lost eight or nine men. Yesterday, they had been called out before sunrise to haul their field cannons down to the Trenton ferry. There were rumors of a Rebeller landing. By sunrise, no such force was evident but before they could return to Trenton, artillery from the opposite shore opened up and inflicted further casualties on the massed troops.

No, he thought bitterly, they would spend their Christmas on the front line in Trenton, this shitty little town, expendable to the British and easy targets for the Americans. Sighing, Georg realized how much he longed for a peaceful night, to sleep from dark until dawn, in a warm bed.

"What do you propose we do?" he asked Andreas, not believing he had even asked the question.

"The only action we can take to save ourselves is to desert or surrender. These Rebellers are assigning Hessian prisoners to work on farms. In the province of Pennsylvania," he offered, as if it were an earthly paradise. "When the war is over, we can stay and have our own land." Andreas' eyes burned brightly at the thought.

Christoph looked to Georg for guidance. Georg shook his head. "I cannot desert," he said. "Nor surrender. It is a matter of honor. And I fear for the consequences to my parents." He nervously looked back at the small stone house. "We must go back inside. We need to store up warmth before we stand picket again."

"Nonsense," Andreas hissed, as they followed the slushy path toward the light. "If we leave during a skirmish or battle, we will be listed as killed or missing. No one will know whether or not we died in some nameless place of wounds we sustained."

Inside the picket house, Georg shared a stool close to the fire with another soldier. They warmed their wet feet through the worn thin leather of their leaky shoes. He yearned to take the wretched shoes off, and gaiters and stockings as well, and feel the heat directly on his blistered, dirt caked feet. It was against orders. Soldiers on picket duty, whether on or off watch, were to be battle ready. Always.

Georg ignored Sergeant Wochler's studied look. Around him, soldiers talked softly as they clustered near the fire, conserving their energy and sharing their dwindling supplies of pipe tobacco. Georg leaned forward with his head in his hands. He inhaled the tobacco smoke around him. Desertion from a battlefield was not possible. They moved in ranks, advanced, charged and maneuvered as a unit. The only time they had retreated was on that narrow road on Manhattan Island, and even then it had been orderly and by Company. How could he desert while on sentry duty? He was as likely to be shot in the back by his comrades as in the front by skulking Rebellers. No, Georg thought. To desert, even if he desired to, could not be done. Nor did he see how they could be defeated by these rabble of soldiers. Troops of the Von Knyphausen Regiment would not be captured or compelled to surrender to these cowardly farmers who lacked the courage to meet them on an open battlefield.

A few isolated shots rang out, followed by two volleys of musket fire. Their Sergeant's command to arms was not necessary. The Hessians grabbed their muskets and dashed out of the picket house. The sky had just begun to lighten behind them.

They raced toward their fifteen comrades at the sentry post. Georg found himself shouting as he ran and others took up the cry "we are coming," to encourage the men less than one hundred yards ahead. There was another volley of musket fire and stabs of flame from the tree line. The silence of the predawn was broken by the screams of wounded soldiers. Once they reached the post, which was nothing more than a clearing, sheltered by tall evergreens, Sergeant Wochler formed all of the able bodied men into ranks between the sentry post and the woods. Bayonets lowered, the twenty-one men charged across the snowy field, the thin crust crunching beneath their feet. They halted at the tree line.

—⁂—

Bant lay behind a fallen log, fifty yards into the woods. Two other riflemen were similarly positioned. Behind them, the militia had retreated. There were less than a dozen of them. Their plan had been to overrun the picket post and then wait for the few remaining Hessians to emerge from the picket house. They had miscalculated, thinking that those on sentry duty represented almost the entire Hessian force. The riflemen had picked off the Corporal and a few others, the militia had fired a volley, reloaded and were preparing to charge when the other Hessians arrived. Now, confronted with more troops, the militia retreated into the darkness of the woods.

It was not over yet, however, Bant thought. He and the other riflemen could take down one or two more. At this range, with the sky becoming lighter behind the Hessians, it would be an easy shot. The rifleman next to him signaled he would target the one who seemed to be in command. Bant shrugged. It made no difference to him which Hessian he shot. To him, they were all the enemy now. He only cared about his targets if he had a choice of killing a Dragoon or another soldier. For him, he would choose a red-coated cavalry man every time.

He picked out a Hessian in the front rank, two in from the one in command. He sighted down from the high brass cap, noting the red pompom on top. He could shoot the pompom off at this distance, as a warning. He wanted to kill him, not give the soldier a close call to talk about with his comrades in the barracks. He moved the barrel down until he found the crossed straps, more of a drab grey than a bright white. This man has been on campaign for some time, he thought. The Hessian held his rifle with the long bayonet at the end, just above his stomach, his right hand holding the stock slightly over his hip. Bant settled on a spot below where the straps crossed, and to the right of the musket stock. He did not want to waste his shot destroying the Hessian's musket. He steadied himself and squeezed the trigger. The man crumpled and collapsed on the ground. He saw the soldier next to him drop to his knees to help. The one in command turned toward the two men as the side of his head exploded in a dark red mist.

—⁓—

Georg cushioned Andreas' head in his lap as Christoph ran back to the picket house for blankets. Using their muskets as carrying poles, Georg and Christoph fashioned a stretcher from a blanket. Andreas moaned softly as they rolled him on to it and screamed when they lifted him up. The men, leaderless but disciplined, covered the retreat of their comrades carrying the dead and wounded. Once inside the picket house, they built up the fire and lay the wounded men close to it. Two soldiers volunteered to dash back to Trenton for reinforcements and a wagon while others established a perimeter around the stone building.

Andreas lay quietly on the blanket. Beads of sweat dripped from his forehead. His face was pale. Georg unbuttoned his friend's coat and pulled up his shirt. It was already soaked red. Blood pulsing feebly from the wound in his stomach. Christoph detached his bayonet, cut strips from a blanket and handed them to Georg. The two of them turned Andreas to bind his wound. Blood covered their hands. There was a dark stain on the back of Andreas' coat that had seeped into the blanket. Georg eased the strips under Andreas' side and felt small pieces of something hard on the stretcher around Andreas' lower back. Bone fragments he thought. They created compresses from a wad of shirt linen another soldier handed them and wrapped the wound, front and back with broad strips of cloth. Andreas moaned and opened his eyes. He grasped Georg's hand in both of his and pulled himself up slightly.

"Promise me," he whispered. Georg and Christoph knelt closer to Andreas. "Promise me you will not die. . ." Andreas tried to say more. The effort was too much and he sank back on the stretcher. His lips continued to move, mouthing words they could not hear.

A horse neighed outside the picket house. The Surgeon's Assistant and several other soldiers from their Company opened the door, letting in an icy blast of cold air. The flames in the fireplace blew and danced from the wind. Georg instinctively shielded Andreas from the gusts of cold air.

"Load the wounded on the first wagon," the Assistant ordered. "And be quick about it, They cannot long stand the cold in their condition."

There were seven wounded men in the room. Georg and Christoph waited until some of the soldiers had been carried outside, and then lifted Andreas, keeping him as long as possible near the warm fire. Without asking for permission, the two climbed on to the wagon and huddled protectively over Andreas, each one holding one of his hands. He lay there, his pale face glistening with sweat, his teeth chattering and his lips turning blue. Georg took off his coat and laid it on top of the blanket, tucking it under Andreas' chin. Georg looked at the other wounded. A man next to him, blood oozing from the bandage on his shattered shoulder, lost consciousness and fell against Georg. Georg, without his coat, welcomed the warmth from the man's body and tucked his arm around the soldier's waist to keep him close and upright.

In Trenton, Andreas recovered consciousness as they unloaded his stretcher. Candle light from the hospital shone from the windows and the open doorway. It was a former warehouse for storing goods brought up river from the south, and for grain and fish from above the Lower Falls to be shipped south.

"Do not die like me for nothing," he rasped. "Do what I said," he nodded, as two orderlies took the handles of the stretcher. "Do it," he repeated and his head fell back on the blanket. They waited outside in the cold as daylight came, until the orderly brought them their muskets. Christoph's stock was stained with Andreas' blood.

When Georg and Christoph returned to the barracks, they discovered they and the rest of the men of the picket line had been given barracks duty for the remainder of the day. Georg tumbled on to his cot and slept until noon, wrapped in two blankets, his own and the one he took from Andreas' cot. In the early afternoon, they were ordered to clean their uniforms and weapons. The men did it in an easy and relaxed manner in the absence of Sergeant Wochler. He had been the one to mete out punishments and his death was not mourned by those who had been on the receiving end.

The entire Company lined up on the drill grounds surrounded by their U shaped barracks. At least, Georg thought, it shielded them from the winds. Once dismissed, Georg intended to return to the hospital down near the river and see Andreas.

They stood to attention under the drab, grey sky, as Major Heckmann and Captain Seckendorf sat on their horses, staring over the Hessian's high brass capped hats at the barracks wall behind them. Lieutenant Reuter stood before the Major, saluted, turned to face the men and took a piece of paper from his tunic.

"By Order of Colonel Von Borck, the following promotions have been made." He read off a list of names. There was a stirring behind Georg when the Major announced one of the Corporals had been promoted to Sergeant. Then - "Private Georg Friedrich Engelhard to Corporal, effective immediately."

Georg heard Andreas' whispered voice as if he were standing next to him. "This promotion will only make you a target for Rebeller riflemen. Commit some petty offense and be broken down to Private again." He nodded in assent and did not notice the Regimental Chaplain approach the Major. The Chaplain stepped forward.

"We will hold services for our fallen brethren tomorrow morning at 9 a.m. The following soldiers have gone to their just reward with their Maker." Please dear God, Georg thought, let it not be Andreas.

The Chaplain read solemnly, intoning the rank, name and cause of death.

"Sergeant Karl Wochler, killed in action." The Chaplain read the names of the other nine men, killed that morning at the sentry post. God be blessed, Georg thought. Andreas is alive and in hospital.

"Private Mathias Gebhardt, died in the field hospital of illness," the Chaplain intoned.

"Private Karl Grub, died in the field hospital of wounds."

Georg strained and watched the Chaplain's finger moving down the piece of paper. He was almost to the bottom. Andreas lives, Georg sighed in relief.

"Private Andreas Felsenheim, died in the field hospital of wounds."

He looked at the solemn ranks of soldiers arrayed in front of him, and then up at the darkening sky. "May the Lord have mercy on all their souls."

Georg and Christoph sat on their cots, for once oblivious to the cold. "We should ask to be part of the burial detail," Georg said. Christoph nodded. "If they let us. We are down to so few able bodied soldiers, they have been using local people or their servants."

"They must let us," Georg said firmly. "Or they can make me a Private again for insubordination. I heard Andreas tell me he does not want me to be Corporal."

Christoph looked at Georg peculiarly. "He told you that?" he asked, his voice rising in disbelief.

"He whispered to me after the Major announced my promotion," Georg insisted. "Maybe he was no longer alive at the time, but I heard him," he asserted vehemently, challenging Christoph to disagree.

The two friends left the barracks, and in the gathering dusk, walked through the bleak courtyard and down the street toward the hospital. It was three days till Christmas, Georg thought. Andreas was dead. It would be a grim holiday, bad enough having constant sentry duty and being harassed by the damn Rebellers, but worse now without Andreas. Maybe he should desert. No, he thought. To whom? To those ragged, ill disciplined militia who killed Andreas and ran away? There was no honor in that. These Rebellers would not meet them on a battlefield. There would be no opportunity to be defeated and honorably surrender. He would fight on. They would cross the Delaware and capture Philadelphia. Then the war would be over and he could go home.

Chapter 16 - On the Pennsylvania Shore

Two days before Christmas, in the waning light of the December afternoon, Lieutenant Holmes pointed the boat toward the landing at Malta Island, above McConkey's ferry. His shoulders, despite being well used to rowing, ached from the constant turning of the thirty-foot long sweep to steer the flat-bottomed Durham boat through the strong river current. He stood on the black as pitch platform at the tapered stern, the sweep hooked into a vertical curved wooden lock, slightly hunched over to get more weight into each push against the water.[1] He thought the rest of the crew would be tired as well. Four of them manned eighteen-foot long oars, while two others, Adam, stocky and powerful, and Solomon, tall and long limbed, stood on the walking boards. They moved along the boat's forty-foot length, poling it out of the current and toward the shore.

It had been his idea to take the boat out on the river, pushing off from the Pennsylvania shore about an hour ago, to get the feel of it, the poles, the oars, the sweep and the current. The six Mariners had come willingly, eager to be on the water. They had poled and rowed upstream, staying close to the land, before swinging out into the middle of the river, catching the current and then putting in toward shore. They repeated the exercise, getting used to the long iron-tipped poles, the narrowness of the walking boards and the shallow draft. He was amazed they could come as close to shore with less than six inches of water under the keel. That would change when the boat was fully loaded, whenever that would be.

As Holmes steered the Durham, the rest of the crew stopped rowing and Adam and Solomon put their shoulders against the poles slanted out in front of the bow and slowed the boat down. They glided slowly into the inlet, hidden once again from prying eyes across on the Jersey shore, and tied the boat to a tree stump protruding from the mud. There were almost thirty of the black, shallow drafted river cargo boats, resting like sleek eels along the shore.

Adam grinned as he rolled his shoulders and dug his fingers into his tired muscles. He flexed his thick neck, turning his head from side to side.

"Why are you so happy," Solomon asked. "That pole has worn a groove in my collar bone."

"I am pleased someone has seen fit to acquire these boats. We know there is nothing left that floats on the Jersey side."

Solomon looked at him puzzled.

"These came from Pennsylvania's shores," Adam said.

"I do not catch your meaning," Solomon said, shaking his head in confusion.

"Lieutenant. What say you?"

The other men stared at Nat, waiting for him to respond to Adam's question. Holmes smiled.

"I think what Private Cooper suggests is these Durham boats will be used to transport troops, and perhaps artillery. I am not privy to any battle plans," he added hastily. "However, if the intention is to withdraw to defend Philadelphia we can walk there in a day. The enemy," he said, gesturing east through the trees, "is across the river on the Jersey shore."

"So, Solomon. You see why I am exuberant. In the near future I believe we will be attacking not retreating." Adam clapped his hands together, making a loud noise. "After all our marching and being chased by the British nipping at our heels like nasty terriers, we are preparing to strike back."

"I only hope it is after Christmas," Solomon replied. "It would be pleasant to be close to a warm hearth with a full belly, at least on that day."

—⟋⟍—

Farther down river, a few miles below McConkey's Ferry, Will sweated from the heat of the blacksmith's forge. The smith had been shoeing the artillery horses with cleats for most of the day. Lieutenant Hadley had given Will the task of checking the cleats and the blacksmith's work before the shoes were nailed to the horses' hooves. "We cannot afford any thrown shoes or lame horses," he had said. Standing in the warmth of the smith's workshop, Will mulled this over in his mind. He found it peculiar. There were plenty of blacksmiths between here and Philadelphia and time to make cleats with winter coming on.

The following morning, when the smith completed his shoeing of the Regiment's last horse, something stranger happened. A Lieutenant from an infantry regiment, together with a squad of four soldiers, invalided but still capable of handling their muskets, placed the blacksmith under house arrest. He was forbidden to leave his home or shop or meet with people, by order of General Sullivan. When the smith protested, the Lieutenant merely told him it was a temporary measure for his own safety. They escorted the irate man to his solid stone home and took up quarters inside to ensure the orders were obeyed.

Will returned to their temporary quarters in the miller's home. The sky was dark for early afternoon, blanketed with foreboding deep grey clouds. The men, crowded around the two large fireplaces, enjoying the warmth of the room, good naturedly shouted at him to quickly close the door and keep out the frigid December wind. He pulled up a stool, removed his worn boots and pointed his stocking feet toward the flames.

Isiah Chandler, barefoot came over and they shared the small seat.

"Here is the latest from Philadelphia," Chandler said, handing Will a copy of The Pennsylvania Journal. It was dated December 19th, five days ago. "Tis by old 'Common Sense', himself." Will glanced at the newspaper, saw the title, "The American Crisis," and read the first two lines. The words mesmerized him: "These are the times that try men's souls. The summer soldier and the sunshine patriot will, in this crisis shrink from the service of his country; but he that stands it NOW, deserves the love and thanks of man and woman."[2]

Chandler wiggled his first three toes sticking out from his right stocking. The fabric was so thin it could have been a layer of his own skin. "While this writing may be good for our souls, it would have been better for our bodies if the good citizens of Philadelphia had sent us new stockings and stouter shoes and boots." He looked down at his protruding toes, caked in black dirt and dried blood.

"And more blankets," another man added. There were shouts for cooking pots, tents, cots, great coats, scarves, all the items the men had either lost during the long retreat through the Jerseys, or now had need of as winter made their lives more miserable.

Will tried to read on through the commotion.

"Here now men," Lieutenant Hadley called from the mantle at the far fireplace. Will had not noticed him before.

"Philadelphia has sent us the essentials to do our duty. We have more gunpowder and grape shot. Tampions to cover the muzzles and touchhole covers to keep our cannons dry." He brushed his long curly hair back from his temples. "Enjoy the fires now. You will be given three days rations. We are to leave shortly." He waited for the hubbub caused by his announcement to die down. "We go north. The Colonel has instructed me to tell you we are carrying the fight to the enemy."

The men cheered loudly. The news created a sense of purpose among them and lifted the long months of retreat off their shoulders. Will looked around at his comrades talking excitedly among themselves. They were eager to strike back.

Levi Tyler joined them at the fireplace and held his gaiters out to warm them before putting them on over his worn black shoes.

"Well," he said to Chandler and Will, but loud enough for others to hear, "as old 'Common Sense' said, we know the summer soldier and the sunshine patriot. We have seen enough of them marching off and leaving us to do the fighting. I suppose now is the time to earn that love and thanks of every man and woman he is talking about." He paused and winked. "Especially the women." Several men laughed. Sergeant Merriam grimaced, his face red from the effort to control himself. Or maybe it was just the heat from the roaring fireplace, Will thought.

Late in the afternoon, with the side boxes fully loaded with shot and the wagons carrying barrels of powder and charges, they formed up and rode north toward McConkey's Ferry. It was an easy pull for Big Red. They brought with them only light field cannon, three, four and six pounders. Close front line support for infantry, Will thought, not the heavy guns for long range artillery duels.[3] They were going to attack the enemy across the Delaware. He looked at the threatening dark clouds to the north. He hoped the weather would hold. He did not relish crossing the river in a storm.

Chapter 17- A Stormy Crossing

The large jagged chunk of floating ice, half as long as the boat, struck the Durham's black hull just ahead of where Adam was standing. The vessel shuddered from the impact. Adam lost his footing on the sleet-covered walkway and lurched forward toward the ice-clogged Delaware. Quickly jabbing his long iron-tipped pole into another floe, he regained his balance. The wind was in his face, coming from the Jersey shore, driving the mixture of sleet, hail and snow in blinding sheets. He barely could see one-eyed Titus, less than eight feet away, on the walkway parallel to him across the open hold. The other four Marblehead Mariners were manning poles behind him, two on each side.

Adam looked down at the Continentals nearest to him. They were more than forty of them, standing in ranks in the hold, their heads and shoulders above the gunnels which partially blocked the cold, wind whipped spray. After boarding, they had instinctively turned away from the wind and now all faced the stern. The newly issued blankets on their backs were coated white, as if the snowy mantles were part of their uniforms. They huddled together, ankle deep in water, hunched over against the lashing sleet.

Two days ago the river had been frozen, although not enough to bear the weight of cannons and horses. Now, because of yesterday's thaw, it was an angry swollen torrent of fast moving water and sharp pointed ice floes, hefty enough to stove in the hulls of the shallow draft fifty-foot long Durhams. The Mariners had switched from oars to the eighteen-foot poles after the first crossing. The oars were useless for the dangerous eight-hundred foot wide river passage. They either scraped across the ice, or when submerged in the water, they became trapped under the floes.

They were approaching below the landing point. The soldiers already on shore had lit bonfires, more for warmth than as signals. Adam shouted above the storm and noise of the crashing ice.

"Lieutenant. More to port. Over there." He pointed with his arm.

Nat Holmes, nodded and yelled something in reply, his words lost in the wind. Adam felt the Durham shift as the Lieutenant leaned into the long sweep steering oar. The bow was now in line with the bonfires and Adam could make out the figures of men standing close to the flames. Holmes brought the Durham around and the soldiers eagerly clambered over the gunnels, slipping and sliding on the craggy blocks of ice that formed a frozen barrier between the boat and the shore.

Adam watched them holding their muskets across their chests, one hand on the flintlock, as they disappeared into the woods. He doubted whether a single soldier had dry powder or flint. He hoped it would be different for the Mariners. They had wrapped their muskets, powder and cartridge boxes in stout waterproof canvas. The guns were still on the Pennsylvania side, stored inside a shed attached to the stone house at the ferry, together with their haversacks. By God, Adam thought, if they were going to attack the Hessians in Trenton, he wanted to go into battle with dry powder.

They poled the empty boat back across the ice-choked Delaware. Holmes positioned more of the Mariners on the starboard side walkway to fend off the cakes of ice moving rapidly downstream. They passed a few Durhams heading in the opposite direction and a wide, flat-bottomed ferry, carrying officers and their horses. Empty, the Durham had a two-foot draft and they beached it just below McKonkey's Ferry, where the ice had been cleared away. This was his fifth round trip. After marching the eight miles from camp to the ferry, the Mariners had been on the water for more than four hours. Most of the troops were across as was some of the artillery.

The storm increased in ferocity. It was still blowing from the northeast, the wind and driving mixture of sleet and hail doing their best to douse the pitch pine torches, guiding the troops to the shoreline. Colonel Knox stood on the slope above the ferry landing, his cape collar pulled high up on the back of his neck. In the swirling sleet, Adam thought he resembled a giant oak tree. His deep stentorian voice roared out instructions to the officers of the embarking troops.

"Massachusetts Continentals. Third Regiment. Divide by companies and move to the empty Durhams. Hurry lads, we do not want to keep the Hessians waiting."

"They will be damn sorry they came to New Jersey," someone yelled from the ranks. "We cannot swim, Colonel. But get us across safely and we will have at them," another cried. The shouts of others were carried away by the gusting wind.

The Colonel recognized Lieutenant Holmes as their Durham struck the shore.

"Holmes," he shouted over the noise of the storm and the crashing ice in the river. "Hold your boat for the cannons." He turned and waved to his right. "Captain Bauman! Load your three-pounders and men on this Durham. Step quickly now."

The men from the New York Artillery Company rolled their three guns down the slope. Adam and the other Mariners held the Durham steady with their poles. The New Yorkers hoisted the three pounders onto the walkway using lever bars through the gun carriage wheels while others lifted from the carriage or barrel. They clambered along the gunnels to lower the guns down into the open hold. There was a piercing scream of pain followed by a stream of curses. One of the artillery men's fingers had been crushed by the barrel against the edge of the gunnel. The injured man shook his head vehemently, tucked his hand under his armpit and refused to leave the boat.

Jeremiah Fisk, his bushy eyebrows coated with frozen sleet, jumped down into the hold and, together with Adam, secured the three cannons with ropes, tying them fast to the now useless oar locks. The sixty-two men of the Artillery Company, quickly gave up the attempt to stand in ranks as ordered. Instead, they crowded around their guns, the lucky ones sitting on the carriages and the sleet slick barrels, preferring the freezing cold on their thighs to the slushy water in the hold. Adam moved along the walkway and pushed off with his pole into the ice choked Delaware.[1]

—༄༅—

Will stood in the woods on the Jersey side with the rest of the Massachusetts Company of Artillery. His pockets were stuffed with hard biscuits and three days cooked rations of salted beef. He had forty cartridges in the box slung over his shoulder and a dry flint tucked inside the second shirt he wore under his blue coat. His canteen was filled with diluted rum. After it was gone he would drink snow water.

The gun crews clustered around the artillery horses for protection from the biting wind, the dropping temperature and the increasing intensity of the storm. Will leaned into Big Red, using him as a shield and feeling the large horse's warmth through the thick matted winter coat. He smiled at Isaiah Chandler who had wrapped his bare hands in Big Red's mane.

"Tis the next best thing to gloves," he said, catching Will's eye. Will nodded. He liked the older man. He shivered, thinking of the big fire in the miller's home they had left on the Pennsylvania shore. His thoughts drifted to other warm rooms and the pleasure of the enveloping, comforting heat, the bright orange-yellow flames casting an hospitable glow and promise of good food and companionship. He shook his head to shake the snow from his tri-corn and immediately regretted it as the flakes fell from the hat, down behind the collar of his uniform and seeped from his neck on to his back.

"I wish I had some of the leather from my tannery," Sergeant Merriam said, standing behind Chandler. The sleet clung to the wisps of his stringy hair. In the dim light cast by the lantern he held, it gave him a ghostly appearance. "I am no boot maker but I can use a leather awl well enough to make thick soles for all of us."

"Maybe when we capture Trenton and defeat the Hessians, we will find some good boots," Corporal Levi Tyler said. "Mine are worn through and I am willing to pull a decent pair off the feet of some dead Hessian, if the opportunity presents." He unwrapped the narrow ratty plain wool scarf under his tri-corn, put his hands over his large ears, red from the bitter cold, and shifted from one foot to the other. "Those brass hats the Hessians wear. Those, I do not want any part of. They do not look as if they serve the purpose. Take the heat of the sun in the summer and bake your brains and do nothing to keep out the cold in the winter."

Will stomped his feet, thinking if his toes were any colder they would break off. His boots, adequately soled when given to him by Colonel Knox in Westfield almost a year ago, were so thin from the long dismal retreat through the Jerseys, he felt every thing underfoot from the tiniest pebble to the smallest branch. Isaiah Chandler had been right. The good people of Philadelphia would have helped the soldiers more if they had sent warm woolen stockings instead of broadsheets of Mr. Paine's "The American Crisis." After reading it, Will had stuffed his copy in his stockings and in his boots. It made no difference. His toes were so numb he was unsure they were still there.

Sergeant Merriam and Chandler left the shelter of Big Red and once more inspected the gun carriage hitch and the six-pounder. Merriam held the lantern close to the breech and then the muzzle. The cannon was still attached by traces to Big Red. Since they had no idea when they would move out, Merriam thought it best to be at the ready. When the two men returned, Will took the horses reins and walked him a few steps. The six-pounder rolled forward slightly, breaking the crust of ice that had formed around the wheels. Frozen droplets of ice shimmered like tiny stars on the brass cannon, reflecting the small flame from the lantern.

The lantern brought back memories of his brother John at the Rising Sun Inn. He had last seen John lying on the barn floor, unconscious but breathing. Adam had hit him with a pistol butt. Will wondered if John was still with the British Dragoons. According to rumors, Trenton was occupied by the Hessians. British troops were further north, in Princeton and Brunswick. Still, Will thought, the Dragoons ranged wide. It was possible he would meet John in battle before the day was over.

"The seals are holding," Chandler stamping his feet forcefully.

"What seals?" Will asked puzzled, still thinking about John and how much he looked like their father.

"All bookbinders know how to make glue, Will" Merriam said. "And Chandler's bindery in Boston was one of the best."

Isaiah smiled at the compliment. "It is a skill I have. Nothing more," he said. "I collected the trimmings from the horses' hooves at the blacksmith's. Boiled them at the barracks before this march." He paused, seeming to remember the warmth of the barracks' fireplace. "I added charcoal which you would never do for book binding of course. But it makes a good enough paste to keep the tampions and touch hole covers in place. We do not want sleet or snow in the barrel before we meet the Hessians, now do we?"

"It must be soon now," Tyler said, gesturing toward the woods and the bonfires. "It appears to me we have as many here as were on the other side before we crossed."

It was true, Will thought. He looked at the nearby bonfire. Troops were crowded around so densely, seeking the welcome warmth in the storm, Will could barely see the flames. The soldiers had pulled down what little fencing and posts they found and built large bonfires to keep warm. They turned their bodies one way and then another, one side barely warm from the heat from the fire, the other bearing the brunt of the strong winds which whipped snow and sleet against them.

Above them on the slope, a horse whinnied, answered by another. Big Red pricked up his ears but remained silent. A New York artillery unit was up ahead. Will could not see them in the forest. When they had disembarked he recognized the uniforms of Captain Hamilton's company. The New Yorkers had two brass six-pounders, like Will's company. The newly arrived soldiers of the Philadelphia Associators, not yet tested in battle, were further into the woods, with their two pair of four-pounders. Will guessed most if not all the artillery was across.

This time, he thought, we will be assaulting the enemy's fixed position. Instead of retreating. Along with the others, he was eager to march on Trenton and attack. Pay the British and the Hessians for chasing the starving, weary army down the length of New Jersey, threatening them at every moment, forced to flee before their overwhelming numbers. He thought of the good patriots and their families in the towns they had passed through and abandoned to the hated Hessians who looted and preyed on these defenseless people.

What did it matter if the Hessians, having slept snug and warm inside their barracks, emerge with powder dry and have at them. The cannons' powder will be dry too and Will knew they had enough grape canister to mow the Hessians down.

Will watched the dark shapes of the latest group of soldiers disembark on the stony shore, form into ranks and march up the slope past the artillery. He could barely make out the black-hulled Durham moving back into the river. After what seemed to him an interminable wait, he heard voices above the sound of the cracking ice and two Durham's returned. The boats came almost to the shoreline and the soldiers on board, lifted cannons over the sides and pulled them across the jumbled broken ice floes and up the frozen slope. The Mariners on the Durhams stowed their poles and tied the boats to trees and boulders. They strode up the slope, haversacks on their backs, muskets on their shoulders. This was it, he thought. The Mariners were here. No more ferrying. He wondered where his friends Nat, Adam, Solomon and Jeremiah were and whether his cannon would be in support of their part of the attack.

"Men, gather over here," Lieutenant Hadley called, waving a lantern to attract their attention. Will joined the less than seventy five men of his artillery company in front of their three artillery pieces. Their commander, Captain Lieutenant Winthrop Sargent sat erect on his horse, his tri-corn pulled tightly down over his head, his shoulders hunched against the wind driven sleet behind him. He cupped his hands in front of his thin, straight line of a mouth, shouting to be heard over the howling wind.

"Our orders are simple. Follow your officers at all times. Be silent on the march, move briskly and no stragglers." He paused and Will thought he was done. The Captain had a reputation of being a man of few words.

"There are other companies in Colonel Knox's Artillery Regiment but we are the only one from Massachusetts." The men strained to hear him, their heads up despite the strong wind, sleet and snow.

"Make the Colonel proud. Colonel Knox intends to have all our pieces up front with our troops. Be the first to get in position, the first to reload and fire, and the foremost unit that clears the streets of the Hessians. Do your duty as I know you will." He turned his horse, leaving it to Lieutenant Hadley and the other three officers to have the men form up.[2]

Will mounted Big Red and pulled the six-pounder up the slope. A soldier ran past with three lit torches and stuck one into a metal ring on each of the gun carriages. Will in the lead, followed Lieutenant Hadley as his company took its position in front of a dark mass of soldiers. Now he understood what Captain Sargent had meant by follow your officers. The Captain, Lieutenant Hadley and the other officers had a piece of white paper attached to the back of their tricorns. It was barely visible in the darkness but when they attacked at dawn, the men would see it.[3]

Will felt the hard sting of hail as the column turned northeast on to a narrow path through a thick forest. The tall trees moaned and bent in the ferocious wind as the column marched into the teeth of the storm. Sheets of snow, occasionally mixed with sleet and hail struck his face and exposed hands. The road, slippery and slick led uphill from the river. It was frozen hard and coated with a thin crusty layer of snow and ice that crunched and cracked under the weight of the horse and gun carriage. At least it made the marching for the soldiers following somewhat easier, Will thought.

Big Red maintained his footing, pulling the six-pounder on its heavy oak carriage and the side boxes loaded with powder and grape shot. Will was grateful the artillery horses had been shod with cleats. The spiked shoes gave the horses a better grip.

The troops emerged from the woods on to a wide level road that headed southeast. The wind was now blowing from behind them. Will wished for a scarf or cape as the icy sleet fell on his shoulders, soaking through the wool, freezing his back and buttocks. He didn't know whether it was better to be sitting up on Big Red, motionless and freezing, or marching on foot, warmer from the exertion, but with frozen feet and aching limbs. Will sensed the soldiers had picked up the pace, thankful to be out of the woods with the howling gusts at their backs. They marched silently but vigorously and with purpose. They were going to attack, Will told himself. For the first time since crossing the Hudson and entering New Jersey they were carrying the battle to the enemy. It will not be long now, he thought.

The quickened pace lasted only for about a mile. Ahead, Will saw a dark mass of troops standing motionless along the road. The soldiers stood in place, stomping their feet and facing forward away from the wind. He pulled back on the reins and Big Red halted. Impatiently, Will peered ahead into the darkness.

Lieutenant Hadley rode toward them. "Bring the cannons forward," he shouted over the noise of the storm, waving his arm. "Move quickly. There is a steep ravine ahead. Unharness the carriages from the horse. We will lower the guns down one side and pull them up the other."

Will urged Big Red on, stopping at the edge of a precipitous decline. His would be the first cannon to be hauled across. It was one hundred feet down to the snow- covered bottom and an equal height up the far side. Through the sleet he saw Colonel Knox ride up with Colonel Glover and the two confer with Captain Sargent. The men of the Marblehead Mariners, easily distinguished by their short blue jackets and canvas breeches, came running back down road from the vanguard

"Men of my company. Break out your drag ropes," Knox bellowed. "Remove the side boxes. Lighten the carriages." He gestured to some of the troops standing on the sides of the road. "You men. Carry the side boxes down and across the ravine. Mariners man the ropes. Gun crews use your levers."

There was a flurry of activity. Will dismounted, tethered Big Red to a tree and fumbled with his frozen fingers to undo the harness.

"Lieutenant Hadley," Colonel Knox shouted. "Ride back down the line and bring up all the artillery. We will move them across this ravine together."

Quickly, the Mariners tied the drag-lines to the six-pounder and knotted the other end to a stout tree near the top of the ravine. Soldiers and Mariners rushed forward until there were more than one hundred men holding on to the frozen ropes, straining to lower the heavy cannon without it getting away from them. Will grabbed a long iron lever bar and slid part way down the steep slope, feeling the wet snow soak his feet and breeches. He thrust the bar between the spokes of the carriage wheels to slow its descent. Isaiah grabbed the bar with him. Levi and Baldwin held on to the bar through the other wheel. With the four of them restraining the cannon's forward motion by the lever bar and the men holding on to the ropes, they inched the gun down, the sleet swirling around them, the skin on their hands cracked and bleeding. Once they reached the ravine floor, the tension in the rope slackened and the troops holding on let go and raced pell-mell, sliding and slipping until the mass of men surrounded the cannon now resting on level ground.

It was darker and the storm was worse at the bottom. The sides of the gully funneled the wind into howling gusts and whipped the snow along the shallow creek into their faces. The creek water rushed over smooth round stones, calf deep in some places and icy cold. Will slipped, fell on one knee and gasped as the frozen water soaked his thigh. He struggled with Chandler and the others to turn the cannon around so that the muzzle pointed back the way they had descended and the thickest and heaviest part of the gun was facing the ravine wall they had to scale.

A few of the Mariners scrambled up the far side, pulling the drag-lines with them and fastened them to trees at the top. Some of them slid midway down and secured ropes on trees and stumps as well. At the bottom, Holmes and Adam crawled under the carriage and made sure the two drag-lines were still securely tied to the cannon's axle.

With the six-pounder in position, Holmes ordered troops up the slope to the midway point. There the men turned to face down toward the creek. They grabbed on to the ropes and strained to pull the cannon up over hidden rocks and snow covered shrubs. Will grabbed the lever. This time he used it as a brake to prevent the cannon from sliding back down on to them. Soldiers jostled each other to get a hand on the cannon or carriage. Some grabbed on to the studded wheels bare handed. Others leaned their shoulders against the depressed muzzle or parts of the gun carriage. Silently, except for the grunting sounds the men made straining against the weight and the occasional oath, they inched the heavy gun up the steep slope. They paused to catch their breath at the midway point while the men on the top of the ravine took in the ropes' slack.

More troops moved steadily past them, climbing up the steep incline, some staggering as they lugged the heavy side boxes, others carrying the wormer and sponge poles, water buckets and lanterns for the cannons.

The last part was the steepest and most treacherous. The snow had been tamped down by the feet of the men who manned the ropes. However, there were more men on the level top with better footing than those on the ice slick slope below. Will felt the strength of many hands pulling on the ropes and an easing of the weight on the lever bar. The cannon rolled over the snowy lip the ravine and the men collapsed on the frozen wet ground. The troops who had helped bring the first cannon across, were ordered to form up and march ahead away from the ravine.

The Company's two other cannons remained on the far side. Together with the Mariners, Will slid back down the ravine and scrambled up the other side. This time, helped by troops from different units, they brought the other two cannons across. It went faster because they were more familiar with the terrain and knew which trees were stout enough to anchor the drag-lines.

After they pushed the third cannon over the top of the south lip of the ravine, Will collapsed on the ground, panting from the effort and exhausted by the cold and lack of food. He rolled over, feeling the icy slush seep through his breeches at the knees. The wind whipped along the plateau, lashing him with a blast of sleet. Nat offered him a hand up.

"Well, Will," Nat said. "Not as bad as bringing the cannons through the Berkshires last December. Worse though in that we have a battle to fight at the end of this march."

Will nodded. It was bad enough, he thought. His palms were raw in places where the skin had been torn off, frozen to the iron lever pole. He pressed his blood streaked hands into his armpits to warm them momentarily and vowed to himself he would load grape shot and charges no matter how bloody and frozen his hands were.

"Nat," he said, as they both turned away from the wind. "I hope it is a straight march from now on to Trenton. If I do not see you before, . . ." He left the sentence unfinished. Nat reached out and grabbed him by the shoulders.

"Remember when I told you on the road south from Albany I felt Providence had plans for you? We have not come so far together as to fail. I will see you after we take Trenton from these Hessians."

Will grabbed his friend by the shoulder one more time before rejoining Sergeant Merriam and the gun crew. Quickly, they reattached the side boxes and stored the poles and levers. The troops formed up and moved ahead down the road. With their three six-pounders on the south side, the horses back in harness and the torches relit, Captain Sargent ordered the Company forward, the storm still at their back.

Mounting Big Red, Will turned to say goodbye to Nat and Adam. The Mariners stood at the edge of the ravine. They would stay to bring across the Army's remaining artillery. He yelled and waved but his friends did not hear him. Will wondered how long it would take for the rest of the Army to catch up, and how much further they had to march to reach Trenton.

Their brief progress was quickly halted and the word was passed back down the line. There was another ravine ahead. When Will approached the edge he saw it was steeper but not as wide. Once again, the horses were unharnessed, the guns unlimbered, the drag ropes brought forward and the side boxes detached. Troops of different companies grimly held the ropes as the gun crews slowed the descent and then wrestled the cannons up the opposite side.[4]

"Hurry men. Get those horses back in harness and fasten the side boxes down," Lieutenant Hadley shouted. He saw Will already remounted on Big Red.

"Will take the lead. Ride forward until you find Captain Sargent. He is in the vanguard of General Mercer's brigade. Position with the other cannons behind our Captain." He waved Will forward. "The rest of you," he said addressed the gun crews on foot. "Keep moving and watch out for each other. No falling asleep. It will mean the death of you."

Will urged Big Red on to the frozen road that climbed through a sparse forest before leveling off. The wind whipped across wide-open fields and pelted him with alternating sheets of snow, sleet and hail. The marching column parted to let the cannons through, the men closing in behind the guns, slogging determinedly forward, silent and hunched over as if bent by the force of the ferocious wind at their backs. He rode for what seemed like forever, his hands frozen to the reins, his inner thighs chaffed and raw. His neck and shoulders ached from the labor at the two ravines. His entire body was cold, wet and stiff. He almost dozed off, lulled by the movement of Big Red and an overwhelming sense of tiredness, when he realized the column had stopped. He sat up in the saddle wondering where they were and how much further they had to go. He thought he could discern, in the uniform grey sky, a faint light in the east. Weren't they supposed to be at Trenton at dawn?

The soldiers around him collapsed, exhausted on the snow covered ground. Will, tired as he was, knew these men were more so, having marched the entire distance that Will had ridden. Eight miles up on the Pennsylvania side and half way to Trenton in the storm.

They were ordered to rest, eat and drink and be ready to move on. Will stayed in the saddle. He chewed a few pieces of cold cooked beef and a biscuit and discovered he had lost his canteen. Probably back in one of the two ravines. No matter, he thought. He wasn't thirsty anyway. There was snow enough to drink should he decide to dismount. He let go of the reins. Big Red dipped his head to the ground and pawed the snow, looking for forage. Will looked down and in the breaking light of dawn saw dark patches in the snow. They were bloody splotches, some in the road, others on the sides where the soldiers were. Puzzled, he traced a line of bloody spots to a group of soldiers huddled against some trees. The poor fellows had scraps of leather bound by rags around their feet. Some were barefoot and their bleeding feet left trails where they had walked, their cut soles and battered toes alternately freezing and bleeding anew. Their uniforms torn and ragged were not mismatched. These were Continentals, Will reminded himself, not unreliable militia.

Will heard horses on the road behind him. He turned in the saddle. Through the wind driven sleet he saw a group of officers, led by General Washington, riding toward him. Colonel Knox was among them. They passed around the three cannons. The soldiers stood up silently and lined the road as the General rode by. He stopped his horse and in a slow deep voice commanded them to keep by their officers during the battle, and then disappeared into the swirling sleet down the road.[5]

Colonel Knox, easily distinguishable by his impressive bulk rode back, accompanied by Captain Sergeant and Lieutenant Hadley. He stopped his horse in front of the cannons.

"Men," he bellowed into the wind. "We are four miles away from Trenton. We will hit the Hessians with the storm at our backs and with a righteous fury that will drive them before us. The watchword is Victory or Death. Victory for us and Death for them. Press on. Press on to Trenton. "

Lieutenant Hadley ordered all lanterns and torches extinguished. They weren't necessary anyway in the dim light of dawn. The troops in the Regiments ahead of them veered left and took a road east past a little hamlet, consisting of a few homes, their grey stones barely visible through the sheets of sleet. As the road widened, with the wind almost directly behind them, the soldiers began to move faster, taking long steady strides, their muskets on their shoulders, one hand covering the flintlocks.

Will kept Big Red in position behind his Regiment's officers who were riding ahead of the three cannons. He hoped there would be no more obstacles. The sky was a dull grey blanket and the sleet had turned to thick flakes of snow. They would be attacking after dawn. Even so, with the wind blowing strongly, the Hessian pickets would have a difficult time seeing them before the army swept out of the storm and were upon them. Will tightened his fingers on the reins. His feeling of drowsiness was gone. He was excited. He knew his place in the gun crew. His duties with the powder charges and grape shot were routine now. He had performed them under fire before. Chandler had been right. You are always afraid but you do your duty. This time they were attacking. No different he thought, with respect to his own fear in battle. But now, when the Hessians ran from them, it would be they who were afraid of surrender, death and defeat. Of being imprisoned, stripped of their dignity and possessions, like the Americans captured at Fort Washington.

Will thought of the marching soldiers following the cannons, leaving their blood stained footprints in the snow. The march through this storm was different than any other he had been on. He could sense a different spirit. Maybe it was a sense of revenge, of striking back. Maybe the men had been inspired by Tom Paine's words. Maybe it was just a desire to get at the enemy. The troops increased their pace, moving at a slow trot, knowing they had covered almost all of the four miles to Trenton. A few scattered musket shots rang out ahead of them. The men surged around the cannons and broke into a run.

End Notes

Part One - Battle for Brooklyn

Chapter 1- Hanging of a Tory

1) Once the British troops landed, Loyalists in New York City planned to capture George Washington and other senior officers and bribe American soldiers to defect. The plot was financed by the Royal Governor, William Tryon, who had been driven out of the city and was aboard the Duchess of Gordon, a British ship of the line in New York Harbor. New York's Tory Mayor, David Matthews, testified after the War, before a Royal Commission in London, "I formed a plan for the taking of Mr. Washington and his Guard prisoners but which was not effected."

Thomas Hickey, a Sergeant in Washington's Life Guards, was the only one of the eleven or twelve conspirators arrested who was court martialed and hung. It is unclear how Hickey, an Irishman and deserter from the British Army several years before, ended up in the Life Guards. According to the record of the court martial, Hickey testified:

"[He] engaged in the scheme for the sake of cheating the Tories, and getting some money from them, and afterwards consented to have his name sent on board the man-of-war, [to Governor Tryon on the Duchess of Gordon] in order that, if the enemy [the British] should arrive and defeat the army here, and he should be taken prisoner, he might be safe."

Also implicated in the plot, were a drummer, a fifer and two Privates in the Life Guards, David Matthews, the Mayor of New York and Gilbert Forbes, a gunsmith and owner of The Sign of the Sportsman. Forbes was alleged to have done most of the recruiting at three New York City taverns, Corbies Tavern, Lowrie's Tavern and The Sign of the Highlander. The other conspirators were briefly imprisoned in Connecticut but it appears they were never tried.

Hickey was tried and convicted on June 26th and hung before a cheering crowd of 20,000 people at 11 am on June 28th. He was the first American soldier to be executed in the Continental Army. He refused a priest, claiming that all clergy were "cutthroats."

General Washington issued an order for all troops, not on duty, to attend the hanging. Apparently fearful of widespread desertions or defections, Washington wrote John Hancock, President of the Continental Congress,

"I am hopeful this example will produce many salutary consequences, and deter others from entering into like traitorous practices."

The arrest of the conspirators and Hickey's court martial gave rise to many rumors. The most prevalent at the time was the plan's goal was to assassinate General Washington and other senior Officers who regularly dined with the Commander in Chief. The story was Hickey planned to add poison to a dish of peas to be served to Washington. This attempt was foiled by the General's housekeeper who threw the peas out the window into the yard where they were eaten by chickens who promptly died. Nothing in the records of the trial or in contemporaneous accounts supports the tale of the poisoned peas and the dead chickens. However, there were many Loyalists in New York City and the threat of them supporting a British invasion was real. The uncovering of the plot and Hickey's hanging resulted in increased anti-Tory activity by patriots in Long Island.

For further reading on Thomas Hickey and the plot against George Washington, see: "Tories-Fighting for the King in America's First Civil War," by Thomas B. Allen, pp. 163-165; "1776," by

David McCullough, pp. 132-133; "The Scoundrel Who Saved The Continental Army," by Donald N. Moran, A Brief History of the Commander-in-Chief Guards with Roster, by Donald N. Moran, www.revolutionarywararchives.com; "226 Years Ago: Irishman Thomas Hickey Executed for Plotting Against Washington, Irish Echo, March 27-April 2, 2002 edition,www.Irisheco.com.

In April 1776, after the American Army arrived but prior to exposure of the Hickey plot, anti-Tory mobs rampaged through New York City, destroying property and tarring and feathering suspected Tories and sympathizers. General Israel Putnam imposed martial law, causing one resident to write:

"We all live here like nuns shut up in a nunnery, with curfews, passwords and sentry posts." (Schecter, "The Battle for New York," p. 88.)

2) Lucy Knox, together with Catherine Greene and Martha Washington were all in New York City before the arrival of the British fleet. Throughout the War, Lucy Knox and Martha Washington traveled to and stayed with their husbands when the Army was in permanent camp. In 1776 Lucy was only twenty years old, had been married two years and had an infant daughter. (Roberts,"Founding Mothers-The Women Who Raised Our Nation," pp. 90-91.)

Chapter 2- A Mighty Fleet

1) New York City in the 1770s consisted of about 20,000 citizens and 3,000 slaves living in a small area on the tip of Manhattan from The Battery (which was an artillery emplacement) to "just below today's City Hall park." (Gallagher, "The Battle of Brooklyn 1776," p. 16.) The slave cemetery was just above Wall Street.

2) General William Howe's army of 9,000 soldiers on 130 ships arrived from Halifax and entered the Lower Bay on June 29, 1776. One observer in New York City at the time stated: "I was upstairs in an outhouse and spied as I peeped out the Bay something resembling a wood of pine trees trimmed. I declare at my noticing this, that I

could not believe my eyes fixed at the very spot, judge you my surprise when in about ten minutes, the whole Bay was full of shipping as ever it could be. I declare that I thought all London was afloat." (Schecter, p. 99.)

Colonel Knox and his wife were having breakfast at his headquarters overlooking the harbor. With the arrival of the British fleet, Knox later wrote his brother, "The city is in an uproar, the alarm guns firing, the troops repairing to their posts, and everything in the [height] of bustle. I not at liberty to attend [Lucy], as my country cries the loudest." (McCullough, p. 134.)

Admiral Richard Howe's fleet of an additional 150 ships and 13,000 soldiers arrived shortly thereafter, prompting another American soldier to write to his son, "You would be surprised if You was here to see what a Mighty Fleet of Ships our Enemies have got; they lie against Staten Island, more than a Mile in Length from East to West, and so thick & close together for the greatest part of the Way, that you can see through where they are no more than if it was a thick Swamp; and the Regulars expect as many more soon and then we expect bloody Work of it." (Schecter, p. 111.) The size of the invasion fleet was the 18th century equivalent of the "shock and awe" tactics of the first Iraq War. It was the largest invasion fleet until the landing at Normandy on June 6, 1944.

With the invasion fleet in the harbor, General Washington wrote to a comrade in arms from the French and Indian Wars, recalling Washington's defeat at the Battle of Fort Necessity on July 3, 1754 and the defeat when he was an aide to General Braddock at the Battle of the Monongahela on July 9, 1755.

"I did not let the Anniversary of the 3d or 9[th] of this Inst[an]t [month] pass of[f] with out a grateful remembrance of the escape we had at the Meadows and on the Banks of the Monongahela. [T]he same Providence that protected us upon those occasions will, I hope, continue his Mercies, & make us happy Instruments in restoring Peace & liberty to this one favour[e]d, but now distressed Country." (Anderson, The War That Made America, p. xix.)

3) In the Continental Army, relations among the units from different colonies, particularly at the beginning of the War, were often acrimonious. The regular and better-trained and equipped regiments had little respect for the hastily assembled militias that had hurried to the cause and left just as quickly when their time was up. On August 1, 1776, twenty-one days before the massive British army landed on Long Island, General Washington issued the following order:

"It is with great concern, the General understands, that Jealousies &c: are arisen among the troops from the different Provinces, of reflections frequently thrown out, which can only irritate each other, and injure the noble cause in which we are engaged, and which we ought to support with one hand and heart. The General most earnestly entreats the officers, and soldiers, to consider the consequences; that they can in no way assist our cruel enemies more efficiently, than making division among ourselves; That the Honor and Success of the army, and the safety of our bleeding Country, depends upon harmony and good agreement with each other; That the Provinces are all United to oppose the common enemy, and all distinctions sunk in the name of an American. . . and he will be the best Soldier and the best Patriot, who contributes most to this glorious work, whatever his Station, or from whatever part of the Continent he may come; Let all distinctions of Nations, Countries and Provinces, therefore be lost in the generous contest, who shall behave with the most Courage against the enemy, and the most kindness and good humour to each other- If there are any officers, or soldiers, so lost to virtue and a love of their Country as to continue in such practices after this order; The General assures them, and is directed by Congress to declare, to the whole Army, that such persons shall be severely punished and dismissed [from] the service with disgrace." (Lengel, "This Glorious Struggle- George Washington's Revolutionary War Letters," pp. 54-55.)

4) Knox had 121 cannons in place in the Brooklyn forts and at The Battery. However, he was short of men for the gun crews. Many of the soldiers in the militias lacked their own individual firearms and instead had pikes. The lack of manpower was solved by an order for each Continental company to "lend" four men to the artillery

regiments. If the designees had muskets, they were given to other men in their militias so the firepower of the company was not diminished. (Gallagher, p. 50.)

5) There was a serious problem of sanitation in the American army, both in New York City and the forts in Brooklyn. Gastrointestinal diseases, spread by the polluted water supply, increased among the men during the warm summer months. General Greene wrote with disgust about the troops "easing themselves in the ditches of the fortifications, a practice that is disgraceful to the last Degree." (David Hackett-Fischer,"Washington's Crossing," p. 87.) Greene initiated the practices of digging "vaults," as latrines were then called, and established some degree of camp sanitation. (Hackett-Fischer, p. 88.)

6) The British landing on Staten Island, while unopposed was not without difficulties. By the time the transport ships were ready to disembark the troops, they were dealing with both the tide and a strong headwind. Some of the ships drifted dangerously close to Long Island but no cannons were brought to bear. There was some musket fire but it did no damage. A rain storm came up in the evening, making the troops wet and uncomfortable. However, the end result was the British landed unopposed on Staten Island. They were welcomed by the local population and four days later, the Staten Island Militia swore allegiance to the Crown, received regular army pay, and a guarantee to serve only as a home guard. (Gallagher, p. 68.)

Chapter 3- On a Secret Mission

1) General Ruggles never returned to Massachusetts. In compensation for his estates, which were confiscated after the War, he was given 10,000 acres of farmland in Wilmot, Nova Scotia where he lived until his death in 1795.

2) There were competing views among the British High Command about how to deal with the rebellion. One faction favored a deliberate strategy of extreme violence and terror against civilian populations as

was common in the wars in Central Europe. The British had applied this strategy in Ireland and Scotland. Both General Howe, and his brother Admiral Howe, opposed the strategy and favored isolating New England as the seat of the rebellion and drawing on the support of Loyalists. General Howe wrote "You are deceived if you suppose there are not many loyal and peaceable subjects in [the colonies]. I may safely assert that the insurgents are very few, in comparison of the whole people." (Hackett Fischer, p. 77.) Howe's plan was to win over American opinion by protecting the Loyalists and granting amnesty to those who took an oath of allegiance to the Crown.

Both Admiral and General Howe issued orders forbidding sailors and troops from attacking civilians and looting and destroying private property. Hackett Fischer, p. 75. However, even the threat of court martials and severe punishment did not deter troops and officers from raping women, regardless of their political affiliation.

One British officer, Captain Francis Rawdon, Lord Hastings, was "cheered" by the number of court martials for rape because it showed how spirited his men were. He wrote:

"The fair nymphs of this isle are in wonderful tribulation, as the fresh meat our men have got here has made them riotous as satyrs. A girl cannot step into the bushes to pluck a rose without running the most imminent risk of being ravished, and they are so little accustomed to these vigorous methods that they don't bear them with the proper resignation, and of consequence we have most entertaining courts martial every day." (McCullough, p. 142, Gallagher, pp. 68-69.)

3) General Washington ordered the reading of the Declaration of Independence to the troops in the hope ". . . this important Event will serve as a fresh incentive to every officer, and soldier, to act with Fidelity and Courage, as knowing that now the peace and safety of his Country depends (under God) solely on the success of our arms. And that he is now in the service of a State, possessed of sufficient power to reward his merit and advance him to the highest Honors of a free Country. . ." (Lengel, p. 51.)

After the Declaration was read, a mob of civilians and militia surged to Bowling Green where they pulled down an equestrian statue of King George III. The lead from the statue of the King mounted on a huge horse was reported to have been melted down into musket balls. The King's head was cut from his body, the nose was amputated and it was hung on a spike outside a tavern. A British engineer, John Montresor eventually retrieved it "and had it sent to England so the ministry might see the zeal of the rebels firsthand." (Schecter, pp. 102-103; McCullough, pp. 137-138.) Ironically, many of the men participating in pulling down were slaves sent out by their masters to do the heavy work.

4) At the time there were six towns which make up the Brooklyn of today: Boswyck (now Bushwick), Breukelen (downtown Brooklyn), Midwout (Flatbush), New Amersfort (Flatlands), Nieuw Utrecht (New Utrecht) and Gravesend. The total population was around 4,100 made up of 2,600 whites and 1,500 blacks, comprising both slaves and freedmen. Brooklyn had the highest percentage of blacks to whites north of the Mason-Dixon line. (Gallagher, pp. 32-33.)

5) The British had very good intelligence already about Long Island. While stationed in New York City, as part of the Royal Garrison, many of the Officers had travelled to Brooklyn and further out to Jamaica to participate in hunting parties, horse races and other social events.

The Americans, on the other hand, had little knowledge of the terrain, and more importantly the passes or chokepoints on the major roads. Washington recognized the need to gather intelligence and took advantage of the natural sympathies of those closest to Connecticut. His spies regularly sailed across the Long Island Sound, responding to signals for pickups and meetings, some as simple as laundry blowing on clotheslines. (Dr. David Robarge Lecture-How the Patriots Used Intelligence to Help Win American Independence, The Society of the Cincinnati, July 26, 2011.)

6) The people on much of the Island were of divided loyalties. Generally, those closer to Long Island Sound and Connecticut supported the Revolution. Those in the rich farmland areas on the

center of the Island were Loyalists. The towns of Brooklyn, Flatbush, New Utrecht and Flatlands were Dutch in heritage and still retained their Dutch population, most of whom were neutral. Hempstead, in the middle of the Island, could not endure the division of loyalties between Tories and patriots. In 1775, it actually split into two townships, with North Hempstead supporting the Revolution and Hempstead remaining loyal to the Crown. Hendrik Onderdonk was a patriotic leader of North Hempstead. The actual names of the two prominent land owning families at the time in Hempstead were Fordham and Carman.

Chapter 4- Encounter at The Rising Sun

1) The Rising Sun, also known as Howard's Halfway House, was a tavern on the Jamaica Road at the junction of the Jamaica and Bushwick Roads, near the Jamaica Pass. At the time of the battle for Brooklyn, it was owned by William Howard, who lived there with his wife and young son, William Jr.

In the very early morning of August 27th, the main body of the British Army, led by General Howe, marched up the King's Highway and began a massive flanking movement of the American Army intending to come through Jamaica Pass and strike the left side of the American line. Generals Howe, Cornwallis, Clinton and Percy arrived at the tavern around 2 am. Seventy years later, William Jr. described the scene, after he and his father were roused out of bed as follows:

"General Howe and another officer were standing in the bar room. After asking for a glass of liquor from the bar, which was given him, he entered into familiar conversation with my father, and among other things said: 'I must have someone of you show me over the Rockaway Path around the Pass.'

My father replied: 'We belong to the other side, General and can't serve you against our duty.' General Howe replied" 'That is all right-stick to your country, or stick to your principles, but, Howard, you are my prisoner and must guide my men over the hill.' My father made some further objection, but was silenced by the General, who said, 'You have no alternative. If you refuse, I shall have you shot through the head.'. . . My father, thus compelled to serve the cause of the enemy, was marched out under a guard, who had orders to shoot him if he attempted to desert, and I was taken along with him. . ."

At 3 am, they guided the British over a trail east of the tavern until they flanked the pass and Howe confirmed it was lightly guarded. The five or so American troops on patrol were quickly captured. This marvelous, gripping description is in Gallagher, pp. 105-106.

Chapter 5- Skirmish at Flatbush Pass

1) In Hesse-Kassel, beginning in 1762 each regiment of the army was assigned a specific district for drafting soldiers. Conscripts, young men between the ages of seventeen and thirty, served twenty-four years. The determination of whether they were indispensable or dispensable was made by the local authorities. Generally, young men were deemed "dispensable" and thus conscripted if they "'were not needed at home' and their departure 'did not hurt farming or other crafts and trades.'" Those exempted from conscription included subjects whose net worth exceeded a certain amount, "sons of landed families, apprentices and journeymen in all kinds of trades, students, miners, men who sold cooking pots, men who hauled salt, servants at the court, and even all liveried servants of the nobility. "(Krebs, "A Generous and Merciful Enemy," pp. 50-51.) Generally, conscription targeted younger sons of poorer farmers and "put a particular strain on rural areas." (Krebs, p.52.)

2) The invasion of Long Island began on August 22nd at Gravesend. Hessian Grenadiers were among the first to land. (Gallagher, p. 89) By noon almost 15,000 troops had been successfully brought from the transports to the beachhead. The Knyphausen Regiment actually came ashore in the afternoon and moved inland toward Flatbush. The rest of the Hessians landed three days later. (Hackett-Fischer, p. 99.)

3) The lyrics of one of the Hessian barrack room songs were:

> Go with us to America.
> There will be enough for all.
> There will be silver, gold and money,
> Everything that a man seeks in the world
> All that a man seeks there
> Is in America.
> (Hackett-Fisher, pp. 62-63)

Hessian officers and soldiers also received prize money for the taking of booty that was approved, and plunder which, while not sanctioned, generally went unpunished. The distinction between booty and plunder is booty was military supplies and stores (ammunition, guns, cannons, tents, wagons and other equipment used by the Continental Army). Plunder was household goods, silver, furniture, bedding, clothing and other furnishings, generally belonging to civilians in the Hessian's path. In addition, Hessian soldiers did not have their pay docked for rations provided by the British, if they fed themselves off the land. (Hackett-Fisher, pp. 64-65.)

4) There was a skirmish at Flatbush Pass between Colonel Edward Hand's Pennsylvania Riflemen and the Hessians posted as guards to Cornwallis' encampment in Flatbush. (Gallagher, pp. 91-92; Schecter, p. 129.) Both sides had been well primed with propaganda from their leaders. The Hessians knew American troops carried tomahawks. The British told them this was evidence the rebels practiced cannibalism on their defeated enemies. In addition, the British made sure the Hessians knew the rebels had resolved to give no quarter to the Hessians if they surrendered or were captured. (Gallagher, p. 119.) The American propaganda emphasized the bloodthirsty characteristics of the Hessians hired as paid mercenaries, by a vindictive King to punish decent men who sought only to enjoy their rights as free Englishmen.

5) During the skirmish, the Pennsylvanians dragged one Hessian corpse back into the woods as evidence of their contact with the feared

Hessians and to dispel some of the myths about them. (Schecter, p.129.)

Chapter 6- The Hessian Bayonet

1) On August 27th, while General Howe with the main body of British troops was making his sweeping flanking movement up the King's Highway and west through Jamaica Pass to come behind the American lines, the Hessians and Scottish Highlanders, the "Black Watch," so called because of the dark colors of their tartans, under General von Heister menaced the center at Battle Pass on the Flatbush Road. (Gallagher, p. 115.) General Grant threatened the American right on the Shore Road. It was here the Americans believed the main British attack was taking place. Both Grant and von Heister were simply making credible demonstrations and keeping up the pressure until they heard the signal cannons from Howe's main body, indicating they had outflanked the American lines. Howe's cannons were heard around 9 am.

British General Grant had boasted in Parliament he could seize the entire continent with 5,000 Regulars. The American General, William Alexander Lord Stirling, a bona fide Scottish Lord, is reputed to have reminded his men holding the Shore Road against Grant of that boast to bolster their fighting spirit. They didn't need it. Stirling had two of the best-equipped and well trained regiments of the American Army in his sector- Smallwood's Marylanders and Haslet's Delaware Regiment.

In one of the ironies of history, after the war ended, General Grant became Governor of Stirling Castle in Scotland. (Gallagher, p.130.)

2) The order for the Hessian Grenadiers to carry their sabres across their chests, was given specifically so they would not get caught up in the thick brush in front of them. It also enabled them to open their heavy jackets in the heat and made it easier to use their bayonets. (Pearfon, "Those Damned Rebels," p. 173.) The bayonet was a

fearsome weapon, three sided which made "gaping wounds that could not be sutured." (Schecter, p.145.)

3) The Hessians were not the brutal killers depicted in American propaganda at the time. There were several instances of false surrenders during the chaotic rout of the American troops.

"Great excitement and rage on the part of the Hessians cannot be denied, but it was chiefly caused by some squads of the enemy, [the Americans] who, after being surrounded and having asked for quarter, fired again upon the unsuspecting Hessians, who had advanced toward them [to accept their surrender.] (Gallagher, p. 121.)

There were also instances of incredible brutality by British as well as Hessian troops. One Hessian Colonel observed, "The riflemen were mostly spitted to the trees with bayonets." (Hackett-Fischer, p. 97.) (Pearfon contains a similar observation attributed to a Hessian officer on p.174.)

4) The Old Stone House was the Vechte farmhouse. General Stirling, learning of the threat from the rear by General Howe's troops, realized the British would cut off the retreat of the American troops battling Grant's ever-increasing numbers. Stirling launched a suicidal attack with between 250 to 400 of Smallwood's Marylanders, led by Major Mordecai Gist, against more than 2,000 of the British, led by General Cornwallis. They made several charges through the orchard toward the Stone House, until their ranks were decimated. General Stirling then ordered them to retreat and fight their way to safety. Stirling himself was captured, but the action of the Marylanders permitted the remaining troops on the American right more time to escape the British trap. The Marylanders did have artillery support to suppress the British cannons at the Old Stone House. I have placed two gun crews from the Massachusetts Artillery with Smallwood's Regiment. This is not an established historical fact.

Smallwood's Regiment suffered grievous losses, killed, wounded and captured. Gallagher states that of the 400 Marylanders involved in the action, 256 were killed and over 100 others were wounded or captured. (Gallagher, p. 130.) Major Mordecai Gist and nine others managed to reach the American fortifications across the Gowanus. McCullough puts the number of Marylanders involved in the assault at no more than 250 and states they valiantly charged Cornwallis' troops six times. (McCullough, p. 177.) Pearfon also puts the number at 250. (Pearfon, p. 176.) General Stirling was captured and surrendered his sword to Hessian General von Heister.

General Washington, from a vantage point in Brooklyn, (one historian states it was from the Cobble Hill fort), watched the Marylander's attack the numerically vastly superior British forces. He is reported to have cried out, "Good God! What brave fellows I must this day lose." (McCullough, p. 177; Hackett-Fischer, p. 95.)

Smallwood's Marylanders fought heroically in the battle. Where they are buried remains a mystery. According to Gallagher, they were initially buried in a mass grave on a farm, belonging to Adrian Brunt that became Brooklyn's Third Avenue between Seventh and Eighth Streets. When Third Avenue was widened in 1910, a plaque commemorating the burial site apparently was removed. The site became the location of a Red Devil paint factory, then an automobile repair shop. (Gallagher, p. 174.) Local Brooklyn historians are convinced the Marylanders are buried beneath a concrete covered lot at the intersection of Third Avenue and Eighth Street. (NY Times, August 25, 2012, "Seeking Brooklyn's Lost Mass Grave.")

5) Colonel Smallwood was absent from the field of battle, having been ordered by General Washington to sit on a courts martial board in New York City. He arrived in Brooklyn, on the morning of August 27th, in time to witness his Marylanders' assault and to plead with General Washington for reinforcements to cover the Americans' retreat. (Gallagher, p.132.) Colonel John Haslet, commander of the Delaware Regiment was also absent from the battlefield, attending the same court martial.

6) Following the disastrous defeat on August 27th, Washington dispatched fresh troops from New York City to the forts of Brooklyn Heights, including the Marblehead Mariners. The move, designed to

boost morale among the despondent troops who had fled the battlefield and the men manning the forts, had its desired effect.

One Pennsylvanian Officer wrote: "The faces that had been saddened by the disasters of yesterday assumed a gleam of animation on [the approach of fresh troops] accompanied with a murmur. . . that 'These were the lads that might do something.'" (McCullough, p. 183.)

7) The battle of Brooklyn was a disaster- a total American defeat. American casualties were 300 killed and 1,000 taken prisoner, including three Generals. (McCullough, p. 180.) Hackett-Fischer has approximately the same numbers but adds there were no reliable estimates of the wounded. (Hackett-Fischer, p. 98.) General Howe claimed his losses were 59 killed, 267 wounded and 31 missing, with Hessian losses five killed and 26 wounded. Howe's inflated estimates of American losses were 1,000 prisoners and 2,000 killed wounded or drowned in the Gowanus.

When Washington wrote John Hancock after the defeat, he reported low morale among the remaining troops and large-scale desertions.

"The Militia instead of calling forth their utmost efforts to a brave & manly opposition in order to repair our Losses, are dismayed, Intractable, and Impatient to return [to their homes.] Great numbers of them have gone off; in some Instances, almost by whole Regiments- by half Ones & by Companies at a time-" (Lengel, p. 63.) Washington reiterated to Hancock, who was President of the Congress, his arguments for a standing army.

Colonel Henry Knox was not in the field with General Washington on August 27th. However, that did not stop him from exaggerating the casualties inflicted on the British. In describing the battle to his wife, he wrote, he estimated the British suffered 1,000 killed and "[w]e lost about the same number killed, wounded and taken prisoners, among whom are General Sullivan and Lord Stirling. . . I met with some loss in my regiment: they behaved like heroes, and are gone to glory. I was not [in Brooklyn] myself, being obliged to wait on my Lord Howe and the navy gentry who threatened to pay us a visit."

By that he meant an attack on lower Manhattan by the fleet. (Drake, *Life and Correspondence of Henry Knox*, p. 29.)

Chapter 7- Retreat Across the River

1) At noon on August 29th, Washington issued orders to confiscate all boats ostensibly to ferry, from Manhattan to Brooklyn, the militias supposedly arriving from New Jersey. (McCullough, p. 185.) It was a ruse. He then convened a council of war in Brooklyn Heights around 4 pm. The weather at the time was stormy with the wind from the northeast, which prevented the British fleet from sailing up the East River and cutting the army off in Brooklyn. The decision to evacuate the Army, with its equipment was made in the late afternoon. To avoid a panic-stricken rush to the Brooklyn side of the ferry, and to enforce silence, the troops were told there would be a night attack, up the East River to outflank the British.

The more inexperienced troops, mostly the militias, were evacuated first, beginning around 9 pm. Sometime around 11 pm the wind shifted to the southwest, enabling some of the rescue ships to use sail. The best troops, manning the front lines opposite the British began their withdrawal around 3 am, August 30th. The last troops to withdraw were General Mifflin's Pennsylvania Regiment. Mifflin took the rearguard assignment because he had suggested the retreat and did not want that proposal to sully his reputation for bravery. (McCullough, p. 185.)

2) By dawn most, but not all, of the troops had been evacuated. A thick fog descended upon the East River, masking the retreat from the British for another critical hour or two. One eyewitness described the fog as "so dense. . .that a man could not be discerned six yards off." (Gallagher, p. 151.) The early light of the rising sun failed to pierce the fog and was described as "a strange yellow light." (Hackett-Fischer, p. 101.)

3) Haslet's troops were highly critical of General Washington's handling of the battle. Colonel Haslet himself wrote to a delegate to

Congress, "I fear General Washington has too heavy a task, assisted mostly by beardless boys." (McCullough, p. 202.) General Charles Lee had originally been charged by Congress with the defense of New York City. When Washington assumed command, General Lee, by letter, lobbied the Congress sitting in Philadelphia, to name him overall commander of the army.

4) While the Battle for Brooklyn was a major defeat, the evacuation of the army and most of its supplies the night of August 29th-30th was a masterful success. More than 9,500 troops were ferried across the East River, primarily by boats manned by the Marblehead Mariners. Still it was a close thing. A Tory sympathizer, Mrs. John Rapalie, the wife of a Dutchman, observed the evacuation and sent her slave to alert the British. Fortunately for the Americans, the slave was intercepted by Hessians who didn't speak English and couldn't understand the slave's Dutch. (Gallagher, p. 164; Schecter, p. 151.)

Gallagher writes that Washington was among the last to leave Brooklyn, although this may be an apocryphal story.

Chapter 8- A Fortuitous Fire

1) The muskets carried by American, British and Hessian troops used a paper cartridge. To load, a soldier used his teeth to open the end of the paper cylinder containing the ball and powder. "Recruits for the American Army at the time were required to have at least four good teeth, two upper and two lower, which had to meet to allow them to bite off the end of the cartridge." (Gallagher, p. 43.)

2) Historians agree the Battle of Harlem Heights on September 16, 1776, was triggered by the British troops who, having encountered the Americans and driven them back, sounded their bugles as if in a fox chase. The effect of this insult led General Washington to order an attack. His Adjutant General, Colonel Joseph Reed described the scene as follows:

"By the time I got to him [Washington] the enemy appeared

in open view and in a most insulting manner sounded their bugle horns as is usual after a fox chase. I never felt such a sensation before: it seemed to crown our disgrace." (Hackett-Fischer, p. 106.) (See also, McCullough, p.218 and Schecter, p.198.)

The confident British troops continued their rapid advance through open fields and ran into Smallwood's Maryland Regiment, Knowlton's Rangers and some Virginia infantry, hiding behind bushes and wooden fences. The American troops forced the British back, Washington committed more troops, a total of 1,800 in all were engaged, and again made the British retreat. At some point in the battle, British troops were fleeing on the run. "[W]e drove the dogs near three miles," one American soldier wrote. (McCullough, p. 218.) By three p.m., the American Army was ordered to end their pursuit. Washington feared they were being drawn into a set piece battle he wished to avoid.

His Adjutant, Colonel Reed, observed, "The pursuit of a flying enemy was so new a scene, that it was with difficulty our men could be brought to retreat." (McCullough, p. 219.) Washington sent his Aide-de-Camp, Lieutenant Tench Tilghman, to bring it about. Tilghman wrote the troops "gave a hurra and left the field in good order." (Schecter, p. 200.) According to Hackett-Fischer, one American officer wrote after the battle, "Our troops were in a most desponding Condition before, but now are in good spirits." (Hackett-Fischer, p. 107.)

3) On September 21, 1776, after the Continental Army had abandoned New York City and the British had occupied it, a fire broke out in the early morning hours on the west side of the city. The estimates are imprecise but the fire destroyed between 10 and 25% of the city's 4,000 homes and businesses. It spread from one wood shingled roof-top to the next, aided by a strong southwesterly wind. The flames reached and quickly consumed Trinity Church. St. Paul's was saved by alert citizens clambering up the roof and extinguished flaming flakes of shingles before they could set the Church on fire. Many of the buildings were looted and plundered, furthering the destruction of the city.

A British officer described the scene as follows:

"The Sick, the Aged, Women and Children, half naked were seen going they knew not where, and taking refuge in houses which were at a distance from the fire, but from whence they were driven a second and even a third time. . . and at last laying themselves down on the Common. The terror was encreased by the horrid noise of the burning and falling houses, the pulling down of such wooden buildings as served to conduct the fire. . seeing the fire break out unexpectedly in places at a distance, which manifested a design of totally destroying the City. . . (Schecter, p 208.)

The fire ultimately died down or burned itself out, being stopped by the grassy grounds of King's College that served as a fire-break at the northern end of the conflagration.

General Howe claimed the fire was started by rebel arsonists. Several people were allegedly caught with incendiary devices and in some cases were forced, at the point of bayonet, back into burning buildings. Royal Governor William Tyron specifically claimed Washington was "privy to this villainous act, as he sent all the bells of the churches out of town, under pretense of casting them into cannon. . ." (Schecter, p. 206.) British marines and sailors who had been sent to help fight the fire, claimed to have caught some "mad-cap Americans," in the act of setting fire to houses or cutting off the handles of water buckets. (McCullough, pp.222-223.)

Although over 200 people were held and interrogated no one was convicted. Some Americans were convinced the fire had been set by members of militias rather than regular Army, while others accused the British of having started the fire themselves in order to loot the city.

Washington himself denied any knowledge of how the fire started. He had written John Hancock, President of the Continental Congress, on September 2nd, in effect asking for permission to destroy the city rather than let it fall into British hands and serve as secure winter quarters. Congress denied his request. In a follow up letter on September 8th, Washington acknowledged their decision, stating "The Congress having resolved that [New York] should not be destroyed nothing seems to remain but to determine the time of [the British] taking possession." (Lengel, p. 66.) On September 22nd, the day after the fire, Washington, wrote to Congress and called the fire an accident. Two weeks later, in a letter to his cousin, Lund Washington, III, he wrote: "Had I been left to the dictates of my own judgement, New York should have been laid in Ashes before I quitted it. . . [T]o this end I applied to Congress, but they absolutely forbid-" He added however, "Providence – or some good honest Fellow, has done more for us than we were disposed to do for ourselves. . ." (McCullough, p. 223, Schecter, p. 209.)

In all likelihood, the fire started accidentally in the Fighting Cocks Tavern, on the west side of Manhattan, near Whitehall Slip. It spread rapidly due to the strong wind that blew pieces of cedar shingles from roof to roof. This seems to be the general consensus of historians, although Hackett-Fischer supports the British claim it was intentionally set because it started simultaneously in many places. (Hackett-Fischer, p. 107.) We probably will never know with certainty. Schecter makes a convincing case that given Washington's deference to civilian authority, it is highly unlikely he would have disobeyed Congress' clear denial of permission to burn the city, and then lied about it in official and unofficial correspondence. (Schecter, p. 207.)

Chapter 9- A Small Victory

1) The Battle of Pelham Bay, named after the place where 4,000 British and Hessian troops landed and began their march inland, occurred on October 18, 1776. Colonel Glover's 14th Continentals, formerly the Regiment of Marble Head Mariners, and two Massachusetts Militia units, totaling approximately 750 men, were guarding the east- west roads that ran from the East River to the Hudson, to protect the American Army from being cut in two as it retreated from New York City.

The narrow Split Rock Road that ran from the beach inland was lined with stone walls. Other stone walls divided the fields. According to Hackett Fischer, the men were placed "in echelon one behind the other protected by the stone walls. (Hackett Fischer, p. 110.) Schecter has the American troops in intervals behind the walls on opposite sides of the road. "Glover enhanced the destructive effect of his small force by coordinating a relay from one unit to the next: After a regiment popped up from behind the walls and fired several volleys at close range, it was to fall back to the new position, farther ahead of the British, while the next regiment, hidden on the opposite side of the road, took its turn firing at the enemy." (Shechter, p. 227.) I have used Schecter's description but in either case, the Americans hid behind the stone walls, firing volley after volley at the Hessians compacted on the narrow road, inflicting horrific casualties and stalling General Howe's advance. Colonel Loammi Baldwin (the Massachusetts commander of a local Militia, apple farmer and later developer of the Baldwin apple) stated that as his men poured musket fire into the mass of enemy troops, they remained "calm. . . as though expecting a Shot at a flock of Pidgeons or Ducks." (Schecter, p. 228.)

Glover's holding action ended with the Americans retreating across a creek, destroying the bridge and engaging in an artillery duel until nightfall. Colonel Glover estimated he lost eight men killed and 13 wounded. The British suffered between 200 to 800 killed, far more than they lost in the entire battle of Brooklyn. General Howe, reporting on the battle to London, stated he lost three dead and 20 wounded, but he only counted British troops. The Hessians bore the brunt of the fighting and were three quarters of the British force in the battle. (Schecter, p.229.)

2) After the battle, the Hessian wounded were brought to St. Paul's Church in Mount Vernon, N.Y. The dead were buried in the Church graveyard.

Part Two- Retreat Through The Jerseys

Chapter 10 - Assault Up The Cliffs

1) The Battle for Fort Washington began at 7 am on November 16, 1776. The attack was three pronged, with General Knyphausen leading 4,000 Hessians who approached the plateau and the Fort

from the north, on both its east and west sides; Cornwallis' 3,000 troops landed below the plateau to the east from the Harlem River; General Percy's contingent of 3,000 men attacked from the south. (McCullough, p. 241; Schecter, p. 248.)

Captain Andreas Wiederhold, of the Von Knyphausen Regiment, reported the General "at all times could be found in the thickest of the fight, where resistance and attack was the hottest, and he tore down the fences with his own hands to urge the men on. He was exposed like a common soldier to the frightful cannon-and shrapnel-fire, as well as to the rifle shots, and it is wonderful that he came off without being killed or wounded." (Schecter, p. 252.) At the time, General Wilhelm von Knyphausen was 60 years old, as compared to General Howe who was 52, George Washington who was 44, and Generals Clinton and Cornwallis who were 38.

2) Although Fort Washington, located on a 280 foot high precipice, surrounded by rivers on three sides and heavy fortifications on the landward side, appeared to be impregnable, it was not. In the opinion of a British officer, the fortifications were "too extensive for the number of troops." (Hackett-Fischer, p. 111.) General Greene, who convinced Washington the Fort could be held, had estimated he needed 10,000 men to defend the entire perimeter. (Schecter, p. 246.)

Schecter's detailed description of the surrender negotiations has Colonel Rall sending English speaking Captain Hohenstein to the Fort demanding surrender and being fired upon by the Americans. (Schecter, p. 253.) The terms were to surrender immediately, lay down all arms and turn over all ammunition, provisions and military supplies and the men would be allowed to keep their personal effects. Colonel Magaw asked for four hours to decide what to do. Captain Hohenstein gave him thirty minutes. In thirty minutes time, the Hessian Captain returned to the Fort and escorted Colonel Magaw out who surrendered his sword to General Knyphausen. (Schecter, pp. 253-254.) The Hessians then proceeded to strip the Americans of their personal possessions, cutting knapsacks from the backs of the surrendered troops.

McCullough writes, after General Howe arrived, Colonel Magaw surrendered with no promise other than their lives. (McCullough, p. 243.)

Regardless of which version is more accurate, the stark fact is Fort Washington was captured and 2,800 American troops, including 230 officers, surrendered and were forced to march out of the Fort between two columns of Hessians and lay down their arms. The British suffered 78 killed and 374 wounded and the Americans lost 59 killed and 96 wounded. In addition, the British seized 146 cannons, arms, ammunition and other military supplies. (McCullough, p. 243.)

3) General Washington is supposed to have witnessed the battle and the capture of the Fort bearing his name from the Jersey Palisades. He came in for severe criticism for his indecisiveness as to whether to defend the Fort or not. General Charles Lee claimed his last words to Washington, before Lee left him at Peekskill were "Draw off the garrison or they will be lost." Lee wrote Dr. Benjamin Rush, a member of Congress, "I must entreat that you keep what I say to yourself, but I foresaw, predicted, all that has happened." (McCullough, p. 244.) Lee also wrote "Oh! General- an indecisive mind is one of the greatest misfortunes that can befall an army." (Hackett-Fischer, p.114.)

Hackett-Fischer states after observing the surrender, Washington turned away and "began to weep 'with the tenderness of a child.'" (Hackett-Fischer, p. 114.) In an interesting footnote, the historian reports this event was told to Washington Irving by men who were with General Washington at the time. Irving initially included it in his five volume biography of George Washington (1855-1859) but it was removed from later editions.

Washington himself, writing to John Hancock from Fort Lee on November 16th, obviously after the disastrous battle, reported on the maneuvers of the two armies and concluded with a plea for more troops and supplies:

"The Loss of such a Number of Officers and Men, many of whom have been trained with more than common Attention, will I fear be severely felt. But when that of the Arms and Accoutrements is added much more so, and must be a farther Incentive to procure as considerable a Supply as possible for the New Troops as soon as it can be done. . ." (Lengel, p. 77.)

4) Cornwallis relied on three local guides in choosing a place to scale the Palisades. They were Loyalists: one owned twenty acres and a brewery in what is now Leonia. His property had been seized by New Jersey patriots. Another ran the Hoboken Ferry and recruited Loyalists for the British. The third owned the property where the British landed. Despite the advice of these three Loyalist guides, Cornwallis doubted the trail they had chosen and wasted several hours scouting the shoreline for another path. Finally, when the troops had scaled the Palisades, by way of this narrow rocky path, they were five miles from Fort Lee. (The Revolutionary War in Bergen County, Carol Karels, editor, "The Invasion and the Myths Surrounding It," by John Spring, pp. 26-27.)

One Hessian observed of their climb up the Palisade, "Fifty men would have sufficed to hold back the entire corps if they had only hurled stones down on us." (Karels, "British and Hessian Accounts of the Invasion of 1776, by Lt. Col. Donald M. Londahl-Smidt, Ret, p. 23.)

5) Historians agree that when Washington received news of the British landing on the Palisades, he rode from Hackensack to Fort Lee and he and General Greene organized the retreat. The Army left in haste, leaving behind provisions, tents, and the heavy cannons. (McCullough, p.246; Hackett-Fischer, p. 124.) One open question is who warned the Americans of the British landing. Hackett-Fischer attributes it to an "American Officer" galloping up to Washington's headquarters at the Zabriskie house in Hackensack. (Hackett-Fischer, p. 124.) Tom Paine was at headquarters that morning and stated they were informed by an officer. McCullough is less sure and attributes the warning to either a local farmer, or a British deserter. (McCullough, p. 246.)

A legend, since discredited, is the warning came from a slave girl, Polly Wyckoff who saw the British approaching while working in a farm-house kitchen and alerted the Americans. (Karels, "The Invasion and the Myths Surrounding It," John Spring, p. 30.)

Accounts vary as to whether the Americans left their breakfasts cooking and fled but do agree some soldiers broke into the rum supply, became drunk and were captured by the British.

6) At Newark, originally settled by Puritans who named the place New Ark for the Ark of the Covenant, Washington sent the sick and wounded northwest to Morristown, a safe and secure area behind the Watchung Mountains. The dwindling remainder of the American Army retreated south toward Brunswick, Princeton and Trenton. (Hackett-Fischer, p. 129.)

In 1776 in particular, and indeed throughout much of the war, the Americans suffered from a serious lack of gunpowder. The Colonies had few places to manufacture it and depended upon foreign sources, primarily the French. (American Historical Review, Vol. 30, No. 2, 1925, pp. 271-281.) Morristown, with about 250 residents, two churches, two taverns and two schools, actually had a black powder mill, run by the Ford family. (Wikipedia, History of New Jersey, New Jersey in the American Revolution.) George Washington had passed through Morristown in 1773 while traveling to New York City. It is probable he knew of Ford's black powder mill from that earlier visit.

While there is no historical evidence of a return mission from Morristown carrying the precious gunpowder, it is a fact the sick and wounded were sent from Newark to Morristown. I have imagined they traveled by wagon and the wagons were put to good use in carrying gunpowder to the Army as it retreated southwest toward Trenton.

Chapter 11- The Powder Mill at Morristown

1) Abraham Van Buskirk was a surgeon with a "considerable practice," in the Teaneck/New Bridge area of Bergen County. He was tried by patriots for working against their cause and in 1776, he fled his home and joined the British Army when they arrived in New Jersey. On November 16, 1776, he was commissioned by General Howe as a Lieutenant Colonel in the New Jersey Volunteers. After the Revolution, his properties were confiscated and Dr. Van Buskirk

went to Halifax, Nova Scotia. In support of his claim to the British Government for compensation, General Cornwallis stated Van Buskirk "rendered very essential services to the British Forces being a Loyalist of the greatest merit and served the whole war with Zeal and Fidelity." (Karels, "New Bridge: History at the Crossroads," by Kevin Wright, p. 59. For a wonderful account of conflicting loyalties, gentlemanly conduct and concerns about Officers as prisoners of war, see "How George Washington Saved the Life of Abraham Van Buskirk's Son," by Todd Braisted in Journal of the American Revolution, September 16, 2014)

I have created the character of Mercy Buskirk Ford to illustrate the historical fact that families were divided and the Revolutionary War in New Jersey was indeed a civil war. Fathers and sons were on opposite sides and in some families, the father deliberately sent one son to the Loyalist Militia and the other to the patriot side, in an effort to protect the family's property. The Ford family were in fact ardent patriots.

2) Gunpowder was made from a mixture of saltpeter, which is potassium nitrate, carbon taken from charcoal and sulfur. During the early days of the Revolution, the potassium nitrate was extracted from manure, either from horses or cattle. Patriots harvested compacted manure from stable floors. "Nitre beds" which were compost heaps, over the course of about a year, produced crystallized potassium nitrate. Another method of obtaining saltpeter was by mining bat dung from caves where it had accumulated over many years. These were called "nitre caves."

I have supposed there were bat caves near Ford's gunpowder mill from which he obtained the saltpeter to make his black powder.

3) As early as August 1775 the New Jersey Provincial Congress adopted a plan for the formation of 26 Regiments apportioned among the various counties and townships. Morris County was to provide two regiments and one battalion. A regiment at full strength was usually ten companies of 60 to 80 men. In addition, there were Minute Men or "Flying Companies," that served four month terms, inactive

but standing by ready to fight where needed to protect the Province. Morris County was to raise one battalion of six companies.

In October 1775, the New Jersey Provincial Congress passed an ordinance calling for all able-bodied men between the ages of 16 and 50 to be enrolled in the State Militia. They were to report with a musket or "firelock and a bayonet, sword or tomahawk," and their pay was regulated by the various towns and counties. Pay was one shilling sixpence for every day or part of a day in drilling. This was good pay for playing soldier. A skilled workman like a carpenter earned about one shilling a day. (Wikipedia, New Jersey During the Revolution-The Militia of New Jersey During the Revolution.)

In the summer of 1776, the Continental Congress established the Flying Camps to serve as mobile reserves. These were militiamen, so called weekend soldiers as compared to regular Continental Regiments and were recruited in New Jersey, Pennsylvania, Maryland and Delaware. (Dwyer, The Day is Ours," p. 19.)

Chapter 12-With the Rearguard at the Raritan River

1) The American Army literally disintegrated on December 1, 1776, decreasing from almost 20,000 in August to less than 3,000 men as those whose terms were up simply left.

One soldier described their leaving from Brunswick as follows: "Two or three days after our arrival at Brunswick, being the first of December, and the expiration of the flying Camp's troop's time, Our Brigade march'd to Philadelphia leaving our brave Gen'l with a very weak army." (Hackett- Fisher, p. 129.)

General Nathaniel Greene wrote, "Two brigades left us at Brunswick, notwithstanding the enemy (10,000 British and Hessian troops) are within two hours march and coming on." (McCullough, p. 256.)

2) While the Army retreated south from Brunswick toward Trenton, Washington ordered the New York State Artillery,

commanded by Captain Alexander Hamilton, to block and hold off the British advancing forces. The battle began around one p.m. British light infantry and Hessian Jaegers, equipped with rifled guns with hexagonal bores, drove back the Americans who were trying to destroy the bridge over the Raritan. The American artillery and riflemen hidden in the stone houses on the south side of the river forced the British advance units to retreat and the British then brought up their artillery. Hamilton engaged in an artillery duel until almost sunset and kept the British Army at bay until the American Army had safely withdrawn. (Hackett-Fischer, pp. 130-131; McCullough, p. 256, Dwyer, pp. 75-76.) By the morning of December 1st, the Americans were retreating south of Brunswick. General Cornwallis' main force occupied Brunswick on December 2nd.

3) Haslet's Delaware Regiment did indeed serve as the rear guard troops at the Raritan River. When they were ordered, around sundown, to follow the retreating army, they had their tents (and presumably some other equipment) but no wagons to carry them south. They had to burn them to prevent the tents from being captured. One of Haslet's Officers describes the event as follows:

"Colonel Haslet came to me and told me to take as many men as I thought proper and go back and burn all tents. 'We have no wagons,' said he 'to carry them off and it is better to burn them than they should fall into the hands of the enemy.' Then I went and burned them-about one hundred tents. When we saw them reduced to ashes, it was night and the army far ahead. We made a double quick-step and came up with the army about eight o'clock. We encamped in the woods, with no victuals, no tents, no blankets. The night was cold and we all suffered much, especially those who had no shoes." (Hackett-Fischer, p. 131.)

By the time this proud Regiment reached Trenton, it had been decimated by disease and even desertions, as they got closer to Delaware. While some troops departed to return home, with permission to join new Regiments, many of them, led by their officers, simply deserted. When the Army crossed the Delaware into Pennsylvania and made camp, Colonel Haslet wrote a friend in Delaware that of the original

700 men in the Regiment only six remained. (Dwyer, p. 120.) Haslet wrote when he informed General Washington, "he declared his intention of having officers and men bound neck and heels and brought back as an example to the army." (Dwyer, p. 120.)

4) The basic details of this burial scene actually took place but on a different battlefield. Private Joseph P. Martin, in his narrative of his service in the Eighth Connecticut Continental Regiment, recounts burying a soldier near a country estate, shortly after the Battle of Harlem Heights, in September 1776. Two young ladies, who Martin thought were sisters, emerged from the house, and upon learning the dead soldier's face would not be covered, one offered a "fine white gauze handkerchief from her neck and desired that it might be spread upon his face, tears at the same time flowing down their cheeks."

Martin goes on to call them "Worthy young ladies. . . deserving the regard of the greatest of men. What sisters, what wives, what mothers and what neighbors would you make! Such a sight as those ladies afforded at that time and on that occasion was worthy and doubtless received the attention of angels." (Joseph Plumb Martin, Private Yankee Doodle, Being a Narrative of Some of the Adventures, Dangers and Sufferings of a Revolutionary Soldier, George E. Scheer, editor, pp. 44-45.)

Chapter 13- Plunder and Revenge

1) The town of Brunswick was incorporated in 1730. It was named after Braunschweig, a city in Lower Saxony, Germany. (Wikipedia, New Brunswick, New Jersey, Origins of the Name.)

2) On November 30, Lord Admiral Howe, General Howe's brother issued a proclamation basically offering amnesty, within the next sixty days, to all who would take an oath of allegiance to the King. In return they would receive a "free and general pardon" and would "reap the benefit of his Majesty's paternal goodness, in the preservation of their property, the restoration of their commerce, and the security of their most valuable rights, under the just and

most moderate authority of the crown and Parliament of Britain."
(McCullough, p.258.) (Hackett-Fischer has the order being issued by
both General and Lord Admiral Howe, p. 161.)

The oath was simple enough. It read: "I _____, do promise
and declare that I will remain in peaceable obedience to his Majesty,
and will not take up arms, nor encourage others to take up arms in
opposition to His Authority. . ." (Dwyer, p. 76.)

Many eagerly accepted the offer, believing the war to be over. A
farmer, John Bray from Raritan Landing wrote to his uncle in Lebanon
Township, New Jersey:

"You are acquainted that the British troops have possession of
this place and you may depend that they will go through the country
wherever they attempt it and [such] great destruction follows wherever
they go that I would recommend it to all my relations and friends to
come in and receive Protection. The Proclamation which no doubt you
have heard is free to all during its limitation. Great numbers flock in
dayly to headquarters which is at this place. You can come down and
receive Protection and return home without molestation on the part
of the King's troops and you best know the situation of the Provincial
Army. Do advise Couzin Johnny and Thomas and Couzin Thomas
Jones for if they do stay out to the last they will undoubtedly fair
the worst. 40,000 Hessians have offered their service to the King of
England of which 24,000 are to embark in the spring but I hope the
matter will be settled before that time." (Dwyer, p. 77.)

About 3,000 rebels, from Brunswick and the surrounding area
pledged allegiance and received their paper of protection. (Dwyer,
p. 77; Hackett-Fischer, pp. 161-162.) There was a religious and class
division among those who signed and those who did not. Generally,
the wealthy and very poor signed the Oath. The middle class did
not. English Calvinists were supporters of the Crown, Presbyterians
in Princeton and Scots-Irish in Essex County were not. The Dutch
speaking Colonials in Hackensack and New Bridge welcomed the
British.

3) General Howe issued a different order on December 12, 1776
from his headquarters in Trenton.

"Head Quarters Trentown, 12th of December 1776. Small straggling parties, not dressed like Soldiers and without Officers, not being admissible in War, who presume to Molest or fire upon Soldiers, or peaceable Inhabitants of the Country, will be immediately hanged without Tryal as Assassins."(New Jersey During the Revolution-The Militia of New Jersey During the Revolution.) This was in response to small militia unit ambushes of British and Hessian troops engaged in patrols or foraging for supplies. Howe's order and subsequent hangings resulted in more American civilians taking up arms and "more British and Hessian regulars died miserably on country lanes in New Jersey far from home." (Hackett-Fischer, p. 180.)

I have moved the order up in time. The attack by the cavalry on Bant and the militia men he was travelling with, takes place around December 2nd.

Chapter 14- On the Water Again

1) In 1776, New Jersey had more slaves than any other northern colony. While the British promised freedom to blacks who fled their masters and joined units such as the Black Pioneers, who served basically as laborers for the army, British troops also seized slaves from patriots as the property of rebels. (Hackett-Fischer, p. 169.) One such rebel property owner, in Upper Freehold, complained a band of Tories "seized on my Negro man, two horses and a wagon, and sent them into the service of the British army." (Dwyer, p. 87.)

New Jersey permitted slaves to win their freedom by serving for their masters in the State militia. Sometimes, these promises of freedom were not kept. Hackett-Fischer cites the instance of Samuel, the slave of Casper Berger of Somerset County, who served in the militia from 1776 until the end of the war. His master then broke his agreement and sold Samuel to another. Samuel "bought his freedom a second time, by twenty years' hard labor." (Hackett-Fischer, p. 169.)

Some American officers voiced their disapproval of even free "blackmen" serving alongside white soldiers. One Captain Alexander Graydon, in describing the Marblehead Mariners (Fourteenth Massachusetts Continental Regiment) stated:

"There was an appearance of discipline in this corps. The officers seemed to have mixed with the world and to understand what belonged to their stations. Though deficient in polish, [the corps] possessed an apparent aptitude for the purpose of its institution, and gave confidence that myriads of its meek and lowly brethren were incompetent to inspire. . . .Even in this regiment there were a number of negroes, which, to persons unaccustomed to such associations, had a disagreeable and degrading effect." (Dwyer, pp. 233-234.)

2) The Pennsylvania Council of Safety created the Pennsylvania Navy in 1775. The Navy controlled the Delaware River, vital to protecting Philadelphia and the crossing at Trenton. There were thirteen heavily armed galleys as well as gunboats, fire rafts and floating batteries. The galleys were the post powerful ships on the river, with one thirty two pounder, four twenty four pounders and eight eighteen pounders on board. On December 8, when Washington sought to cross the Delaware to the safety of the Pennsylvania shore, Commodore Thomas Seymour sent nine galleys to transport the men and equipment across the river. (Hackett-Fischer, pp.134-135.) There actually was a galley named Camden, as well as Congress, Franklin, Ranger and Washington. (The Pennsylvania Navy, Wikipedia.)

3) The fear of rape, by both British and Hessian soldiers and officers was real. As the British Army descended through New Jersey, the stories of atrocities in the towns and countryside they had passed through spread quickly. Accounts of rape and pillage were exploited by the Americans and admittedly were useful propaganda. But, unfortunately, many of the atrocities committed were true enough.

An investigation was ordered by the Continental Congress and the Governor of New Jersey. Testimony taken by county justices and local clergy showed incidents of rape were common. In the town of Pennington, Mary Campbell testified before a local Justice she had been raped many times by soldiers although she was at least five months pregnant. Another woman, Rebekkah Christopher testified she had been raped several times by British soldiers, escaped and only to discover her ten year old daughter being raped by five or six other soldiers. "Three women were most horribly ravished by [British soldiers], one of them an old woman nearly seventy years of age, whom they abused in a manner beyond description, another was a woman considerably advanced in her pregnancy, and the third was a young girl." (Hackett-Fischer, pp. 178-179.) General Greene, writing to his wife, reported the New Jersey Tories "lead the relentless foreigners (British and Hessians) to the houses of their neighbors and strip poor women and children of everything they have to eat or wear; and after plundering them in this sort, the brutes often ravish the mothers and daughters and compel the fathers and sons to behold their brutality." (McCullough, p. 261.) Dwyer makes the point "that at a time when it was considered shameful to disclose such things, [women] would swear under oath that they had been raped by British soldiers." (Dwyer, p. 187.)

4) The Army's need for horses and wagons was urgent. In Princeton and the surrounding area, many of the people were trying to escape the on coming British Army while simultaneously avoiding the "press men" from Washington's Army seeking to confiscate the very means they needed to escape. According to Joseph Galloway, a New Jersey Tory, in his testimony to Parliament in 1779, General Washington "got few carriages but what he took by force. The people hid their wagon wheels. He compelled them to produce them. They then broke their wheels and disabled their wagons, which rendered it very difficult for him to be supplied with wagons." (Dwyer, p. 87.)

In another incident, a scholar at Princeton, anxious to get away from the oncoming British, was at the home of a Mr. Johnson, when Washington's press men showed up.

He wrote in his journal, "with much difficulty we put them off for this time. Soon after, they came again, when we had little hope of keeping the wagons and horses. But knowing unless we got off our things while we had our wagons, they must necessarily fall into the enemy's hands, I took the opportunity while the press men were debating with Mr. Johnson, and took the wagons out of the stable and went off with them into the woods, and though they ran after me, they neither found me nor the horses.

After they were gone we packed up our things. I carried them by hand to the woods where we had concealed the wagons. Near daybreak we got all the things ready to move and drove to Amwell where we arrived a little before sundown." (Dwyer, pp.87-88.)

5) The description of the ragged army struggling past the huge bonfires to be ferried to safety across the Delaware is attributed to the famous American portrait painter, Charles Wilson Peale. Peale wrote "that it was 'the most hellish scene I ever beheld. All the shores were lighted up with large fires, boats continually passing and repassing, full of men, horses, artillery and camp equipage. . .The Hollowing [shouting or halloing] of hundreds of men in their difficulties of getting Horses and artillery out of the boats, made it rather the appearance of Hell than any earthly scene.'" (Hackett-Fischer, p. 133.)

Both McCullough and Hackett-Fischer describe the poignant scene of Charles Wilson Peale encountering his brother James, an Ensign in Smallwood's Marylanders, on the banks of the Delaware. As the troops went past Peale, "a man staggered out of line and came toward me. He had lost all his clothes. He was in an old dirty blanket jacket, his beard long and his face full of sores. . .which so disfigured him that he was not known to me on first sight. Only when he spoke did I recognize my brother James." (McCullough, p. 263; Hackett-Fischer, p. 133.)

His brother must have changed dramatically since Charles, a portrait artist trained in observing and painting facial details, was unable to recognize him. James also became a portrait painter after the war.

Chapter 15- Death Along the Delaware

1) General Howe arrived in Trenton on December 8 and, passing through the town, rode down to the river. American artillery on the Pennsylvania shore opened up with a furious cannonade. Captain Friedrich von Munchausen, a Hessian aide to the British General observed:

"Howe rode with us all around, stopping from time to time. He stayed there with the greatest of coolness and calm for at least an hour, while the rebels kept their strongest fire going. Wherever we turned, the cannon balls hit the ground, and I can hardly understand, even now, why all five of us were not crushed by the many balls." (Dwyer, p. 111.) A cannon ball did, in fact, sever the hind leg of the Captain's horse and he suffered a bruised knee. Among the troops, thirteen soldiers were killed or injured. (Hackett-Fischer, p. 135.)

There was some confusion as to the number of American cannons involved. A British Lieutenant claimed eight or nine artillery pieces, another German Officer reported there were eighteen heavy guns firing at them, and Munchausen counted thirty-seven guns. (Dwyer, p. 110; Hackett-Fischer, p. 135.)

2) At the time, Buck's County was populated mainly by Quakers, who were opposed to the war. Many of the locals refused to feed the ragged soldiers unless paid in sterling. A Sergeant in the Massachusetts Artillery wrote the first night in Pennsylvania, they were quartered in the rear of a tavern. The tavern keeper had food but "refused to take rebel money, as he called it." The Sergeant brought it to the attention of General Israel Putnam who authorized the men to take what they needed without paying for it, if the tavern owner refused to accept Continental money. When the tavern owner complained to General Putnam, he ordered him arrested with the words "Take this Tory rascal to the main guard house." The men then feasted on "a ham of bacon one large cheese, and a bucket full of cider-royal." (Dwyer, pp.115-116.)

I have used the incident, changed the location to a miller's home and substituted Colonel Knox for General Putnam.

In addition to the lack of food, many of the soldiers slept in the woods without tents, shelter, blankets or cots. The army was melting away due to desertions and sickness.

General Washington had expected reinforcements from Philadelphia and the Pennsylvania counties. Outside of 1,200 Philadelphia Associators and two hundred or so militia from Bucks County, no other troops arrived. On December 20th, from his headquarters above Trenton Falls, Washington wrote John Hancock in Philadelphia:

". . . In short, the present exigency of our Affairs will not admit of delay either in Council or the Field, for well convinced am I, that if the Enemy go into Quarters at all, it will be for a short season, but rather I think, the design of Genl Howe, is to possess himself of Philadelphia this Winter, if possible, and in truth, I do not see what is to prevent him, as ten days more will put an end to the existence of our Army. . . (Lengel, p. 81.) In a letter to Lund Washington, earlier that month, the General wrote:

". . .our numbers, [are] quite inadequate to the task of opposing that part of the Army under the command of Genl Howe, being reduced by Sickness, Desertion, & Political Deaths (on & before the first Instant, & having no assistance from the Militia) . . . (Lengel, p. 79.) A more vehement and emotional reaction to the lack of volunteers flocking to the cause to aid the ragged army came from John Bayard, a Philadelphia merchant who was serving as a Colonel in the Pennsylvania Militia. On December 13th, he wrote to the Philadelphia Council of Safety:

"We are greatly distressed to find no more of the militia of our State joining General Washington at this time. For God's sake what shall we do? Is the cause deserted by our state, and shall a few brave men offer their lives as sacrifice against treble their number without assistance? . . . Are our people fast asleep, or have they determined basely to give up the cause of their country? . . . You cannot expect that our few citizens, join'd to the small remains of General Washington's army, will offer up their lives without a prospect of success, unless joined by a proper force. For God's sake, exert yourselves." (Dwyer, p. 163.)

3) The brutal pillaging, plundering and rape in New Jersey, of both Whig and Tory, and the neutral Quakers, served to turn what had been a pro-British population into a hornet's nest of militia and snipers engaged in hit and run attacks on British and Hessian foraging parties, baggage trains, couriers and small patrols. On December 10th, General Howe's Hessian Aide, Captain Friedrich von Munchausen,

reported the Americans had "captured a small escort with eight baggage wagons." This was followed by the capture of "several patrols and individual dragoons with letters," as well as "700 oxen and nearly 1,000 sheep and hogs from our commissariat." (Dwyer, p. 113). On December 14, 1776 , the German Captain concluded: "It is now very unsafe for us to travel in Jersey." (Hackett-Fischer, p. 179.)

Hackett-Fischer devotes an entire chapter to "The Rising of New Jersey." He details the spontaneous uprising of the men of Hunterdon County, led by Philemon Dickinson, a gentleman farmer who organized the militia of the county. From mid-December, near Coryell's and McConkey's ferries and south to Pennington and closer to Trenton, the Hunterdon County militia engaged in numerous attacks on foraging parties and other small bodies of enemy troops. Another militia band of approximately six hundred men, led by James Ewing, conducted numerous raids on the South Trenton Ferry and the Hessians in Trenton. To the south, a militia band harassed the Hessian forces at Mount Holly and Blackhorse. (Hackett-Fischer, pp. 191-199.)

These guerrilla tactics wore down the Hessian occupying forces, unnerved them and contributed to their subsequent defeat at the Battle of Trenton. In retrospect, had General Howe wished to cultivate the Loyalist instincts of the Jersey population, he should not have quartered Hessian troops in small garrisons throughout the State.

4) On December 13, General Howe made the decision, due to the weather turning much colder and a "hard frost," to halt the campaign and send the troops into winter quarters. (McCullough, p. 267; Dwyer, p. 114.)

The Hessians were spread along the Delaware River from Mount Holly, south of Trenton through Bordentown, to Trenton. General Leslie commanding some British troops, made Princeton his winter quarters. General Grant, overall British Commander in New Jersey was based in Brunswick. General Howe removed himself from the frigid southern New Jersey winters to New York City.

It is unclear whether Colonels Rall or von Donop still thought the army would cross the Delaware when it froze, capture Philadelphia, the largest city in America, and take up winter quarters there. Colonel

Rall, when questioned by another officer as to whether the cramped quarters in Trenton were the "good winter quarters" they had been promised, replied that he would lead the troops "across the ice of the river Delaware and straight into Philadelphia." (Dwyer, p. 166.)

The regular Hessian soldiers certainly believed this was the plan and they only had to endure the wretched conditions until the severe winter made the river a highway into Pennsylvania and on to Philadelphia. Initially, they had expected to spend Christmas in the rebel capital.

The Hessians regarded their winter quarters as less than satisfactory. Lieutenant Andreas Wiederholdt of the Knyphausen Regiment described their entry into Trenton as follows:

"We marched to that famous place, Trenton, which I shall never forget in my life. . .

Nice winter quarters, in truth! Our poor, worn-out soldiers, could relax even less here than in the field for duty was extraordinarily heavy; watches, details and pickets were endless. . . When the details and pickets were relieved, only then could the soldiers wear or not wear hose, shoes, shirt and such things." (Heckert, "The German-American Diary, Notes of Related Historical Interest, Including Translated Excerpts from the Wiederholdt Diary, American Revolutionary War, p. 142.)

5) The fact General William Howe had a mistress in New York City was hardly a military secret. Her identity was known. One popular ditty, which I assume was familiar to the Hessians and British troops going into winter quarters in New Jersey, and therefore a matter of gossip among them was:

Sir William, he, snug as a flea,
Lay all this time a-snoring;
Nor dreamed of harm, as he lay warm
In bed with Mrs. Loring.

Elizabeth Lloyd Loring, described as a "flashing blonde," was the wife of Joshua Loring, a New England Tory from a prominent Loyalist family. (Hackett-Fischer, p. 72.) Their affair began during the British occupation of Boston.

The dark side of the story is her husband, Joshua Loring, Jr., was rewarded, by General Howe, with the position of head of the commissary for rebel prisoners. (McCullough, p. 75.) He abused his office, starved the American soldiers, left them ill-clothed and malnourished, and pocketed the money provided for their well-being. The stories of the horrid conditions aboard the prison ships in New York harbor are appalling. From 1776 to 1783, an estimated 11,000 American prisoners are estimated to have died on board these pestilent, crowded, hellish containers of human misery. (The Battle of Brooklyn, August 27-29, 1776, Marilyn H. Pettit, pp. 25-26, published by Old Stone House of Brooklyn, available on line at www.theoldstonehouse. org)

"In the words of a contemporary Loyalist . . . 'Joshua had a handsome wife. The general . . . was fond of her. Joshua had no objections. He fingered the cash, the general enjoyed madam." (McCullough, p. 75.)

Chapter 16- On the Pennsylvania Shore

1) The famous painting of Washington Crossing the Delaware is wildly inaccurate in many respects. The General appears to be standing in some sort of flimsy row boat being poled through the ice floes.

In actuality, Washington's army was transported across the Delaware primarily in Durham Boats, so called because they were used to transport pig iron from the Durham Iron Works near Philadelphia, as well as other freight on the Delaware River. Unlike the inappropriate boat depicted in the famous painting, they were "pointed at both ends (the steering oar could be mounted at either, making it unnecessary to turn the boat around when it reached shore), . . . forty to sixty feet long with a beam of eight feet." (McCullough, p. 274.) With their flat bottoms, they drew two feet of water fully loaded. They were high sided, meaning the gunnels came above a soldier's waist as the troops, as many as forty men at a time, stood in the boats. They had regular oars and eighteen-foot long poles that the Marblehead Mariners used to push against the ice and river floor, as they walked along the wide planks on the side of the boats. All historians agree the troops crossed standing in the boats, Durhams were painted black and were propelled by both oars and the long poles. (Dwyer, p. 233; Hackett-Fischer, pp. 216-217; McCullough, p. 294.)

General Washington had his men commandeer the Durham boats beginning in mid- December. They were hidden on the Pennsylvania side near McConkey's Ferry, in preparation for the main American attack on Trenton, the day after Christmas, 1776. While it was possible for the Officers' horses and the field cannons to be carried across on the Durham boats, the high sides would have made loading very difficult. It is probable, flat-bottomed scows or even the ferry may have been used for this purpose.

2) Thomas Paine was part of Washington's staff during the retreat through New Jersey. He was known among the soldiers as "Common Sense." (Hackett-Fischer, p. 139.) Paine was motivated to write The American Crisis, by troops leaving at the end of their enlistments and the failure of others to support the patriotic cause, as well as by what he perceived as the general air of panic, despair and defeat. "By his own account, he started to work on 'The American Crisis,' when the army reached Newark and 'continued writing it at every place we stopt,' scribbling by firelight in makeshift camps along the road while exhausted soldiers slept around him." (Hackett-Fischer, p. 140.). It was published on December 19, 1776 in the Pennsylvania Journal and reached the soldiers of the Continental Army along the Delaware River within a day. (Hackett-Fischer, p. 142.)

3) Colonel Knox had taken the brief time since crossing the Delaware to integrate field cannons, the three and six pounders, as close "assault weapons," for the infantry. (Hackett-Fischer, p. 153.) In order to bring the light artillery up, on icy winter roads, I have assumed, the Colonel would have required the horses to have cleated shoes to give them better traction.

Chapter 17- A Stormy Crossing

1) General Washington's plan was to surprise the Hessians in Trenton just before dawn on December 26, 1776. His timetable called for all of the troops and artillery to be across the Delaware River by midnight so "that we might easily arrive at Trenton by five in the Morning [December 26], the distance being about nine miles." (Samuel Stelle Smith, "The Battle of Trenton," p. 20.)

About 2,400 troops left their camps around four p.m., on the 25th, a half hour before sunset, and marched the eight miles up the Pennsylvania side to McConkey's Ferry. The weather, sunny but cold at the beginning of the march, turned foul, starting as rain and by eleven p.m. was a fully fledged nor'easter. One of General Washington's aides described the weather as follows:

"It is fearfully cold and raw and a snowstorm settling in. The wind is northeast and beats in the faces of the men. It will be a terrible night for the soldiers who have no shoes. Some of them have tied old rags around their feet; others are barefoot but I have not heard a man complain." ((Dwyer, p. 228.)

Worse for Washington's plan, the Delaware was choked with large ice floes, carried downstream by a swiftly flowing current. Washington put Colonel Knox in charge of the crossing. The dangerous task of ferrying the entire army, horses and eighteen pieces of artillery to the New Jersey shore fell primarily to the Marblehead Mariners. Several sources credit Colonel Knox and his booming, stentorian voice over the noise created by the storm and the crashing of ice in the river, for the successful crossing. The Mariners skill was such that not a single cannon or man was lost, although Colonel John Haslet fell into the water and was rescued. He marched to Trenton and took part in the battle. (Dwyer, pp. 232-233; Hackett-Fischer, pp. 218-219.) Haslet's comment on his misadventure was:

"I fell into the water and have been suffering from piles ever since." (Dwyer, p. 233.)

One of the soldiers wrote briefly about the crossing and in more detail about the terrible weather, while waiting on the New Jersey side:

"Over the river we then went in a flat-bottomed scow [a Durham].
. . . and we had to wait for the rest and so began to pull down fences
and make fires to warm ourselves, for the storm was increasing rapidly.
After a while, it rained, hailed, snowed, and froze, and at the same
time blew a perfect hurricane, so much so that I perfectly recollect,
after putting the rails on to burn, the wind and fire would cut them
in two in a moment, and when I turned my face to the fire, my back
would be freezing. However . . . by turning myself round and round I
kept from perishing." McCullough, p. 275.)

Colonel Knox, in his letter of December 28, 1776, to his wife
Lucy, whom he addressed as "My Dearly Beloved Friend," described
the crossing as follows:

". . .a part of the army, consisting of 2,500 or 3,000, passed
the river on Christmas night, with almost infinite difficulty, with
eighteen field-pieces. The floating ice in the river made the labor
almost incredible. However, perseverance accomplished what at first
seemed impossible. About two o'clock [in the morning] the troops
were all on the Jersey side; we were then about nine miles from the
object [Trenton]. The night was cold and stormy; it hailed with great
violence; the troops marched with the most profound silence and good
order." (Drake, p. 36.)

If Knox was correct as to the time when all the troops were across,
it must have taken another hour to get all the artillery over, which is
what Smith reports in "The Battle of Trenton." The march did not
begin until four a.m. four hours behind schedule and too short a time
to arrive at Trenton just before dawn. (Hackett-Fischer, p. 225; Smith,
p.20.)

2) The Mariners ferried eighteen guns with Knox's Artillery
Regiment across the Delaware. Four cannons were at the head of
the leading brigades of each division of the troops during the march.
Hackett-Fischer notes that the ratio of guns to troops was unusually
high, seven to eight guns for every one thousand muskets instead of
two to three per thousand. (Hackett-Fischer, p. 223.) One advantage
to having field artillery as part of the attack, was they could be reliably
counted upon to fire even in the storm, because their vents and muzzles

were plugged, whereas, muskets were more prone to misfire with their exposed flash-pans. (Dwyer, pp.234-235.)

I have speculated that the Artillery Regiments, short on supplies, may have had to improvise in making covers for the vents and muzzles.

3) Hackett-Fischer quotes General Washington's orders for the Officers to "have a white paper in their hats to be distinguished by," and "notes this custom has endured in the United States Army from the banks of the Delaware to the coast of Normandy, where officers and non-coms had white stripes painted on the backs of their helmets." (Hackett-Fischer, p. 208.) Also see, McCullough, p. 273, "officers were to have a white piece of paper in their hats to distinguish them," and Tom Hanks on Omaha Beach in *Saving Private Ryan*.

4) The map on p. 229 in Hackett-Fischer's "Washington's Crossing," shows Jacob's Creek and another ravine on the Bear Tavern Road to Birmingham, the route of the Army's march. He then describes the difficulties and speculates on how the cannons were lowered down one side and up the other, only to encounter the second ravine and have to repeat the process. Colonel Knox had brought fifty-nine guns from Fort Ticonderoga over the Berkshires to Cambridge in the winter of 1775-76. His experience must have been invaluable, although unlike the trek of the "noble train of artillery", on this night, time was of the essence and the army's advance was definitely slowed by getting the guns across the two ravines.

5) The army reached Birmingham, roughly four miles from Trenton, around six a.m. Here according to plan, the army divided, with General Sullivan's Division, including Colonel Glover's Brigade with the Regiment of the Marblehead Mariners, taking the lower or River Road to flank Trenton and encircle it from the south. General Greene's Division, including the artillery attached to General Stirling's Brigade, had the longer route, turning east until they met the Scotch Road that joined with the Pennington Road less than a mile from Trenton. General Washington rode with General Greene and there are several reports by soldiers that throughout the march,

their Commander in Chief urged them to press on and "in a deep and solemn voice," "to keep with their officers." (McCullough, p.277; Hackett-Fischer, p. 228, "Soldiers keep by your Officers. For God's Sake, keep by your Officers.")

Miraculously, both sections of the army arrived at Trenton at the same time, and even though it was well past dawn, around eight o'clock when the first shots were fired at the Hessian pickets, they caught the Hessians by surprise. The men of General Greene's Division swept out of a driving snow storm at the top of the town.

I have placed Knox's Massachusetts Artillery in the vanguard of the attack. The artillery were to be rapidly positioned among the troops to sweep the streets clear of the enemy and to break up their formations.

Author's Note and Acknowledgements

This is the second in the series of historical novels about the Revolutionary War. John Updike, one of the most acclaimed authors of the 20th century, disdained historical fiction as "vigorous fakery." Henry James referred to its "fatal cheapness." I think both are wrong. I am passionate about history. I believe that well-researched, accurate historical fiction will reach many more readers and teach them more about American history than "straight" history books. I take seriously the responsibility to depict events accurately and to create an atmosphere around my fictitious characters that is true to the times in which they lived.

So, where in "Tories and Patriots" does history end and fiction begin? First, I will not alter history- have a battle where there was none, place historical figures where they were not, or put words in the mouths of General George Washington, General Howe and other historical figures. Second, I do extensive research and try to provide the accurate details of clothing, shoes, food, drink, furniture, books, music, uniforms, weapons, weather, and especially language to engross the reader, not only in the story, but the time and place of the events described. It is not all just about battles. While Will Stoner, Adam Cooper, Lieutenants Hadley and Holmes, Elisabeth Van Hooten, and Privates Georg Engelhard, Christoph Weber and Andreas Felsenheim are products of my imagination, I hope the reader will become immersed in their daily lives and recognize them merely as examples of the real people who struggled with loyalties, love, friendship and war during "the times that try men's souls." Third, I have included Notes for each Chapter at the end of the novel. They provide historical context and include quotes from correspondence or contemporaneous articles from newspapers or broadsheets to give more of a voice to the principal participants through these writings (and very imaginative spelling) of the times. I point out where I have moved up the date of an order or described an event that seems preposterous but actually happened (in 1776, storms and unusual weather seem to have played a large role in preventing the annihilation of the Continental Army.)

The saga will continue with the third in the series, "Blood Upon the Snow." I hope this and the subsequent novels provide both compelling and interesting historical reading. While each one stands on its own, many of the characters are present from the beginning in "Cannons for the Cause." I have tried not to include too much background for those readers who first became acquainted with Will Stoner and Nathaniel Holmes on the road from Ft. George to Cambridge. An astute reader will also recognize Will's gradual maturing as he develops from a young recruit to a soldier all too familiar with the horrors of war.

I could not have written any of these novels without the encouragement and assistance of numerous friends. They read the manuscript in several versions, offered many helpful comments and simply supported me by being my friends. They know who they are and I treasure their friendship.

I am extremely grateful to Ben West, my editor, who raised many questions about assumptions and leaps of logic I had made, details I had assumed, and fulsome explanations that, upon reflection, were unnecessary. The final version is much better because of his efforts. Special thanks also to Priscilla Drucker for once again providing editorial assistance. Of course, any remaining errors are my sole responsibility.

My good friend John Carp provided vital advice about Dutch names and language. He saved me from memorializing my ignorance in print. We had been friends since we met in Somalia in the late 1960s. He and his wife were there under UN auspices and we were serving in the Peace Corps. Over the following four and one half decades, although they lived in The Netherlands and we in the States, our friendship deepened and the bonds between our two families grew. We saw each other frequently and took many marvelous road trips together, both in Europe and the U.S. John passed away suddenly at the end of October, 2014. I wish he could have lived to see this book published. I think he would have enjoyed it.

My son's devotion to my writing, his commitment of time and incisive criticism, continues to amaze me. I am deeply indebted to him, not the least for his sound artistic advice and his admirable sense of design. The cover, the internal artwork and easy readability of the text are all his doing.

Finally, my beloved wife continues to encourage me to write, reading the various iterations of the manuscript, praising me when praise is due and providing constructive criticism when necessary. I cannot say more than I did in the Notes and Acknowledgments for "Cannons for the Cause" – My gratitude to her is exceeded only by my love.

Martin R. Ganzglass
Washington, D.C.
December, 2014

Bibliography

The following are books, blogs or websites, I have read for historical background. Private Joseph Plumb Martin's stands out among the first hand accounts. His plain prose is a compelling account of an ordinary soldier's suffering from hunger and extreme cold, as well as the horrors of war and battlefield butchery. In addition, his sense of humor, sarcasm, and puncturing of some officers' pomposity makes his memoir well worth reading.

Since it is easy enough to search a book online by author and title, I have omitted the customary reference to publisher and date of publication.

Allen, Thomas B.,
Tories: Fighting for the King in America's First Civil War

Anderson, Fred,
The War That Made America: A Short History of the French and Indian War

Braisted, Todd
How George Washington Saved the Life of Abraham Van Buskirk's Son, (appearing in the Journal of the American Revolution, September 16, 2014)

Chernow, Ron,
Washington, A Life

Dohla, Johann Conrad,
A Hessian Diary of the American Revolution (Edited and translated by Bruce E. Burgoyne)

Drake, Francis S.,
Life and correspondence of Henry Knox: Major-General in the American Revolutionary Army

Dwyer, William M.,
The Day is Ours: An Inside View of the Battles of Trenton and Princeton

Gallagher, John J.,
The Battle of Brooklyn, 1776

Hackett-Fischer, David,
Washington's Crossing

Heckert, C.W.,
The German-American Diary, Notes of Related Historical Interest, Including Translated Excerpts from the Wiederholdt Diary American Revolutionary War

Karels, Carol (Editor),
The Revolutionary War in Bergen County, The Times That Tried Men's Souls

Krebs, Daniel,
A Generous and Merciful Enemy-Life for German Prisoners of War During the American Revolution

Landahl-Smidt, Donald,
British and Hessian Accounts of the Invasion of 1776 (appearing in The Revolutionary War in Bergen County, Carol Karels, Editor)

Lengel, Edward G.,
This Glorious Struggle: George Washington's Revolutionary War Letters

McCullough, David,
1776

Martin, Joseph Plumb,
Private Yankee Doodle: Being a Narrative of Some of the Adventures, Dangers and Sufferings of a Revolutionary Soldier (George E. Scheer, Editor)

Moran, Donald N.,
The Scoundrel Who Saved the Continental Army

Pettit, Marilyn H.,
The Battle of Brooklyn, August 27-29, 1776 (appearing on the website: www.theoldstonehouse.com

Pearfon, Michael,
Those Damned Rebels

Pfister, Albert and Seume, Johann Gottfried,
The Voyage of the First Hessian Army from Portsmouth to New York, 1776 (Project Gutenberg E Book)

Robarge, David,
How the Patriots Used Intelligence to Help Win American Independence (Lecture at The Society of the Cincinnati, July 26, 2011)

Roberts, Cokie,
Founding Mothers-The Women Who Raised Our Nation

Schecter, Barnet,
The Battle for New York

Sellers, James L.,
The Supply of Gunpowder in 1776 (appearing in the American Historical Review, Vol. 30, No. 2, 1925)

Sloane, Eric,
Sketches of America Past

Spring, John,
The Invasion and the Myths Surrounding It (appearing in The Revolutionary War In Bergen County, Carol Karels, Editor)

Smith, Stelle Samuel,
The Battle of Trenton

The New York Times,
Seeking Brooklyn's Lost Mass Grave (August 25, 2012)

Wright, Kevin,
New Bridge-History at the Crossroads (appearing in The Revolutionary War In Bergen County, The Times That Tried Men's Souls, Carol Karels, Editor)

The thrilling saga of our War for Independence

continues with . . .

Blood Upon the Snow

Corporal Georg Engelhard was thankful his Knyphausen Regiment was not the Regiment of the day. That duty fell to Colonel Rall's Regiment, quartered in brick buildings midway up King Street. It was one of two broad and long cobblestoned roads that sloped down the length of Trenton, from the heights at the top to the road at the bottom that led south to Bordentown.

Georg was exhausted. This entire Christmas week the Seckendorf Company had either been on patrol freezing in the snow covered fields, or on sentry duty stationed in small huts and makeshift outposts covered by tree branches. On Christmas Eve there had been no respite. They had been awake all night under arms and ready to muster at any alarm. Georg was worn down by the incessant rounds of night sentry duty followed by daytime patrols, through the deep snow and thick woods where they could be ambushed at any moment.

Even when they were officially on relief duty in their barracks, the soldiers slept in their uniforms with their cartridge belts strapped on. It was an old U shaped stone building, three stories high and almost as cold inside as out. Now, at breakfast in the common room on the ground floor, the fire barely warming those lucky enough to sit close by, they were only permitted to unbutton their powder blue jackets. Their muskets, bayonets affixed, were at the ready, stacked on wooden racks, at the entrance door. Georg longed to undo the knee high black gaiters, which pinched his calves when he sat, but it was forbidden.

"This has truly been the worst Christmas week, I have ever spent," Georg said to his friend Christoph, sitting beside him on a wooden bench. "After we buried Andreas I cannot sleep. I see only his face before he died as we carried him to the wagon."

Christoph nodded. They both remained silent, thinking of their last patrol with their friend, the rifle shot coming from the dark woods, Andreas crumpling to the ground, his white waist-coat quickly soaked red with his blood, and dying slowly in agony from his stomach wound.

Andreas had spoken often of his wish to be captured or the opportunity to desert in the confusion of battle. He had encouraged Georg and Christoph to join him. Georg had refused. It offended his sense of honor. He wanted to win the war and go home. All it would take would be to cross the frozen Delaware, a half a day's march to Philadelphia, capture the Rebeller's capitol, gather up loot and plunder and return to Hesse, richer than his family could imagine. No, he would not leave his comrades and desert to the ragged, ill-disciplined mob of farmers and tradesmen who ran when the Hessians charged them, bayonets at the ready.

"Shh," Christoph hissed, quickly glancing at the other soldiers bent over, seated around the table eagerly spooning porridge from their bowls to their mouths.

Georg was so tired, he was unaware he had spoken. He tried to remember what he had said.

"Georg. You must. . ."

Christoph's words were interrupted by the sound of musket volleys in the distance. The soldiers looked at each other confused, awaiting orders. There were shouts in the street.

"Heraus! Heraus! The Rebellers. The Rebellers. Turn out. To the alarm posts. Hurry, hurry."

The men scrambled to their feet and ran for their muskets. The kettle drums beat urgently for them to form up. Outside, it was sleeting. The wind, gusting down from the top of the town, picked up already fallen snow and swirled it around them in clouds, obstructing their vision. Georg, as the Corporal in charge of the two lines got his files of men in order. His Company, led by Lieutenant Reuter, quick marched in ranks down the lane leading from the barracks to the bottom of King Street. Their alarm position was less than a hundred yards away, in the field past the Presbyterian Church and below the apple orchard. As they crossed King Street, Georg looked to his left. The men of Colonel Rall's Regiment, distinctive in their mustard colored breeches, were forming up. At the top of the hill, where King Street met the Pennington Road, through the wind blown sleet and snow and the smoke of musket fire, Georg could barely see figures of soldiers. They seemed to him to be an indistinct mass of blue-coated troops. His Company turned on to Queen Street. George could more clearly see the Rebellers at the top and some at the junction with the Princeton Road. As they marched up Queen, Georg thought there were too many of the enemy for a harassing raid. He heard the volume of musket fire increase but whether it was the Rall Regiment returning fire or the rebel force, he could not tell.

—⋙—

"Will. Bring the gun over here," Lieutenant Hadley cried, pointing with his arm to a level area among the soldiers. Will urged Big Red forward. He leaped off the horse and ran to detach the traces. Isaiah, Levi and Baldwin, unlimbered the six-pounder and together they turned it around. Will joined them as they rolled the gun forward through the soft snow. They were at the top of a wide street. Below them was the town. Some of the troops formed up around them, and fired a volley toward the Hessians midway down the street. Others raced through the snow-covered fields behind the buildings seeking to get closer and fire into the enemy's flanks.

"Aim low. Keep your muskets low. Leg them. Leg them," an officer nearby shouted to his men before they fired another volley. The smoke from their muskets blew down the street, blending into the nearly horizontal sheets of sleet and snow.